THE KEEPER
OF THE DIARY

JUDITH
DIANA
WINSTON

CHEWUT PRESS • 2012

Chewut Press
3435 Ocean Park Boulevard, Suite 107 –37
Santa Monica, CA 90405

www.TheKeeperOfTheDiaryBook.com

ISBN – 978-0-9643282-1-1

1. Visionary – Fiction. 2. Mystical – Adventure – Fiction. 3. Egypt – Fiction. 4. Sacred Sites – Machu Picchu – Easter Island – Stonehenge – Callanish, etc. – Fiction. 5. Metaphysical – Spiritual – Fiction. 6. Extraterrestrial – Pleiades – Fantasy – Fiction.

Published in the United States of America.

10 9 8 7 6 5 4 3 2 1

Book Design: Benjamin Cziller, www.ImageDriven.com

Cover Photograph – Judith Diana Winston
Back Cover Photograph – Jon Perachiotti
Interior graphics - excerpted from the book Meditative Magic,
  The Pleiadean Glyphs, Chewut Press © 1995
Design – Benjamin Cziller / www.ImageDriven.com
Printed in United States of America

Dedication

With great love and appreciation I dedicate this book to Carole Foley, my editor and collaborator who, with one of those incredible synchronicities that has always guided this project, came upon the scene at the perfect moment to help expand the book's horizons.

You proved to have the uncanny ability to climb right into the story I had been living with for almost twenty years. You often tugged on my brain and managed to pull out ideas I didn't even know I had.

Thank you for your attention to detail, creative input, knack for giving the characters a sense of "place" and your wonderful ear for everyday conversation, which often found its way directly into the characters' mouths.

Without your commitment, belief in, and steadfast devotion to the ideas and scope of the project, this book might never have seen the light of day.

Or, if it had, it would not have been nearly as good a read. ~JDW

SPECIAL THANKS TO:

Julie Stone for being my Guiding Light and Mentor on story structure, character development and zany right brain ideas.

AND

Leah Kalish
Debra Winston-Levin
Selma Winston
Michael Perlin
Joan Danto
Ron Levy
Dr. Gary Berman
Jon Perachiotti
Salomon Bonilla

For your general support and love for me and this book and its "bigger picture" perspective. You each held the vision with me and, in your own way, contributed something unique. I couldn't have done it without you!

In addition, many thanks to Benjamin Cziller, my talented graphic designer, for his beautiful work and commitment above and beyond the call of duty.

It has been said that in The Dark Time, when the old ways no longer held and confusion reigned, there would come Way-Showers to lead Mankind out of the turmoil and doubt, and into a New Era of Light.

So it is in these days of deep questioning, when many go within to search for answers, that the ancient legends and stories of a Great Brotherhood of Light, whose members walk amongst Man, begin to surface once again.

This Is One Of Those Stories....

Part One

CHAPTER 1

Day 1 - Night

I do not know anything except what I have been told. I am lying on a cot in a small, cement and steel house in an Arab village close to the Sphinx on the Giza plain near Cairo. The night is hot and dry, and the air is thick with dust. The locals say that I was near death from exposure and dehydration when I was found two days ago lying near the Sphinx.

I am awake again. I have no idea whether days or only moments have passed. It is pitch black, and except for the flickering flame of a small candle casting patches of light on this page, I cannot see anything. My fingers feel stiff and sticky on my pencil stub as they struggle to form these words. My eyes burn and my head is pounding.

I do not know how long I have been here or how long I was in the desert before they found me. I do not know who I am....

My whole body shuddered as I put down the diary I was reading. For some unknown reason, I had been trembling since the moment I opened it. Some kind of strange altered state had overtaken me the instant I spotted the unexpected object in my camera case. My hand still smarted from the electric-like shock that burnt my fingers when I first touched the small, soft, leather-bound book.

I know it sounds crazy, but it felt like the diary was alive! It was like seeing a ghost, except the ghost was real. Real – and somehow familiar! That was the bizarre part. I had never seen it before, but it seemed like an object I had known all my life. I felt, literally, compelled to open it, to look inside.

This is insane! One moment I was calm, in complete control of my mind and emotions, and the next? Suddenly a new and crushingly obvious thought slammed me. *This book doesn't belong here! Where could it have come from?* I knew I had just taken it out of my camera case, but it was the same camera case I had packed at home in Los Angeles, hand-carried through four airports and never let out of my sight. *How could it have gotten here?* I quickly checked out my film and equipment. Everything seemed fine.

I looked back at the book lying close to me on the bed. *I don't know whether I even want to touch you again.* I shut my eyes for a long moment. Finally, I forced them open and looked – really looked at it. Clearly what I was seeing was simply an ordinary, rather worn leather-bound notebook, nothing to get excited about. It was just an old notebook that someone had used as a diary, and somehow it had landed in my camera case. So why did it create such a real and visceral reaction in me even before I read a word of it?

It was just plain eerie. I went into the bathroom, splashed cold water on my face, and stared blankly at my image in the mirror. *What am I sup-posed to do with the damn thing now?* I closed my eyes once more. My head began to throb. I sat back down on the bed. *Okay, this whole thing is absurd!* What I had just felt was probably my imagination – or maybe my surroundings. After all, I was in Egypt, one of the most enigmatic places on earth. Yesterday was the first day of our trip, and we were in Cairo, home of possibly the most famous and mysterious structures in the world, the Great Pyramids of Egypt. A sudden quiver ran through my body.

I was too exhausted to think, but I forced myself. *Of course, that had to be the answer…my imagination…or even hallucinations! Because I've been sick, really sick, fever sick!* The week before I left had been filled with frenetic activity alternating with a virus-induced numbing fatigue. Nonetheless, I had pushed myself forward, moving mechanically through each day. I had to because I had made a commitment. I was to be the photographer for a group of people touring ancient Egyptian sacred sites as a part of their spiritual quest. I had never been interested in anything even remotely connected to spirituality. *I don't belong here! I'm not on any kind of spiritual quest! What a mess!*

I had thought the virus was over, that I was well enough to travel, yet clearly I was still very sick. The last minute preparations, two airplane rides and a five-hour layover had been entirely too much for me. So I guess it had to have been the sickness and the excitement that made me feel lightheaded – a bit like I was in another reality. That, and getting up at six o'clock in the morning to catch the plane for Luxor. The group might have been ready to start a day of touring, but I wasn't. I needed to rest. *I'm sure the fog will clear after I get some rest.*

Curling up on the bed, I tried to relax. I took in a deep breath, heaved a sigh of relief, and felt grateful – grateful to be lying down, grateful to be able to rest and let my nervous system quiet, and grateful that I had been able to photograph the pyramids in Cairo the day before. In fact, that was the real reason I had agreed to come to Egypt.

I closed my eyes and images of the Great Pyramids, shining majestically, flooded my inner vision. Perfect pictures of the Great Pyramids bathed in the late afternoon sun carried me off to the land of dreams.

Knock! Knock!

The thumping of someone at the door thundered through the darkness and jolted me back to this world.

Knock! Knock!

"It's me, Melissa," a voice called through the door. "Are you alright, Cassie?"

I rolled over, willing myself to wake up.

"Yeah, I'm fine," I half yelled, half mumbled automatically. "Come on in."

I heard the lock release as I sat up, leaned back on my elbows and blinked my eyes into focus. The smiling face of my roommate felt like a jarring blast of energy.

"Sorry for the banging, but I didn't want to just barge in on you. Are you sure you're okay," she asked, concerned. "You don't look so great. Your eyes are awfully glassy."

"Oh, my god, Melissa, I had the strangest dream. It was something about the pyramids and a diary.... It was so strange."

"Well, my dear Cassie, stop dreaming and get up. It's really late, nearly two o'clock in the afternoon, and the group is meeting up in an hour to go to Karnak Temple. I don't want you to sleep the day away like you did yesterday in Cairo."

"Yesterday...Cairo...." I yawned, still blinking the sleep out of my eyes. "I was exhausted. And, thank you sooo much for handling everything with the luggage this morning. Sorry...I was still completely out of it." I looked around and spotted our unopened suitcases stacked neatly in one corner of the room. My camera case lay open on the bed beside me.

"No problem. But you're sure you're okay? Do you want me to call a doctor or something?"

"I'll be fine as soon as I take a shower and change my clothes. I have to load some new film into my cameras and mark the stuff from yesterday. I'll be down in a few minutes. Is there somewhere in the hotel where I can get a cup of coffee?"

"Yes, thank goodness. They're serving coffee, tea and biscuits in about half an hour in the lounge. It's an early version of the whole British Tea thing! I'll put something aside for you. Do you want another knock, or are you positive you're up?"

"I'm definitely up, thanks," I answered, making a mental note to take some special pictures for her.

"Okay, see you in a bit." I watched as Melissa, in her flower-print dress and sturdy sandals, walked out the door, letting it swing closed behind her. I took a deep breath and started to get up. I glanced around the bed at my strewn camera equipment, and then I saw it – the diary! My eyes locked onto the worn, brown leather notebook, and I froze. I was hoping it was only a dream. But it was certainly real – and it was sitting right there next to me. *I still don't get it…where could you have come from? Things don't appear out of thin air.*

I knew there was a simple explanation. There had to be! But I couldn't think about it now – I had a job to do. Hustling toward the small bathroom, I unbuttoned my sweaty cotton shirt and flung it on the floor. I reached into the water-stained tub and shower unit, and turned on the hot water full blast. I tore off the rest of my clothing letting it fall where it may, and quickly stepped into the steaming shower.

I stood enveloped in the wet warmth, enjoying every moment. Suddenly the answer hit me like a rock. I stopped mid-motion, soap in hand, water streaming down my face. I knew exactly where the diary had come from. *It has to have been Rashid. That's the only time the camera case was out of my hands or sight.*

Memories of the previous day rushed back at me. I had woken up in the hotel in Cairo feeling hot and tired. I squinted at my watch and was shocked to discover it was three o'clock in the afternoon. *I've lost the whole day! The group has seen the pyramids and everything.* This was the only day we were spending in Cairo and my one chance to see and photograph the Great Pyramids. So although I still felt feverish and my throat was sore, I had quickly put on some clothes, grabbed a hat and my cameras, and raced up the road and over the sloping sand dunes toward the pyramids.

"Lady, want to go for a camel ride? Nice camel. Very friendly! See."

Dear God, the last thing I need right now is to be hassled. I swirled around ready to defend my privacy. Standing in front of me was a diminutive, ageless slip of a man holding the reign of a very decorative camel. And the camel was, literally, smiling. I was completely disarmed. The weather-lined face of the man twinkled up at me, and the camel showed a toothy grin. I burst out laughing. The pent up tension and exhaustion made me almost hysterical. I snorted as tears rolled down my cheeks and sweat beaded my brow.

"You American?" asked the little man.

I could only nod.

"Where from?"

I squeaked out, "California."

"Cal-E-Fornee-a! My camel name is Cal-E-Fornee-a. Nice lady want to go for camel ride, see pyramids? Pyramids very special. Very much mystery."

It was then that I stopped long enough to look up at the largest of the Great Pyramids and, with a sense of panic, realized the light was completely wrong. It was a perfect morning shot, but now it was afternoon, and the light I needed was gone. My mouth dropped and disappointment shot across my face.

"Don't worry...my name Rashid. I am number one camel driver. I take good care of you!"

I was so disoriented that my guard was down, and almost in spite of myself, I began to confide in the strange little man. "I'm a photographer and I've come all the way to Egypt to photograph the pyramids," I blurted in frustration. "Now I've missed my chance...the light is all wrong, and the people I'm traveling with are leaving for Luxor early tomorrow morning."

Rashid listened attentively, nodding his head up and down as though he understood every word. When I finished, he was still nodding and twinkling. Half smiling, he closed one eye in a kind of wink. "Don't worry, Missy, everything *juuust* fine. This is *puuufect* time for taking picture of pyramids!" he went on to say in his halting English but with a great deal of assurance. "You just see! I know very best place for photographing pyramids."

It turned out that the spot he was referring to was on the other side of the pyramids, but far enough over the dunes to get a full shot of all three Great Pyramids. He explained that he knew this place because he'd seen a guide help a French television crew. They had spent the entire day watching the light "everywhere" and had chosen "...very same place," at exactly this time of the day. I had my doubts and didn't want to get taken, but there weren't exactly a ton of options, so I put myself in his weatherworn hands.

I almost gasped as we approached the other side of the Great Pyramids. The light was perfect – in fact, gorgeous! After shooting an entire roll of black-and-white as well as color film, including a few prize shots of Rashid and California against the backdrop of the pyramids, we took a flying camel ride across the dusk-lit sand down to the Sphinx. Rashid helped me slide off the camel, and I walked over to the giant monument. I felt wildly alive and experienced an aching sense of familiarity – and peace. I even had the odd impression that this entire strip of ground, with its "very much mystery," was trying to tell me something. *But I'll be damned if I can figure out its message.*

Rashid's voice broke into my thoughts. "It's getting late. I would like to take you to my family for to share traditional Arab meal."

"Oh, Rashid," I exclaimed, deeply moved. "I would love to join you, but I have to get back to the hotel. I'm the photographer for a group of people and I haven't been with them all day."

Rashid seemed disappointed but understood. He helped me pack up my camera gear and took me back to the hotel. He had given me the gift of perfect light for my photographs.

But, why...why had he given me the diary?

CHAPTER 2

Deep in thought, I towel-dried my hair and scurried toward my suitcase. My eyes involuntarily zeroed in on the diary still lying on the bed. Time screeched to a halt as I stared at it long and hard. I knew I needed to hurry to meet the group downstairs, and even though I was a bit afraid of the diary, the pull was overpowering. Almost like a marionette, controlled by a will other than my own, strings seemed to move my fingers – to pick up the diary and open its pages. Before I could stop myself, I had begun to read – again. *I'll only read a page or two,* I promised myself as I sat on the edge of the bed with the book cradled in my hands.

June 1

It would seem that three days have passed since my first entry. These three days are all that I know of my life. I cannot remember anything before waking up here. I have tried very hard to remember, but my mind is a complete blank. I believe this journal is my path of recovery. It is also my sanity. It is the only tie I have to any sense of myself.

June 3

I will start by recording what I do know. I am of medium height and very thin. I have dark hair and an olive complexion. I would guess my age to be somewhere in my mid-twenties. I look much the same as the other young men here except I have blue eyes and am a bit taller than the average. However, I do not feel like I am one of them.

I cannot put my finger on why that is. Perhaps it is because nothing here has the slightest ring of familiarity. Also, it is already obvious to me that my knowledge of people and places goes far beyond that of anyone I have met here.

June 7

I took a short walk around the crowded village today and I overheard a group of European tourists talking amongst themselves about hiring a guide for a private tour of the Great Pyramids. They spoke in their own language, but I understood every word they said. Many villagers know a variety of languages, however they have only mastered enough to get by with the tourists. I appear to be the only one who has a real command of several different languages.

I am different in another way. I am literate. I can write. For reasons of privacy I am choosing to write in English. Most of the adults here, and even many of the younger men around my age, cannot write much beyond their own name or the names of other family members. Now the children must attend school for six years, so that has improved somewhat.

June 14

I still become lightheaded and dizzy and I tire quite easily. Occasionally, Rashid stays here at night to look after me. When I feel up to it, I sometimes work with his nephew, Hakim.

Wait a minute…Rashid! You mean he's a part of this story, too? No…it's probably a different Rashid. Knowing I should be getting dressed but too curious to stop reading, I turned another page.

June 19

It is very strange to have no past. I feel like one newly born. Everything around me holds great interest, even fascination. I have come to love the complete stillness of the desert as the sun moves so very slowly across the sky. I relish the constant earthy smell of the animals and most of all, the sight of the night sky – dark and mysterious. At night the air is dry and crisp, almost electric, and the sky a mass of starry light. I draw a great reassurance from the simple and tangible presence of the physical world.

June 25

I have been walking around the village. It seems to be quite prosperous. It is primarily made up of extended families, including a great many children. Constant exposure to the intense sun prematurely ages the villagers' skin. Their faces are deeply lined and weathered, making even the young appear older.

Tourism is the main source of income. The men work as guides and sell souvenirs. Many of the younger men work at a nearby stable. Life here is quiet. Only the intervention of Allah breaks up the monotony. The entire family comes together at three o'clock in the afternoon when the large meal of the day is eaten.

Afterwards, during the heat of the day, the men rest while the women clean up. In the evening the men go out to the cafés and drink black tea or the dark, vicous Turkish coffee flavored with cardamom. They sit and talk or pass the time playing dominoes and backgammon.

The life of the women has probably not changed in generations. They cook and wash clothes as well as make shawls and jewelry and saddles. Their sole entertainment consists of visiting each other's homes where they sit and gossip, frequently poking fun at the men and howling with laughter. Only rarely do they leave the village, and when they do, it is in groups to shop at the market. Their lives are quite restricted, but they do not seem to notice. Or, if they do notice, they do not mind. Everything is accepted or explained away as "the will of Allah."

The first time I walked around the village, I came across a group of women dressed in black and clustered around the front porch of one of the houses. They stood wailing and putting mud and dirt upon their heads. I was shocked. However, having now seen this more than once, I have come to understand that it signifies a funeral and is the traditional way for women to show their support and grief for the family of the dead.

In their own way, all of these people are highly religious, even spiritual. They cannot conceive of anything that is not God and make frequent reference to Heckmit Rabina or "the will of Allah." They seem to feel Allah as a living presence within which they dwell, much like the desert itself.

June 29

As I've become more acquainted with the villagers, I've noticed that there are a few men who appear to be different from the rest. Even though they have families, they come and go, spending long periods of time in the desert. They have an ageless quality about them and an air of mystery. These "Desert Men" will stay in the village for a few days, or even weeks, before one or another disappears again into the vast ocean of sand. However, even when they are here, they seem to stand out.

They seldom participate in the same chores as the other men. Also, they command a level of respect, not for anything they do but simply by their presence.

July 23

Weeks have passed. I am no longer considered an oddity, but I still feel like one. On the surface I fit in quite well. However, for me, the difference between myself and the others becomes more apparent with each passing day.

July 25

The Kebir el Bellad, or acting elder of the village, is a man named Rashid. He was the one who found me in the desert by the Sphinx and has acted as my benefactor ever since. His sister and her large family have taken me in. I have been given a small "house" to live in by myself, as it would not be fitting for a stranger to sleep under the same roof with the unmarried nieces of Rashid. My "house" is little more than a storage closet, consisting of only one room with unused items stacked along one of the walls.

July 28

Rashid is very different from the others. In a sense he is some what like me. He seems to fit in but does not. He has a secret. I have no idea what made me write that, but in the moment of writing I know that it is true. Also, I try my best to quietly fit in. I cannot say why exactly, but I feel it is best for now not to reveal what I have been learning about myself.

August 6

I find I am intensely preoccupied with the passage of time. And I have a strange sense of foreboding. I feel that somehow time is running out for me, and I don't know any more than when I first awoke.

The shrill ring of the telephone jolted me back to reality. I had become so completely absorbed in what I was reading that I'd lost track of my surroundings. The phone rang again. I dropped the diary and jumped up, losing my towel in transition and almost tripping. I ran to the phone.

"Hello," I croaked.

"Cassie...pleeez don't tell me you fell back asleep!" said Melissa.

"No, no," I answered, a bit breathlessly but trying to sound natural. "I'll be right down. I kind of got lost in a long shower." *I can't believe I let myself get sucked in...again!*

I hung up the phone and dashed over to my suitcases. I quickly unzipped the large one, rifled through to find comfortable sandals, shorts and lightweight cotton knit shirt, and hurriedly dressed. I put new film in my cameras and darted toward the door. Then I remembered the diary. I dashed back to the room, grabbed it and purposefully stuffed it in the deepest recesses of my suitcase, zipping it shut. In a matter of moments, cameras in tow and hair still wet, I raced toward the lobby.

We made the short journey to the ancient temple complex of Karnak in small horse-drawn carriages. The route hugged the muddy banks of the Nile, and I stared off into the water, mesmerized. The syncopation of the horses' hooves on the pavement brought back to mind images of the pulsating energy at the Cairo airport, where we had arrived two nights earlier.

Although I hardly remembered the change of planes in Rome, I was wide-awake when we landed in Egypt. As we made our way through the airport, I couldn't help but get caught up in the tremendous sense of the exotic. Everywhere I looked, there were dusky-skinned men with flashing eyes and black beards, dressed immaculately in three piece suits and turbans. Other men wore the traditional long *galabia,* their women walking behind them, faces veiled and bodies entirely hidden beneath layers of heavy clothing. The women balanced large suitcases and heavy packages on their heads with amazing grace, leaving their hands free to hold the sweaty palms of small children or clutch an infant to their breast.

At one point I was surrounded by Muslim pilgrims, swathed in yards of white cotton cloth, all making their once-in-a-lifetime journey to Mecca. The whole panorama had the intrigue of a forties film set in "The Mysterious Middle East."

Weaving in and out of the hoard of bodies was an endless stream of roving cats. I overheard two women in my group talking excitedly about them. One said, "These cats are probably descendants of the ancient temple cats, guardians of the inner mysteries, and instruments of the Cat Goddess, Bastet." *No,* I groaned, *what have I gotten myself into?*

The night sky was inky black by the time our weary band of twenty travelers reached the Mena House Hotel at the foot of the pyramids. At one time, it had been a palace and it had a long and exotic history. Now it lay in a sort of tarnished splendor but still maintained a captivating presence, much like that of a dowager queen who carries herself with a certain grace, even though her days of great beauty and power have passed.

As I stood outside gazing up at the Great Pyramid, it seemed to glow. It was so huge that by comparison I felt small and vulnerable but, in some strange way, protected. Peculiar as it sounds, it seemed to talk to me. And for an odd brief moment, I had the eerie feeling that I belonged there – as though I were home.

CHAPTER 3

As our carriages drew to a halt in front of Karnak Temple, a chorus of Ooo's and Ah's brought me out of my reverie. I sighed as I realized how much of a blur the events of the last few days had been. Two things did stand out though – Rashid and the diary. But as I looked up at the ancient temple complex, my attention was pulled back to the present. The site was huge and appeared very complicated. It contained three main temples enclosed by enormous mud brick walls. There was an open-air museum across from a sacred lake and a vast number of powerful columns that seemed to reach to the sky. I studied the many hieroglyphic-covered walls and obelisks. Although the temple lay mostly in ruins, it was easy to sense the massive power it once held.

I followed along as the group leader, Gabriel, shared bits and pieces of information about the ancient place. He was a stout man of medium height with silver hair and beard. He so perfectly fit the picture of a spiritual teacher, he could have been sent directly from Central Casting. He had a compelling voice that sounded both sage and trustworthy – and he certainly knew how to spin a good yarn. He had the group in the palm of his hand. As I listened to him talk about the ancient *this* and spiritual *that*, and how life must have been for the temple initiates, he almost got me as well. Almost – but not quite! *He can't possibly know any of this stuff for sure. He's probably making it up as he goes along. That's enough for me!*

I left the group of woo-woos to walk around and capture the beauty of Karnak Temple on film. That was my job – to photograph the people and the places. *I don't have to buy the stories!* However, once I was out of the circle of Gabriel's voice, I found I could not concentrate. My mind kept drifting back, back to Rashid – and the diary.

That night, although I was exhausted, I couldn't get to sleep. Eventually I got up and fumbled around in the dark until I felt the soft cover of the diary between my fingers. Then, with quiet deliberation, I stowed myself away in the tiny bathroom.

Flashlight in hand and my back against the door, I opened to the spot I had marked earlier in the day.

August 10

They call me "Ghareb." It means stranger, and so I am. I still remember absolutely nothing about my past. Rashid's nephew, Hakim, and I have become friends, of sorts. He is probably a bit younger than I, but he looks a good deal older. The sun has already aged him.

Hakim is very spirited and this often gets the best of him. We were to take a large American lady and her two small sons out for a camel ride. When it came time to pay us, the Egyptian money confused her. Hakim ended up getting twice the amount of money Rashid had told her it would cost. Rashid was very angry with him. He did not say a word to me, but looked at me with great intensity as if to say, "You should know better."

I find it curious that he would expect more of me than of one of his own family. Given the same situation, many of the village fathers would have been proud of their son, or in this case nephew, for getting more money from a tourist. Most consider the tourists open game and, although there is nothing malicious about it, they try to get as much money as they can. But not Rashid! He seems to have a genuine respect for the tourists that come here.

The nephew was not dishonest, just young. In fact, Hakim loves the Americans. I think he would work for them for free. He uses every chance to practice his English and boasts he will go to the United States one day. He even named the family camel California, which he pronounces Cal-E-forn-E-a. It always makes me laugh. No one knows that I understand English. I am constantly amazed at my knowledge.

A camel named California! Rashid had a camel named California. It has to be the same Rashid! Now that I know where the diary came from at least I can give it back. But I rationalized – I think I'll just read a teensy bit more to make sure this guy Ghareb is okay.

August 17

I am feeling very frustrated and alone. Lately I have been waking up remembering snatches of dreams, mere wisps of images that vanish before I can fully grasp them. That no man's land between sleep and waking has become very difficult for me. Often I am confused and disoriented when I do wake up. It takes a while before I am able to remember exactly where I am.

I experience a deep loneliness and sense of separation. There is no one here I can talk to, and I feel an almost desperate need to talk to someone. I have thought of approaching Rashid, however I am not quite ready. Also, I cannot help but notice that he purposely avoids being alone with me. At times, if I turn around quickly, I catch him staring at me yet he avoids direct eye contact. It is very disconcerting. He does not talk very much, nonetheless, I have the sense that his keen eyes do not miss anything.

August 22

I cannot believe how long I have been here and how little I still know about myself. I feel like there is a wall, a barrier in my mind that I keep slamming up against whenever I try to remember things. It is useless for me to force my memory. Sometimes I lie in bed at night and will my mind to go backward. I can go to a certain point where there are some fuzzy images − then a door slams shut. If I try to push past that point, I get an intense throbbing headache.

August 26

I have taken to observing Rashid rather closely of late. He is the only one here who interests me. I have been watching him interact with the tourists, and the result is so often surprising. It is never what I would expect. He seems to have a special power over people. It is as if he knows more about them then they know about themselves. They open up to him in ways they never would with the other guides.

The type of tourist Rashid attracts is different, too. Most of them seem to be looking for something. They have a peculiar kind of animation and a similar look in their eyes, very alive and probing. It is the kind of alertness you generally see in small children or birds, but rarely in adults.

They are of all ages and come from all over the world, but they seem to have a common language. It is as though they all belonged to the same family, yet were not aware of it. They have a way of recognizing each other once they meet. Rashid has brought many of them back to the house for dinner. He often sits outside and talks with them late into the night, and I am certain he does not do this for money.

After one of these visits, Rashid will frequently vanish for a few days without saying a word to anyone. I keep feeling he holds a key to my identity. I am certain he knows something about me that he is not revealing.

September 3

This place is beginning to wear on my nerves, I feel haunted by it. Frequently, I find myself in possession of strange bits of information and history about the Great Pyramids and the temples. Images and thoughts flicker through my mind like scenes from a movie seen a very long time ago. I have no idea what they mean or if any of it has a personal connection to my life.

September 7

Today Rashid sent me out as a guide with a group of people from Atenne Deux, a French television network. They were scouting locations for a film. Still needing to keep my "uniqueness" a secret, I protested vehemently to Rashid that I would not be able to communicate with them.

But of course, there was no fooling him. Rashid did not exactly confront me on the issue. Rather, as has become usual in our exchanges, he looked at me with a sly smile and said, "Ah, Ghareb, my little friend, I am sure you will find a way." In that instant, any doubt that I might have had about his deeper knowledge of me vanished. What does he know? Why must we play this cat and mouse game and why can I not make myself demand that he tell me?

Of course, it all went fine with the French tourists. I acted the perfect Egyptian guide. I greeted them with "Ehlen waseh'len" and imitated the pidgin French I have heard the other guides use. But, because I understood every word they said, I had to watch my facial expressions and remember not to laugh when they joked amongst themselves.

The tourists were very pleased and gave me a big tip. When I returned in the evening I gave most of the money to Rashid's sister, Hadiga, in whose home I have been living these many months. What need do I have of money? Hadiga made quite a fuss over me and said I might want to think about starting a family of my own, now that I was becoming "rawgilh shatiru," a successful businessman. I know exactly what she has in mind. She has been hinting for weeks about a match between Gameleh, her sixteen-year-old daughter and me.

Hakim shrieked with glee, teasing his sister relentlessly. She blushed a bright beet red and ran out of the room giggling, trying to hide her face. I know it was all meant as a great compliment, but it only made me sad. I cannot imagine spending the rest of my days here. Besides, my mind was elsewhere. I need to find out who I am.

Rashid was gone when I returned this evening. I wonder if anyone else notices his strangeness.

    I fell asleep on the bathroom floor. Fortunately, I woke up before dawn. Melissa was still breathing deeply as I stuffed the diary into my suitcase and slipped into bed. *Two hours to sleep,* I groaned, *if I'm lucky.*

    Morning came quickly.

    "Okay Little Miss Dreamer, time to wake up," called Melissa. My mouth would not work. I felt like I had just fallen asleep.

    "If you remember we're going to visit Luxor Temple today," she said cheerily. "It's within walking distance of the hotel."

    "Mmmm," I finally managed to mumble. "You know what," I continued, trying in vain to wake up, "I'll meet you at breakfast. If I'm not down in time, I'll meet you at the temple."

    "Well…alright. All you have to do is go out the front door of the hotel and turn left. You can't miss it."

    "Got it! Turn left…can't miss it," I repeated, trying to sound cheery myself. I was definitely not fully recovered and way past merely being tired. I closed my eyes, cursing my decision to come on this ridiculous trip. Then I remembered the young man from the diary. He was the stranger, the "outsider." Unable to stop myself, I drifted off to sleep again thinking, with some discomfort, that I, too, was feeling very much the outsider amongst my group of airy-fairy traveling companions. And feeling like an outsider was exactly what I had spent my entire life trying to avoid.

CHAPTER 4

I am in a dark room. I search and search for the light switch. It's not in the usual place, so I slide my hand across the wall until I find it. I flick it on, but nothing happens. I try again, still no light. Then I try a third time, but even now it doesn't work. Then I hear soft laughter coming from across the room. I toggle the switch back and forth many times, willing it to shed some light. Finally, I give up and lean against the wall for support. At that moment the light flashes on. I see that I am the person standing in the dark on the opposite side of the room.

I awoke from the dream with a start, feeling muddleheaded and not much better than I had in the morning. But something had shifted – I was starving. Since it was already mid-afternoon, I decided to go in search of food rather than trying to catch up with the group. I dressed quickly and was about to leave when I remembered – *the diary!* I pulled it from my suitcase and glared at it, not quite sure what I wanted to do. *Oh, well....* I shoved it into a small backpack with one of my cameras, grabbed a hat and left.

Sitting under the tattered umbrella at a small outdoor café, I reached for the diary and put in on the table in front of me. I experienced the same push-pull sensation I felt every time I picked it up. *This whole thing is so strange...but addictive! I feel like an intruder in someone else's life.*

As I gazed transfixed by the diary, my thoughts took off in another direction. Events of the past year and a half flooded my memory, and I suddenly realized how much my life had changed in that short span of time. It was almost as if some kind of outside force had been at work in my life. Of course, I knew it was ridiculous, but in a way, that's what my life had become – ridiculous. I certainly had no plans to either move from a city I loved or to travel. *Yet I'd made the move and here I am sitting at an outdoor café...in Egypt!*

As far back as I could remember, I had been searching for "something." I couldn't wait to leave home, to be out on my own and explore. I headed for San Francisco, the picturesque city I had dreamed of living in since a short visit years before. Oddly enough, when I finally arrived I had no idea what to do with myself. I felt weighted down, as if a force was blocking me from becoming who I was meant to be.

I spent a few years trying my hand at one thing then another, but nothing seemed to quite fit. I would move on, always looking for what felt "right." I was often forced to take jobs I hated just to pay the rent, but I stuck with my search, determined to find my "true calling." Eventually I discovered photography – then fashion photography. It was pure love right from the start! After only seven months of art school I began making a living doing something I adored. I had arrived – and it had only gotten better from there.

Apparently I had a gift – and it turned out I had the Midas touch, as well. Clients couldn't get enough of my work. Soon I even had two New York clients who loved the way I used San Francisco as a backdrop for my shots. I was a sure bet for major success. Then the strangest thing happened. I woke up one morning and, out of nowhere, felt compelled to move to Los Angeles. What made the idea truly insane is that I didn't even like Los Angeles.

I tried not to think about moving, but the feeling wouldn't go away. I didn't discuss it with anyone for several weeks. Then one day I was walking in Golden Gate Park with my friend Lisa. It was a typical foggy November day with the sharp smell of eucalyptus in the air. The sun peaked out from the clouds and it became warm. I turned to my friend and said, "I've been thinking of moving to Los Angeles."

Lisa stopped dead in her tracks, stared at me and burst out laughing.

"You've got to be joking, Cassie!" she said, unwinding the hand-made, multi-colored scarf from around her neck.

"No, Lisa, I'm serious," I countered.

"Why would you move there? It's a horrible place...too many people...too many cars...and way too much concrete. We went there last year and you hated it. Remember?"

"Of course I do! It's bizarre, but I can't stop thinking about it," I answered, unzipping my jacket. "It's weird, but it's like it's been calling out to me. I think I'm just tired of wearing so many layers of clothing."

"That's ridiculous! And speaking about clothing, you're building a great career here as a fashion photographer. Everyone loves your work! You're a genius at finding locations, and your shots are so intriguing and moody...so sophisticated!

"Who else do you know who's actually working at what they trained for? And what they love doing! Especially in the arts! You're not only working, for god's sake, you're getting paid so well. You're on your way. Another six months and you'll have a great portfolio to take to New York. That's where you said you wanted to go...where all the big fashion magazines are. Fashion editorial work, that's your specialty, all the creative stuff. Don't you remember, that's what you said you were born to do," Lisa said, sounding a bit like my mother.

"I know, I know," I answered, "It's just that I have this feeling.... I can't explain it," I signed, "I'm kind of bored and restless. Maybe I'm supposed to move to L.A. to get me in the mood for New York...kind of prepare myself," I mumbled, realizing that what I was saying made no sense at all.

"But Los Angeles doesn't even have a fashion industry. It's nothing like New York. Nobody will understand your work. It's too avant-garde. Who are you going to work for?"

And she was right! After nine lonely months in Los Angeles, hard as I tried, I had still not landed one paying job. I not only felt I was losing my mind – I was losing my identity, as well. *But if I hadn't made that move and hadn't been completely stymied in my attempts to get work....* I shuttered when I thought about what had happened next.

It was a typical day of my life in L.A. – loaded with frustration. I had just finished one more interview at an advertising agency where the art director said he loved my work, but thought I wasn't quite right for the job. The truth was he didn't love it – he didn't even get it. His suggestion was that I rent a studio and shoot some models against generic white background paper, so we could "see the clothes."

My work was artistic and creative and set a mood. That was what sold the clothes. *Every art director here has the mentality of a catalogue designer.* I felt sick and humiliated as I remembered the meeting, but was determined not to give in to defeat. I knew I could do it. *I simply need to stick it out...try harder. That's worked for me before and I'll make it work now!*

I came home to the small, airless West Hollywood apartment I shared with another woman photographer who was also not finding any work. Rather than get into one more inane discussion about how bad things were, I made a beeline for my tiny bedroom. I plopped my portfolio on the desk I had rescued from the Goodwill, looked out my one viewless window and then down at my ratty, hand-me-down futon and orange-crate nightstand. "I deserve better than this," I groaned, as I dive-bombed onto the little mattress.

I was starting to doze off when the phone rang. *I hope it's that guy from Los Angeles Magazine.* He had said he would get right back to me about the editorial on L.A.'s young designers. *It's got to be him! I know it's him. He loved my portfolio....*

As I sat up and reached for the phone, I automatically smoothed back my hair and answered in my most professional voice, "Cassandra Wolfe here."

"Cassie, is me...Jean Luc. Remember? We work on the Armani ad together last year in San Francisco?"

"Of course I remember you Jean Luc. How are you?" I said, my heart sinking. And how could I possibly have forgotten him? He was this gorgeous European model I had used in an ad that had brought him a lot of attention. He had stayed on for a week in San Francisco, and we had had a mad passionate love affair. The relationship never went anywhere which was, unfortunately, much more typical of my romantic life than I cared to admit. Still, there was something special about him.

"I apologize for not calling sooner but this year, it has been crazy! I can talk only for a minute now, but I will be in L.A. next week and we can have dinner, yes?"

"Yes, definitely," I answered, sounding much too eager. *Jeez...! I'll never get this man-woman thing right. I should have hesitated a bit.*

"Good! I will call you Monday. But, right now I am calling you with a job offer. It's something remarkable!"

"A job offer! Great! I'm all ears." *I knew it! It was just a matter of time. Perseverance...and time!*

"This spiritual teacher I have been studying with, he is taking some students to Egypt and is looking for a photographer to make a slide show of the trip. Is not much money, only a couple thousand dollars, but he would pay all of your expenses, including airfare and meals. It would be for three weeks and is a fantastic opportunity."

"Are you serious? You want me to go to Egypt to shoot a slide show for some Guru guy? I'm a fashion photographer. I don't...."

"But Cassie, he's a fantastic man, absolutely brilliant, and you would get to go to Egypt for free."

"Thanks Jean Luc, but I don't think so. As a matter of fact, right now I'm expecting a confirmation call from *Los Angeles Magazine* to shoot an editorial on L.A.'s young designers. I can't just go flying off for three weeks to Egypt. I have my career and...."

"Whoa! Stop for a second. Think about it Cassie, it would be so good for you. I know a beautiful model who's going to be on the trip. You could shoot some pictures of her in front of the Great Pyramids. Or even shoot the pyramids as a location shot. It would be a great piece for your portfolio. Two birds with one stone, you know. I have a plane to catch, so I will call you on Monday. Promise me you will at least go to a travel agent and get some brochures, and please…think about it! You have my American mobile number if you have any more questions."

"But I…." I heard the phone click off, and I was talking to the air. A model at the Great Pyramids would make a great shot, and any photos of them would be terrific, but I couldn't go flying off to Egypt and leave my responsibilities – my career. Before I could catch my breath, the phone rang again. *Now, this one has to be Los Angeles Magazine!*

It was – and I was summarily told that I did not have yet another job. They had decided to use a "name photographer." Of course, they're always so polite and say, "But we will be sure to keep you in mind for next time." *Blah, blah, blah! It's always next time! It's bullshit!* At that moment my roommate Gail poked her head into my bedroom.

"I can tell you've had a bad day and I hate to bother you with this right now, but I need to get last month's rent and we just got a huge gas bill."

"I know, I know! I'm working on it." *God, doesn't this ever end? Okay…how much did Jean Luc say that gig would pay?* There certainly wasn't anybody else knocking on my door with exotic offers. *I have to take it…but they better let me shoot film. I so prefer it to digital.*

I remembered having seen a funky little travel agency close-by. It was almost hidden between two buildings and hard to spot. Vines trailed over it, and it looked like it had been there forever. *Okay, I'll check it out tomorrow.* I heaved a sigh of resignation.

* * * * * * * * * * *

On my way to see the travel agent the following morning, I pondered the irony of it all. I was half Jewish and half Arab. My great-grandfather was from Egypt, but I had never thought of it as my "roots." I had never even been particularly interested in anything Egypt-ian – except for my grandmother's delicious *basboosa*.

I arrived at the agency right after it opened. The matronly travel agent was on the phone. She signaled me to the chair in front of her desk, which was near the front door. After a few minutes of waiting, I mouthed the words, *Egypt! I'd like some information on Egypt.*

With her hand over the mouthpiece of the phone she whispered, "Wouldn't you like to go to Israel, too?" The half Jewish part of me flinched. *Great! Now instead of doing my "real work," I'll be visiting both of my ancestral homes. Not!* Before I could say a word, she plopped a couple of brochures on the desk in front of me. Then, very efficiently, she swiveled her chair around and pulled out yet another brochure from a small cabinet behind her.

"I have a trip coming up to Egypt and Israel," she whispered again, handing me a glossy brochure with a picture of the Great Pyramids on the cover. "Look this over. I'll be off the phone in a sec."

My hand had barely grasped the brochure before my eyes were drawn to the picture of the pyramids. I immediately went into a kind of reverie. Multiple images passed before my eyes so quickly, I could not identify them. Then, for one brief moment, I clearly "saw" a face – a face of a man with black curly hair and piercingly bright blue eyes that seemed to lock directly onto mine. My eyelids began to flutter and I felt like I might pass out. When I came back to myself, my eyes were still riveted on the Great Pyramids – pyramids that were alive and glowing. I dropped the brochure like it was on fire and half ran, half stumbled out the door.

I walked mechanically toward my apartment, trying to make "logi-cal" sense out of what had happened, but of course, none of it was "log-ical." *I hope Gail's not home...I have to clear my head,* I thought, opening the door. But there she was, sitting on the sofa dissolved in tears.

"What's the matter?" I asked, dropping my purse on a chair and running over to her.

"It's the electricity," she sobbed, dabbing her eyes with a Kleenex. They've shut it off! That's what happens when neither of us has any money."

"Don't worry," I said, taking her hand in mine and allowing the motherly side of me, which was in short supply, to come out. "It's going to be all right! I'm taking this job in Egypt, and I'm going to have some money for you right away. You need to call your mom. I know you hate doing that, but I also know she will front you the money for now."

"In Egypt?"

"I'll explain later...just phone her." Then I called Jean Luc's cell and fortunately got in touch with him immediately. I told him I'd take the job and asked for half the money up front. He heard the tension in my voice and said, "If you need the money right now, I front it for you. I got a lot of work from those shots you took of me."

That was less than three weeks ago, and now I am sitting in a café in Egypt. I leaned back and gazed across the road at the Nile River. Well, the last year and a half had certainly been a "trip," but I hadn't been the one in the driver's seat. And I didn't much enjoy being a passenger in my own life.

"More coffee, Miss?"

The waiter's voice shot through my thoughts and I nearly jumped out of my seat.

"Sorry miss, excuse please."

"It's okay, I'm fine," I said, more snappishly than I had meant to. "Yes, I would like more coffee, thank you." I glanced down at my barely eaten sandwich. In truth, I was not fine. I had lost my appetite. I touched my forehead. *I think I'm still running a fever. Damn it!* Then I looked at the still unopened diary lying patiently on the table. I was almost afraid to pick it up again, but I felt compelled, and at this point I was hooked – too enchanted not to read more.

I reached for the diary, and as my fingers touched the cover, an image passed before my eyes. It was a young man with black curly hair and piercingly bright blue eyes that stared into mine. *My god...that's exactly the face I saw at the travel agency when the agent handed me the brochure with the picture of the Great Pyramids on it. This can't be what I think it is....*

I opened the diary to the first page and reread it.

———————— ✦ ————————

Day 1 – Night

I do not know anything except what I have been told. I am lying on a cot in a small, cement and steel house in an Arab village close to the Sphinx on the Giza plain near Cairo. The night is hot and dry, and the air is thick with dust. The locals say I was near death from exposure and dehydration when I was found two days ago lying near the Sphinx.

I am awake again. I have no idea whether days or only moments have passed. It is pitch black, and except for the flickering flame of a small candle casting patches of light on this page, I cannot see anything. My fingers feel stiff and sticky on my pencil stub as they struggle to form these words. My eyes burn and my head is pounding.

I do not know how long I have been here or how long I was in the desert before they found me.

I do not know who I am....

CHAPTER 5

My fingers slowly closed the diary, holding it gently in my hands. *Oh, my god! It's definitely the same face I saw at the travel agency. And I remember that somewhere in the first few pages, he even described himself as having blue eyes.*

It had all gotten much too bizarre. In fact, it was crazy! Rashid, the camel named California, the face with the blue eyes! I tried to think it through, to make some kind of sense of it all, but of course I couldn't. However, I knew one thing for certain – if I hadn't moved from San Francisco to Los Angeles, for no fathomable reason, I would not have been out of work and would never have accepted Jean-Luc's proposal. *And if all of that were true, I also wouldn't have been at the travel agency that morning, and I wouldn't have had the vision of the familiar-looking, blue-eyed man whose diary is now in my hands.*

I stared at the diary, tapping it nervously with my fingers. *This is downright creepy! Things like this just don't happen in my life! Why now?* I searched for answers that didn't come. Then with a sense of resolve, I opened the diary to the place where I had left off that morning. *I have to read it…the answer to all of this has to be in here someplace!*

September 14

Three and a half uneventful months have passed since I first began this diary. In the past few days I am aware of a marked shift in myself. It feels like the very air itself is intensely charged.

All at once, I have such a deep premonition of change. Tonight I was unable to sleep, and as I lay tossing on my little cot I began to feel the walls closing in on me. It became so oppressive I had to go outside.

I have brought my little journal with me and have wandered over by the Great Pyramids to look up at the stars and rest my overworked mind. The moon is full and the entire plain feels alive and throbbing with energy.

September 16

This afternoon I went to the Mena House, a large old hotel that was once a palace. It lies within walking distance of the Great Pyramids. Rashid had sent me to pick up some tourists. While I was waiting for them in the room used by the porters, I glanced at the television set that plays incessantly. It was tuned to a news program that featured an Arab archeologist and an Israeli scholar discussing some artifacts recently found in the Negev Desert. I stood transfixed. The face, the voice and even the mannerisms of the Israeli were vibrantly familiar to me. I know him! I am positive of it.

As I stood there completely immobilized, an entire scenario passed before my eyes. I saw the Israeli and with him a small, dark-haired boy. They were in a wood paneled office, lined with old leather bound books. The man was smoking a pipe, and the young boy, with glazed eyes and waving arms, ran around the room shouting in some strange and guttural language.

Then, without warning, everything went black, and I must have lost consciousness. When I opened my eyes, I was lying on the floor. A lot of people were around me and one of the bellhops was leaning over me, and shaking my shoulder. As I think about it, even now, my heart begins to race and my mouth goes dry. It is definitely a memory - my first. So this is how it begins!

September 21

I have been asking questions about the television program for days. The bellhops at the Mena House are convinced I am "magnoon, which amounts to a crazy man, or at the very least "ghaby, a fool. They want to know why I should care so much about "some Jew" on television. I have been careful to conceal the true depth of my interest - or my exhilaration and I have learned some things. I found out the man is a famous Israeli professor, the head of Hebrew and Jewish Languages at the Hebrew University in Jerusalem. I have written him a detailed letter telling him about my situation and asking him many questions. I have no idea how we are connected, but I am certain that I know him.

I am filled with hope. For the very first time, I feel confident that this endless period of waiting and wondering will soon be at an end.

September 28

This waiting to hear from the professor is very difficult.

October 19

Weeks have passed and I have still not heard from the Israeli professor. I do feel like a fool for putting so much expectation on that connection. No matter how hard I fight against them, feelings of frustration and despair are beginning to overtake me again.

October 24

I am still unable to remember anything before awakening in the desert. I have finally decided I must speak with Rashid, although I have no idea what I will say. I have approached him a number of different times. I do not understand why, but it is clear he does not want to talk with me. He never exactly avoids me, but it seems to happen that every time I try to talk to him about what is on my mind, he starts talking about something different. Or else, whenever I am about to approach him, one or the other of us is called away by somebody or something needing our attention. This has happened five or six times, so I am certain it is no accident. I do not know how he does it, but I do know that he makes it happen.

October 27

Today I was with Hakim at the stables. We were preparing two horses for a show in Aswan. I had a very odd, prickly feeling on my back. I felt I was being watched. I turned around very quickly and there was Rashid. However, when I blinked against the sun he was gone. For a split second I felt as if I was losing my sanity.

I live with a constant sense of doubt about everyone and everything. Things cannot go on this way. A persistent feeling of urgency weighs on me more heavily with each passing day.

November 3

I know I am being watched almost constantly now, but I can never catch anyone in the act. When I turn around, there is no one there. Last night I was abruptly awakened from a sound sleep by the murmur of voices deep in argument. I could hear angry hissing whispers right outside my window, and I was able to make out the words, "You must let the boy remember!" There was the sound of scuffling followed by a bright, lightening-like flash. I ran outside, but there was not a soul in sight. I looked around, expecting someone from the village to have been drawn by the argument and the light. No one came. I appear to be the only one who heard any-thing unusual. Intuitively, I know who "the boy" is.

November 5

Rashid was gone when I looked for him the morning after the flash of light. No one seems to know where he is. And no one seems to be concerned. As Hussein, the father of one of my new friends said, "Rashid comes and Rashid goes sometimes for weeks at a time. Rashid is like the wind. But he is always here when someone needs him." I kept my commentary on his statement to myself.

November 9

I had a very strange dream last night. It is the first one I have remembered in such detail. I saw a beautiful lush val-with rolling green hills. The sky was a vibrant blue and the air was pure and sweet. A great number of brilliant glowing lights appeared. They grew in size until they were quite large. They were spherical in shape and pulsated with an intense brightness. Within the sphere I could make out a form, almost humanoid, but lacking in definition. At first the images were very faint and I had to strain my attention to make them out. They seemed to be made of smoke or mist.

As I continued watching, the forms became more and more dense, until they were almost solid shapes. The figures were very tall with light skin and silvery-blond hair. They appeared to have human faces with long foreheads and unusually large glowing blue eyes. I felt their rhythmic pulsation inside of my own body, keeping time with my heartbeat.

November 16

Night is the only time I feel truly alive. The daylight hours pass uneventfully, like the shadows of dreams. I feel uninvolved. But the nights - the nights are vibrant with images and intense emotion.

Last night I had another very detailed dream. I have no idea where it was, but the place was familiar to me. I was by the sea and a wild storm was raging. The earth shook and the wind blew fiercely. There were great tidal waves rolling in upon the land. As I stood on a spot of scorched ground, gases from within the earth's core erupted in spontaneous fires all around me. There was also fire in the sky. I was wearing a flowing, metallic robe with small crystals woven into the fabric. Others, dressed in a similar fashion, ran about in aimless terror. I stood very still with my arms stretched upward, as if in an invocation.

Abruptly, the earth gave a great and violent shudder, and a trench of water opened beneath me. At that instant, I felt myself swooped up off of the ground and into the air. I floated high enough to see one last great wave pour over the land, inundating everything in its path. Then I floated even higher until I could see the entire outline of the landmass below me. An island was being ripped in half and the half I had been standing on was literally drowning. I heard a great wail as the larger potion of the huge island and all of its inhabitants sunk beneath the waves. I felt damp and clammy when I awoke. My face was streaked with tears and my jaw was tightly clenched.

November 21

It is beginning to turn light outside. Again, I have awakened in the middle of a dream. Each detail was so vivid it was like watching a movie that was running at a slightly slower than normal speed. In my dream, I saw a woman in her early twenties holding a small child. It was the same child I had seen with the Israeli professor in my vision at the Mena House. However, in this dream the child was younger.

The woman was very agitated and her eyes red and swollen from crying. She gently rocked the child who lay exhausted in her arms. She was trying to dial a number on the telephone, but her hand shook so violently, she was forced to hang up and redial many times. Somehow she managed to complete the call and heard the line begin to ring. She sat biting her lower lip and rocking the baby. Finally a man answered.

"Benjamin?" she sobbed.

"Yes," answered a male voice. "Sara is that you? Speak up, I can hardly hear you."

The woman moved her lips but nothing came out. Then, almost inaudibly, she managed, "Yes, I...it's David...it's happened again...." The words caught in her throat. She took a quick gulp of air and squeezed her eyes tightly shut to hold back the tears. "I'm so afraid, Ben. Do you think he's psychotic or...." Moments passed before she whispered "...or possessed?"

With the words out, her body softened and she gently rocked the child in her arms. "Ben...Ben, I thought it was all over. He's been so good, so normal. He's been just like any other child for almost three months. Now the nightmare is starting all over again. I'm so worried about him. His little body can't take much more of this."

That was all I saw before I woke up, but this time my dream was not sketchy at all. Every nuance was completely familiar to me. I have gained access to a whole new world at night. It feels like I am reaching into a very deep part of myself. I do not yet fully understand what is happening, but I am truly, truly grateful.

November 26

It is dawn. I am sitting, chin propped on my hands, elbows on my knees, staring out through the open shutters as the first light spreads over the Giza plain. It is unbearably beautiful. It is quiet and the air is still with only the faintest hint of morning sounds coming through the thin brick walls. The chill of the night remains around me. I can hear the lone bleating of a goat and the voice of the muezzin as he proclaims the call to prayer.

I am in this world, but I am not a part of it. I feel a wrenching sense of nostalgia for another time and another place - neither of which I can name.

⊰⊱

I forcibly stopped myself. I hadn't realized it, but the afternoon had swiftly passed, and it was rapidly growing dark. Again I found myself feeling guilty for not having been with the group all day. Like the author of the diary, I also felt I was living in two worlds. The diary held a deep fascination for me, but the strangeness of its story and the way it came into my possession were very disturbing. I had no idea how to solve the mystery. However, as I returned to the hotel, I promised myself I would put the diary aside for a while and try harder to fit in with the group. The bottom line was, in spite of everything, I had been hired to do a job, and I intended to do it!

CHAPTER 6

The following morning, with a little assist from Melissa in the wake-up department, I joined the group. The highlight of the day was to be an initiation ceremony in Luxor Temple, which was scheduled for that evening. In preparation for the event, Gabriel had suggested we go on a shopping trip to purchase *galabias,* the long cotton caftans traditionally worn by Egyptian men. He thought that all of us, both male and female, might find the simple cotton robes to be more ceremonial in feeling than our ordinary clothing. The whole thing seemed a bit silly to me but I held true to my resolve to fit in and tried to at least pretend I was interested in the event.

Before sending us off on our outing, Gabriel had us meet in one of the hotel's small lounges for another of his "history lessons." As Melissa and I rushed down the corridor to the lounge, we passed a tall, thin man carrying large charts of some sort under one arm and metal stands under the other. Even though he was laden with equipment, his back was ramrod straight, and he took such long, smooth strides he seemed to float down the hall. When we reached the double door entry and heard him behind us, I realized he was probably headed for our lounge. I turned, held the door open for him and watched as he glided into the room.

"John! Great, you're right on time. Let's set them all up right here," said Gabriel, reaching for the stands. "Perfect! Thank you. All right everybody, sit down and make yourselves comfortable.

"We're going to spend a little time this morning talking about our initiation ceremony in Luxor Temple tonight but before we do, I want to introduce you to John Smith. John is our liaison with the tour company, so if there is anything you need, any logistics, problems or anything else that comes up, John is the man to talk to."

The tall slender man with thinning black hair and a pronounced Adam's apple smiled and nodded. "I'm sorry I couldn't be with you in Cairo, but you can count on me for the remainder of the trip. You have a wonderful tour guide in Gabriel, but if you need anything just let me know. I can see you're all waiting to hear what Gabriel has to say, so I will leave you in his capable hands." He nodded at Gabriel then at us and glided out of the room. *Look how long his arms are. No wonder he could carry those charts so easily.*

"So let's begin," said Gabriel enthusiastically. "How many of you know about the seven *chakras?*"

Most of the hands in the room went up.

"That's a good start. Now, when you think of the chakras, what is the first one that comes to mind?"

"The heart chakra," called a chorus of voices.

 "Right! What's another one that comes to mind?"

A young man named Thomas spoke up. "Um...I think the second chakra has to do with having good sex."

A self-conscious chuckle flitted about the room.

"Well, there's certainly some truth to that, but let me step back for a moment and bring everyone up to speed. What we all see and relate to as our body is only the physical form. We also have an invisible *energy body.* And in the same way that our physical body, with its organs and tissues, is fed by the energy in oxygen, our invisible body is fed and run by energy from the Cosmos.

"There are more similarities. Much as our various organ systems, the lungs, heart and kidneys for example, have a particular physical function to fulfill, there are seven invisible energy centers, or chakras, that have a specific vital role as well. Their subtle, invisible energy underlies every atom of our physical body. This energy infuses our body and extends out from it in what we call the *aura.*

"The important thing to understand is that each of the chakras has a physical, mental, emotional and spiritual component. When any of them are blocked, the energy in that part of your life will be blocked as well. If you want to move forward in your life and in your spiritual development, an understanding of the chakras and their function is essential. So those of you who aren't interested in moving your life forward might want to go out and take a walk right now."

Everyone laughed.

"Ah...I see that no one is getting up to leave." There was even more laughter. "All right then, this might be a little dry but bear with me...."

"Here we go," Gabriel said, as he pulled the two chart stands forward. The first chart showed a simple outline of the human body with seven small red circles beginning just above the head and running down the spine. The second showed the human body in skeletal form with a series of squares and rectangles superimposed over it.

"You can see a similarity in shape between the two charts, can't you? That was the intent. The first chart is obvious. It's the human body. The seven circles represent the seven chakras. The second chart shows the skeletal form of the human body, and the squares and rectangles represent the floor plan of Luxor Temple.

"The temple was specifically designed to resemble the human body and was known to the initiates as the Temple in Man. It is believed that as the initiate passed from room to room during their initiation process, the energetic frequencies built into each chamber would stimulate the rising of the *kundalini* and move the initiate toward enlightenment."

The room buzzed with the word *kundalini*.

"Hold on a moment! I realize all of you want to hear more about kundalini. We'll get to it, I promise. But before we go there," he said, pointing to the first square, "this is where we began our tour of Luxor Temple yesterday morning." Then, pointing to the very top of the last rectangle, he said, "This is the end of the sixth room where we saw the alter on the far wall. I'll explain why there is no seventh room when we get there.

"Now," Gabriel said, indicating the human body on the first chart, "we are ready to talk about these seven red circles, or chakras. Those of you who think you know about the chakras, don't fall asleep, because I'm going to do a little review, and then I'm going to take you quite a bit deeper into their meaning.

"The seven chakras represent invisible energy centers. A chakra is the focal point for receiving energy. It brings in the 'energy of aliveness' from the Cosmos and the collective unconscious, and merges it with the physical, mental and emotional worlds of each person. Under the proper circumstances, it then sends that energy up the spine and out to animate the physical body, bringing about self-awareness and spiritual awakening.

"The word *chakra* literally means 'wheel.' And like a wheel, its spin will speed up or slow down to match a person's inner condition and level of awareness. If the energy of a chakra becomes clogged or stagnant, it can cause any combination of physical, mental, emotional or spiritual distress. The chakra system represents a very sophisticated understanding of the whole of person…body, mind and spirit.

"Now, here is where kundalini comes in. Like chakra, kundalini is a Sanskrit word. It roughly translates as 'coiled up' or 'coiled like a snake.' Basically, kundalini is dormant energy that resides within all of us. It lies right below the spine, coiled like a snake, around the first chakra. It can be activated by various spiritual practices such as yoga, meditation and chanting. However, it can also be brought to life by situations of intense stress or a near death experience. Once awakened, the kundalini begins its journey snaking up and around the spine piercing and opening the chakras. You can't talk about the chakras without also talking about kundalini."

Gabriel paused. "Okay, aside from the kundalini, are there any questions so far?"

Suzanne, a woman in her early thirties, said, "I've taken yoga and been meditating for a few years, but some of what you've said already is completely new and the connection to the temple is fascinating. I'm sure I'll have some questions later, especially about kundalini."

Gabriel chuckled. "Sounds good! All right then, let's go on and spend a few moments talking about each individual chakra. Don't worry about remembering all of the details. I will simplify it as much as I can while still giving you a basic foundation.

"Starting from the bottom, the first chakra is located at the base of the sacrum, below the spine. It is related to our will-to-live. This is life at its most basic. When we think of primitive people, like the proverbial cave man or those living in abject poverty, we see people who are in survival mode. All they can think of is where their next meal is coming from.

"The second chakra, located at the actual base of the spine, is concerned with creativity, identity, self-image...and yes, it encompasses one's sexuality. The same energy that can create a baby when operating purely on the physical plane of the body, can also bring forth a great work of art or a new way of harnessing energy from sun.

"So then, on we go. The third chakra is located on the spine, four or five inches below the shoulder blades. It is related to desire, and is the vitality and emotional center. Most people in the Western world live in the third chakra. Our immediate needs are taken care of, and we have the luxury to be able to think about the future...to make choices. It is here that one chooses either to feel emotions or shut them down. When this chakra is in balance, we feel a positive emotional connection and relationship with others, and a sense of our place in the world. When it's not open...well, you've heard the expression, *I feel like I've got a knot in my stomach?* That is the exact location of the third chakra, and the knot is telling you that there is an emotion trying to get your attention...to be acknowledged and worked with.

"Now, not only do most people in developed countries live in the third chakra, but they usually don't progress much beyond it. What life is calling on us to do at this time is move into the fourth, or heart chakra. This chakra is located between the shoulder blades. It is the love center. The heart chakra is where we experience compassion, love for another, and of course, self-love."

Hands flew up. "Ah! Very good! I knew that would get a rise out of you...if you were listening. And I know what you are going to say. What do you mean that most of us don't live in the heart chakra? I love...my mother loves...my children...my husband. And it's true, you do love...and you are loved. The problem is most people live a restricted form of love. It's conditional. I will love you if you love me. Look at how many people promise to love and then get divorced. Friends love one another until one of them doesn't perform the way the other thinks they should. Often it's not even talked about. The friendship simply breaks, and they both move on until the same situation arises again with someone else.

"Even love within the family is complicated. The most unconditional love is between a parent and child, but even then there is often a sense of responsibility, of obligation and the need for approval or the culturally correct way of doing things. Now this isn't true for all families, but how many of you know someone who dreads the holiday season because it means family time? Or, has an in-law who treats them badly, because they didn't approve of the marriage? Living in the fourth chakra, the heart chakra, means unconditional love. You love and you don't need anything back. When fully developed, it allows us to sacrifice ourselves for a higher cause. An example would be when doctors, nurses and clergy risk their own lives to care for people during a dangerous epidemic.

"As I said, the chakras are complex because they overlap as they weave their way through the physical, mental, emotional and spiritual realms of a person's life. But the fourth chakra, the heart chakra, is important because it is the bridge between the chakras dealing with the physical world and those that have to do with one's spirituality. I know you still have questions, but you only need to have a general sense of how the chakras interconnect, so for brevity's sake, let's move on.

"The fifth chakra is located at the back of the neck. This chakra is about communication...listening inside to hear your inner truth. It's also about surrendering your personal will to the higher will of God or Source. Has anyone here found themselves in a situation where no matter how hard you try, things aren't going the way you had planned?" Groans filled the room. "Well, life is presenting you with two choices. Either you can go into battle and continue to swim against the current, or surrender and trust there is a reason things are not working out...that there is higher purpose at play. In the second case, you give up trying to control how things 'should be' and move into trust. This is where the saying, *Let go and let God* comes in.

"The sixth chakra is located within the head, right above the eyes. The ancient teachers called it the 'third eye.' It's about seeing but on a much deeper level than just the physical. Those people we think of as wise, not necessarily educated, but wise, are seeing with their third eye. It is about the capacity to see things as they really are. It's only when you are willing to see things clearly that the third eye opens. When the third eye is completely open, a person can 'see' energy. Interestingly enough, the sixth chakra is associated with the pineal gland, which contains rods and cones just like your two physical eyes do.

"This chakra opens when the kundalini energy we spoke about earlier has snaked its way up from the first to the sixth chakra. This chakra then acts as a hyper-dimensional doorway to the seventh chakra, or cosmic consciousness.

"The final chakra, the seventh, is located right above the head. It governs the activity of the upper brain and is all about connecting to our Spirituality. When completely opened, our consciousness moves beyond the ordinary human realm and into the spiritual one. Many people occasionally dip into the seventh chakra and have moments of amazing clarity and brilliant insight, but in general, they cannot sustain it."

There was a rustle in the room and someone ventured to ask, "Does anyone actually reach that level...and stay there?"

"Yes, there are those who reside at the level of the seventh chakra. People like Jesus, Buddha, the author Eckert Tolle, to name a few. And of course, the great spiritual teachers throughout the ages reached that level. But in addition, there are a surprising number of people whose names you might never know who have experienced an awakening through what I can only call Grace. These remarkable souls can be found in all walks of life and in all parts of the world...working in offices, doing menial tasks or even being amongst the homeless on the streets. Yet, despite outward appearances, these people live in a profound state of Oneness." Gabriel paused, as if considering something before continuing thoughtfully, "Some believe this state is the next step in human evolution.

"Well, that's it for the lecture."

"Gabriel, you were going to talk about the second chart."

"Right! Thank you, I almost forgot. Okay, let's look at the second chart now. Gabriel moved it slightly forward. You can see that the floor plan of Luxor Temple corresponds to the human body. Each 'room' parallels one of your body's invisible centers. Therefore, as we move through the temple tonight, each of you will also be taking a journey through your own body and nervous system. But as some of you may have already noticed during the tour yesterday, although there are many small sanctuaries, there are only six main areas, or 'rooms,' within the temple. At the end of this last room, where the entrance to a seventh room would ordinarily be, there is only an altar.

"Now, looking back at the chart with the seven circles, you can see that the seventh chakra lies completely outside of the body, floating above the head. Therefore, the corresponding room for the seventh chakra lies outside of the temple, beyond its physical boundaries. It may be invisible, but it is definitely there.

Gabriel looked at each one of us before going on. "The purpose of this evening's initiation at Luxor Temple is for each of you to begin to create a conscious connection to your own chakras and start to feel how their energy functions in your life. And because the temple holds the energy... the frequency...of many who have gone before with the intention of becoming enlightened, that energy can act upon you as well. It offers an opportunity, if you choose, to free up energy...to awaken the kundalini...and to remove blocks that might be preventing you from being more fully present in your life.

"Remember, don't worry about the details. All you need to understand is that the upward progression of the opening of the chakras signifies the awakening of your inner spiritual awareness. If you have a constriction in a chakra, you will also have a restriction in that area of your life. For example, if you have a blockage in your second chakra that, among other things, involves sexuality, you may unconsciously not allow yourself to become involved in a truly intimate relationship. Or, since the second chakra also deals with creativity, if you are a writer, you may find yourself too often stymied by writer's block.

"This initiation is not something that I can do to you or for you. And it is not something that you can force yourself to do, either. However, if any of you are at a place in your lives where movement is ready to happen, I can help to clear away the debris. So I want you...all of you...to think seriously about this. You are the expert on what is appropriate for you at this point in your life. Each of you must decide on your own. I cannot assist you without your inner consent. But remember, there are no bad choices, only honest ones."

Gabriel glanced at his watch. "Okay now," he said, rubbing his hands together with delight, "Those of you who want to talk about kundalini stay right here." Then Gabriel said, "For the rest of you, it's time to go shopping for your galabias. I want you to take your time and find the one that feels right for you, the one that speaks to you. Tonight's ceremony will be a very special event, so I want you to approach it that way. Keep your groups small, two or three is best. I will meet you back in the lobby at seven this evening. Have fun this afternoon." Then he shooed us out like a flock of pigeons.

CHAPTER 7

The group was abuzz with excitement as we paired off and set out on our quest. Melissa had asked me to join her and I agreed, glad to be feeling at least somewhat a part of things.

"What do you think?" asked Melissa enthusiastically. "Are you all ready to make any giant leaps in consciousness?"

I hesitated before answering, thinking about the diary and my life at the moment. "I'm...I'm not really into this stuff," I said, with some reserve.

"Well, I am. There are so many things I feel stuck about, especially my relationship with my boyfriend Chuck," Melissa said, rolling her eyes, her red curls bobbing in the sunlight. "I am definitely giving my inner consent."

For a few moments I almost envied Melissa's uncomplicated nature and wished some of it for myself. It didn't last long, but it did get me thinking. "I might have some stuck areas to work on as well," I ventured quietly. *I can't believe I said that...this group must be getting to me. I don't agree with any of this crazy woo-woo stuff!*

Night finally arrived. Everyone was excited, although most were a bit nervous about what might occur. Many of the group had meditated and fasted as a part of their preparation for the ritual. I purposely made sure I had a hearty lunch. We gathered at the appropriate time and, under the magical light of the full moon, formed a single-line procession. Slowly, we filed down the avenue of sphinxes leading toward the Temple's entrance. Each of us wore our galabias and carried a lighted candle. We were all silent. I was surprised that even I felt a sense of awe instilled by the solemn ritual and the powerful nighttime presence of the temple itself.

I stepped aside to photograph the group and then turned to shoot a picture of the entrance of the temple reflected in the moonlight. I saw our tour liaison, John, leaning against the wall by the entrance. He turned quickly and disappeared into the darkness. *He probably didn't want to mess up my shot.* I started to take some more pictures, but Gabriel suggested I put the camera away and give myself fully to the proceedings. He was my boss, so I had to rejoin the group, but personally, I would have been much happier just being the photographer.

We snaked our way through the first five rooms, our long galabias softly brushing against the stone floor. We paused in each of the small rooms. Gabriel suggested we do our best to connect with the energy of our own bodies. *What energy? This is getting seriously stupid!* It was late by the time we reached the last room, the sixth chakra or "the third eye," what Gabriel had called "the bridge to Cosmic Consciousness." Now, before the altar at the end of the room, we formed a circle with Gabriel at the center. Then, with the glow of the many candles lighting our faces from below and casting strange and haunting shadows, we began a deep and sonorous "Om" chant. One by one, we were called into the center of the circle. We put our candle on a tray Gabriel had brought and closed our eyes.

When it was my turn, I tried desperately to opt out, but Gabriel gave me an odd smile and beckoned me forward. I took a deep breath -- of dread – and stepped up to face him. *I so do not belong here,* I practically said out loud.

First Gabriel touched me gently on the forehead, the third eye, as he had each of the others. "This is to assist you in releasing the issues of the past, so that you can see things differently," he said softly. Next he tapped the top of my head, saying, "This will aid you in connecting with the higher realms and taking responsibility for what you see." Then, from somewhere very far away, I heard, "*...for you this is a graduation, both a death and a rebirth. It is time for you to take the next step.*"

I stood as immobilized as a statue for an unknown period of time. The glowing candle-lit faces began to shift and change, and the stone walls seemed to swirl about me. I felt myself being pulled down into a vortex. Images appeared – memories from my childhood.

I am a girl of seven. I know that life is deeper and more mysterious than anything alluded to by either my parents or teachers. I know, just as certainly, that I am deeply connected to these mysteries. I feel a great sense of excitement and understand that my life is meant to take a different path than that of parents and friends.

A beautiful lady visits me at night. She listens to me and understands the way I think. She tells me I have an antenna that will always warn me when truth is not present. She teaches me how to do things with my mind and tells me I can do these things because I am special. She tells me other people will not be able to understand me and that I should not expect them to. This makes me feel different — but in a wonderful way.

I want to have friends, but it is hard to always have to hide myself. Sometimes I forget and tell the other kids things I know I shouldn't, like about the beautiful lady and what she teaches me. Then they make fun of me and call me a liar. One time it gets so bad I feel like the laughing stock of the school and slink away, taking my secret path home to avoid them.

Now I am entering puberty. The experiences that earlier had made me feel "special," now only make me feel different. I feel more and more the outsider, even in my own family. I try my best to fit in and manage to obliterate my true feelings most of the time. Soon I forget them altogether. I feel very alone – and confused – and frightened.

My eyes flew open. I was slumped in Gabriel's arms. I glanced around. Everyone's eyes were fixed on me, wondering what was going on and why and how I'd become so lost. I was very self-consciousness – just like I 'd been as a child when I had told my friends about the beautiful lady. *They stared at me then like I was some kind of freak…and that's exactly how they are staring at me now.*

✳ ✳ ✳ ✳ ✳ ✳ ✳ ✳ ✳ ✳ ✳ ✳

I have no idea what happened that night, but something inside me seemed to move and click into a new place. I experienced a profound change – a change I was not in the least bit happy about. The diary, my secret companion, seemed to have altered everything. Like its author, I too felt frightened, alone and out of control. That enraged me. Logic, which had always been my strongest tool in life, now seemed to be failing me. I felt vulnerable, very much the child again, ancient shadows lurking in the corners of my mind. Much to my chagrin, I found myself with a continuous questioning chant, *Damn it...why me? Why is all of this stuff happening to me? Why was the diary given to me? Was the diary given to me or was it an accident?* And then an even more shocking thought, *If I can make some kind of spiritual connection, will I be able stop all of this questioning?*

Although I continued to run a low fever and feel "out of it" the entire time we were in Luxor, I forced myself to photograph, as well as participate in, the group's activities. Not only was it was my job, it was paying the rent. So when we visited the Valley of the Kings and Queens, and then went on to Alexandria, I trooped right along with the others, snapping pictures as I went. While in Alexandria, I thought briefly about trying to locate any living relatives of my paternal great grandfather, Bashir, who had been born there. But with neither the time nor the energy and only the common surname Nadim, to go on, that idea soon vanished.

Our last stop in Egypt was a return trip to Cairo, but only in order to catch the plane that would take us on the next leg of our trip, Aman, Jordan. Since we did not plan to get into Cairo until late afternoon and had an early morning flight, we stayed downtown near the airport - miles away from the Great Pyramids.

The bus trip back to Cairo was long and monotonous. We moved through barren stretches of desert broken only by a lone mud-brick house, an occasional human or donkey, and a scattering of palm trees. I stretched my body over the empty seat next to me and stared vacantly out the window.

"How about joining us for a game of gin rummy?"

"What?" I spun around, startled.

"I didn't mean to scare you," Melissa said, putting her hand on my shoulder. "You looked so forlorn sitting there by yourself."

"No, I'm...I'm fine. You just caught me by surprise. Guess I was kind of sleeping with my eyes open," I responded with an awkward smile. *God, what I would give right now to be back in San Francisco, taking one of my lone walks in Golden Gate Park.*

"So how about it?" she asked again. "Come and join us in the back. We're playing for one Egyptian pound a game. You might get rich!"

"Thanks," I answered, "but I think a nap is what I need."

I stretched myself out further, bunched my jacket under my head and closed my eyes. However, the second I closed them I saw a strange, sharp geometric form. The image was so clear, I was compelled to draw it. I reached down for the little notebook I used to keep track of my various rolls of film. It took a few tries, but after a while I was able to draw what I had seen. *Interesting! This almost looks familiar.* Then my weary eyes closed again. However, before long, my hand found its way into my backpack and fished out the little diary.

Should I or shouldn't I? I was still nervous reading the diary. *After all, it isn't really mine.* On the other hand, the way the diary had come to me, and because I had met Rashid and the camel named California, I was beginning to feel a mysterious tie to it. For some unfathomable reason though, I didn't want anyone else to know about it, so reading it on the bus made me uncomfortable. But, as usual of late, I was absolutely driven to read on – almost as if it were a foregone conclusion. And I had to admit I had become curious. *I can't wait to see what's going to happen next.* So finally, with a bit of trepidation – but even greater curiosity – I opened the diary, removed my bookmark and began to read.

CHAPTER 8

November 29

It is the six-month anniversary of my being discovered in
the desert, but it feels more like a year. Last night I had
a very strange experience. During the night I was awakened
from a deep sleep, or what felt like a deep sleep, by a high
pitched whirring sound. As I opened my eyes and sat up, I
thought Rashid was standing by the side of my cot. I
blinked to clear my vision then realized it was not Rashid,
but rather a tall figure whose facial features were almost
completely hidden by the deeply draped hood of its long
dark robes. Only the eyes showed, like two brilliant blue
stars in a night sky. The scent of roses filled the air,
and although there was no light, the phantom was illuminated
by a greenish-gold glow that seemed to emanate from
within the cowl of its robe and surround it like a halo.

I opened my mouth to speak, but before I could utter a
sound, the apparition put a finger to its lips, signaling
silence. It then spoke in a low, clear masculine voice.

"I have very little time, so I want you to listen carefully,
David. Yes, that is your name, and you are at the center
of warring forces that you have no way of understanding
at this time. You could say that you are in the eye of the
hurricane. It is very quiet where you are, but a great storm
rages around you. For now, you must take what I am about
to tell you on faith. You must trust that I am here to

help you. Later, you will remember who I am, and all of this will begin to make sense.

"It is important for you to know that there exists an ancient drama, older even than Mankind. It is a drama in which you now play a pivotal role. In fact, it is one in which at an earlier time you yourself chose to participate. You have long since forgotten that decision, but it has not forgotten you. How you handle the tasks ahead will determine the future of the Hu-man Race as you know it, as well as that of Planet Earth, itself.

"There has been a clamp put on your memory while the warring forces were aligning their positions. That clamp is now being loosened, and you will begin to remember things quite naturally and quite quickly. At first, you may feel overwhelmed by so much information coming back to you at once, but there is a Spiritual Law in place that states, 'We are never given more than we can handle.' I have known you for a very long time and I know how strong you are. Whatever emotions you may experience in the coming weeks and months, keep in mind what I have just said."

Then, I involuntarily closed my eyes as I tried to understand the full meaning of the words I had heard. When I opened them, the apparition was gone. All that was left was the smell of roses.

I ran outside and looked around. It was still an hour or more before dawn, but a few members of the village were already beginning to stir. However, my visitor was nowhere in sight.

I stood alone in the night, my body shivering from the cold desert air. In that moment, all of the nameless fears I have lived with for months, since the minute I regained consciousness, pulled together and settled upon me like a great weight.

Who was this strange visitor? I thought about his words and the urgency in his voice. Everything was familiar and yet nothing made sense. Even my name, David, seemed right, but I could not say for sure that it was true. However, it certainly is not an Arab name. So all along my feelings of displacement have been accurate. I am not from this place. Nonetheless, these monuments, the Sphinx, the Great Pyramids and even the land surrounding them are in no way new to me.

All of a sudden, I became aware of Hakim beside me. He was speaking to me, but I could not hear his words. I had no idea how long he had he been standing there.

"Listen to me," he said, tugging on my sleeve. "We have to go to the stables. They are bringing in the three new horses today and we need to clean up and make a place for them."

I nodded, went back inside and put on a warm sweater. Then I mutely followed him in the dark. It was fortunate for me that we were busy all day, and I had no time to think. We had quite a lot of cleaning to do. Then it was necessary to move some horses from our stable to another down the road. After that, the new horses needed to be exercised and groomed.

It was after dark by the time we finished. Hadiga had

saved food for us. I asked, but of course no one had any idea where Rashid was or when he might be back. Exhausted, I returned to my little "house." I lay down and quickly fell fast asleep.

December 1

Two days have passed. I am more confused than ever. The stranger said that I would begin to remember, but I have not. His words about "warring forces," "ancient drama" and a "promise" that I had made keep going round and round in my head. At times I can almost remember something, but it is only a faint shadow. Even my nights are dreamless once again. I feel more alone and forsaken then I did before. The stranger's coming seems little more than the cruel joke of some ill fate I still do not understand.

December 2

Nothing....

December 3

Nothing!

December 4

Another day and night has passed. Nothing! Maybe the stranger's coming was not real. Maybe it was only a dream.

December 5

Still nothing! I don't know if I can go on. I feel as if this life has no purpose for me. I feel numb and spend my days as if I am moving in a dream.

December 6

Once again I was abruptly awakened in the night by the high-pitched whirring sound. Again, not quite awake and not quite asleep, I thought it was Rashid standing beside my bed. However, as soon as I registered the smell of roses, I knew it was "The Stranger."

"David, I am sure you have been puzzled these last many days, but there were things that needed to be settled before I could be at liberty to tell you more. As I said earlier, an ancient drama is being played out. It is a story that is even older then the existence of Mankind. It is imperative that I relate its history to you and that you understand it."

The hairs on my arms stood up straight and a chilling cold ran down my spine. I felt I knew the words that were to follow even before they were said. I had desperately wanted answers, but now that they were forthcoming, I was filled with dread.

The Voice continued. "The first thing I need to tell you is how Hu-mankind came to be. You will understand the significance of this as I proceed. Before there was any 'thing,' there was only Oneness — or Spirit. Over eons of time, Facets of Curiosity developed within the Oneness. Those Facets pulled themselves out of the Oneness. However, the Facets knew they were of the Oneness and always returned.

"Inherent in the nature of Oneness, there existed a potential for all possibilities. One of those possibilities was the Process of Materialization – the method by which Spirit becomes Matter. This process is what later resulted in the development of Mankind. Spiritual essence eventually coalesced into physical form – the Hu-man body.

"But I am getting ahead of myself. My story begins long before Hu-mans appeared – back when the Facets of Curiosity first pulled out of the Oneness for exploration. As I just said, in the beginning they knew they were of the Oneness and always returned. Eventually however, they became so preoccupied with exploring, they forgot they were the Oneness.

"The Process of Materialization then became activated, and since the end product of materialization is Matter, the result was a profound and fundamental change. No longer would there be a single element, Oneness, or Spirit. Now there were two elements – Spirit and Matter. This comprised the most basic of dualities. Once these primal forces were established, they would forever pull upon one another.

"You can think of these forces as two magnets. The Materializing Force will perpetually pull upon Spirit to create more Matter. And the essential nature of Oneness will ceaselessly tug upon Matter to return to Spirit. The two forces managed to remain in balance until shortly after the time of Man's creation. However, since then the duality has taken the form of a battle – a battle that has been acted out both in the Heavens and on the plane of Earth many times and in many ways. Finding the appropriate balance between the two energies has been the eternal quest.

"The battle is now reaching its fulcrum. In order to have a fuller understanding of how all of this has played out for the Hu-man Race, we have to go back to the beginning of Hu-mankind.

"The duality that exists between Spirit and Matter also exists at the very core of Man. At the time of Mankind's creation, he knew himself only as Spirit and also saw the world around him as imbued by Spirit. Originally, Hu-mans could come and go between the state of Oneness, or Spirit, and that of Matter, or Form.

"Hu-mans had full and constant awareness of the interconnection of all Life throughout the Cosmos. Of course, this is the true state of things. Unfortunately, this primal 'Knowingness' did not last long.

"As Hu-mankind evolved on Earth, most of your race became mesmerized by their own individuality and their physical form. They also became overly enamored of their vast ability to create in, and interact with, the material world. Almost all Hu-mans finally came to believe that Matter was the only thing that existed. In fact, Matter itself is only an illusion. Underlying all Matter is energy. This was known 'in the beginning,' and your modern day quantum physics understands it once again, but that gets us off my main point.

"When Hu-mans finally came to believe that Matter was all that existed, they forgot their true essence as Spirit and began to perceive of themselves exclusively as separate physical beings. They lost all sense of interconnection.

"Finally, at some point, the Hu-man Collective made a perilous choice — it over-identified itself with Matter. Thus, the Hu-man Race began its long descent into Darkness, or Matter. In the process, Mankind sorted itself out into two distinct groups — those who remembered their Spiritual essence and those who did not.

"Now, I want to be perfectly clear. Neither Spirit nor Matter is inherently better than the other. They simply 'are.' Nor is the Process of Materialization itself bad. Identification with Matter to the exclusion of Spirit is what creates problems.

"That will be all for tonight. We will continue at another time. Until then, think upon these things, my boy." With those parting words, he was gone.

CHAPTER 9

December 8

I was abruptly awakened by the now familiar, high-pitched whirring sound. I blinked against the darkness and recognized the tall stranger whose facial features were almost completely hidden by the deeply draped hood of its long dark robes. As before, I was mesmerized by the brilliant blueness of his eyes.

The voice began immediately. "To add to the complexity of the duality between Spirit and Matter, Hu-mans are not the only intelligent Life Form in existence. As a matter of fact, they are one of the newest. And they were not the only Life Form to become divided. Extraterrestrial beings — Star Beings — from many different parts of the Universe also came to identify themselves either with the energies of Oneness-Spirit-Light or with those of Darkness. These Star Beings have greatly impacted events on Earth.

"The Star Beings who followed the Forces of Darkness, or separation, saw Earth as a prime piece of real estate. This was in exact opposition to the viewpoint held by the Star Beings who followed the Forces of Light, or inter-connection. These two groups, in their way, have fought numerous territorial battles over Earth. The same two groups have also fought to control the hearts and minds of Man. Since the Hu-man Race has Free Will — the power and ability 'to Choose' — it was imperative to win them over.

"Both types of Star Beings understood the strengths and weaknesses of Mankind. For the moment it is necessary that I focus your attention on the Star Beings who followed the Forces of Darkness. I will call them the Dark Star Beings. They knew that as Hu-mans increased their identification with Matter, two important changes would occur. First, they would lose their sense of inter-connection and feel isolated. And second, that isolation would then cause them to feel protective of themselves, their territory and their possessions.

"The combination of isolation and the need to protect creates Fear and Greed. Due to Hu-mans' emotional make-up, when they are in a State of Fear they give up their true personal power and become easy to manipulate. The Dark Star Beings knew that if they could make the Hu-man Race feel afraid, they would be able to control them.

"I will say more about that at a later time. For now it is important for me to emphasize that, although the Dark Star Beings have had their influence, they have not been Hu-mans' biggest problem. Hu-mans themselves have always been their own worst enemy. Time and again many have freely chosen to misuse their vast intelligence and infinite imagination to exploit one another and the planet. To that end, on more than one occasion throughout their history, Hu-mankind has developed highly sophisticated and powerful technologies. As with so many other things, technology in itself is neutral. It is when technologies are based on science without morality that they become extremely dangerous.

"This happens when there is a failure to recognize the inter-connection and Oneness of all Life. With the loss of connection, there is also a loss of understanding that whatever one does, or even thinks, affects everyone and everything. An individual, or group, that does not feel "inter-connected" does not feel a responsibility beyond its own personal needs and desires. In cases like this, the mind becomes completely detached from the heart. And that is the situation Earth finds itself in today."

December 12

Night after night, my mysterious visitor returned, telling me more and more each time. Then one night his voice sounded different, more serious — almost distressed. "My boy, it is important to know that Man's challenge — the fact that he is both Matter and Spirit — is also his greatest strength. By its very essence, the Hu-man Race is the Earth-Sky connection, the inherent bridge between Spirit and Matter or Heaven and Earth. You will notice, David, that I have always separated the two syllables of the word Hu-man. This is purposeful. The name, itself, came from the ancient sacred tongue. 'Hu' is one of the names of God, the Creative Force. Hu-man translates as God-man.

"The Hu-man Race, in fact all Life, is the essence of God in physical form. This is the great secret that the Race of Man keeps from itself! However, even the name Hu-mans call themselves is a constant unconscious reminder of their true nature, which is God, or Spirit, in Matter.

"And so the battle rages on maliciously to this day. Those who run your world hold in their hands such massive powers of destruction that even those in the distant sectors of your Universe have become alarmed. There is a web of consciousness that connects all Life, and the Hu-man Race holds vital keys. But as long as there is conflict inside of Man, there will continue to be conflict around him. If the various groups of Hu-mans continue to see themselves as separate, different and in rivalry with other groups, they will end up destroying all.

"This is a very important time. The Hu-man Race is moving out of its infancy. It is on the cutting edge of evolution, but stands on a perilous brink. It must finally choose — and choose consciously — Will it evolve or perish? David, this is where you come in. The destruction you saw in your dream the other night was, in fact, a memory. Your other dreams were memories, as well. They were a deliberate bleed-through to prepare you for what is to come next. You re-experienced the sinking of the continent of Atlantis. You were a priest in that time, and in that past life you were called A-Ta. You tried to protect your sisters and brothers from the rising tide of Darkness and separation that threatened to envelop them.

"Unfortunately, the Dark Star Beings were so powerful you were unable to succeed. Consequently, great explosions, similar in nature to nuclear fission, eventually destroyed the entire continent of Atlantis. These eruptions caused massive damage including a pole shift as well as enormous weather changes all over Earth. This is preserved in racial memory as the story of 'The Flood.'

"The destruction was a direct result of the separation from Spirit I have been talking about. A self-seeking group of Atlanteans ignored their connection with the All-That-Is and became obsessed with power and control. They misused their mind's great abilities for manifestation and directed the force of their will toward what they selfishly, and ignorantly, perceived to be their own benefit.

"Things appear very much the same today. However, there is one great underlying difference. Both Earth and the Hu-man Race are going through a period of great cleansing and are in the process of a frequency shift. But in spite of how things might currently appear, in its evolutionary journey, the Hu-man Race has already passed through its descent into Darkness, and the turning point back toward the Light is in process.

"In fact, a new planetary vision already exists energetically. It is waiting for individuals to align with it, so that it can be channeled into Earth and the plane of everyday life. In other words, the energy pattern of a New Era, an evolutionary leap for Mankind, is at hand. Of course, some Hu-mans are far more prepared to be a part of this process than others.

"Many of the souls who were involved in earlier power struggles on Atlantis have returned to Earth, once again, to deal with these issues. Karmically, the pull is very strong to repeat their old patterns. They are drawn to those same arenas of power wherein they fell from grace in the past. And they are easily preyed upon by the self-seeking Fields of Darkness, which they themselves set in motion so very long ago. The similarities are that strong.

"David, although you do not now remember, in earlier times you chose to play a role of leadership in the grounding of these new energies. But I must warn you — you will encounter forces that are here to work with you as well as forces that want to see you destroyed. Both are very ancient.

"Your choice to help Hu-mankind has automatically made you a threat to those driven by fear and separation, those reincarnated from so long ago. It has also brought you to the attention of the Star Beings who follow the Forces of Darkness. They feed on chaos, fear and confusion and would like things to stay exactly as they are. They want nothing less than total control of Earth.

"Also, it is important for you to understand that there is a side of you that doubts. You must always be on your guard. It is this part of your Hu-man nature that the Forces of Darkness will try to use. Fortunately, regardless of how situations may look, you will always have a choice.

"This is enough for now. The essential thing to remember, now listen carefully David, the essential thing to remember is that you are never alone. There are many of us here to help — you need only to call upon us."

Then the Being, with his large, glowing blue eyes, leaned over me, kissed me on the forehead and vanished.

His face was familiar!

Had I really made a choice to help the Human Race? Was I in danger because of it? I didn't know what to think, but I knew one thing for certain — with that visit my life changed. The days of idle play with Hakim and the simple life of the village were over.

His last words whirled around in my brain. I felt both utterly fascinated and profoundly shaken by what I had just read. *This is so intense but....* Something about it struck a deep chord in me. Like David, it was almost a memory – but a memory I couldn't quite remember. My temples began to pound and my whole body stiffened into a state of hyper-alertness. A number of moments passed before I realized the bus had stopped moving and people were beginning to gather their belongings and leave. We had arrived back in Cairo.

CHAPTER 10

I stood impatiently amongst the woo-woos, running my fingers nervously through my hair, waiting for our luggage to be unloaded. *I'm way out of my league with this diary. Maybe I need to tell Gabriel about it. He's a spiritual guy...he'll be able to make sense of it!*

I spotted one of Melissa's bags and called out to her. Then mine appeared. I grabbed them, dropped them off in our room and headed out to find him– rationalizing as I went. *I mean, really, I have enough going on as it is...I don't need this!* Moving fast and deep in thought, I rounded a corner in the hallway and almost bumped into him.

"Gabriel I...uh...I need to talk to you, "I blurted out, feeling very foolish. He looked at me with a strange smile, a smile I hadn't seen before.

"Of course, but I have to take my bags to my room and make a few calls. See me at dinner."

Dinner! I can't wait until dinner! My thoughts ran on like a high-speed locomotive.

Had I imagined the strangeness of Gabriel's smile? I'm beginning to imagine all kinds of things. I need to remember it's only a stupid diary. I took a deep breath and reasoned with myself. *Even though it sometimes seems like the diary is describing me, it isn't me, and it has nothing to do with me. It doesn't even belong to me...it belongs to Rashid.* That was clearly the answer. All I needed to do was give the diary back to Rashid and whatever hold it had on me would be over.

Why hadn't I thought of that before? It was such a simple solution. Gabriel had said that John, our tour liaison, could help us with anything. I went back to the room and called down to the front desk, but John was not booked into the hotel for that night. I told them I needed transportation to the pyramids. They suggested I try their tour director, Amir, and gave me directions to his office.

I washed my face, slicked back my hair and elongated my body as I had so often seen my models do. Then I made my way down to the lobby and over to the tour director's office.

"My name is Cassandra Wolfe and I'm traveling with one of the groups staying at the hotel. What is the best way to get to the Giza area and the pyramids?" I kept my voice calm and contained.

A large man with a gentle face looked up and extended his hand. "My name is Amir. Sit please. When do you want to go to the pyramids," he asked, smiling.

I sat on the edge of the chair in front of his desk. "Right now!"

"Now! That's impossible."

"What do you mean, impossible?"

"Right now is the middle of rush hour traffic."

"I don't care if it takes a long time…I still need to go now."

"Impossible!"

"I'll pay whatever it takes."

"Is not about money…is about rush hour," Amir replied, in his heavily accented, melodic voice. Rush hour traffic here is insane. They all drive like madmen," he continued, with a dramatic wave of his hand. "I grew up in Cairo and I, even I won't go to drive there now. No, not in rush hour! Besides, it will be dark already by the time you would arrive to the pyramids."

I stood my ground and in a very measured voice said, "But I have something…something that's not mine. It belongs to a camel driver named Rashid, and I need to give it back to him before my group leaves in the morning."

"Rashid," he smiled, rolling his eyes. "Lots of camel drivers named Rashid. Is a very common name, like John or Tom in your country. We can never even find him."

"No, you don't understand, this Rashid is different. He has a camel named California."

"California...for sure," said Amir, breaking into a hearty laugh. "All the people here love California. Everyone knows Hollywood!" He held up his hand like a gun. "Bang, bang! What you think? You think they going to name their camels...Nee-bra-ska?"

"I...I didn't know," I whispered, feeling considerably less certain. "Is it really that common of a name?"

"Yes...absolutely! Now can you relax?"

"This *is* me relaxed! You should see me when I am really hyped up," I replied defensively. Then in a more subdued tone, "Are you absolutely sure there's no way to go there now?"

"I'm sorry, no. It is not possible."

I guess he would know about the time and traffic. And we're leaving at six in the morning for Jordan. There's no way I can return the diary tomorrow. Again I felt the strange sensation of being at a total loss. *I didn't want this damn diary in the first place and now I can't give it back.* I shut my eyes, fury and frustration battling inside me. *Like it or not...at least for now...the diary is mine.*

Amir's melodic voice seeped into my thoughts. "My girl, everything will be fine. I know you love the pyramids. All the people do. But the pyramids have been here for thousands of years. You will come back to Egypt again, and they will still be here waiting for you. I promise."

He thinks this is about my wanting to see the pyramids again. It was all so absurd even I burst into hysterical laughter. Amir's large friendly face was full of concern.

"It has been a long, hard trip. All the people get tired. Don't be embarrassed," he said, getting up from his desk coming to my side. Towering over me like a gentle giant, he patted me on the cheek and said, "Why don't you go wash your pretty face and join your friends for dinner. A good meal will cheer you up, and you'll feel much better. You'll see."

I left Amir's office, went up to my room to compose myself, then reluctantly went back down to dinner. I could not help myself – I double-checked his information with the concierge on the way. But his answer was the same, and I had another disappointment at dinner. There was no opportunity to speak privately with Gabriel.

We left Cairo early the next morning and flew directly to Amman, Jordan. After checking into the hotel, we left our suitcases and boarded a chartered bus for Petra. I tried to beg out of the long day trip, saying I was too ill, but Gabriel convinced me that, as a photographer, I would never forgive myself if I did not go. He was right.

Petra is a place completely isolated from, and suspended in, time. Located in the Jordanian desert, the ancient Edomite city is surrounded by a ring of almost impenetrable mountains and is accessible only by mule. We mounted pack mules and slowly began our descent into the canyon below. The path snaked between two high vertical walls of rock. It wound so tightly that we could only see four or five mules ahead of us. As we neared the bottom of the path, emerging from between walls of rock that had blocked our view, stood a magnificent Nabataean temple, the Khazneh, carved out of the living red rock face.

When we entered the ancient city itself, a hushed stillness filled the air, and a sense of gentleness seemed to enfold us with loving arms. For the hour or so that we were within its protection, the voices inside my head stopped, and I felt – peaceful. The commonly known history of Petra is that it was a major trade center and a crossroads of civilization. However, Gabriel had another story that more closely fit my bodily experience of the place. We gathered around him as he told of a Petra that predated its more conventional history.

"In about the second century before the birth of Christ, the Essenes, a faction of Jews who were unhappy with the secularization of the Jewish Priesthood, physically separated themselves to lead a simpler and more spiritual life. Believing that the Jewish temple itself had become too much a place of worldly affairs, they formed their own communities. The most well known was at Qumran, located between the limestone cliffs of the Judean desert and the maritime bed alongside the Dead Sea. That was where, in 1947, the first of the Dead Sea Scrolls was discovered.

"Within this group of ancient people, a few were so motivated by Spirit – and their trust in the Power of God to work through them – that they took to healing the sick on a one-to-one basis. These wise healers, so filled with God's love, established a community right here. They would retrieve the sick, mostly lepers, who had been cast out of the cities and towns. The healer and the person in need of healing would isolate themselves and set up residence together in one of the many caves of Petra. The healer dedicated his or her life to restoring the health of the other. They would stay there until the illness was cured or both died of the disease. Miraculously, in most cases, the sick person was made well, and the community of healers grew."

In spite of myself, I was deeply moved by this tale of love and faith, and pondered it as we explored the ancient city. *It must have been a very different world. I mean…what could give someone the kind of motivation to put his life on the line for someone he didn't even know?* We wandered about on our own for nearly forty-five minutes, which gave me ample time to photograph the all but abandoned city, then the group came together on a hillside near what was once the town center. The site appeared to be an open-air amphitheater. We gathered in a circle and closed our eyes. Gabriel did an invocation, calling in the Light and asking for a healing for any of us who were in need.

I opened my eyes and was surprised to find Gabriel gently gazing at me. He nodded and I experienced a wave of love and understanding. I realized how very alone I had been feeling amongst the group of woo-woos with a body that had a mind of its own, a fever I couldn't seem to kick, and my strange "secret companion," the diary. It was a moment of incredible sweetness. All my frustration seemed to lift, and I was completely at peace. At least for the time being, all was exactly as it should be.

However, when we returned to the hotel in Amman, I was not at all as I should have been. My sense of peace had completely vanished, replaced by exasperation, once again, at the state of my body. I was sweating and burning up with fever. I gave up and asked John, our tour liaison, to call a doctor. John risked the "infectious den," called room service for tea and juices, and stayed with me until the doctor came.

I told him he didn't have to stay, but he insisted. "Thank god, Cassandra, you don't have the symptoms of that horrible disease that seems to be popping up. Nobody knows what it is or what is causing it. It seems to start out with nausea and vomiting, but it's not food poisoning. After those symptoms are over, people start having emotional problems." He paused before saying, "I shouldn't be worrying you about this when you're feeling so poorly. Try to rest. The doctor will be here soon."

John threw a light coverlet over my shivering body. As he did, my eyes were drawn to the strange-looking tattoo on the back of his wrist. It was small but distinct. I had noticed it before but was not close enough to see it clearly. *Well, not this time either.*

He sat down quietly in a chair across the room, and glad for the blanket, I curled up on my bed, trying to stay awake until the doctor came. John sat with his eyes closed, as though to give me privacy. I tried to keep mine open to stay awake. I sighed, wondering how long it would take for the doctor to arrive.

The English-speaking doctor appeared surprisingly soon and diagnosed me as having bronchitis and strep throat. He prescribed antibiotics and antihistamines and chided me on waiting so long before seeking medical help. "You're a lucky girl that it's not anything worse, like that horrible mental disease. All of us doctors are on the lookout for it, especially amongst tourists. We can't be sure if it's airborne and contagious, like a virus or bacterial infection. It may be an electromagnetic disorder for all we know. It seems to be confined to this region, but you don't have any of the symptoms associated with it. You'll be fine, you just need to take it easy."

I was embarrassed – and relieved. I thanked him profusely as he gave me a stinging shot of penicillin. John arranged for my medications, brought them to my room and then left me to drift off into a hopefully healing sleep.

The next morning, we flew to Tel Aviv and took a bus directly to Jerusalem. I was momentarily revived but completely "spaced-out" from the prescription drugs. I joined the group on a visit to the Wailing Wall, but then needed to go back to the hotel and rest rather than continuing with them into the labyrinth of the Old City.

After a quick shower, I sprawled out on the bed and fell asleep immediately. One hour later I was awake again and felt the pull of the diary. My mind said no, but I picked it up anyway.

CHAPTER 11

Sometime late December

I cannot say why, but immediately after my night "visitor" left, I absolutely knew that it was time for me to leave as well. Quietly on that moonless night, without a word to anyone, I stole away from the village that had been my home for over six months. Strange as it may sound, I began to miss it even as I left. Yet, I knew that it was my Destiny that called. I took with me only my diary and the small pencil I had been using.

With no conscious decision, I found myself directed to the footpath leading down to the Sphinx. During the entire year I had lived in the village, I had avoided going anywhere near the Sphinx. I never thought about it. I simply never went in that direction. Strangely enough, I had even turned down well- paying guide jobs that might have takenme there. Now my feet almost flew over the shifting sand. I could not get there fast enough. I stumbled over the rocks, shredding my hands as I fell, and climbed over the wire enclosure surrounding the Sphinx.

Feeling as though I was following some predetermined set of instructions, I sat down by the right paw of the Sphinx. Suddenly I heard, or rather felt, a loud popping noise inside my head, and my life opened up before me.

I was born outside of the Old City of Jerusalem. Although my parents were middle class Jews and not overly religious, my mother took a certain pride in being able to trace her lineage back to the House of David, hence my name. I was the first child of what was intended to be a large family. At the time of my birth there was an unusual concentration of planets in the Zodiacal sign of Aquarius. This was to be much commented on later in my childhood.

My first few years were very ordinary. When I was about two years old, my father, an award-winning teacher of mathematics, was offered a teaching post at the Hebrew University in Jerusalem. My parents were delighted with the increased status and money, and we happily moved into the city. Shortly before my third birthday, as my mother would later say, "David began to have problems." Very unexpectedly, I was given to intense periods of hyperactivity. My eyes would become glazed as I ran wildly about, out of control, shouting a sort of gibberish.

During these fits, my physical strength was so great that my mother could not subdue me by herself. If an outburst occurred while my father was at work, my mother would have to run to the neighbors for help. A group of them would hold me down and wait for it to pass. It was always the same. First the activity, then I would become rigid. Finally my body would go completely limp, and I would fall into a deep and comatose sleep. I would sleep that way for hours. When I awoke, I had no memory of what had happened.

In the months that followed, the intensity and duration of these attacks increased until most of my time was spent either in this altered state or asleep. My parents were frenetic in their concern for my well-being and began seeking the advice of psychologists and neurologists. None of these specialists offered any real guidance or even hope. The best they could offer was that I would probably grow out of it. Fortunately, the experiences themselves seemed to leave me untouched. Whatever my body had lost appeared to be replenished by the long hours of sleep that followed. During the time periods when I was awake and lucid, I was completely normal.

Although my strange illness did not seem to be harming me, it was consuming my parents' life. By one of those interventions of fate that seems ever to have been my friend in this life, my father happened to have a small tape recorder turned on right before one of my attacks. Of course, he then forgot about it. The following day he was sitting in his temporary office in the Humanities Department, drained by the events of past weeks, when he turned on his recorder to listen to what he thought was the tape of a recent lecture. I can only imagine his surprise when he heard the guttural ranting and raving of his small son.

At that precise moment, Professor Abraham Hoffritz, a great bear of a man and the head of the Department of Hebrew and Jewish Languages, was walking down the hall. He stopped and listened for a moment, then excitedly barged into my father's office.

"Well Ben, what have we here?" asked the graybeard in his heavily accented Hebrew.

My father, caught off guard, sat unmoving, too embarrassed to answer. Both of my parents had confined discussion of their "problem" to the immediate family and the experts they had consulted. It was a situation of great anguish to them, and they considered it too personal to share with outsiders.

The tape played on, and Hoffritz, still listening with rapt attention, cocked his head and knit his brow. "Hmm, this is very interesting," he mused. "I don't think I have ever heard anyone capture the accent in such a well defined manner. It is a very tricky accent you know, and it almost sounds like a child's voice. Where did you get this tape?"

Again my father was at a loss for words. It was all he could do to sputter out, "What do you mean...accent?"

"Don't you understand what you are listening to my friend?" he asked, incredulously.

My father shook his head. "Well, if I am not mistaken, and I rarely am," he chuckled, "this is a speech from the Old Testament in ancient Aramaic, and word perfect, I might add. It was a speech that King David made to his warriors during the greatest battle he ever fought. In case you are wondering why I happen to know this very esoteric piece of information, only a moment ago I was going over the syntax of this speech with one of my graduate students. I was coming in here to see if you had an up to date dictionary. I wanted to show this student of mine — such a hard head but a good boy, very bright — how the interpretation has changed as our language has modernized.

"Now tell me, Ben, what are you doing with such a tape? A little moonlighting perhaps? Trying to steal my job?" He good-naturedly cuffed my father on the shoulder. My father blinked and shook his head again, still speechless. For the first time, Hoffritz noticed my father's distress.

"I only kid you Ben. It's okay. But tell me, where did you get this tape?"

My father was so stunned he did not know whether to laugh or cry. He sat motionless, then eventually broke down and sobbed.

"Ben, what is wrong? Let me help you. Wait, I'll be back in a minute. I must go and tell my student to come back tomorrow."

My father had not moved an inch when the professor returned a moment or two later. He steadied himself, then told Professor Hoffritz the entire story. Then they met with my mother. Professor Hoffritz clarified the sounds I had made during my attacks. He felt the only logical conclusion to be drawn was that I had been experiencing episodes of "past-life memory." The three of them had several more discussions, and my parents took me to see him many times as well.

Of course, I had no recognition of this until my memory was jarred when I saw him on television in the porter's room at the Mena House Hotel. That is when I had the "waking dream" and then passed out.

The best medical experts had been of no help to my parents. Although the idea of my having past-life episodes was difficult to accept, it was easier than a diagnosis of insanity. Unfortunately, one of the local newspapers got hold of the story, destroying my parent's life once again. They found themselves besieged by curiosity seekers, ranging from the mildly inquisitive to the religiously fanatical. To maintain any privacy at all, even though jobs such as my father's were difficult to come by, they were forced to change their name and flee the city. We settled down in Tiberias, near the lake, and lived a quiet life.

By the time I was four, the attacks had greatly lessened in intensity and duration. Before my fifth birthday they ceased altogether. Whatever purpose they had meant to serve in my life had apparently been fulfilled.

Mid January

About a month or so has elapsed since I left the village. I have never returned. The last set of memories came in a flood – but that is not always the case. I cannot force myself to remember – the memories come when they come. Sometimes I get pictures that I don't fully understand. I have to be very patient with myself or I block the process altogether.

There have been some very dark moments when I have felt terribly lost and alone. I have put out my hand to many tourists to get money for food, but I know that it is important that I stay alone in the desert, remembering....

My god...what a story! I closed the diary and shut my eyes. I was gone again. The medications from the doctor in Aman had not yet kicked in. I touched my forehead. *Damn! I'm still running a fever.* Resigning myself to the fact that I was definitely going to spend the day on my own again, I lay back on the pillow and dozed for a while. Amazingly, I saw a geometric symbol similar to the one I had seen on the bus ride from Luxor back to Cairo. I forced myself awake and grabbed my note pad so that I could draw it. As I stared at it, making sure I had drawn exactly what I had seen, another one appeared, and I drew it as well. I felt a strange sense of exhilaration as I stared at my little doodles. *How interesting...I'm becoming an artist!* Then, even though I was tired, my ever-present curiosity got the better of me.

CHAPTER 12

The following day

Another doorway of memory has opened for me. I am still trying to absorb what it means in its fullness. Right now I think it is important for me to keep putting pen to paper. The act of writing helps me sort things out.

A rather uneventful period followed my fifth birthday. My father's income had lessened considerable when he left the University and my parents kept putting off having other children, until one day it simply did not seem important any more.

My mother had, on a number of occasions, pulled out the newspaper articles about me. Each time she asked whether or not I had any memories of what had happened when I was a little boy. I did, but everything was foggy and jumbled.

In my next significant memory, I was about twelve years old. I saw myself outdoors playing with the neighbor's dog. Then the scene shifted dramatically. What came next was a vision — a very profound vision. I was in the same place but the houses had vanished. Everything looked different. Even I looked different — and older. I looked about seventeen — but I was seeing it through the eyes of my twelve-year old self.

I was walking beside a bearded man in his twenties or early thirties. We were both dressed in plain un-dyed linen robes. His face was young but his eyes were very old. They looked like they had seen everything there was to see and more.

Even though it was strange to have such a vision, and even though I was so young, somehow I instantly knew that this was "He," the one who was known as Jesus. He was both softer and more commanding than he has been painted in both pictures and words. Waves of a gentle but unmistakable power flickered off of him like electricity.

He called me "Beloved," and I knew I was greatly honored.

However, before I could take all of this in, the scene changed, and once again, I was the twelve-year-old with the dog.

I looked on helplessly as the dog darted out into the street and into the direct path of an oncoming truck. Just as quickly, I leaped out to catch him. There was a screeching of brakes and a moment where the entire scene seemed to freeze - the truck, myself, the dog.

"Everything will be all right now, David," said a soothing voice beside me. I watched, as everything appeared to move in reverse motion. I, the young boy, looked up and saw a tall, strange-looking man leaning over me, his large, brilliant blue eyes staring into mine. There was a moment of blackness then everything returned to normal. The dog began to lick my face. I stood up and the three of us moved out of the street. Even then, there was something familiar about this odd-looking man, and I felt instantly drawn to him.

As curious as I was about what had just occurred, I was too surprised to ask any questions. I felt calm and completely safe with this stranger.

Quite casually, as if we had known one another all of our lives, the stranger turned to me and said, "David, I know about the vision of Jesus you had right before the dog ran out into the street. I also know about your 'strange ravings' as a small child. Both of these things were meant to happen, as well as today's accident. They were to give you an experience of two of your earlier lifetimes, one as the disciple John and one as King David. The accident today was the perfect way for me to enter this, your current life. Do you understand what I mean by earlier lives?" I did not know what to answer.

"Do not worry, David. We have only begun to talk. There are many things I will explain to you about your life, both past and future. In time you will understand." It was in this way that Zev Moab, who was a Man yet more than a Man, first entered my young life. He became the secret tutor of my childhood, and I began to lead a double life. If my parents suspected anything unusual going on, they never said a word. I believe they had come to accept that their son would always be different.

Now it made sense that the visitor who appeared in the night, leaving only the faint sent of roses, was familiar. He had been my friend and teacher – Zev Moab.

Two days later

Zev Moab taught me things I would never have learned in school. We always met in the same olive grove, about two kilometers from my parent's little whitewashed house. We never set a time, but instinctively I would know. And Zev Moab would always be there, waiting for me. Sometimes we would walk. Sometimes I would sit in the low branches of my favorite olive tree. But always I would learn.

I began to understand even then that this boy, David, was only one point in a series of lifetimes – both past and future. Indeed, time itself was an illusion. Everything I had ever done in this lifetime – or any other – was as much a part of me now as when it first occurred. In one way it made life much more complex, but in another way it simplified things.

There was no person or thing in my life that I had not invited in. Everyone and everything was there for a specific reason. Sometimes there was a lesson I needed to learn. Other times there was some unfinished business, either from my current life or from the past. That past might be five minutes ago, yesterday or many lifetimes ago. There really were no accidents. Everything was cause and effect. It was all a giant mosaic in which each piece had lovingly been put into place.

Studying with Zev Moab helped me re-experience many of my past lives. I felt, in great detail, events I had lived before. I realized why I had earlier seen myself beside the one known as Jesus, and I returned time and again to that sojourn with Him. That lifetime had been pivotal for me, because I had so loved and trusted the one called Jesus, that I had never doubted my spiritual path. I came to know and understand what it meant to love unconditionally – to practice complete acceptance.

One day, while peeling an orange, Zev Moab turned to me and said, "By now, you must realize that I am not like other men, yet you have never asked who I am. Would you like to know?"

"I know who you are," I said, skimming a pebble across the ground, avoiding his eyes – and the subject. "You are my teacher."

"Yes, David, that is my role in your life," he replied. "But I am also from a different Race of Man. I am not Hu-man, so to speak. My race comes from another star system, the Pleiades. My planet is much older than Earth, and my race, too, is older than yours." He paused a moment, waiting for this to sink in. Then he stopped, seeming to re-think what he was about to say.

"Perhaps it would be best to leave off for today. You have been an excellent student, but the next subject that needs our attention is rather complex. It is important that you spend some time simply being the boy that you are." With that he turned and walked away, hands folded together behind his back, his long robes swaying as he moved.

CHAPTER 13

A few days later – I have no idea what the date is.

I remember being rather taken aback at the time by Zev Moab's abrupt halt to our conversation. My feelings were hurt. Now that I was almost fourteen, I was not much used to thinking of myself as a boy. In fact, I was not even sure what that meant any more. Also, I was curious. After all that we had discussed, including "past lives," I could not imagine anything that would come as a shock or be more complex.

I spent my time away from Zev Moab impatiently waiting his call. After what seemed an eternity, but was only about ten days, I sensed it was time to return to the olive grove. As in the past, Zev Moab was waiting for me. To say that I was excited to hear what he had to say would be a vast understatement.

""Welcome back, David." Zev Moab smiled broadly for the first time since we had met. "I see that our little break has had the anticipated effect, and now you are ready to hear the rest of the story." I was all eyes and ears, waiting for what would come next.

"If you remember, when last we met I told you that I am from a different Race of Man - that I am not Hu-man. I also told you that my race comes from another star system, the Pleiades, and that my race and my home planet are older than yours."

I nodded silently, unwilling to break the moment as I took my usual seat in the low branches of the old olive tree.

"All right then, we will continue," Zev Moab said, glancing up at me. He clasped his hands behind his back and began to pace back and forth as he often did when he was deep in thought. "My people, the Pleiadeans, knew that as your race developed there would come a time of crisis and trial on Earth, a time in which the Hu-man Race would face great challenges - and great possibilities.

"There was conflict among us. You see, we abide by a Galactic Law of non-interference. That means we cannot directly interfere with individuals or events on another planet. However, we all understood the uniqueness of the Race of Man and knew that developments on Earth would affect the entire Galaxy.

"We were at an impasse. Some thought we should help Hu-mankind. Others thought we should not interfere under any circumstance. The dilemma was solved by a majority vote. We decided to establish – in potential – the ability to be of assistance, as needed, in the future. To this end, we chose to use our knowledge to seed the Hu-man bloodline with particular genetic codes. This has provided us, over the ages, with the ability to offer Spiritual Teachings and guidance to your young, evolving race.

"However, we were not the only Star Beings, or Galactic Visitors, as we personally have enjoyed thinking of ourselves, who were interested in or have visited Earth. Many different Star Beings and Entities from other sectors of the Galaxy have also visited Earth and contributed to your genetic makeup.

"Unlike my race, not all were benevolent. Unfortunately, there were those who clearly did not have Earth's well-being in mind. Those Dark Star Beings were motivated by their own vested interests and seeded your bloodlines with their own in order to make control of Hu-mans easier. A part of what they injected was a program for Evil. They knew that Evil would create chaos amongst Hu-mans, and that's what the Dark Star Beings live on – the frequency of chaos. This is their food. They wanted to ensure that a certain level of chaos, confusion and fear would have its time on Earth.

"Those who study the timetable of Earth's development can see evidence of this. They can trace the instances of chaos caused by that early genetic encoding of Evil, an Evil that has time and again resulted in the decimation or enslavement of great numbers of the Peoples of Earth. Hu-mans have always had Free Will as to whether or not to follow a Path of Evil, but this encoding has made the choice much more difficult.

"Fortunately, we and others who did have Hu-mankind's best interest in mind foresaw the dangers and challenges that would befall Earth. That is why we, the Pleiadeans in particular, have been so diligent in keeping our bloodlines intact. Your planet is now in the period where you need our assistance."

At that point, I jumped down from the tree and stood at its base, staring up at Zev Moab.

"David," he said, his deep eyes peering into mine, "It is time for you to know the truth about yourself. Although you are Hu-man, you personally are a direct descendant of my race, the Pleiadean's bloodline. That is why we came together as we have. And, that is why an exception has been made to permit me to be your personal guide."

In spite of myself, I had been completely surprised by what Zev Moab had told me, and it took some time for its relevance to fully sink in. I had thought there could be nothing more important or exciting than experiencing past lives and learning about cause and effect, but I was wrong. Although learning more about Zev Moab and how I was connected to him and his race was utterly thrilling, what he had to say about Evil was very scary. It was the hardest thing yet for me to believe. But I did under- stand the importance of what he said and had listened with rapt attention to the words that followed.

"In order to better comprehend the unfolding times on Earth, it is necessary for you to learn about the very beginnings of your race. Mankind has been on this planet much longer than your scientists even suspect. There are many aspects of Hu-man development that the majority of your race cannot comprehend because they look at things from a particular viewpoint that, unfortunately, is very limited.

"The history of Mankind is very complex. In the earliest time, although Hu-mans had physical bodies, they were not as physically dense as yours are today. Also, there was no separation of male and female. All beings were hermaphroditic and carried the duel polarity of male and female energy in equal balance. And there was no need to reproduce because the earliest Hu-mans were eternal."

"But, Zev...?"

"I know how hard it is to believe David, nonetheless that is the way it was. The reason the earliest Hu-mans were eternal, that they did not age or die, is because they were not individuals in the sense that you now think of them. You see, they did not have an individual continuing essence. Instead, they had a group soul. Therefore, they could not individually die as you understand it. But they could not individually grow, either.

"And so it happened, through the eons of time, that Hu-mans evolved. Now there exists separation of the sexes, individual souls, and mortality. Although the Hu-man Race has maintained a larger group soul, they now also have an individual continuing soul, or essence.

"It is important to know that the Hu-man Race was

never left to develop aimlessly on its own. Long before they developed individual souls, in fact, long before Hu-mans even existed on Earth, Beings in the Highest Realms, higher than my race or any of the other races that seeded your bloodline, established a definite "plan" for planet Earth."

"But Zev, do you mean that seeding the Earth's bloodline with Evil was a part of a plan?"

"That is an important question, David, but it is a hard one to understand, and there is not a simple answer. Let me try to explain why Evil has been important in Hu-man evolution," he said, resuming his pacing. "Mankind's basic nature is such that he learns by contrast. For instance, Hu-mans can recognize the satisfaction of food by experiencing hunger. They can understand the benefit of shelter by being exposed to the elements of nature. Hunger and the elements are not 'bad,' because they have led man to develop new skills.

"In the same way, Evil, as a possibility, is allowed to exist. In fact, it has an important function. Since Hu-mans have Free Will, they can see for themselves what occurs when they choose to follow the Path of Evil. If they are not pleased with the consequences, they can choose another path. In fact, Mankind's ability "to Choose" has forced him to think, to analyze - to grow. It builds his character."

"I never thought of it that way, but I still don't understand...."

"You will soon. Parts of the original plan must remain hidden for a while yet. However, I am permitted at this time to sketch the broad outline of the overall project in order that you may come to a deeper understanding of the unique role that Mankind plays in the Cosmos. But that will wait until the next time we meet."

CHAPTER 14

Later in the afternoon

The memories keep coming. It was a week before I sensed Zev Moab's call. Once again, he had left off at a critical point in his lesson to me. Looking back now, I understand that these breaks were to give me the opportunity to absorb all that he had been saying. Not only were the concepts strange, they were also vast in their implications. It was good that I learned these things when I was little more than a child, when my mind was still malleable. I cannot imagine how I would have been able to embrace them had I not heard them until I was a fully formed adult with experience in the world. For that matter, I cannot fathom how any adult, growing up in the everyday world, would react to such information.

The things Zev Moab went on to say only became more and more complex and intense. However, as I said, I was still young and I had come admire and trust Zev Moab deeply. Therefore, my imagination wrapped itself around his words, and I pulled them deep down inside of myself. I was ready for anything — or so I thought.

"You are the only race in your part of the galaxy that can experience emotions. Although there are a great variety of planets sustaining Life in your part of Galaxy, the Concept of Emotions is unknown to them. Beings from the other planets, such as my own, cannot fully understand the meaning of hate, fear, pity, greed or even love."

"So then you don't feel anything?"

"Many of us do feel something – something akin to what you might call empathy. That is why we can care for you and your planet the way we do. You see, David, as a rule, the course of our development has led us to become Beings of enormous mental power, but it has come at the expense of emotion. For instance, we can mentally comprehend the concept of the Creator's Love for us. We understand it to mean there is no separation between the Creator and us. And that this Love entails the ultimate in compassion – a compassion with no conditions or expectations. However, we are not capable of returning that Love. It is not that we are purposely uncaring. It is that, for us, that level of feeling is quite impossible.

"Instead, we Pleiadeans understand and operate under the Universal Law of Karma. This law states that whenever a person takes any action, the consequences of that action will eventually return to him. Therefore, throughout our worlds, one Being will never deliberately do harm to another because he does not want the effects of that harm returning to him. Feelings are generally not a part of the equation. Restraint is exercised, when it is, not as a result of caring or regard for other creatures, but rather out of common sense.

"Hu-mans are different, and importantly so. The fact that they can feel emotion is no accident. Indeed, granting Mankind that ability was a major step in the larger plan. It was the only way Hu-mans could feel Love. Of course, the animal Kingdom can feel Love, but that is of a different nature and not what we are discussing here.

"You see, it was recognized by the Great Entities close to the Source of Creation, that the ability to love was essential. Therefore, it was decided that there should be at least one civilization at the developmental level of Man who could learn to manifest not only Love, but Ultimately, Divine Love. Eventually, this race would be in a position to show the other more mental races such as my own, what Love could accomplish and why it was so crucial. That is why the Hu-man Race is so important to us.

"The Path to Divine Love would require that a race walk through the full range of possible emotions. It was understood that the path would not be an easy one. The soul group that was to become the Hu-man Race was consulted, and it agreed to accept the challenge.

"Thus, the Hu-man Race was given the capacity for Love, but they had to develop, on their own, an understanding of its great worth. It would have been meaningless to bestow the Gift of Love without giving Hu-mans the choice to not love. It was decided that the only way the Hu-man Race could truly come to Know Love – and to 'Choose' it – was by experiencing, over eons of time, what is created by the Distortions of Love.

"It was always Known there would be many pitfalls and a great amount of self-inflicted pain as Hu-mans learned about emotion. In truth, Love is all that really exists.

However, until Hu-mans once again establish a deep sense of relationship within themselves, remember their true essence is Spirit and understand that interconnection is the basis of all Life, they will be tossed hither and yon by emotion. They will not understand what powerful creators they are and how Love can manifest all of their true needs.

"Now, as I've said before, when it comes to negative emotion, Fear is the real culprit. Hu-mankind would never take the Path of Evil if he were not motivated by Fear. Fear grows out of faulty beliefs. A major cause of Fear in Hu-mans is their belief in scarcity. They think there isn't enough of whatever it is they desire. This is not true. It is only an imprint put into the Hu-man energy field by the Dark Star Beings to control the Hu-man Race. In fact, as we view your planet, we see great abundance. There is more than enough for all.

"Caught in this false belief, Hu-mans horde, deceive and strike out in a vain attempt to get their needs met. Once the Cycle of Fear begins, it always creates more Fear, and an emotional rampage erupts."

"I understand...in a way, but I still don't...." My words trailed off. I knew I hadn't fully understood what Zev Moab was telling me, but these ideas were so new and foreign that I could not formulate a simple or direct question. As usual, Zev Moab was patient with me, letting his words sink in.

"I'm sure this will all become more clear to you as I continue. You see, David, the concept of Evil is very complex — but the function of Evil is crucial. The Dark Star Beings who seeded Hu-mans with Evil did it as a means to control them. What they neglected to take into consideration was the positive role Evil can serve. They did not think Human Kind was strong enough to overcome Fear, to 'reconnect,' but of course they are – and that is their journey.

"As Mankind's understanding of his true nature and his belief in the power of Love grow stronger, he will learn how to better deal with Fear. Understanding that even Fear is a choice, he will be able to exercise his Free Will and choose how he wants to respond in different situations.

"Each of these Love-based Choices, on an individual basis, allows not only the single individual but the entire Hu-man collective to grow and to evolve into something greater – something even more beautiful than it already is. These choices will bring Hu-mankind to the next level of its evolution – and this evolution is open ended. That, my young friend, is the great role that Evil plays in the bigger picture, and the importance of Hu-Man emotion."

"Oh Zev, I would never have imagined that Evil could do such amazing things. But Mankind has had to work so hard for its Gift of Love."

"Yes, it certainly has. We knew the journey toward Love would be a thorny passage. It was for this reason that Helpers, such as those of my race, have kept so close to you of Earth. Most of the time we are not in physical form, but we have always been with you. You are our younger brothers, yet, in the deepest sense, you are also our teachers. It is ironic that we, who could not experience Love, should have been sent to assist you in not destroying one-another, so that in your process of learning about Love you could also teach us how to feel it."

"I think I am beginning to understand. I never realized there was so much to emotions."

"Yes, David, and I have only begun to talk about all that was involved in Hu-mans being able to experience them. But none of it would have been possible without Mankind developing a unique identity and an individual soul. Each Hu-man needed to be responsible for his own growth.

"There is one more thing I want to mention today, David. Along with an individual soul, Mankind was also given the Gift of Death."

At this point I winced.

Zev Moab, who notices everything, did not even change his tone as he continued.

"Those on Earth hold such strong concepts of separation that I know it is difficult for you to see Death as a gift, but that is exactly what it was. Without Death there would have been no opportunity to return to Spirit, assess the life you had just lived, and make conscious choices as to what experiences would be needed next. It took many sacrifices on the Higher Realms to make Death possible."

Death as a gift! Give me a break! This whole thing is way too weird...fascinating but weird. It's written like a true story, yet it can't possibly be true.

I needed a break myself, so I got up, put the diary away and crawled back in bed. It had been two days since I had seen the doctor in Aman. It was ridiculously hard to be so sick so far away from home. There were moments when I contemplated getting on a plane and going back to California, but aside from the pride issue, it would have taken far more energy than I had at that moment. *Clearly this is not the best way to heal...or to travel!* We had been moving so quickly from one place to another that it was a relief to be staying in Jerusalem for the next few days.

The following morning I stoically joined the group and took my promised pictures. Unfortunately, by the time we reached our second stop, the Garden of Gethsemane, I was, let's just say, "lagging a bit." Gabriel took one look at me and told me to go back to the hotel. "You're never going to get over this thing if you don't rest for a couple of days." I sheepishly agreed.

So once again, I "dropped out" and took to my bed, like some nineteenth century damsel with the "vapors." I was definitely on a journey all my own. I slept and I sweated and I questioned. Occasionally I ordered room service, although for the most part my fever was so high, I did not have much of an appetite. I felt so overloaded by the diary and my thoughts that I just put the damn thing away for a while. But even in my sleep, I could not escape my utter fascination with the diary or the knot in the pit of my stomach and the now familiar mantra, *Why me... why has this diary come to me?*

I am in a cave and I know that I am walking over snakes. A voice tells me, with great certainly, that I will be protected as long as I keep looking up.

I woke up with a start but the symbolism of my dream stayed with me. I was clearly being told that I would be safe if only I could hold a higher perspective. *But, could I?*

CHAPTER 15

A day and a half of resting seemed to do the trick. I felt a bit better, and standing in the steaming hot shower, I committed to staying on the trip. I marveled that today was Yom Kipper, the most holy day of the year for the Jewish people, and here we were in Israel. Yom Kippur, the Day of Atonement, is a day of fasting and prayer. Since the hotel dining room was closed, Gabriel had made special arrangements for food.

The group gathered together in the empty dining room. I was the only one who was Jewish, or rather half Jewish, since my mother was Jewish and my father Arabic. With this background, I had always been more than a bit ambivalent about religion. But no matter how you looked at it, I was pretty certain I'd been doing quite enough fasting and praying on my own over the past week.

As a child, I was taught that Yom Kippur was the Day of Atonement, a day in which we were to ask forgiveness for all of our sins, and that God would then wipe the slate clean so we could begin a new year. This had been very problematic for me as a kid, because I never thought I'd done anything that bad. Consequently, I did not "atone" but felt guilty and worried that my slate would not be wiped clean. Now, as we seated ourselves around Gabriel and munched on cold cereal and fruit, we learned the true meaning of Yom Kippur. Gabriel, who had chosen to fast, explained the significance of the High Holy Day in very simple terms.

"Yom Kippur is, in fact, the Day of Atonement. However, the original meaning of atonement is at-one-ment. Yom Kippur was established as a day to recognize and reaffirm our Oneness with Spirit, to re-member our true essence. It gives us an opportunity to look more deeply into our inner lives. While it is a solemn day, it is also a day of celebration."

If only I'd known that as a child! I felt a small burden lift from my shoulders, one that I hadn't realized I was carrying. He continued talking but my attention drifted. *Oneness with Spirit! True essence! That sounds a lot like what I've been reading in the diary....*

Something Gabriel said caught my attention, and I tuned back in. He was talking about Jewish mysticism and the process of enlightenment. "*Kabbalah,* the mystical branch of Judaism, is a living tradition that goes back thousands of years and embraces the very act of creation itself. The oral tradition of *Kabbalah* says that the purpose for human existence is that God wished to behold God. In other words, Man was created in God's image, One with Spirit. However, humans are complex because they can experience emotions, so being human is both a gift...and a problem. *Kabbalah* talks about the process of Man's losing and gaining enlightenment, or Oneness with Spirit. It describes Mankind's initial descent from Spirit into Matter, as well as his assent from Matter back to Spirit."

Oh...my...god....

"My interpretation of this is that God is not Matter, God is Spirit. I believe that God has created us humans with the ability to learn from our experiences and 'to choose' the way we want to live our lives. I also believe that God created humans with the ability to evolve to the place where, like God, we can express Divine Love."

Matter...Spirit...Emotions...Divine Love...! The diary talked about how Man had lost his Oneness with Spirit and it said that humans were created with emotions so that they could manifest Divine Love. Now Gabriel was saying the same thing. Gabriel's voice went on, but I was much too lost in my thoughts to hear his words.

If people have been studying Kabbalah for thousands of years and the

diary is saying some of the same things…then…at least a part of the diary
might be true. But, I definitely don't buy the "extraterrestrial" bit!

I was surprised when the others began to get up and move away from
our table. Apparently, the lesson was over. In honor of the High Holy Day,
we were given one of the few free days on our schedule. Everything in the
Jewish section of the city was closed, but Melissa and a few others were
going to explore the Arab quarter of the Old City. Although I was not exactly up to it, I was suffering from "cabin fever," so I joined the group.

It was incredible to actually be in Jerusalem where David had spent
his early childhood. It did not seem so much the historical Israel I had heard
about in Sunday school. Rather, it was a very active, ancient-modern place,
a Jewish, Christian, Muslim city. I became very aware of the presence of
all three faiths, their cultures and the common threads that ran between
them. It brought back memories from the happier days of my childhood.
Our large boisterous multi-ethnic, multi-religious, extended family would
put differences aside and gather together to celebrate birthdays, weddings
and various "rites of passage" with song, food and drink.

Strolling the bazaar later that afternoon, I stopped to admire some jewelry at one of the stalls. When I looked up my tour-mates were nowhere in
sight. I began to search for them, but the more I wandered amongst the
labyrinth of corridors on my own, the more disorientated I became. I was
startled when an Arab boy of about fourteen approached me and, in very
broken English, beckoned me to come with him.

"Over there, more big!" he said, tugging at my arm and pointing up
some stairs. Then he pointed to my ever-present camera. He seemed to be
saying there was something that I should photograph.

I could not make out what he was trying to say, and I was reluctant to
follow him, not because I felt unsafe, but because I was sure he was going
to try to sell me something. However, he was so persistent and looked so
sincere that I gave in and followed him.

He led me up some steep steps to a church, running a monologue in
Arabic the entire time. Then he turned me around and pointed down,

insisting that I take a picture.

I was confused. "I don't understand…what do you want me to photograph?"

"Over there, more big!" he kept repeating as he pointed to the street below.

This time I looked more carefully, and, indeed, it was a wonderful panorama of the Old City from two stories up. Despite my tiredness, the photographer in me did appreciate the view.

"Thank you," I said, handing him the few shekels I felt he had earned. He smiled broadly. "This for you," he said, handing me a small pouch,

"But I…."

He saw my bewilderment and shook his head. "No…no money…is gift for you," he said, pointing again to the crowd below. "See, more big!"

I dropped the pouch in my camera case and turned back to look once again at the broad view of the teeming Old City with its exotic Middle Eastern flavor. I had a 90 mm close up lens on my camera and held it up to my eye, ready to frame the perfect shot. I looked through the viewfinder and was stunned to find a familiar face – a slender man somewhere in his early-thirties. He had dark curly hair and shocking blue eyes, and was staring right up at me. I quickly snapped a picture then turned toward my guide. He had vanished. I looked back through my camera lens. The young man had also vanished. *Was it David?*

I raced down the stairs toward the street below, but the crowd was milling around me. I frantically ran this-way-and-that, but if the young man was there, I couldn't spot him. *Damn it!* Exhausted, I stumbled through the Old City until I somehow found my way back to the hotel. I was about to flop down on the bed when I remembered the little pouch. I rummaged through my camera case, found the pouch, opened it and poured the contents onto the bed.

There was a small handful of seed crystals, a piece of malachite and a scribbled note that said, "For you from Egypt." *How strange!* I slowly put the stones back in the pouch and stuck it in one of my suitcases. My mind kept going over and over the experience. *There's something about his face...those deep blue eyes and curly black hair...that haunts me. I feel with every fiber of my being that I must find him!*

The image of the man who looked like David, an image I had only seen in my mind before that day, stayed with me as our group moved around Israel. We visited many spots right out of the Old and New Testaments. Somehow, I was able to do my job and to snap the required pictures. Finally, alone in my room one evening, I had the opportunity – and the ability – to stay awake long enough to re-open the diary.

CHAPTER 16

Some days have passed

I began my studies with Zev Moab shortly after my twelfth birthday. So much happened in the following years that it is difficult to remember everything and even more difficult to record it all. For now, it will suffice to say that, with Zev Moab as my teacher, I learned to travel in my consciousness through both time and space. My understanding of life and death grew immeasurably, and my concept of time was forever altered. I barely resembled the boy I had been, and I, at least, considered myself a man — and a very unusual one at that!

One day, when I was nearly sixteen, Zev Moab met me once again at our usual place in the olive grove. The moment I arrived I could sense an urgency that I had never felt from him before. "David," he said, "the time for action is growing near. You will soon be learning more about your personal task in this lifetime. In order for you to make appropriate choices it is important that you understand the current condition of the Hu-man Race.

"As you know, far too many Hu-mans have lost their connection with Spirit. This has put the Hu-man Race at a crossroads because Mankind's ability to develop advanced technology has vastly outpaced his moral understanding of its implications. Man must now choose between two conflicting options.

One path is 'to Choose' cooperative living, whereby he uses power in a positive way — a way that enhances Earth and all Life upon it. The other path is to continue to live with collective greed, using power in a negative way — which might benefit a few but could destroy all. Will Hu-mankind choose 'power with' or 'power over' others? Choosing the second path could mean the demise of the Hu-man Race and horrible damage to your magnificent planet.

"Remember, I once told you that there was a plan set out for Mankind even before his appearance on Earth. As a part of that plan, Hu-mans were to act as stewards of the planet as well as parent and protector to the animal kingdom.

"Hu-mans have had numerous challenges in their evolution, and the use — or misuse — of power has been the most difficult one. It has come up time and again in many ways. One of the earliest ways it showed up had to do with Mankind's sexuality.

"Now, before we go any further, it is important for you to understand the gift and great creative power of Hu-mankind's sexuality. Sexuality in and of itself is a magnificent thing. Unfortunately, then as now, there was a misunderstanding of the real and profound meaning of sexual energy. It is much more than a means of pleasure and procreation. In truth, it is a pathway to the Divine.

"However, in its lowest form, the sexual act can be used as an instrument for power and control. The Star Beings who followed the Forces of Darkness understood and used this knowledge to their advantage.

"During the time of Atlantis, there was a particular species of mammal that no longer exists on Earth. It was similar to Hu-mans in many ways but very different in others. The Dark Star Beings urged Hu-mans — often in subtle ways — to impose sexual relations upon those vulnerable creatures.

"Since the role of Man was to 'protect', the situation became a true test of character. Many Hu-mans, in their blindness, followed the ill-meaning direction of the Dark Star Beings, thus failing this all-important test. In the end, Mankind's use of 'power over' these creatures engendered a deep sense of separation within the Hu-man Race.

"The separation took two forms. The first was a separation from their inner knowing. The second was a separation from one another. Separation creates feelings of aloneness and ultimately — Fear. So, it was in this very calculated way that the Dark Star Beings gained a greater level of control over the hearts and minds of Hu-manity.

"This sexual misuse had profound ramifications. In your recorded history, sexual relations between Hu-mans and another species did not produce progeny. That was not always the case. In earlier times, Hu-mans procreative abilities were quite a bit more powerful and those encounters were able to produce offspring.

"Out of those inter-species sexual unions were born strange mutated creatures. Some were quite wonderful and have lived on in myth, but most were badly deformed. According to the ancient guidelines, they were now the responsibility of the Hu-mans. Some honored this charge, aiding and loving the odd creatures, lifting their vibration and helping them to evolve. Others, in the throes of their new egos, saw an opportunity for power and exploitation. They abused the Things, as they called them, turning them into beasts of burden — and worse.

"This sexual misuse started slowly, with a few cases here and there, but it escalated over time. It was similar to a low-grade infection in the midst of a glorious expansion of Spiritual Technology, an infection that resulted in a true polarization of the Hu-man Race. Had it been noticed and halted in its earliest days, events may have turned out quite differently. However, time passed and the rift between those who opened their hearts to the Things and those who felt they had the right to exploit them grew ever deeper.

"And so it finally happened, during the age of the great

flowering of Atlantis, that two powerful opposing groups began to emerge. They divided into what you might today think of as two political parties.

"One group continued to remember their origin in Spirit and therefore, their connection to all that exists. They protected and nurtured the Things. The second group, having followed the Dark Star Beings, lost their connection to Spirit and felt justified in controlling others — whoever they might be.

"This second group became so obsessed with power that they were the ones who eventually destroyed Atlantis, the very place they called home. A heavy burden of Karma came onto the planet. And, since nothing is ever truly forgotten, these events have been retained in racial memory as The Fall.

"The same kind of power struggle is in play on Planet Earth today, and both sides will soon be vying for your attention. As with all things, this tug of war is actually taking place on the Spiritual Planes. However, what is experienced collectively on the inner planes of thought and imagination must always manifest on the physical plane as well. Such is the creative power of Hu-mankind's Emotions.

"Now David, as heart braking as this scenario sounds, it has not been in vain. It is true that at one level, this sexual misuse was a breaking of The Law. At another level, this infraction was perfect, because it was a part of the Great Plan. It offered Hu-mankind opportunities for learning and ultimately, 'Choice'. At still another level, all that happens can never be other than perfect. I know these paradoxes are all but impossible for the Hu-man mind to grasp nevertheless, as you continue learning, your ability to hold the biggest possible picture will become easier.

"My dear young friend, your role in all of this will soon become apparent. It is the personal test your soul chose — and it will be your Final Initiation. From now on, the events of your life will begin to move rapidly. Try to remember what I have said. David, the times ahead will challenge you, but your spirit is very strong. You are a part of the larger plan that was set in motion so long ago. And even as we have been watching over Earth, we will be watching over you."

Zev Moab looked deeply into my eyes, touching my very soul. He moved forward and held me in a tender embrace, then stepped back and whispered, "I believe in you!" In that instant, my tutor and friend of the past four years vanished.

CHAPTER 17

We reached Tiberias, our second-to-last stop in Israel, late on a warm and slightly windy afternoon. We stayed at a hotel on the lake. The wind rolled over the water creating gentle ripples, and a few small sailboats moved silently across its surface. I stared idly at the picture-postcard scene. Some of my tour mates donned their bathing suits and jumped into the pool, however my fever was still up and down, so a swim was out of the question for me.

I wrangled my way out of my sweatshirt for the umpteenth time that day and groaned as I sprawled across a lounge chair. *Ah, this feels so good,* I thought, relaxing in the winter sun. I had long since given up trying to keep track of where we were on our ever-moving itinerary. Consequently Tiberias, famous as the Roman Israel, was merely one more pit stop to me.

Tiberias! I sat up with a start. This is where David lived – where he studied with that Zev person. Great! Now I was thinking about the diary as if it were true! My mind froze then began to slowly move forward. *But what if it is true? What if he still lives here...or what if his family does? I suppose it's possible that I could find him...or them...or somebody...anybody...who knows him.*

I threw my sweatshirt over my head and yanked it down, grabbed my hat and shouted to the swimming Melissa, "I'm going for a walk. I want to explore the town." Then I turned and quickly left before she had a chance to even think about it and try to persuade me to stay and rest.

Passing through the gates of the hotel's pool area and onto the street, I noticed our tour liaison, John, getting out of a taxi. *That's who I should ask! I bet he would know how to find someone...he seems to know everything else.* I raised my hand and was about to call out to him, then abruptly stopped. *No! No, no, no!* I still didn't want anyone who was a part of the group to have any kind of information about the diary. I couldn't wait to talk to Gabriel about it in Cairo, but that was when I still thought I could give it back. *Now...I don't know...I just don't want to talk to anyone about it.*

I walked toward the center of town until I found a tourist kiosk. *Damn, three groups before me! This is going to take forever!* I looked around for another kiosk, but none were in sight. They would all be busy so there was no use searching for another one. That was why they were there – to give out information. *Well, as long as I'm waiting I may as well read something.* I reached for one of the brochures written in

English and thumbed through it. It described the seventeen natural mineral hot springs in Tiberias and explained that the area itself was more than six hundred feet below sea level.

I looked through a few of the other brochures, keeping a sharp watch on the tourist agent. When I caught his eye and he nodded that he saw me, I was better able to focus on the brochures. One gave the colorful history of the town. I hadn't realized that the lake was the Sea of Galilee so often mentioned in the New Testament. The Jewish population called it Lake Kineret. Again, I was struck by the importance of the area to Jews, Christians and Arabs.

Eventually it was my turn, but when I started to ask if there was any way to find out about a young man named David who had grown up in the area, I realized how ridiculous I would sound. The town had more than 30,000 inhabitants, and I did not even know David's last name.

What am I going to do...tell him I found a diary in Egypt that was written by this David guy and it talks about the sinking of Atlantis and Star Beings who follow Forces of Light and Dark? What am I thinking? This story can't be true. I was mired in doubt again – and since I hated doubt, I turned it right into certainty. *This diary is just some weird joke Rashid put in my camera case to drive me insane.*

As I turned to leave, I noticed some kind of commotion beginning right beyond the kiosk. Apparently a man had passed out and a young woman was kneeling beside him, crying and yelling for help. Soon the air was punctured with the shrill sound of sirens. "I don't know what is going on," said the man who ran the kiosk. "That's the fifth person this week...young people, too. And it's not even that hot now. They don't all pass out. Two of them had to be carried away, because they were acting crazy."

I hope it's not related to that sickness John and the doctor in Aman were talking about. I took quick long strides directly back to the hotel, determined to do something to find out if the diary was true, but by the time I got back I couldn't even think. My "something" turned out to be getting the key to my room, going up the elevator and collapsing on the bed.

The next day we were scheduled for a bus ride to the Jordan River where Gabriel was going to perform a ritual Baptism. Again, the theme was leaving behind the old and embracing the new. Many members of the group had carefully chosen symbolic names. A few had even decided to change their names, deciding their birth names had never exactly held the energy of their true essence. *Whatever that means,* I thought, feeling comfortable in my re-found skepticism.

Once again, I was feeling very much the outsider – but this time happy for it. When we reached the riverside I watched lethargically as my tour mates, wearing their galabias, the simple cotton robes appropriate for such a ritual, hurried out of the bus. Wearing jeans and a T-shirt, I dragged myself out. *I have a job to do,* I reminded myself. Regardless of how I felt physically, I knew that, as on so many other occasions during the trip, I could still photograph whatever I needed to – and do it well. It always amazed me that no matter how I was – or how bored – the photographer in me was able to go on automatic.

But this time was different. In spite of myself, I caught their rush of excitement. I stood on the muddy bank of the river as my tour mates waded into the water, and one-by-one approached Gabriel. *Something special is taking place here!* I quickly put on a close-up lens to capture the rapturous expressions of the participants as Gabriel dunked their heads into the cool water. They came up with eyes wide open and a child-like look of wonder.

Suddenly I felt hazy and lightheaded – absolutely *pulled* in the direction of the river. Barely aware of what I was doing, I placed my camera on a dry patch of bank and plunged in. Not until I was knee-deep in water did I become conscious of what was happening. It didn't matter that the water "burned" like ice against my hot skin. I kept moving forward, almost as if I were being led by a will greater than my own. I didn't stop until I was standing next to Gabriel, water up to my chest. He turned to me, a smile crinkling at the corner of his eyes.

"Are you willing to let go of those things that no longer serve you?" he asked, in his deep melodious voice. I nodded. "And are you ready to stop living your life in a mechanical way?"

"Yes, I am," I all but shouted.

"Do you want to take a new name to signify your renewed connection with Spirit?"

"Diantha," some part of me called aloud.

Then Gabriel gently dunked my head into the water, and I saw a silvery pyramid illumined beneath a full moon. Gabriel helped me up and out of the water. I was stunned. I had no idea where that name had come from or what it meant, but the more I repeated it over in my mind, the more I liked the sound of it – and the more it seemed to somehow fit me.

Now I truly was on overload and something deep inside me must have let go, because that night I had a most unusual dream. I dreamed I was high on a mountaintop. Twelve tall figures were in a circle ritualistically smoking a pipe they passed from one to another. I stood off to one side. Many of my tour mates stood scattered along the side of the sloping mountain. I was talking to a girl named Beth. She was someone with whom I had hardly exchanged a word during the trip. Unlike most of the other participants, her main objective on the journey seemed to be shopping. Every time we made a stop, she made a beeline for the gift shop.

In the dream, I was purposely engaging her in conversation. I had an almost desperate need to question her about her purchases and insisted she take them out one by one and show them to me. Unexpectedly, Gabriel appeared and tapped me on the shoulder. With a solemn air, he handed me the pipe. I accepted it casually, continuing my conversation with Beth. I put the pipe to my mouth to draw on it, but Gabriel stopped me. He shook his head and uttered only one word – "Choose!" I stopped what I was doing and looked him in the eye, still holding the pipe clenched in my hand.

At that moment I woke up – hand poised in front of my mouth as if it were clutching a pipe. I understood that I was about to make a momentous decision. Very consciously, I inhaled deeply on the invisible pipe.

I have never had a dream like that before or since. I know I was asleep, because I know I woke up, but there was an aliveness to the dream that felt more awake then actually being awake. I think it's the kind of dream one has only once in a lifetime. In it, certain events are sealed and cannot be changed – a direction is chosen. Even at the time, I was aware that I had chosen a life-path in the dream, and, as a consequence of that choice, there were things I gave up. Although I understood the dream's metaphor immediately and was somewhat awed by it, I was in for an even deeper shock when I picked up the diary two days later.

CHAPTER 18

Many days later

I know it has been over a month since the night I left the Arab village and made my way to the Sphinx. In that time I have wandered about like a true nomad, living hand to mouth with no place to call home. However, periodically I have returned to what I consider "my station" beside the right paw of the Sphinx. That is where I am right now as I write this. Instinct keeps calling me back – but I have no idea why. Mostly I feel completely lost in time, floating on a vast sea of events where the recent past, the distant past, the present – and possibly even the future – keep washing over me in endless waves.

I keep trying to sort through the jumble of images and extract those from my childhood. I remember studying with Zev Moab from the time I was twelve until I was nearly sixteen. I endured an intense loss when he left. I felt completely devoid of faith and constantly questioned the direction of my life. To make matters worse, although I had always lived with my mother and father in my boyhood home, it was not an ordinary existence. I had been so involved with Zev Moab that it had been a very long time since I had any real connection with either my parents or the events of the everyday world. I had experienced my life as if I were living in another dimension that had become superimposed on the daily life that surrounded me.

For weeks, or possibly months, I wandered around my parents' house, going aimlessly from room to room, touching things just to see if they were real.

There were many days during which I never even got out of bed. I would spend the entire day, from morning until night, lying there staring out of the window at the endless blue of the Mediterranean sky. I would lie unmoving, my hands clasped behind my head, staring – and waiting. As the harsh bright sun climbed higher and higher, I felt the present burning itself so deeply into my consciousness that everything else was gone. There was no past and no future – only a huge and faceless void.

I have no idea what my parents thought about my behavior. When I look back, I realize they must have been stricken with helplessness. Occasionally one of them would quietly open the door of my bedroom a few small inches and peek in. Often I would hear a deep sigh, then very quietly the sound of the closing door, followed by a soft shuffling of slipper-clad feet down the little tile stairway to the rooms below. I suppose I must have been conscious of their concern, but I was much too apathetic to say anything that might have reassured them.

I think I really expected to die. I almost hoped I might. I was so lethargic and disconnected from life that it was impossible for me to imagine the dramatic turn of events that was about to occur. I now understand that, however bleak things may seem, life is never static. On the night of my sixteenth birthday, during an electrical storm violent even for that time of year, I had a remarkable dream. The entire experience was so dynamic and the images so clear that, although it was a dream, it was as if I were more conscious and alive then I had ever been before — or have been since.

In my dream I am high on a mountaintop. The night sky is an opaque black, punctured by bright stars that appear close enough to touch. I stand at the edge of a circle of Twelve Beings. They appear to be made of granite and look like giant, seated stone statues. Their bodies seem to be covered with flecks of quartz crystal glistening in the starlight.

Standing somewhat below me on the mountainside are my parents and the few boyhood friends I had managed to make. I am engaged in senseless conversation, struggling very hard to talk with all of them at once. I yearn to physically hold on to them. The dark night flashes and the mountaintop is alive with thunder and lightning. My family and friends seem unaware that anything special is taking place as they idly talk of mundane matters. My friends are planning a party, and my mother is telling me what we will have for supper.

Then everything becomes quiet. I notice that the large stone creatures have become smoky and vaporous. Streams of cloud-like mist begin to swirl and turn around the megaliths, and snake down the mountainside. Then, before my eyes, the stone figures become luminous, animate Beings. They are very pale and their bodies are taller and more stately than any ordinary man. The area of the forehead is elongated, and their eyes are unusually blue, bright and shining. The air is very still, and the Man-like creatures glow against the dark night sky.

Slowly and ritualistically, a pipe is passed around the circle. Each Being takes the pipe into his hands and very carefully draws on it. The entire scene is lit by some kind of internal luminescence. Finally the pipe is handed to me. I casually reach out my hand to receive it, continuing a conversation with my friends. The Being standing closest to me shakes his head "no." His eyes fix on mine and he says only one word — "Choose." Slowly, consciously, I reach my hand out to his and take the pipe. I know that by this act I am sealing some sort of a pact, making a commitment. Very deliberately, I raise the pipe to my lips.

At that moment, I found myself awake. Dream and reality had merged. I was still holding the pipe. Zev Moab, the radiance from his partially covered face, glowing brightly from beneath the hood and cowl of his dark robes, was standing above me. Deeply and with great care, I drew in the contents from the bowl of the pipe and handed it back to him. As his large, glistening blue eyes met mine, I realized that he looked exactly like those "Twelve" in my dream. For the first time I understood, deep within my being that, in truth, Zev Moab was no Hu-man. He smiled gently and said, "Tomorrow I will take you to Egypt, and the next step of your journey will begin."

My hands began to tremble and the diary loosened from my grip and fell to the floor. I felt disoriented – as if I were in two places at the same time. It was like looking into the mirror, but instead of seeing my own familiar face, there was a completely foreign one staring back at me.

Who is this David anyway and why...why did I have essentially the same dream as this mythological character? I could not even speculate on what this newest bit of information might mean. I have no idea how much time passed. I felt like I was struggling with my sanity. *The diary has to have been meant for me...it wasn't an accident!* But that only opened up a much deeper set of questions – questions that hurt my brain to even think about. Now it was my former life in California that had become achingly unreal. It seemed to have no connection to me, nor I to it.

After two weeks in the Middle East – which seemed more like a year – we moved on to Greece. The group was scheduled to travel by bus to a ferry bound for the Isle of Patmos, where it was said that John the Beloved wrote Revelations. Four days in the Greek Islands was supposed to be the fun part of the trip, visiting the sights and frolicking on the beach, but not to me – not now. With Gabriel's permission, I checked into a hotel in Athens. *Let them have their adventures. I need time to be alone...to finish the diary. I have to sort out what the "coincidence" of David and I having the same dream is...and what all the rest of this means!*

I went up to my room with the intention of pulling out the diary and digging right in, but the moment I put down my suitcases, stowed my camera gear in the closet and got comfortable on the bed, I was gone. Sometime in the wee hours of the morning, I moved from dreamless exhaustion into an intense dream.

> Someone is calling out to me. I think it is a man. He is trying to get my attention, but a dense blanket of fog lies between us. Although I try very hard, I glimpse him only intermittently and cannot make out either his face or any of his words. Then I see the camel named California. He is smiling at me.

I awoke with a start. Was David calling out to me? I dozed again for a couple of hours, but once I was awake – and alert – I pulled out the diary and thrust it open. With no place to go and no one to answer to, I sprawled myself out on the creaky old bed and tore into it.

CHAPTER 19

One week later

About a week has passed since my last entry, but the memories keep coming. I remember the experience that happened shortly after my sixteenth birthday in particular. As promised, Zev Moab returned and took me on a journey from my parents' house in Tiberias to Egypt, home of the Great Pyramids. I was overjoyed to have him back in my life, but had no idea what lay in store for me.

First we went to the famous pyramids themselves. Then we walked down the Giza Plain to the Sphinx. Three structures were within the fence that protects the ancient site. Zev Moab took me directly to the Sphinx and told me sit beside its right paw.

"David, I want you to close your eyes for a moment and recall all that you have learned."

I did as Zev Moab asked and immediately felt a rush of energy course through my body, and with it, the deep knowledge of all that I had been taught. I quickly opened my eyes.

"Very Good," he said. "You understand. I knew you would. And, as you sit here quietly in meditation, you will understand so much more. My dear boy, this is where I leave you once again. I realize it must be distressing, but let me assure you there will be another to guide you on the next step of your journey. And remember, my David, you are never alone." Then, once again, Zev Moab took his leave of me.

I recall only too well my anticipation at that time. What Zev Moab told me was true. I had received a great deal of training. I had learned how to control my thoughts and my bodily states. And after that last moment with Zev Moab, I understood — on a deeper level — what I had to do, and I put my skills to good use.

I looked around until I found a comfortable spot, shaded

from the sun by the shadow of the Sphinx, and here I began my vigil. I sat very still, as I had been trained to do. I allowed myself to experience the desert around me, staying alert and present but uninvolved. I waited, poised like a cat, totally relaxed yet ready to spring into action at the slightest provocation. I felt the approach of dawn but did not move. I knew that by sitting motionless and controlling the pace of my breath, I could make myself invisible to ordinary sight. Thus, I would be protected from the wandering eyes of any guard patrolling the area.

I stayed in this state for three days and two nights. I had brought a canteen of water and a few dates with me. I did not require any other nourishment. My body was in a state of suspended animation. On the third evening, about an hour after sunset, I felt the hairs on the back of my neck begin to bristle. I held my breath. Then I heard a slight shuffle in the sand behind me. Very carefully, with an almost invisible movement, I turned my head. There was nothing.

I returned to my original position and continued my vigil. In order to keep my energy focused, I allowed it to fully merge with that of the Sphinx. I was immediately in touch with her history, and was shocked to discover that she is much older than the Great Pyramids and had been built in alignment with the star system Sirius.

I actually saw her being built, but then my focus was broken again. I felt my consciousness deliberately wrenched by an outside force and anger began to rise within me. Once more, with deliberation and determination, and without moving so much as a muscle, I pulled my attention back. Carefully and meticulously, I expanded my own field to encompass the surrounding area.

When I picked up no vibration, human or otherwise, I once again relaxed my focus, allowing my awareness to diffuse and float, bringing back the image of the Sphinx. Then, snap! My concentration broke again like a dry twig. For the first time in many years, I experienced a lurch of fear, followed by an anger I could not control. I calmed myself as best I could, intentionally making a mental note of what I was experiencing without dwelling upon it. Methodically I began my exercise once more. This time I could not do it at all. I broke out in a cold sweat. I was fighting desperately for self-control — and I was losing!

I felt consumed by a dark chilling fear, when abruptly, without being able to stop myself, I began to question the validity of my entire life. Why was I here? How could I possibly know the truth? Who was Zev Moab really — and how did I know I could trust him? Even if the things he had told me were true, how could he think it possible for me to withstand the Forces of Darkness he spoke of?

He had said there were forces on both sides. Maybe he was testing me, leading me here to expose me to the Dark Ones. Maybe "he" is one of "them." I tried to fight against the onslaught of terror, but it was useless. Fear had become a tangible substance, thick, dark and heavy, completely surrounding me. I could smell Evil lurking in the air.

I became so fidgety that I got to my feet and began to pace back and forth. I felt a compulsion to leave immediately – before something horrible happened. Then I thought I heard the voice of Zev Moab telling me that I was "not my body and not my emotions." I knew I was alone. That meant that the voice was only in my head. It must be Zev Moab. That was the way he had always spoken to me when he could not be physically present.

"This has got to stop!" I shouted, feeling completely out of control.

"You must take care of yourself, you know," replied a matter-of-fact voice. "If you don't take care of yourself first, you cannot possibly be of any help to others." The voice was soothing and gentle, and I began to relax.

The voice continued, "There is so much of life that you do not know. You are only sixteen. There is plenty of time for you to take on the responsibilities of a man once you truly are one."

Immediately, I realized that this voice was not inside my head. This voice was coming from somewhere else – somewhere outside of me. I swung around and there, leaning against the other paw of the Sphinx and smoking a thin European cigarette, stood a strikingly beautiful young woman. Her crimson lips were full and her dark eyes sultry and mysterious. I was startled. "How did you get in here?" I asked, shakily.

She crossed one long shapely leg over the other and a

portion of creamy, white thigh peeked out through the high cut slit in her narrow skirt. She inhaled deeply on the dark slim cigarette then closed her eyes for a moment. She slowly exhaled a long stream of smoke before responding, "The same way you did," she said, gesturing slightly with her head. "I came in under that gate, over there."

"But, uh, I never saw you." The words stumbled awkwardly out of my mouth. I felt like a schoolboy, utterly self-conscious and ridiculous. My mouth was dry, my lips caked, and I had no idea what I might say next. I noticed she was smiling. Was she making fun of me? No. Her eyes were gentle with understanding.

A flood of relief rushed over me. Here was a friend! It was as if she knew me, knew everything I was thinking. Then I noticed that there was something about her, the way she moved her head, used her hands, that struck a deep chord in me. I was mesmerized by her every gesture. My knees were so weak I almost fell over. I stared at the ground, mumbling, "I guess that was kind of a dumb thing to say."

"No, it wasn't. I know you're not very used to being with girls. You're just a little shy," she said huskily. She was still smiling.

"Yeah, I guess that's it." I couldn't seem to keep my mouth shut and looked away to hide my embarrassment. It was as if I were in another world and the ground rules completely unfamiliar. I did not look at her, but I could still see her delicate profile and full breasts out of the corner of my eye. What was happening to me? I was lightheaded and felt like I had been drinking strong wine.

"Why don't you come a little closer, David, so I can see your face while we talk," she almost whispered.

I took a few steps toward her. "How do you know my name?"

"What difference does it make?" Her voice was as smooth as velvet and just as textured. I wanted to touch her very much. I was wildly magnetized to her and wanted to feel her silken skin against mine. She opened her arms to embrace me, and I moved a little closer. "Well, David, that's more like it. You don't want to deny yourself the pleasures of life, especially before you've even tasted them, now do you? You don't owe anything to anyone. Other people aren't your responsibility."

I stopped dead in my tracks. I could literally see right through her — almost like an x-ray. I understood everything! She had been sent by "them" — the Ones who followed Forces of Darkness!

"I know who you are," I shouted, "and it won't work! You can try to manipulate my mind all you want, but I will not be deterred from my path."

"David, are you so sure? You know you could be wrong. There is still so much for you to learn," she said, slowly unbuttoning her filmy white blouse. A wave of curiosity propelled by desire flushed my body. "We could make love right here by the Sphinx…it would be like nothing you've ever experienced," she continued, as the mounds of her full, untethered breasts began to emerge from beneath her clothing. Then, taking her blouse completely off, her nipples hard in the soft breeze, she whispered, "Touch me, David, I want you to touch me...."

I tried to speak, but couldn't. My hands trembled and I could almost feel the softness of her skin as she closed the space between us. I backed up and bolted myself against the stone behind me. I mustered every ounce of my will to resist embracing her.

"David, can't we be friends? Wouldn't it be better to talk for a while...find out more about me?"

"There's no point in talking. I don't want to hear anything you have to say," I answered with a voice of steel.

Wave after wave of desire flowed through my body as she continued to entice me. I could feel her energy radiate toward me, warm and viscous, almost as if I could touch it. But I stood firm. I closed my eyes, clenched my fists and focused my mind as I had been taught. Slowly, I began to feel my strength return. As it increased, her energy — her power over me — diminished. Then, very slowly, a slight mist began to rise up from the sand and she seemed to disappear into it, fading before my very eyes. I experienced a choking sensation deep in my throat, and my legs almost fell out from under me.

So that is how it would be. The attacks might take on very seductive forms and be very subtle. They might play

with my mind as well as my senses. With a deep sigh of relief, I realized how close I had come to losing my way. Instinctively, I knew that if I had allowed her to touch me, even
once, it would have all been over. I would have lost my will and
been under the spell of the Forces of Darkness forever.
Without warning, the mist turned a greenish-gold. It rose
and surrounded the Sphinx, bathing it in a luminous glow.
Then everything went black and I lost consciousness.

CHAPTER 20

A few days later

I have no idea how long I remained in that deep sleep-like
state. It seemed that I went in and out of dreams – or
possibly I traveled to other places in my consciousness.
When I managed to open my eyes again, it was completely
dark. Then, very slowly, a mist began to form once again a
few feet from where I lay. A figure dressed in gilded robes
stepped towards me. I know this man, but where do I know
him from?

"My name is Ha-Hotep and I am a member of The Sons of
Thoth, a part of The Great Brotherhood of Light," he
said in a serious voice but with a smile and a look in his eyes
that I could not quite read.

"But...."

"My name is Ha-Hotep, and I am a member of The Sons of Thoth," he repeated gently, pausing until he was certain he had my full attention. "We are a secret Brotherhood created during the time of the building of the Great Pyramids. We vowed, long ago, to protect this holy plain and we have been the keepers of these structures and their Mysteries throughout the Ages."

I gazed at him, still wondering who he was. At last, it was the look in his eyes that gave him away. I recognized this man as Rashid, the one who rescued me in the desert and brought me to live in the village. I was so glad — so relieved — to see a friend. Were there no characters in my drama that had only a single identity? What a silly question I thought, watching myself in my own past, looking around trying to get my bearings.

"We are in a secret chamber inside the Sphinx. The fact that the Sphinx has hollow spaces is generally unknown in your time, and we have made sure that it has stayed that way. There is a hidden entrance in the right paw that opens onto a passageway leading to this room.

"We have protected this very chamber — and others like it — from modern archaeologists and from explorers of the past. They would not have understood the knowledge — the meaning, purpose and contents — within these chambers. We knew that many would only have been interested in plunder. These rooms have not been physically entered since the time of The Christ. He came here to re-learn the ancient secrets and pass through the rites of initiation."

As he continued to speak, the chamber became brighter, and I saw that we were in a very small stone room with a low ceiling. I could not help looking around, studying the carved and painted walls with their strange and mysterious markings. The walls were covered with carved images that seemed to move and change as an odd greenish-gold light – a light that had no source – played upon them.

"I am here to take you to the Great Guardians, the Galactic Visitors who have guided us. They will explain many of the things you see around you," he said, taking notice of my wandering eyes. Ha-Hotep led me to the opening of a narrow passage that seemed to descend straight into the very bowels of the earth. As if in a daze, I followed him.

After walking down what seemed to be hundreds of feet, we wove our way through a series of winding tunnels that connected the Sphinx to the Great Pyramid. We were preceded by the same greenish-gold light, which still had no apparent source. We passed through room after room filled with strange machines and apparatuses and chambers whose walls were lined with sheets of gold. Upon those golden walls were engraved long texts of hieroglyphics.

Finally, after climbing upward again, we reached a room within the Great Pyramid itself. Ha-Hotep explained that this specific chamber had also been kept secret throughout the centuries. This yet undiscovered room lay about midway between those vaults known as the King and Queen's chambers. The room was not large, but it had a soaring ceiling.

My eyes were immediately drawn to a huge multi-faceted, three-dimensional, star-like crystal, which floated in the center of the room, hovering some five feet above the ground.

"Ha-Hotep, what is this? I've never seen anything like it."

"It is a sixty-four tetrahedron crystal. It derives its name from the fact that it is composed of sixty four separate, three-dimensional crystal pyramids. Each one is four-sided and has the same proportions as the Great Pyramid itself. The design was first brought to Earth many eons ago by Star Beings, but it is a pattern that is woven throughout the Cosmos. This particular cluster of crystals is over four feet in diameter and is not only a free energy device but also a time machine."

Still hovering in the air, the giant crystal began to slowly rotate, gaining momentum with every turn. Before long, and despite its size, the crystal was revolving at a tremendous speed. Transparent, water-like energy poured from the sphere and, as it swirled, formed a donut-like vortex around it.

The "water" was then somehow drawn back up through the center of the crystal and recycled out the top. From within this brilliantly shimmering "donut," brightly colored shafts of light flew off in every direction. The crystal itself glowed a cold, luminous white and seemed to pulsate. There was a faint smell of ozone in the air and a feeling of intense energy.

I almost gasped when I tore my eyes from the crystal and looked around the inner chamber – the scene was so familiar. The night before Zev Moab brought me to the Sphinx, I had a dream unlike any other in my life. In it twelve strange Beings were seated in a circle, passing a pipe amongst themselves. Now those same strange Beings were in this chamber, sitting on cushions arranged in a horseshoe shape around the giant revolving crystal.

At first, like the crystal, the Beings were glowing and almost transparent. I could see right through them, like pottery being fired in a kiln. Slowly – slowly – the turning of the crystal all but subsided, and, as it did, the Beings became fully solid and animate.

Studying them with great care, I experienced a sudden jolt of recognition. My friend – my teacher – Zev Moab was seated amongst them. He looked different, more solemn and remote, but it was certainly him. He nodded at me, the barest glint of a smile in his blue eyes, then returned his gaze to the slowly revolving crystal. Once again, I remembered my searing loneliness when he had left me in the olive grove. I had thought I would never see him again. I understood so very little then.

I forced my attention back to the other Beings. In unison, they said, "Hello David, welcome!" Although I had thought of the Beings in my dream as men, upon hearing their voices I realized that was not true. Although the voices were clearly both male and female, the beings carried such an exquisite balance of male and female energy that it was almost as though they had no gender at all.

Zev Moab turned to me and pulled back the hood of his long, dark robe revealing whips of short, silvery-blond hair. I realized I had never, in all the years I studied with him, thought about what he would look like without his hood.

"David, we have a seat for you," he said, indicating the empty cushion directly opposite him. "Please sit. Make yourself comfortable." Lost in thought, I automatically took my seat, still amazed at the way Zev Moab looked. After I was settled, physically and emotionally, I looked back at him, then at the other Beings sitting around the crystal. They had also removed their hoods.

All of them had the same brilliant blue eyes and silvery blond hair, and emanated both strength and vulnerability without in any way communicating masculinity or femininity as it is generally defined. They seemed full and complete unto themselves, while at the same time being entirely open and present. They were very beautiful.

I watched in awe as the crystal lowered itself to my eye level and, still turning slowly, began to glow anew. It formed pictures within pictures. I saw scenes of great primeval turmoil — stars being born while other stars were dying. There were immense and violently beautiful eruptions of energy. It came out of The Great Oneness, the Creator Force, and was the process of Creation itself.

Then I heard the comforting voice of my teacher, Zev

Moab. "We welcome you, David," he said, motioning toward the other Beings in the room. "By now you must have realized that we are Galactic Visitors, and in this particular instance all of us are from the Pleiades. I want you to look carefully into the crystal. You are going to see your past in the time of Atlantis and early Egypt. It will help you to understand who you are, who you have been, and what you now need to do."

CHAPTER 21

I focused on the Great Crystal and, like a camera coming in for a close-up, saw the Earth growing large before me. It was green and blue and fresh. I saw strange and unusual forms of plant and animal life that have never been seen by present day human eyes. There were giant plants that moved of their own volition and great flying creatures with golden feathers. Their wings spanned twenty feet and glistened in the sunlight as they glided sleekly and gracefully through strangely colored skies. I saw the stuff of myths — giant griffins and winged horses.

Before my eyes, great silver spaceships and flying discs were carrying many types of Star Beings, some similar in appearance to those in the room. I saw them land on Earth and materialize whole cities, even instant architectural wonders, out of barren rock. I watched as they

transported giant boulders, first by making them weightless, then easily moving them and finally placing them gently
and precisely into position. Once in place, the boulders resumed
their former massive weight.

The Star Beings were able to perform these feats
effortlessly by collectively focusing the vast power of both
their minds and voices. At times, in order to sound a particular tone, they enhanced their voices by using small machines.
During those times, their voices rose in unison to such a high
and harmonious level of vibration that they could suspend
gravity. They were also able to create extensive rock
carvings by projecting an image directly from their minds
onto the rough face of the rock.

Among the variety of creatures I saw in the crystal were
the great apes, those associated with the ancestry of
Man. I watched as some of them became illuminated by the
glowing light and were transformed, becoming more and more
Hu-man-like.

I saw other life forms that came into being in a different
way — exactly as they had in my dream in the Arab village.
They began as pure light. As time passed, they grew more
and more solid, then more and more dense. Eventually, they
became humans.

I watched as two highly developed civilizations emerged and
later, vanished. The first Root Race was destroyed, and
the second one simply disappeared. This second Root Race,
the Lemurians, occupied a magical Island-Continent located in

the Pacific Ocean. Only a very small part of its land mass continued in physical form when the Island sank beneath the sea, and most of its inhabitants vanished.

The Lemurians were a highly spiritual, proud and beautiful race. They were unique in the history of Earth, because they had bodies that were never entirely physical in the sense that ours are. They had the ability to transform from an almost-solid state into a state of pure energy – and back again – at will.

Before the Lemurian Civilization ended and its inhabitants disappeared, I saw them encode thousands of tiny "seed crystals" with information – spiritual, historical, and technical – that would be helpful to future generations. They were able to program the crystals in such a way that their data would be available in a time-release, energy pattern. Then, according to The Plan, they scattered the crystals over the face of the Earth, insuring that they would be found by future generations.

"The Plan!" My mind flashed back to what Zev Moab had told me about a plan laid out for Planet Earth before the arrival of Hu-mankind. Could this be a part of that same plan? I pushed these thoughts away. It was hard enough to keep up with the images flashing in the crystal.

I forced my mind to refocus and saw that when the Lemurians' purpose here was complete and their Island was about to sink into the sea, they had lifted en masse, with some specific exceptions, and departed the plane of

Earth, never again to incarnate in physical form. Those few who chose to remain behind, as guides and guardians for the generations of humans that would follow, established settlements in the mountains of Tibet.

Images from the giant crystal faded, and I had a moment to close my eyes, but once I opened them, events passed quickly. After a time, the images began to slow down and I was witnessing what seemed like a somewhat familiar scene. It was the civilization of Atlantis with its sophisticated technologies. I saw Beings of the same race as the Twelve sitting with me now. They were Galactic Visitors, Pleiadeans, who were working with the Atlantean priests. They wanted to teach the priests what they knew about Earth's powerful geometric grids and its natural electro-magnetic energy patterns.

Before long, the peoples of Atlantis appeared. The general population was made up of many different types of Hu-mans. Some were extremely tall, others exceedingly small. The hues of their skin were as varied as the colors of the rainbow. This was a result of the genetic seeding and intermingling of a great variety of extraterrestrial races. Although the greatest number of them had light skin and red hair, they all blended together into a beautiful medley of color, size and shape.

The Atlantean Prince-Priest A-Ta emerged from the crowd. He was wearing robe-like metallic clothing with small crystals woven into the fabric. I realized I had glimpsed him in my long-ago dream in the village near the Sphinx. He was the one who had floated above the waves and watched in horror as the Island of Atlantis disappeared beneath the waves. Now my dream began to make sense — I knew I was Prince A-Ta in that past life.

It took a few moments before I could bring my focus back to the Great Crystal. Finally I was able to see that we Atlantean priests, the Lemurians, the Galactic Visitors from Pleiades, as well as other Star Beings who followed the Light, all worked harmoniously together, drawing huge maps to chart the surface of the Earth.

Occasionally, I saw some strange shadowy figures in the background. It was difficult to make them out, but they seemed to emanate darkness. Wherever they appeared, the people seemed to be less animated, even less alive. However the crystal never focused on these ones, so it was not easy to know much about them. I was only shown enough to know that they were there, no more.

Our teachers showed us how to work with the two types of energy that were vital to the health of our planet. The first was the energetic currents that flow down from the Center of the Universe. It was these powerful energies — flowing from Heaven to Earth — that shaped Earth and held the planets in orbit.

The second was those energies that were generated deep within the Earth itself and were electromagnetic in nature. Those energies moved both under the ground and across its surface.

These two energies, one from the Heavens and the other from deep within the Earth, came together at specific locations. The Galactic Energy joined and replenished the Terrestrial Energy, creating the planet's Energy Body. That energy then radiated out across the planet, forming the Planetary Grid System.

The importance of the grid system was explained to us priests in great detail. We saw that the unimpeded, balanced flow of these energies was vital to the health of the Earth. If the lines became blocked, the result would be earthquakes, floods, drought, famine, pestilence and all types of Hu-man illness.

We learned that this grid system acted as the Earth's nervous system. We saw how the union of energies behaved as a catalyst in the construction of all Matter. In addition, we discovered that the grid system could be used to achieve instant communication, travel, Hu-man healing, weather control, the health of plant and animal life and much more. And finally, we Atlantean priests worked with the energies until we could feel them deep within our own bodies, for it was necessary that we be on intimate terms with all we had seen.

We Atlantean priests spent many hours each day teleporting ourselves to distant parts of the Earth. We communed with the Devic Kingdom, the Great Nature Spirits that protect the land, forests, mountains and lakes. With our "inner eyes," we could see the Earth's true energetic form – a giant crystal. And we became one with the vital energy grid that criss-crossed our planet. I continued looking into the crystal and watched as lines were carefully drawn on large maps, tracking patterns of energy. The Galactic Visitors then placed their hands over the maps to experience the potency of the various energies.

After some consultation, they marked all the spots where the energies came together. Thus, they were able to determine the locations of the Earth's strongest energy centers. When all was ready, the Galactic Visitors and the Lemurians, as well as we Atlantean priests, accompanied large expedition parties that were sent to these designated sites.

Once there, we tested the latent powers of different types of stone. It was an important job, because it was understood that certain kinds of stones had the ability to amplify the energy that already existed in an area. Other stones had the ability to attract specific energies from the Heavens. In many cases, we were seeking stone that was composed of a high level of quartz crystal. Quartz has the ability to attract and accumulate energy from the Heavens and infuse it deep into the Earth. Some types of stone were discarded and others put to use, until exactly the right electrical fields and frequencies were created.

Then, according to plan and responding to the energies, we created precise geometrical structures of stone, guided in their placement by Earth itself. We raised giant boulders — often levitated from some distance away — and placed them in magical circles. I saw the first stones put into position in the structure that would later become Stonehenge.

I also saw giant boulders arranged across an island in the North Atlantic off the northern tip of what is now Scotland. Large standing stones were carefully set in place across the small island. Many were set in specific alignments to mark off the rising of the sun on the Summer and Winter Solstices, the rising of the Pleiades and other astronomical events of importance. This site would later be known as Callanish. Contained within its structure were certain activation codes that would later be found — and felt — by a certain few who would know what to do with the information.

Still gazing into the crystal, I watched as early Hu-mans connected with the Planetary Grid System. Since all of the vital connections to celestial activity were purposefully marked in stone, shamans could foretell when the sun's energy would be at its weakest or when it would be eclipsed altogether. They could then plan for those times and keep energy stored in reserve, thus avoiding both drought and famine.

There was a wonderful spirit of cooperation between the people and the land. When Hu-man thought joined with the inherent terrestrial energies, potent Force Fields were created. Objects could then be materialized and de-materialized, the sick cured and the land made fertile.

Often we worked with local shamans, further initiating them into the Earth Mysteries and speeding up the development of their cultures. In other cases, we quietly came, set up visible stone markers to be used later, and left. The Lemurians were especially helpful with their ability to build in stone — the visible markers of invisible energy.

Within the crystal I saw "vortex points," places on the Earth where energy lines criss-crossed one another in a distinctive way. It was in these scattered locations that the Earth created the most intense energies. The vortex points were specifically used by the various Star Beings to transfer from one dimension to another. There are many of these entry and exit points in the lands now known as South and Central America and Tibet.

But even amongst vortex points, I could see that not all were alike. At certain spots on the planet's surface, the Earth's electromagnetic energy combined itself with inert gasses that seeped up from the planet's core, forming a vortex with unique properties. Shamans would prepare a Hu-man Initiate to receive and work with this special energy. At the appropriate moment, when the Initiate stood over the vortex, his or her own energy field immediately expanded to include all time and all space — giving the Initiate the ability to see into the future.

The most famous of these was located at a place that, during the time of the High Greek Culture, came to be known as Delphi. People made pilgrimages to hear the Initiate, the Oracle of Delphi, make prophecies. They listened with rapt attention and planned the events of their lives around the wisdom of the Oracle.

In later times, as Hu-mans lost their deep connection to the Earth and the Earth's energies, they also lost their knowledge of the energetic origin of those words. They continued to visit the Oracle, but mistakenly thought that the person known as the Oracle had magical powers.

Without warning, the crystal grew dark and murky. I could no longer see into it.

CHAPTER 22

Weeks later

I have not written for a long time. It seems that my nervous system can only handle so much information at a time. Given too much, it begins to shut down and all memory comes to a halt. I have been recuperating at my station by the Sphinx. It is unnecessary to describe in detail what has been happening for me in what we think of as "real time." I will only say that since I left the Arab village my view of everything has undergone a total change.

However, I now feel ready to allow my memory to open again and to write what comes forward. I have reviewed my last entry, and I remember that the crystal became dark and murky and I could not see anything. When it cleared, events proceeded at a jagged pace. The Atlanteans had lost their light and airy quality, and the magnificent radiance they had possessed. I watched as they strolled the wide, tree-lined avenues and sailed the waterways of Atlantis, dressed in their silver-blue crystal garments. They were still physically beautiful — but different. A certain kind of purity was gone. I felt a deep sadness at the loss.

Strange new creatures now appeared on the scene — part man, part beast. They were the result of Mankind's abuse of his power and his sexuality. Zev Moab had spoken to me about those sexual unions at great length during one of our talks, but now I was seeing the results — the Things. Some of the Hu-man hybrids were badly deformed. Many had difficulty moving, and it pained me to look at them. However, on the inside, they were still gentle, simple, child-like creatures.

There were many "normal" Hu-mans, even some of my close Atlantean friends and neighbors who, giving in to their own dark side, acted with cruel treachery toward these poor unfortunate ones. They refused to remember that these Things, as they referred to them, were a part of them — products of their ancestors' sexual unions. Many people turned them into beasts of burden and even used them for strange genetic experiments. In some instances, they were corralled together like cattle, enclosed in encampments and treated like criminals. It was horrible to watch, yet so riveting I could not pull my eyes away.

The Dark Star Beings understood the evolutionary process of the Things and that knowledge became a part of their strategy to gain control over Earth. When the Dark Star Beings first encouraged Hu-mans to abuse their power and sexuality, they knew exactly what would happen. They understood that if the mutated Things were left on their own, they would rapidly reproduce. The Dark Star Beings also knew that the offspring of the Things would be monstrous — and frightening in appearance. As the numbers of Things soared into the hundreds of thousands, it looked as though they might overrun Atlantis. The Hu-mans became afraid and life on Atlantis became unstable.

It was a terrible time of fear and confusion. The Dark Star Beings realized that their planned opportunity was at hand. Pretending to befriend the Hu-mans, they took advantage of their fears. They appealed to the masses, promising to make them safe. The way they intended to make them safe was to demand the destruction — the complete annihilation — of the Things. The Dark Star Beings became bolder and bolder in their manipulation of the crowds. Not only did they play upon the Epidemic of Fear, they fed it further for their own purposes.

As the Dark Star Beings gathered more followers, they grew bolder still. The tension of the times made it possible for them to recruit some members of the priesthood. Once a priest succumbed, he became the Hu-man mouth-piece for the Dark Beings. Moreover, being priests, they were able to lull the people into a false sense of security and encourage them to give up any personal responsibility for what was happening. These Dark Priests presented themselves as a New Order and assured the people that they would handle it all — in the name of Hu-mankind.

Within the crystal, I saw another group of Hu-mans. I saw those of us who still kept the memory of our spiritual origin, for we understood — at the core of our being — the Oneness of all Life. And we knew that included our Hu-man responsibility to care for the Things. We tried in vain to explain that Earth itself would be devastated if so great a destruction as that planned by the Dark Star Beings was carried out. The crowds, operating entirely out of fear, were in no mood to listen. They wanted simple answers and they wanted someone to blame for their frustration and their fear. The masses, in their frenzy, turned on us.

Late one night, a secret enclave of High Atlantean priests was called. I was amongst those gathered. I was called Prince At-Ta. All of us realized how events must turn out. The die had been cast. Enough Hu-mans had made their Choice to follow the Forces of Darkness. The energy field created by this Dark Choice was far too strong for our priestly arts to combat. There was no time to look back, to consider what might have been — or what we might have done to prevent the unthinkable. Our Island would be destroyed.

It was of the utmost importance to save the knowledge of our great Culture, to assure that it would not also disappear. We high Atlantean priests who followed the Light had the ability to see that not all was lost. We knew there would come a future civilization, a time when Man would, once again, understand the spiritual concepts upon which our civilization was founded. They would be able to comprehend and utilize in a positive way the sophisticated technologies that gave us our vast power.

Our power came from our ability to discipline and focus our mind in such a fashion that we could pull "free energy" from space. Then, using our minds as a tool, we could use that free energy to create, as well as alter, Matter. Since all Matter was "alive," inter-connected and contained all possibilities, we simply "chose" the result we wanted and tapped into the Universal Life Force. In this way, we were able to harness the energy of aliveness to produce all of the creature comforts we desired.

We greatly enhanced the power of our minds by the use of certain devices, such as quartz crystals. Since our minds run on a frequency that crystals can receive, we were able to use quartz crystals much like a computer. We could encode our thoughts directly into the crystals, which in turn would absorb them in the form of an energy charge.

Some crystals could hold more energy — more information — than others. However, in many cases, a single crystal could hold the combined thought of many powerful and focused minds. The ability of crystals to store energy for use at a later time was of great value to us. Crystals also have the ability to condense and focus energy, much like a laser. Once a crystal was programmed by our mind, we could use it as a tool.

We also had another tool — the toning of certain sounds. We would use those sounds to levitate and move heavy slabs of stone from one location to another across great distances. Then we would use the laser-like ability of particular crystals to make cuts in those same stones so precisely that they would fit together without the use of mortar. That is how we built our Great Pyramid on Atlantis as well as other structures.

Focusing our minds on the crystal, we could transmit energy, amplify and direct thought, even heal and pro-tect our environment and ourselves. With the power of crystals,we were able to run a very sophisticated and advanced culture.

It was clear that there was not always a correlation between "conscience" and "power." The Life Force, the Power of Creation, in and of itself has no conscience. In the wrong hands, it could be as destructive as it was potentially constructive, and that was what I was now seeing in the crystal. the Forces of Darkness – at this point composed of both Earth Beings and Star Beings – wanted control of our technologies, especially our crystals, so that they could have control of Atlantis.

Now, with the imminent destruction of Atlantis upon us, we had to act fast. Our first concern was to safeguard the essence of our civilization. We briefly considered the daunting task of removing the gold and crystal capstone from atop our Holy of Holies, the Great Pyramid of Atlantis. However, to do this all-but-impossible task, we needed a male and female initiate. They must both be direct descendants of the ancient lineage, and they also must have undergone the full rites of initiation.

Even if we were able to find two such initiates, we were not certain that it would be possible to remove the capstone without destroying, not only the Great Pyramid itself, but all that it contained. Since there were three male priests who qualified but no priestesses, we were forced to leave the capstone where it was. It was a painful choice to leave such a powerful device behind. Our only consolation came from knowing that the Dark Star Beings and their Hu-man recruits could not use or remove it either.

Since time was of the essence, we concentrated on what was realistically possible for us to accomplish. We knew we needed the tools necessary for running our world. This meant not only our crystals, but also the other psychotronic capacitors that stored Hu-man energy and ideas. Some of those devices stored the energetic patterns of the various techniques we had developed for empowering our minds. Other devices stored our values and belief systems.

Both were kept inside the Great Pyramid of Atlantis. However, retrieving them was extremely difficult, because the Pyramid itself had been all but overtaken by the Dark Star Beings. With great stealth, we managed to remove most of this equipment and prepare it for transport to safety. Unfortunately, although we tried, we were unable to enter the Hall of Crystals and thus could not retrieve our functional crystals - the ones used for electricity and power throughout the Island.

We then sent our most skilled and creative engineers to quickly build vast underground chambers in a number of locations around the planet. The chambers were to contain giant vaults that were meant to house and protect the sophisticated knowledge and technology rescued from our endangered Atlantean world.

Since we knew that Egypt was – and always would be– the geophysical center of Earth's landmasses, it was the perfect location to be the new Motherland and hold the Spiritual Link for the planet. We recognized that in the future the entire area would concurrently be both a beacon of tremendous Light and a portal for great Darkness. Obviously, it was important to immediately establish powerful frequencies of Light in that location.

Therefore, our largest architectural crew went to Egypt, where a vault was created in the form of a giant subterranean pyramid below the Giza plain. My father, also a High Priest on Atlantis, left with this group.

Other migratory parties of enlightened Atlantean citizens left to establish additional outposts of Light in preparation for the dark times we knew would soon come. Some migration parties went to the Andes and Himalaya mountains. Others, led by a High Atlantean Priest, Iltar, went to the land that would be known thousands of years in the future as Yucatan. It was here that he and his fellow priests built a great pyramid, the Temple of Iltar. They embraced and educated the local inhabitants about the inter-connection of all Life. Beneath this temple another major vault was established.

The remaining Lemurians, who had acted as guides to

we Atlantean priests, chose to retire to the non-physical planes where they would remain free of the Earth-binding webs and shadows. From there they could easily act as funnels of Light to those of us who remained on Atlantis.

This was also the case for the Star Beings who followed the Light and who had also been our teachers. We understood that some would visit from time to time while others would return far in the future when they would have tasks to perform once more. In the meantime, they would serve as intermediaries between Earth and the Higher Planes. However, we knew that they would always be available to us as guides should we choose to call upon them.

It was a difficult time for we priests who chose to stay on in Atlantis. We wanted to be available to the people who needed us, for it was clear that the Dark Priests held great power over Hu-mankind. An oppressively heavy and menacing cloud of energy formed itself over the land, blocking the light of the sun. We knew this came from experiments being performed by those who had chosen to join the Forces of Darkness.

Every day it grew worse. Both physical and mental illness ran rampant as the patterns of energy became more and more distorted. Unfortunately, it was the average Atlantean citizen who suffered the most. They had neither the tenacity nor mental strength we priests had learned and practiced. They fell like flies.

CHAPTER 23

Sometime later

There has been so much to absorb as these memories return that I often leave my station here at the Sphinx and wander about for a time in an attempt to keep my bearings on this Earth.

My next set of memories is very complex. I hope that writing about them will help me to better understand all that happened during that time. I remember that I looked into the crystal once again and saw myself on Atlantis. I had cycled through many lifetimes since the early days of Atlantis, each time as the Atlantean Prince A-Ta.

In this cycle, I was only nineteen years of age. Even though I was very young, so many of the priesthood had left Atlantis to head up the new settlements that, almost over-night, I became an Elder. One day, a young priestess came to see me. She was little more than a child, but was already well known because of her beauty and her psychic abilities. Her name was A-Lan, and she came with an unexpected plea.

Suddenly I felt a tremendous jolt and had the weirdest sensation. It was almost like being hit by a flash of lightening – but from the inside out. I was so shocked I didn't know what to do. My whole body felt like jelly. I shut my eyes tightly, wondering if I were going to dissolve – afraid I would disappear altogether. Then slowly – very slowly – like a giant wave being pulled back out to sea, the feeling receded.

That was horrible! Overcome by an almost senseless blast of rage, I slammed the diary shut and threw it across the room. "I won't stand for this anymore!" I yelled.

I jumped out of bed, paced the room, looked out the window then paced again. I crawled back into bed, not knowing what to do – or even what to think. My mind was a blank for a long time before a childhood memory abruptly emerged. I was about ten and my best friend Janet had a desk next to me at school. I had dropped a pencil on the floor, and, as a game, showed her how I could pick it up with my mind. This was something the beautiful lady who visited me at night had taught me to do. But, right after I did my "trick," Janet had moved to a desk on the other side of the room and wouldn't talk to me for the rest of the day.

Later, when I was leaving the schoolyard to go home, a bunch of kids formed a ring around me blocking my way and yelling, *freak*. I was in tears by the time a teacher came out and broke up the growing crowd of children. She took me into her office and called my mother who came immediately to pick me up.

The teacher had quickly learned of the day's events and informed my mother. On the way home my mother said something very strange, something that scared me so much I had never thought of it again all these years – until now.

"Cassie," she said, pulling the car over to the side of the road and looking at me sternly. "You must never do anything like that again. Not ever! It will lead to very bad things. I know what I'm talking about. When I was your age, I did something like that too, and they took me away from my family. I had to go to a special kind of hospital. I was not allowed to see anyone...not even my parents. You have no idea how horrible it was! They gave me tests every day...day after day...until I got really sick. I couldn't come home for over two months. A doctor and a lawyer had to sign papers, or they would never have let me out. Even after I came home, I was sick for a long, long time.

"That's all I am going to say, but you must never...never do anything like that again! Do you understand? You must try to be like everyone else. Even if you think you can do special things or know things that other people don't, you must keep it to yourself!"

I was shaking.

"Do you promise!" she demanded, in a voice I had never heard before.

I nodded, trying to control my crying. "Mommy, did...did you see the lady, too?"

"No, of course not! And neither did you. We are never going to talk...or think...about this again. I'm telling you this for your own good."

We drove the rest of the way home in silence and no one ever spoke of it again. But I spent a week sleeping on the window seat in my parents' bedroom – and the door to my room always had to be open.

Remembering the event from my childhood left me with a deep sense of confusion – and betrayal. I could not open the diary for the rest of the day and half of the next, but I did manage to retrieve it from the corner of the room and put it on the bedside table.

I have no idea why or how, but I slowly came around to the conclusion that, if I kept reading, everything that had occurred might somehow end up making some kind of sense. So crazy as it as seemed, I propped up the pillows on the bed and resolutely settled in for what I hoped would not be another bumpy ride. I started at the part where I had left off – the part where the young priestess had come to David – or Prince A-Ta, as he had been called then.

"Prince A-Ta," A-lan said softly, "Thank you for seeing me on such short notice."

"I am here to be of service," I replied. "Tell me how I might help you."

"Dear Brother of Light," she beseeched me shyly, placing

her hand over her heart and then touching it to her forehead in the gesture of greeting. "I hope you will not think it too forward of me, but I have seen another way for Atlantis."

Her large aquamarine eyes, smudged about by dark, thick lashes, glazed over for a moment, then looked deeply into mine. For one instant she was no longer a maiden. In her unselfconscious gaze, I could feel the intensity of raw, untapped power. What a gifted High Priestess she would have made one day, if Atlantis were not doomed! I was surprised that she had not gone on to Egypt or one of the other New Lands, where her abilities would have been honed and developed and where she, in turn, could have given to and taught so many. I said as much to her.

She held me in her gaze with a fixed look as she answered. "No, my place is here. As I told you, I have seen other things for Atlantis." Then her eyes dropped and she became shy again.

I studied her before responding. Her energy felt very clean. Her statement was made innocently. It did not come from vanity or ego. This was not a manipulative young woman. I doubted that she ever suspected her power, her charisma or her beauty. I was disarmed.

"Sit down, my child, and tell me what is on your mind," I offered, calling upon my priestly training, as I gestured for her to sit beside me.

We were in an open-air pavilion within the Ancient Garden Temple. The surrounding walls were made of marble and quartz crystal, the floors of travertine. This temple was quite a distance from the Great Pyramid. It was the one place on Atlantis where the pure Spiritual Energy, which had once filled the entire island, could still be experienced. Even as the air over Atlantis was darkening, the air over the temple remained pure and clean.

There was a fountain in the center of the courtyard. The effect of the sunlight, as it mixed with the dancing water, was greatly amplified by many crystal devices. This created a field of low gravity, which was also rich in negative ions. The lighter gravitational pull allowed one to be relatively free of the encumbrance of the body. The ion field gave an enhanced clarity of thought and vision. It also created an overall feeling of well-being. This was not a place where one harboring dark thoughts or manipulative energies would have been comfortable for any length of time. Nevertheless, my lovely guest looked around furtively, a flash of concern showing in her otherwise fathomless eyes.

"It is all right to speak," I said, encouragingly. "There is no one here who would abuse your confidences or harm you in any way."

"Dear Brother, you are wrong. There is one nearby who plots my ruin, though he does not yet know I know his name," she said, her voice betraying none of the tension she must have felt.

I looked around carefully but the courtyard was completely empty. "I know the times are difficult and confusing. However, we are within the Temple courtyard and...."

"What?" she said, seeming to snap out of a daze. "I'm sorry Prince. I must have drifted off."

"Do not apologize. I said nothing of great importance." I hid my surprise at her other earlier statement. "Tell me child, what it is that you have seen?"

"It is...difficult...to know where to begin," she said haltingly, as she sat on the large marble bench, crossing and uncrossing her ankles and folding her hands in her lap.

"Since I was a small child, I have seen many things," she began. "That is why my parents sent me early into the priesthood. I have had many readings with the Great Mother, but even she would never say whether or not I carry the ancient genetic lineage or the Star Seed Codes of Light."

"Perhaps the answer to that question is not important and that is why she did not speak of this to you."

"Yes, that is what I have thought, too. Although in these times of change and uncertainty, it seems that everyone wants to understand everything. There is so little faith in what cannot be easily explained." She paused again, as if she were looking for the right words.

And people do not listen to explanations when they are given, I thought silently, remembering the futile attempts of the priests to save Atlantis.

"I know what you are thinking," she continued quietly. "I can also read thoughts, though none save the Great Mother ever knew to what degree I have this talent. I know that you and the rest of the priesthood, have accepted that Atlantis is already lost. But I wonder if you would feel that way if you could see what I have seen?" Once again she brought her eyes up to meet mine and resumed the gaze that seemed to look into the very heart and soul of my being.

"I know how the Forces of Darkness will destroy Atlantis — and I know when they will do it." She said these words quietly and clearly, without any particular emotion.

The statement seemed to echo loudly all around us, though I knew that she had not raised her voice. I sat very still while I allowed her words to sink in. My fellow priests and I had seen what was to occur, at least in the broadest sense. We felt that the Hu-man collective had been forever altered by the influence of the Forces of Darkness and that Hu-man beliefs and actions had set irreversible laws into motion.

We accepted the inevitability of ensuing events and had taken steps accordingly. All of our important instruments had been retrieved and sent on to Egypt. We moved swiftly, for we could see that Atlantis would fall — and we all thought the time would be soon. However, none of us had seen exactly how that fall would occur. Many had tried, but none had been successful. Our most gifted psychics had found their powers failing due to the great dark and looming thought forms created by the Forces of Darkness and their multitude of followers. Even the Star Beings who were our guides had been unable to interfere with the choices made by the free will of the majority of the Atlantean populace. They were only there to act as Teacher and Spiritual Guide.

Until this moment I had assumed that the fate of Atlantis was not a probability, but rather a certainty. Now this young woman was talking about a different vision for Atlantis. I was not sure I wanted to sit with her and listen to words that might tamper with those Spiritual Laws that I knew so well. She felt my reticence and sat quietly, eyes downcast, not saying a word.

"Why did you not speak up about these things earlier?" I finally asked, my voice stern.

"I had not seen it all, Great Prince, until this very morning, and then I came right here to you." She shut her eyes tightly and I saw a tear roll down her cheek. My heart went out to her. Surely, brought up in the Temple, with such respect for those further along in their initiations, it could not been easy for her to come to me with such a statement.

"A-Lan, tell me exactly what you have seen," I said softly.

"There is something I must tell you first. It is a strange story. On the day that I was born, my mother's younger sister died. I was named after my late aunt. Many stories surround her life and death. No one save The Great Mother, the High Priestess, and now I, myself, know the truth of the mystery that was her life. My mother, against all warning, insisted upon naming me after her. My mother was a good but simple woman. She died when I was only five. She loved her younger sister almost more than life itself.

"My aunt was also brought up in the inner temples from childhood. Even though my mother seldom saw her, she was quite attached to her. They were so different that many could not believe them to be sisters. My mother was a warm and loving soul but plain to look at and showed no particular psychic gifts. My aunt, on the other hand, was very beautiful and exhibited incredible talents from a very young age. They say I resemble her." At this point she cast her eyes down and once again became the shy young girl.

When she looked up, there was an almost painful expression in her eyes. It was apparent how very much she wanted me to understand and believe her words. "My aunt was very special, but she had one great flaw — a profound insecurity and doubt about her own worth. This was very dangerous in one so talented, because it made her vulnerable to flattery."

A-Lan looked away, her eyes shrouded in a deep sadness that she fought mightily to control. She sighed deeply and audibly. When she looked back, her eyes were clear and strong again. "It could be that her insecurity was due to the fact that her own mother had died in giving birth to her. You see, I know all about her. Sometimes it feels as if she and I are one and that I am here to atone for her mistake." She gazed intently into my eyes again, willing me to comprehend her words.

"My aunt was very talented in working with crystals, and respect for her abilities grew. She personally developed the process by which the power of lightening could be harnessed and its energy used. With this accomplisment, my aunt became a master at her craft, and although still fairly young was awarded the highest honor, the position of Master Crystal Technician. She worked in the Great Hall of Crystals and was put in charge of all of the energy that ran our Island World.

"However, because of her deep insecurity, she was always pushing the limits in her work with the crystals. She was warned many times by the High Council of the devastation that forcing too much energy through the crystals could create. They thought she was merely headstrong, but the problem went much deeper. She felt a need to do more – always more. She needed to prove her worth.

"This was at the time when the Atlanteans had already become extremely afraid of the Things and when the factions of Light and Darkness had become apparent and openly divided. There were many on Earth who followed the Forces of Darkness out of fear and desperation. However, there were others who took this path because their separation from the Light of Oneness left them with nothing but a lust for power. They had aligned themselves with Dark Star Beings who planned to take over Earth in order to harvest the planet's rich natural resources. They especially wanted the large reserves of gold for themselves.

"These Dark Star Beings promised many things to their Earthly followers. But regardless of their power, they still needed a very particular Hu-man emissary on Earth to carry forth their plan of world domination. They wanted to find a Hu-man who carried strong genetic encodings of the Lineage of Evil. Finally, they chose an errant Atlantean High Priest who had the intelligence, patience and — ambition — required. He was to continue to live among the people, gain their respect and rise to a position of power. And it was power he was after. He had forgotten how to distinguish between his personal will and the Will of Spirit. But he knew well how to wait — and to watch — for exactly the right moment to exercise the assignment with which he had been charged.

"The right moment arrived when my aunt was awarded the position of Master Crystal Technician. This priest knew of her weakness and her insecurity, and he feigned love for her. He constantly praised her great talent and soon became her confidant and then her lover.

"The priest, operating under the directions of the Dark Star Beings, told her to increase, again and again, the amount of the power she was running through the crystals, and that together they could save the world from the Things. He made her believe that the High Council and the entire priesthood were weak, ineffective and jealous of her gifts.

"In an effort to please her lover and win his approval, she made a fatal mistake. She did exactly what the other High Priests had warned her against. She attempted to force too much power through the Master Crystal in the Great Hall, and the crystal cracked. This was the beginning of the destruction you now see taking place around you.

"When my aunt realized what she had done and how it had shifted the balance of political power, she was in anguish. In her grief and mourning for a sin she felt could never be forgiven, she threw herself into the sea. All of this was kept secret, for the times were growing dark. Even my mother believed she had met with a boating accident. But I know such things. I have never met my aunt, yet I understand and grieve for her. Sometimes I feel as if I am her, resurrected on the day of her death, to right her wrong."

She looked directly up into my eyes again before continuing. "At this very moment, those same crystal technicians, many of whom worked under my aunt but now under the control of the Dark Priests, are powering up all of the crystals in the Great Hall. They have activated and moved into place another Master Crystal, one that is almost as powerful as the one that was cracked by my aunt. Even worse, they have somehow managed to activate the gold and crystal capstone atop the Great Pyramid, and are pulling in vast amounts of energy from the sun.

"Soon the crystal capstone will contain more energy than it has ever held before. They are using energy dangerously – exactly as my aunt did – and it will backfire. This is why I understand it all so well..." she mumbled more to herself than to me.

Then, capturing my eyes in her steady gaze, she continued. "My poor aunt innocently misused the power of the Master Crystal. But this time the crystal technicians, under the tutelage of the Dark Priests, are doing it on purpose – and they have a sinister plan."

"And what is that?"

"The Dark Priests, who now call themselves The New Order, intend to use the crystal technicians to accomplish their long awaited elimination of the Things. On the night of the Dark Moon, when there are no natural defenses and Earth's magnetic field is at its weakest, the technicians will send this vast amount of energy back up through the crystal capstone of the Great Pyramid. They will aim it directly at the Things. And since they do not care if they destroy the Great Pyramid itself, you know what will happen when they do this?" Her eyes bore into mine.

Yes, of course, I knew. It would mean the destruction of Atlantis. I found myself seeing into the mind of this young woman. She was thinking that the destruction of the Things, and concurrently, the destruction of Atlantis, could be prevented. Was that possible? Conceivably what we all had seen was what could happen if nothing were done to stop it. I watched myself thinking this last thought, for already I knew what she was planning. She was planning to save Atlantis — with or without my help.

In a flash, I saw the two of us climbing the Great Pyramid of Atlantis on the Dark Night of the Moon, retrieving the precious gold and crystal capstone and thwarting the plans of the Dark Ones. I knew that she held this vision too, and for one wild moment, it did seem as if the act had already been performed and Atlantis saved! I opened my eyes, still entranced. I was not surprised to find her gone. It was just as well, for I had much to think about. I made no effort to look for her but instead retired to my quarters.

CHAPTER 24

I passed the next day in deep meditation. I was not missed by any of the remaining priests, for Atlantis was a land in suspended animation. What was left of the priesthood had been reduced to waiting and watching. I could not come up with a clear answer to my questions, and there was no one left of those who had been my mentors with whom I could consult.

We priests had assumed that the Great Pyramid — and all of Atlantis — would be destroyed. We had been told that charging the gold and crystal capstone above the Great Pyramid temple required both a male and female initiate. I could not figure out how the Dark Priests were managing to do it by themselves. Nevertheless, my instincts told me this young woman was right. If this was true, I needed to join her. It would be great folly to allow her to do it alone. My head went round and round, filled with questions.

Given my priestly training, I might have considered that when an answer does not come easily and of its own accord, it is probably best to leave things as they are. However, I was not in my usual state of mind. The disorientation of the times was unlike anything I had ever experienced. And, I suspect, it was the strong effect this young woman had upon me. Whatever the reason, unclear as my mind was, I decided we had nothing to lose. In truth, it was our only hope of saving Atlantis.

It was curious that I had chosen to stay behind when so many of the other Atlantean priests had left, yet there had never been any doubt in my mind about that decision. Perhaps, unknowingly, this had been the reason – my destiny. No sooner had I made up my mind than I found her standing quietly outside the door of my chamber. I invited her in without saying a word. She was the first to speak.

"You have decided." It was a statement.

"I have decided," I repeated after her. There was very little to discuss. The Dark Night of the Moon fell on the Winter Solstice, which was only three nights hence. It was most probable that the Dark Ones would attempt their magic at exactly the midnight hour. This would be the time of the lowest magnetic field and therefore, the time of least resistance. We agreed to meet the night before, when the moon was dark enough that it would shield us as we retrieved the capstone but before the priests would gather to do their nefarious deed.

Our plan was to climb the Great Pyramid together and remove the gold and crystal capstone from its top. This was a highly dangerous act for a multitude of reasons. Not only was the state of the capstone so unstable that it could crack of its own accord, but such a cracking of the capstone could create a vibration that would knock us off of the Great Pyramid and we would be killed. Moreover, the cracking of the crystal could provoke the very act we were trying to avoid — the destruction of Atlantis.

However, we knew it was possible that the combination of our priestly energies — the blending of the masculine and feminine lines — could make our effort successful, and we would be able to save Atlantis from demise. I suspected that A-Lan was of the ancient lineage, but at this late hour was that really of concern? She had seemed so certain of her vision. Circumstances being what they were, the choice seemed obvious.

We knew that we must not see each other until the agreed upon night. We needed the time on our own to perform rituals of purification. And most importantly, we needed time to align our energies to one another in order to be able to handle the capstone without it harming us, or we it.

Everything seemed as if it was meant to be. The time of preparation flew by. Once I had made up my mind, I never allowed myself to doubt. Such was my training. If I had, it might have occurred to me that I was crossing a very thin line.

I spent my time in deep meditation and cleansed myself in dedication to the Light. In the moments that were not thus occupied, I found I was caught up in a flurry of daydreams. Clearly, though I do not believe I realized it at the time, I had fallen in love with A-Lan.

We met as we had planned at the base of the Great Pyramid on that shadow-less night just before the Winter Solstice. I was trembling with excitement and anticipation. We embraced quickly and began our ascent. A-Lan felt cool and calm in the darkness beside me. At one point, she motioned for me to be still. She cocked her head as if listening, but I heard no sound. We moved on more cautiously. "He is near, I can hear him," she whispered almost inaudibly.

"Who?"

She waved her hand to silence me, and we continued climbing. I reached the top before her and stopped to catch my breath. As I kneeled, waiting, I was shocked. The place where the capstone should have been was empty! A-Lan reached my side panting and staring intently in front of her. She spoke only one husky word — "Now!"

I followed her lead, having no idea what she was doing. We stretched our arms toward the empty space. Our fingers searched. We did not feel anything but, for a moment, the capstone glowed before our eyes.

It was magnificent, an object of rare beauty. The capstone consisted of a series of interlocking vertical gold and crystal pyramids, diminishing in size as it rose, all perfectly geometrically formed. At its top stood the smallest pyramid of all — and the true capstone of the capstone. It was pure quartz crystal and threw off beams of dancing light encompassing all the colors of the spectrum.

Suddenly, A-Lan was thrown violently backward, as if hit by lightening. A loud screech tore through the night air, followed by mocking laughter.

"Thank you, my Dears, our plan worked! We've been waiting for you! You two have done what we could never have done by ourselves. We needed two descendants of the ancient lineage to perform this task. We may have activated the capstone, but you have ignited it — and now it is ours to use." Their laughter continued to thunder through the night sky.

I saw a glint of light and looked up. The gold and crystal capstone had reappeared. I watched as the first small sparks flew from its point. Then the sparks grew larger and larger, out of control, lighting up the dark night sky.

I scrambled down the side of the Great Pyramid as fast as possible. Miraculously, I was not hurt at all. I called out for A-Lan and followed her whisper of a voice. When I reached her badly burned and broken body, she was close to death. I leaned forward toward her, tears streaming down my face. I saw her lips move, trying to form words. I leaned in yet closer.

"Do not worry, my Love," she implored. "There will be another time when we will come together to complete this work. Do not blame yourself. It was meant to be."

A long shadow cast itself across her torso. "Well! Well! Well! Look what we have here," barked a sardonic voice that pierced the silence of the night. My eyes shot up and I saw a tall figure dressed in the robes of the Dark Priests. I looked more closely and realized it was Carmac, a High Priest who had worked with my father. I thought he had gone to Egypt with one of the relocation parties.

"You look surprised, A-Ta! Did you think I was one of the weak ones like your father?" he spit out. "I know how to seize the moment and take what is mine. The entire Earth will soon belong to the Forces of Darkness. It is better to join what you cannot defeat."

I wasn't surprised — I was astounded. I had always thought Carmac a true priest who followed the One Light. Now, however, it all became clear. This was he whom A-Lan had sensed, the very one who had led her aunt astray! No wonder she knew of this man.

"For one with so much training, you have such little imagination, A-Ta," Carmac hissed, as he bent to look over the shattered body that had been A-Lan. He laughed in glee, his mouth twisted into a horrible smile.

As he reached out his arms to gather her up, a bolt of firelight tore through the night sky. In those moments of intense light, a tattoo was clearly visible on the inside of his left wrist. I recognized it immediately. It was very distinct — a black Celtic cross with an open circle in its center and a black slash of lightning running across it. It was the insignia that marked all of those priests and government officials who had chosen to follow the Forces of Darkness. Before I had time to respond, Carmac's voice rattled again. "This will give you something to think about," he smirked, as he rose and strode off, carrying the lifeless body of A-Lan.

Very soon, the sky became truly menacing and the earth shook. I cowered as I ran for what small protection the stone walls of the Garden Temple might afford. "I am a priest. I should have known better," I berated myself. I had already forgotten A-Lan's last comforting words. I was beside myself with grief.

Within moments, the first episode of what was to be the slow breaking up and sinking of Atlantis occurred. The skies got darker and darker, and the earth revolted against such abuse. There were terrible storms and tidal waves. I was desolate. A-Lan had been killed for nothing — and I was saved. My life had served no purpose. Despite our efforts, we could not prevent the destruction of Atlantis.

CHAPTER 25

Although it took a great number of years for the sinking of Atlantis to be completed, it was only a matter of months before a noticeable amount of destruction began to take place. In that short time, I came to understand that Atlantis had been doomed even before A-Lan and I had met.

And so the time passed, and as it did I began to age very rapidly, for the Dark Energies were destructive of all Life. I listened to the great rumblings as chunks of our beautiful Island sank beneath the sea.

I withdrew into the bowels of the Ancient Garden Temple. One dark, horrible day, I heard a single huge and terrifying sound. I am sure it was the very moment that the Great Pyramid itself finally crashed to the ground. However simultaneously, a strange and astonishing thing occurred. The actual gold and crystal capstone materialized on the marble alter in front of me. I was so shocked that at first I could only sit and stare at it. Slowly, very slowly, the thought began to enter my mind – perhaps that night with A-Lan had somehow magnetized the capstone to my vibration.

My whole body clicked into gear. A feeling of vigor returned. With dawning clarity, I began to see that our task that night had not been to save Atlantis. It had served an-other purpose – to save the capstone!

A-Lan had given her life and now the capstone was in my hands. I remembered her last words, "It was meant to be." How could I have been so foolish? There was much to ponder about A-Lan and I, but this was not the time. The important thing now was to get the capstone out of Atlantis and deliver it to Egypt, the new Motherland. The question was, how?

The skill of bi-location, learned so long ago from the Galactic Visitors, was useless in this time of tempest. Travel by sea was impossible and much too slow. I needed to move quickly, lest my priceless possession be discovered. There was only one way, but it was risky. I could try to use the Lighter-Than-Air-Ship that had been left behind for just such an emergency.

I made my way to the hidden spot where the air-ship had been secretly stowed. A quick examination revealed that one of the many pumps that maintained the anti-matter in balance was punctured. The pumps, combined with the electromagnetic field coil, were the mechanisms that allowed the ship to de-materialize in one location and instantly re-materialize in another. However, with even the smallest leak, the ship — as well as I and the capstone — could all be blown into oblivion.

Panic overtook me. But almost immediately I realized that the only way to plug the leak was with my mind. I had to hold the visualization so strongly that in fact, it would be fixed. This would have been an easy task at an earlier time — but not now. I felt old and worn. My mind had been all but shattered by the events with A-Lan and the years of turmoil surrounding Atlantis.

However, there was no other option. I had to do it! I steadied my mind in all the ways I had been taught, but still it began to wander. I brought my focus back to the task at hand. My mind wandered again. My awareness that the clock was ticking only made me more anxious. Thoughts of A-Lan filled my mind, followed by a flood of remorse. Then I remembered the capstone. This was my mission — what I had been saved to do. I focused my mind again and finally, it held. The puncture sealed and the pump returned to normal function. I entered the air-ship and was instantaneously transported to Egypt.

My father and the other High Priests who had fled Atlantis to establish the new Motherland were waiting for me. I placed the capstone into their safe hands. They stowed it in one of the deep underground vaults, hidden by heavy insulation from the prying eyes of any Dark Ones who might seek it out. There it would remain until a new enlightened civilization emerged.

After delivering the capstone, my work as a priest brought me back to what little was left of Atlantis. Fear and panic ran rabid. I did what I could to help those in need. The people who had followed the Dark Ones were not inherently bad — they were simply weak and allowed themselves to be misled. As they realized the folly of their ways, they were overcome by grief and shame. One thing was certain — the heinous plans of the Dark Ones had backfired. Instead of controlling Atlantis, they had destroyed it.

A-Lan — my Love — was never far from my thoughts. I wondered if she had known the outcome all along. I still did not understand why her life was taken, unless it had to do with what she had told me about her aunt. There were so many unanswered questions. However, amidst all of the death and destruction, I took solace in the knowledge that what she and I had done together allowed me to save the capstone for future generations. And so it was that I lived – and died – in the body of Prince A-Ta.

It was strange to witness my own death. It happened exactly as I, David, had seen in my dream in the Arab village. My spirit had departed my body just as Atlantis broke apart and a major portion of the island-continent was ravished by the sea.

CHAPTER 26

Sometime later – who knows how long....

It was overwhelming. I had gazed into the crystal and witnessed my former life – and death – as the Atlantean Prince-Priest A-Ta. I witnessed the glorious past of Atlantis. I felt spent and it took some time be-fore I was willing once again to continue my journey of remembrance. Finally the memories returned and....

I, along with the Twelve Beings, was still in that hidden room within the Great Pyramid of Egypt. The crystal had grown clear for a few minutes, giving my eyes a rest.

The Beings did not say a word. It was as if they were deep in meditation. Then once again images began to appear within the crystal. They moved forward in time, and I observed the more recent past, events that took place after my death.

The scene shifted from Atlantis to the new Motherland, Egypt. My father was now dead and a new civilization was being born. I focused in on the last surviving Atlantean priest whose name was Ha-Tor. He was one of the Great Brotherhood of Light and a friend to the Galactic Visitors who followed the Light. In many ways he strongly resembled those in the room around me. This led me to believe that their blood also ran through his veins. Later he would be remembered in myth and legend as Thoth-Hermes, the Master Builder.

The Great Pyramid of Egypt was being built, and I saw Ha-Tor, who had drawn the initial plans, supervise its construction. He used Atlantean technology to precisely cut large blocks of stone according to his exact specifications. He then transformed the massive stones to a weightless state, moved them many miles, and positioned them so exactly that they have endured without mortar for centuries. The entire process took only a few months.

The largest of Egypt's new pyramids was an exact copy of our own Great Pyramid in Atlantis. When this pyramid was completed, I saw Ha-Tor remove the gold and crystal capstone from its hidden vault and set it in place on the flat surface atop Egypt's most famous Great Pyramid. To the uninitiated eye, it looked as if there was no capstone – but I knew better. Although it was now invisible, it was the same capstone that had materialized before me on the marble altar on Atlantis – the capstone I had transported to Egypt.

I was shaken when I realized the vital part I had played in the drama that was now unfolding within the crystal. However, I had been an Atlantean priest and, as such, was relieved to know that not everything had been lost after all.

It was clear that the Great Pyramid in Egypt, like ours in Atlantis, was built to serve many purposes. The temple secretly incorporated our advanced knowledge into its very structure. Its dimensions were built to contain key mathematical relationships between Earth and the Cosmos.

The internal structure of the passageways and rooms delineated the spiritual development of Mankind, from his earliest appearance on Planet Earth to a time in the future when Man would again reconnect with his full knowledge of the One Light.

Just like our Great Pyramid in Atlantis, the primary function of the Great Pyramid in Egypt was to be a Temple of Initiation. This was where Ha-tor prepared young men and women for initiation into the priesthood through teachings in meditation and concentration. Two of the most important lessons were the ability to remain centered regardless of outward circumstances, and the ability to differentiate between the personal ego and that of the Higher Self.

A select few of this group were given the opportunity to continue the initiation process which, if they succeeded, would allow them enter the highest levels of the priesthood. Those who chose to continue had to transverse the many passageways of the pyramid, learning as they went, until they arrived at the King's Chamber. The chamber was empty except for the great stone sarcophagus.

The final step of Initiation always began in the pre-dawn hours. When a candidate was ready, he or she would lie in the sarcophagus, head facing north. Then the initiate would intone the ancient, sacred and secret sound. This sound — older than time itself — was originally brought to Planet Earth by a very special group of Star Beings. The intoning of the sound caused the initiate, the sarcophagus, as well as the entire King's Chamber to vibrate in harmony at exactly the same number of cycles per second as Earth itself, creating a Harmonic Convergence.

With this Harmonic Convergence in place, a window in the fabric of space-time was created. The gold and crystal capstone would materialize for an instant, and the celestial energies would be channeled through it. That caused the initiate's individual spirit to leave his body and travel through the highest realms of Spirit. The initiate was then confronted by his greatest fears. He had to rise above the level of personality and experience himself as a multidimensional Being. This was a supreme test of trust, faith and ultimately, of Love.

The process was so intense that the majority of candidates were unable to complete it. The challenge involved was so great that the effort expended would destroy the candidate's nervous systems and cause death. However, those few who did survive, returned with Universal Knowledge. They earned the title of "Master" and became Initiates into the Mysteries and members of the Great Brotherhood of Light. And so the ancient Lineage of Light, a lineage that existed even before the time of Atlantis, was maintained and the Brotherhood grew.

I closed my eyes, remembering when I, too, as the Atlantean Prince-Priest A-Ta, had gone through my initiation. When I looked again, the scene had shifted. I was shown the Egyptian Hall of Records, a special room buried beneath the Great Pyramid. I had been in this large room before.

When I was sixteen, Zev Moab had brought me to Egypt, specifically, to the right paw of the Sphinx. That is where I met the young woman who tried to seduce me. Then I passed out and woke up in a secret room inside the Sphinx. Standing in front of me then was Ha-Hotep, who I had known as Rashid, the mysterious Arab camel driver who had found me unconscious in the desert.

Ha-Hotep had led me along underground passageways lined with sheets of gold upon which long texts of hieroglyphics were engraved. Then he took me through the inverted pyramid known as the Hall of Records. Eventually, we reached the hidden room inside the Great Pyramid where I now sit.

The records I had then seen inscribed on the golden walls were sacred — and priceless. I now recognized them as Atlantean originals on metallurgy, art, law and history.

The script covering the walls was partly early Egyptian hieroglyphics and partly Atlantean. One day this script will act as a Rosetta Stone for deciphering unknown symbols of Atlantean origin around the world.

Light faded from the crystal until it grew completely black. Before long, hot sparks erupted from the darkness, and from time to time I could see massive destruction. I could make out huge waves, great fires and earthquakes. This was the final destruction of Atlantis – the end of an era. It culminated in a change in Earth's axis of rotation and a shift of the North and South Poles, changing the face of the earth dramatically.

The crystal cleared slightly. I saw that although the great system of terrestrial engineering appeared all but destroyed, many structures and giant stone formations still survived.

I watched as time passed and saw that much later, those same ancient stone sites were repeatedly rebuilt by new emerging religious cults whose shamans sensed the potent energies of those special places.

Millennia later, especially in Europe, patches of land, sacred by their very location along the Earth's Crystal Grid, were rebuilt in the form of churches and cathedrals. In many places, like that of Chartres Cathedral in France, memory of the original purpose of these spots became lost in the mists of time, yet their magical attributes endured.

When the crystal cleared completely, my eyes were once again drawn way back in time. The final sinking of Atlantis had caused great changes on the planet, and

now a very different Earth came into view. Not only did I
see the formation of the great polar ice caps, but the
creation of the Sahara and Libyan Deserts as well.
Egypt had been ravished. All save the head of the
Sphinx was buried under great quantities of sand.

Although much of the three Great Pyramids were also
encased in sand, they were structurally intact. They
had been built with the foreknowledge of all that was to
come. Only the limestone casings of the huge stone blocks
used to build the pyramids showed evidence of what had
taken place. Their exteriors were covered with water-
marks and the interiors contained salt deposits. Both
were a testament to the fact that this once grassy-
plain had been engorged by the sea. Now, only desert
remained. I knew that the precious capstone, though
undetectable, was perfectly intact.

What little civilization survived in Egypt fell to the level
of hunters and nomads. Quietly, the Galactic Visitors
returned. Fortunately, many of the Brotherhood, now
known as the Great Brotherhood of Light, lived on. The
Galactic Visitors and the Brotherhood worked together,
their hearts and minds united by their understanding of
the One Light. Using the ancient wisdom and technology,
they endeavored to raise these people back to the level
of civilization.

Now time moved swiftly within the crystal, and I saw the
beginning of the Egyptian dynasties, about 3200 B.C.
The sudden cultural explosion that is associated with
ancient Egypt was, in large measure, due to the assistance of the Brotherhood and the Galactic Visitors.

Finally, the Galactic Visitors chose to withdraw from the planes of Earth — to wait — and to watch. They remained just out of sight, but always available to those who knew how to call upon them.

The Brotherhood, however, continued to intercede in the affairs of men through the end of the Fourth Dynasty. After that, they no longer felt their work could be done openly, and they withdrew into secrecy. From time to time members would resurface, and legend continued to tell of a Secret Brotherhood, now in one location, now in another. In fact, the Brotherhood has continued to exist, in secret, on the physical planes to this day. Bits and pieces of the ancient knowledge survived within the Western Mystery Tradition — a path of mystical knowledge and spiritual development that parallels that of yoga.

Gazing into the crystal, I saw that many of the most powerful Druids in the British Isles, alchemists of the Middle Ages and the Knights Templar were all members of the Great Brotherhood of Light. The Brotherhood was also well entrenched in the legacies of India, China and Tibet, as well as that of The Essenes — the splinter group of Jews from whom Jesus arose and who wrote the Dead Sea Scrolls. Signs of the Brotherhood appear as well in the legacy of the Gnostic Christian sects.

Then the crystal grew clear, and Zev Moab leaned toward me and said, "David, it is time for the next phase of your education to begin in earnest. And we..." he said softly, indicating the rest of the Great Beings with a sweep of his hand, "we are proud to be your teachers."

CHAPTER 27

Growth does not happen in a day, a week or a year. Following that last vision in the crystal, the Great Beings took me with them to visit other worlds, other dimensions and other states of being. It felt like all of this had occurred in the span of a few days however, when we returned, I was shocked to discover that almost five years of Earth time had passed.

Once again, I sat before the horseshoe of the Twelve Beings in the secret room within the Great Pyramid. This time I was allowed to review, within the giant crystal, my recent past in this life as David. I saw that after four years of studying, experiencing and remembering with Zev Moab, I was brought once again to that hidden room in the Great Pyramid, the one that is now sealed but lies in the very center between the King's and Queen's chambers.

I watched as the pictures within the crystal quietly faded. But a moment before it became completely clear, I was taken one more time on a visual journey down those ancient and familiar corridors, beneath the shifting sands of the Sahara. I saw the arched en-tranceway to the great underground pyramid, The Hall of Records. A green-gold luminescence lit a golden plaque just above the arch. I had not noticed it before.

Its image now filled the crystal, and I saw the words:

DAVID
Light of The New Era
Who has been accordingly prepared
That he may bring forth
The Ancient Wisdom
From Darkness into Light

There was a sudden flash of white light and instinctively, I closed my eyes. When I opened them, I was startled to find myself sitting on a grassy mountaintop. It was broad daylight, and I was surrounded by the Twelve Beings. Everything was very quiet. I looked around and slowly realized that this was the same mountaintop I had seen in the dream on my sixteenth birthday. I remembered it all so vividly – the starlit night, the circle of Beings and the pipe that had been passed from one to another. Zev Moab had offered me the pipe, saying that one, all-important word, "Choose" – and I had chosen.

"So David, now you know."

I turned toward the voice and our eyes met. It was Zev Moab. "Yes, David. That night, when you made your all-important choice, your Higher Self acknowledged and accepted your birth-path. Had you not made the choice you did, you would have remained in your parents' little house in Tiberias. Past, present and future history would have been rewritten. Even I could not have opened these dimensions to you without your conscious knowledge and consent."

"But Zev, do you mean that all of this...?"

"Once again, the answer is yes. It was all to prepare you. You are one of those for whom these ancient chambers wait. There will be only three of you in this time. Together you will open the Great Halls connecting Past to Future, retrieve the ancient energetic keys, and reactivate the Earth-Power System."

A feeling of panic engulfed me. "But I'm not...I haven't even...."

"Now David, stay calm. You are right. This task requires an Initiate. But you are a man of twenty and one, wise beyond your years and well trained. You are truly ready for your Final Initiation.

"However, the times have changed. It is no longer appropriate for a candidate to go through the process of Initiation in the protected environment of the Great Pyramid. Now, the equivalent of these same challenges must be met as a part of one's lifework in the everyday world. Your self-chosen assignment is your Final Initiation. In fact, it is your gift to the world."

One of the other Star Beings leaned toward me. "David," he said, concern and kindness apparent on his voice, "your assignment is of the utmost importance. What we are about to tell you is not meant to frighten you. It is merely an accounting of conditions as they exist at the present time."

Now another of the Beings spoke up. "The outlook for Planet Earth is very precarious. The energies of a New Era are at hand and beginning to make their way into your solar system. This is a period of rapid change for your race, your world and your entire universe. In fact, a dimensional shift is underway and the pace will continue to accelerate exponentially. What should have been a time of natural growth and flowering for your planet and its peoples is now a time fraught with danger. The reason is simple. The planet itself is in a weakened condition, and the powerful energies of this shift cannot manifest safely onto a weakened planet."

"What we are trying to say David," exclaimed still another Being, " is that Earth is now in crisis. You see, since the very beginnings of Planet Earth, long before Hu-mankind's arrival, there have been periodic cycles of change. During those natural evolutionary movements, Earth experienced a lowering of its protective magnetic field. This lowering of the magnetic field was normal and purposeful, and in the past enabled new energetic patterns to permeate Earth. In this way, the energy grid and all Life upon Earth were periodically replenished.

"A number of factors have combined to create this altered and unsafe state of affairs Earth now faces. The main one is quite simply due to Hu-man behavior – or I should say – misbehavior. You have witnessed in the crystal and seen with your own eyes, the way in which Hu-mans have disconnected from Spirit and blindly followed the Forces of Darkness. As a consequence, they have forgotten their interconnection with all Life — especially that of the planet itself. Their acts of planetary abuse, along with their deadly thought-forms, have caused Earth's energetic grid to become dangerously blocked.

"Another contribution to Earth's dire situation is the diminished power of the Native Shamans. Traditionally, they were the caretakers of Earth's energetic grid system — the ones who kept the lines of energy open.

"Remember, you saw in the crystal how we Galactic Visitors, with the help of the Lemurians and your own Atlantean priests, long ago mapped Earth's energetic grid. We understood that the places where two lines of energy crossed were the planet's energy centers and act as its acupuncture points. Thus we marked — mostly in stone — the exact location of the main centers.

"The shamans of the original native peoples all around the world understood how to use these power centers, as well as the individual lines of energy, to preserve the balance of Earth. Through prayer and ceremony, they made periodic adjustments that kept the energy within the grid flowing freely and harmoniously. This, in turn, automatically maintained Earth's protective magnetic field at a safe level.

"However, for some time now, the indigenous native peoples have made up a very small percentage of your planet's population. And unfortunately, their numbers are no longer large enough to compensate for the rest of Mankind's limited perspective.

"The result is that Earth's energetic grid system – the very Life Force of the planet – has become dangerously clogged and the protective magnetic field has fallen lower than it has ever been."

Zev Moab spoke up once more. "David, we know that the energies of this New Era are already flowing into your solar system. But as you can well understand, the power of this new energy is causing many shifts within and amongst its planetary bodies. This movement is creating a terrific pull on your planet. And with its present rate of deterioration, Earth's protective magnetic field may soon be completely dissolved, leaving Earth defenseless. If that were to happen, Earth would have no way of handling the force of such powerful incoming energy.

"Of course, the energies would enter nonetheless – but in a cataclysmic way. There could be a slight tilt of Earth on its axis and a shifting of the magnetic poles, ushering in a new Ice Age – much like what happened after the final destruction of Atlantis. The planet would survive, but the jolt to its surface could devastate much of life upon it. Tidal waves and earthquakes are possible. Entire landmasses might be swallowed up by the oceans as new continents are being born. What would have ordinarily been a natural evolutionary movement could become a disaster and Life on Earth – as you know it – would be over."

"Is...is there nothing that can be done?"

"There is one way, and one way only, to safely facilitate the shift of which we have spoken. The vibrational frequency of Earth must first be carefully raised. This in turn will elevate your planet's magnetic field so that the energy can safely enter into Earth."

"How can we make sure that takes place?"

"It will happen automatically as Hu-mans remember who they are and choose to take responsibility for their world. When they see themselves and their planet from the eye of their hearts, stress will be taken off the magnetic field, allowing it to rise to a level where the energetic grid can be safely worked with. Once the grid is cleared, the Earth-Power System will reactivate on its own, the magnetic field will fully restore itself – and the extreme cataclysm of a polar shift will have been avoided."

"Zev, I'm afraid to ask! Who is it that is going to clear the energetic grid...?"

"Well my young friend, that's where you come in. You have been brought to a place of development where you may work with Earth's energies without being damaged. However, there is, as you say in your time, only one 'catch.' Even though Earth's energy grid must be unclogged in order to maintain the magnetic field, the field is currently so weak that merely circulating enough energy through it to do the job could trigger the shift itself.

"But I don't understand. If that's the case, how am I

supposed to clear the grid without destroying the planet and...?

Zev Moab gently raised his hand, and I instantly fell silent. "David, you are forgetting the fullness of all you have learned. You saw in the crystal how Earth and its people glowed with health and vitality in earlier times, and you understand the condition they are in now. You have witnessed it happening and the difference is dramatic.

"When Hu-mans lived the interconnection of all Life, the understanding that everything was part of the One, they knew that the Source of Creation was alive in them. Therefore, they naturally lived in a state of what I can only call Love. What came out of this feeling of connection were acts that benefited all. People worked only for the common good. They would never do anything to harm one another or Earth. They understood — at a feeling level — that by harming another they were harming themselves.

"David, it is impossible to underestimate the importance of this interconnection. For you see, this interconnection — Love — has a particular frequency. It is this very frequency of caring that Earth, as a living being, needs to feel in order to raise its vibrational level and, in turn, its magnetic field.

"So my boy, let me give you your assignment. First and foremost, you have to believe, with every fiber of your being, that Earth and its peoples can be healed. You must hold this thought every waking hour and even in your dreams. You need to visualize the peoples of Earth remembering who they are – remembering their deep interconnection with all Life and remembering they can make the Choice for Love.

"But having the ability 'to Choose' does not mean anything if a person does not know he has it. Therefore, the next part of your assignment is to spread this awareness across the planet. For many Hu-mans, this will seem like a new idea, but the understanding is in the cells of their bodies.

"You have learned well. Now it is important for you to recognize that you are a great teacher – that you have the ability to affect many lives. Occasionally, you will encounter people who have so internalized your message that they, themselves, will carry it forward. In this way you multiply yourself. You will know the ones who can hear your words. Thus, you will be instrumental in the easy grounding of this New Era.

"The planet will then be ready for the final part of your assignment – to enter the ancient vaults and retrieve, not only information from your cherished ancestral culture, but also the energetic keys to reactivate the Planetary Grid System. You will recognize when the time is right."

"It sounds like an overwhelming task...."

"For someone who is unprepared, it would be overwhelming. However, your lineage as well as your training over many lifetimes has provided you with the capacity — and the obligation — to accomplish these goals."

I must have looked confused and frightened. My head was spinning and I closed my eyes. I thought about everything Zev Moab and the others had said. I thought about all that I still had to do.

Zev Moab's voice continued, softer and gentler than ever before. "David, we understand your concerns, but the world is better prepared for this change than you think. Daily, more and more people question their way of life and ponder their connection with Spirit. They visualize and meditate on the idea of a more perfect world, and they understand that small actions they take — on a daily basis — can make this happen.

"A great majority of young adults across the planet are old souls and already in tune with these frequencies. Like you, they were here in the last days of Atlantis. In a deep part of themselves, they remember the destruction and do not want it to happen again. They will become your students, the channels through which this New Era will be anchored both onto and into Earth.

"Do not think you have to do this on your own. We and many other Star Beings are in direct telepathic communication with everyone and everything on your planet and will be here to guide the peoples of Earth.

"However, as with all things, it is a question of choice, and only those Hu-mans who so desire will be able to hear us.

They will be the ones who see that they are not alone in the universe and will therefore be willing – eager – to change their current belief systems.

"My boy, you must stay in the moment and trust. Follow your inner guidance, put one foot in front of the other, and those you need to find will find you. There are others you will never meet. However, merely imagining that someone like you exists will inspire them to do great works. And there will be a special one – but that is for later."

Zev Moab's voice trailed off. My conscious mind was unable to absorb another word. I stopped all thought and surrendered to the deep dark waves of exhaustion that flowed over me, carrying me out over a sea of soothing dreams. I felt warm and cared for and loved in a way I had never known. I dreamed I was in a great desert with wild flowering cactus. I was walking beside Zev Moab – much as I had in my boyhood days.

That sight brought tears to my eyes. I realized all of my great gifts, my ability to travel in time and space, my ability to focus my thoughts, my ability to work with energy – the list could go on and on. These were not only gifts I had earned, but also ones I had been given. And then, as in my childhood, Zev Moab put his arms out to me and said, "It is once again a time for leave taking."

CHAPTER 28

I have now come full circle. Sometime after that last visit with Zev Moab and the other Star Beings, I woke up in the Arab village with no memory of my past — the event that opened this diary. I have no accounting of the actual time I had wandered — and lived — in the desert before they found me, but I know it was years. However, I now understand that amnesia was my choice. I needed time to rest — time for all I had learned and experienced to integrate within my psyche.

There is something else I understand. I could have stayed within the warm folds of amnesia and led a simple life along with Rashid and the others in the little village. But Zev Moab taught me well. I recognize now what all of this means — and what I must do. And once more, I am aware that time is of the essence. On the deepest level of my being, it was my decision to keep this diary, my vehicle of remembrance. I pushed through the Darkness and chose to embrace my destiny.

However, it has become clear to me that, regardless of my experience, I am still vulnerable. Even now, if I were to allow myself one second of true doubt, I could be stripped of all my powers. I would become defenseless against the Forces of Darkness that seem always to lie in wait for me. There are no easy tricks here. Constant vigilance is the price of my freedom. It is all or nothing.

To be continued....

* * * * * * * * * * *

POSTSCRIPT

I am Rashid, the camel driver, the one who put the diary into the camera case. I am also known as Ha-Hotep, and it was I who came to David at the Sphinx and brought him to the secret chamber within the Great Pyramid. There he was mentored, for five years, by the Twelve Star Beings.

The amount of information he received was indeed overwhelming, and the Star Beings were well aware that he needed time to process it all. Amnesia - and the writing of his diary as an aid in the long slow process of remembering - allowed him that time.

Once David was ready, he began to walk amongst Mankind to help them prepare for the coming of the New Era. But just before he began his mission, he entrusted me with his for-now completed diary. I have added an entry - a conversation that occurred immediately after David's tutelage had ended, and he was dismissed by the Twelve Star Beings.

"So, you didn't tell him?"

"No," Zev Moab said. "The boy has enough on his mind without knowing all the details."

"But don't you think he should know that the Dark Forces will never allow the New Era to enter? They thrive on chaos, confusion and fear. That's how they control people."

"The boy is smart. He'll figure out what is going on – and what he has to do."

I flipped through the rest of the diary. Empty – all empty! Is this how it ends? I felt I was hanging in mid-air. It can't just end like this…there's still so much I want to know! And I still had no idea what it was all about – both the diary and my having it.

Thoughts of Rashid, David, the camel named California, all of the images and dreams, and most unsettling, the memory of my mother's childhood warning, raced through my mind like runaway trains. I glanced down and lightly rubbed my fingers over the worn, leather bound book. *So… what am I supposed to do with you now?* But I already had the answer. There was nobody to leave the diary with. It would only get thrown out – and there was no way I was about to let that happen! *I'll have to take you home with me.*

My mind shuffled between the past and the present, then back to the diary resting in my hands. It was unbelievable! *If I hadn't made that crazy move from San Francisco to Los Angeles, I would have been busy working as a fashion photographer and would never, never have considered going on this trip. But then, I wouldn't have seen the face of the man with the curly black hair and piercing blue eyes in the travel agency...and I would never have found this diary. And if I hadn't been so sick, I would not have had time to read it.* I knew all of that had to mean something.

I stared at the diary for an interminable amount of time. I was awestruck, fascinated, confused and overwhelmed all at once. Unable to sort out my jumble of emotions, I quickly shoved the diary into my suitcase. *That's it! I don't want to look at it, and I can't possibly give it one more thought.*

The following day the group returned from the Isle of Patmos. I was feeling somewhat better and welcomed the company and diversion they provided. We spent two days visiting some of the sites in and around Athens, including Delphi. On the third day, we boarded a flight bound for Rome, then New York, and finally back to California. As the plane lifted off the ground in Athens, I felt a sense of great relief. I was going home. I could let go of this madness, heal my body, and be "normal" again.

Part Two

CHAPTER 29

It had only been three weeks, but those three weeks changed my entire life. The Cassandra who returned from Egypt was a very, very different person. Before I left, I knew exactly who I was and what I wanted in life – success as a fashion photographer. I was a smart pragmatic woman, a talented, tenacious photographer – and I was going to succeed if it killed me!

I came back a good deal less certain. In fact, I came back full of questions – pounding questions – questions about things that had never before even entered my mind. Pretty much every one of my values and truths had been challenged or was being held hostage in some sort of suspended animation. Yes, I had visited amazing places, but more confusing was the fact that I had also been to places not marked on any map. I realized I had somehow stepped into another world, but I could not decide if I were more enlightened than I had been before, or whether I had truly lost my way – gone over some dangerous precipice from which I might never return.

It took a little while, but once I had rested and gotten my strength back, my mind slowly began to sort itself out – or so I thought. At some point it occurred to me that if what was written in the diary were actually true, David might need it. There might be something in it that was vital to his being able to save the world – or whatever it was he was supposed to do. After all, he had written the diary in order "to remember." Maybe he wouldn't have total recall without it.

I heard my own words and my mind flipped. *What makes me think that any of this is even true?* I picked up the diary from my nightstand and looked at it for the umpteenth time that morning. *I don't know! I just don't know....*

But, if what you say is true…holding you is like holding a piece of David's brain.

Try as I might, I could not get over the thought that David might really need the diary. Clearly there was nothing else to do – I had to find him! I had to return the diary, ask him if it was true, and why – why in the world it was given to me? It was crucial to my mental health to make sense of everything I had been through. Accomplishing that mission, however, brought up two big questions.

The first was, *How would I find him?* The second was, *What would I do for money?* The first question boggled my mind and led me nowhere, so I put my logic to work on the second one – at least in the daytime. I kept the telephone busy searching for work, but no matter how much effort I put out, I kept coming up short. I heard variations on, "We don't have anything right now." "Call back next week." And the infuriating, "Sorry!" It was exactly as it had been before I left for Egypt.

My nights were equally frenetic and frustrating. I found myself tossing and turning in my sleep, searching for some idea, some way to find David. When sleep evaded me I sat up in bed in the middle of the night thinking – worrying. Whatever I did, I just could not formulate a game plan – and this was definitely not my style. I'd always had a game plan. Or more accurately, I always used to have one until I moved to this stupid city.

After a few days and nights of this routine, I began to feel brain-dead. I was focusing all of my mental power on figuring out how or where I could create some income. At the same time, I was contemplating searching for a man who I didn't know and wasn't sure really existed, who was wandering in the desert somewhere, thinking he could save the world from the Forces of Darkness. *Crazy! Thinking this way is enough to have me locked up. And, if I don't figure out where to find my next job, I'll be the one wandering homeless… somewhere.* I walked over to the window and peeked out. Everything looked normal. *It's me! I've become certifiable!*

One night, as I sat alone in the small, West Hollywood apartment pondering the incredible changes in my life, I discovered something truly shocking – I had absolutely no interest in my former career. I realized that I would be quite content if I never again had to shoot another model or item of clothing. A month ago, a thought like that would have completely freaked me out. Now it brought a sense of relief, as if I had been released from some sort of bond.

I had taken over the dining room table, slides from Egypt fighting for space with stacks of bills. *How am I supposed to get the slides ready for Gabriel with these bills staring me in the face?* The ringing phone jarred me from my numbed concentration. I was surprised to discover it was Rebecca, a pretty, dark-haired woman from Northern California who I had met on the trip. I didn't know her well, but I had been impressed by the quality of questions she always asked Gabriel. It was clear she had a deep interest in the ancient sites.

She was calling to tell me about a group she was organizing to tour sacred sites in Peru and Bolivia. It would leave in about a month and she offered to cover all expenses in exchange for my photographic services. She couldn't pay me any additional money, so I was about to say no when she casually dropped in the line, "Our group will be meeting up with another group for most of the trip. I haven't met the other tour leader, but I've heard a lot about him. He's Israeli and only in his mid-thirties, but has been traveling the world for over ten years giving spiritual talks. His name is David, and he's an expert about all of the ancient stone sites. And Cassie, I saw his picture on the flier. He has the most gorgeous blue eyes!"

I felt like a heat bomb had hit me. My head pounded and my throat went dry. I tried to speak but my mouth would not work.

"Cassie, are you alright…it sounds like something just fell?"

"Yes, I'm…I'm fine," I answered, picking up the phone from the floor. It, along with my jaw, was what had just dropped. "Great! It's great! I…I would love to do it!"

"Wonderful! That's what I hoped you'd say. I saw how persistent you were in Egypt. Even when you were so sick you were practically dropping dead, you kept on shooting. I couldn't have done it, that's for sure. I would have just crawled into a bed somewhere and told everyone to go on without me." Then, in an apologetic voice she added, "How are you…I'm sorry, I should have asked sooner. I've just been on such a high since the possibility of the Peru trip opened up, I've become somewhat of an imbecile."

"I'm fine, but now that you've invited me on this trip, I'm fantastic."

She told me she was still tying up the details but promised to get back to me with specifics in a few days.

"Yes," I shouted, as I hung up the phone and pranced around the room. "Oh my god, yes!" I didn't know if I had clicked off before I yelled, but I didn't care. *A young Israeli guy named David who's been traveling the world for years giving spiritual talks and has the most gorgeous blue eyes.* "David! It's my David! I'm sure of it!" *Now I can give him back his diary, get my questions answered and move on with my life. What a relief!*

Bang! Bang! The neighbors in the apartment below expressed their displeasure at my good fortune by banging on the ceiling. They did this whenever they thought Gail or I were making too much noise. The problem was they were always home and it seemed that, no matter how hard we tried, we were always making "too much noise." They were two really big guys and, though I would never have admitted it, I had always been a bit intimidated by them. But today I put a heavy boot on and pounded back. I was in heaven!

It was a very short stop in heaven – reality struck swiftly. I had just committed to an I-don't-even-know-how-long-of-a-trip with no money coming in. But I knew I couldn't let anything stop me – I had to go. *I absolutely have to get to the bottom of this whole David business.*

An even more amazing thing soon happened. A model I had worked with on a photo shoot called. "Hi, Cassie, this is Kayla. We did some test shots together at that old mansion in the Hollywood hills. I'm the blond with the awful boyfriend."

"Of course, I remember you...and him. How are you?"

"Good...and by the way, Roger and I broke up. But there's something I wanted to ask you."

"Sure, what's up?"

"Well, remember the black and white shots we did outside by the pool with that cool loungewear?"

"Yes." *How could I forget!* We had spent most of the day waiting for the light to be just right, and her boyfriend was looking at his watch the entire time. "Glad to hear you've broken up with Roger. What can I do for you?"

"Do you still have the negatives?"

"I certainly do."

"Great! I was wondering…have you ever seen the hand painting they do on black and white photographs? It's kind of like a cross between a black and white photo and a colored one…but kind of dreamy."

"Yes, I know exactly what you're talking about. I love the look of them." I had wanted to try the technique for years, but I'd always been too busy pushing my career forward.

"Well," Kayla continued, "My mom's birthday is coming up and I love those shots. I thought it would be cool to blow one up really big, have it hand-painted and give it to her for her birthday. Can you do that kind of stuff?"

I hesitated – for about a heartbeat. "Absolutely, of course I can do it."

"Sweet!" said Kayla. "I'll call you back once I decide which one I want to do. What do you think you would charge?"

I was clueless. "You decide which one, then we'll talk about size and I'll give you some numbers."

"Great! I'll get back to you." *What did I just get myself into?* I would have to make some fast tracks on this one, but money was money. Besides, I could call in some favors from my artist friends to get me started. They certainly had no problem asking me for photographs.

Kayla called back later in the day. When I gave her a price, she decided to order two prints. *Damn, I probably undercharged her!*

But then she asked if I could shoot some headshots for her new boyfriend, Chase. "He's an actor," she said, with extra emphasis on the word "actor."

"Of course I can." *Great!* She put him on the phone and we settled on a price and time.

We hung up and I sat still, letting everything sink in. *What's happening to me?* This was very weird. My life had never worked so easily. It was such a strange sensation. I knew I should be thrilled, but someplace deep inside of me I sensed a knot of fear – almost a premonition. I pushed it aside and forced myself to go to the art store and buy photographic paints and dyes. I stopped by a friend's studio for a few tips – then I was on my own.

Starting with a couple of old black and white fashion reject photos, I experimented, adding a touch of color here and there, getting used to the brushes as well as the dyes and paints. To my surprise and delight the whole process seemed to come very naturally. Somewhere along the way, I got a call from Rebecca giving me the date we would leave for Peru. *Three weeks. It's going to be pretty tight!* But I forced myself to relax and focus on developing my technique.

I did the first painting with small brushes using liquid photographic dyes. The second photograph was larger, and I ended up putting oil paint into a gel medium. Then using bits of cotton baton, I worked the color into the paper. To get into the smaller areas of the oil painted photographs, I would roll the small pieces of cotton onto a toothpick. I combined colors in non-logical ways and the results were stunning.

I could not believe how much I loved the painting and how easily it came. I seemed to move into an altered state, a kind of creative frenzy, and the painting would just come through me. Occasionally I looked up from my work, shocked to discover hours had passed. The painting brought a whole new life, a new dimension to my photographs. I was in ecstasy, much like the period of time when I had first discovered my passion for photography. I ate, slept and dreamt the hand-painting – but I never forgot that I was about to meet David.

As my confidence built, I started work on the first blow-up print for Kayla. It came out great, and I was excited to begin the second print, which turned out even better. It was totally bizarre. In a matter of just over a week, I had become a master at something I had never even tried before. And I was making money at it! I also made money shooting the head shots of Kayla's boyfriend. He was so pleased, I ended up photographing two of his friends, as well.

Time seemed to warp itself to accommodate me, and amazingly I was able to finish all the work several days before I left for my trip. I was so excited about the painting, I blew up a very large, thirty by forty inch photograph of the Sphinx, and painted it in turquoise, antique gold, and lilac. The colors were unusual, but the way I did it nobody thought to question them. *I am definitely taping into another dimension here.* Then I blew up an equally large shot of the Pyramids and painted it fuchsia, yellow-gold, and deep blue. It was like I had brought those ancient places back to life.

The three weeks passed in a flurry of activity, and before I knew it, it was time to go to Peru.

CHAPTER 30

Our group was not scheduled to meet David until the fourth day of our trip. I tried hard to keep my curiosity, excitement and nervousness subdued, but I felt like a child waiting for Santa Claus. I had stowed the diary in one of my suitcases, ready to return to David. I would simply pull him aside, find out what this has all been about, and give the diary back to him.

Rebecca did a great job of organizing our various tours. The first day our group went on an extended bus tour around Lima, but I was impatient and not too interested. The second day, however, was fascinating. We piled onto the bus early in the morning for a ride to the Pampa Colorado desert. Then, in groups of five, we boarded a single engine plane and flew over a huge archeological site called the Nazca Lines. Believed to be the work of a pre-Incan race that lived in the area about three thousand years ago, the four hundred square mile site has remained intriguing – and inexplicable.

Those early artists were able to create huge line drawings on the desert floor – drawings that only made sense when viewed from the air. "Maybe they have something like a blueprint...nobody know," said our pilot, Pedro, as we flew over the Lines. Trying to further explain what we were seeing, he added, "First the desert, the ground, she's all dark and hard. Those early peoples dig up the ground taking away...maybe thousand of pebbles and small stones. That leave only light dirt below to making lines...pictures. Look...there...and there," said Pedro, pointing out different shapes on the desert floor below.

The lines etched into the ground extended as far as the eye could see.

There were lines that formed geometric patterns, as well as curvilinear lines forming giant figures of animals, men and strange symbols.

Pedro went on to explain that the site remained in such good condition because of the dryness of the desert. "We get, thanks god, maybe twenty minutes rain each year. No sands blow and no waters wash away. Ancient people make pictures...they stay forever. Make for Pedro a good job!"

Then he became even more enthusiastic. "You people very lucky...you come up here with Pedro. On the ground... nothing...you cannot see pictures. For long time people very curious, but nobody understand. When airplane in 1920s come...fly over this place and people so surprised...they see pictures for first time. Now many peoples come here," Pedro continued, nodding. "They walk down one Line when time of equinox, another when time for solstice. When you walking the Lines, you see rising or setting of sun and also many different stars. All these things...all marked by the Lines." Pedro laughed. "Now even people fly over Lines in helicopters and even a hot air balloon!"

The tiny plane lurched and trembled, and some of our group looked like they might be sick at any moment, but I was much too interested to feel any such discomfort. "How do you suppose the people on the ground knew how to make these Lines?"

He shrugged his shoulders. "Some peoples use word *enigma*. But me," he said pointing up, to the sky above his head, "For me...I think maybe the flying discs."

"You mean to say you think extraterrestrials guided the making of these Lines?"

He turned and smiled at me. "Who do you think made them?"

Good point! I thought about the diary – and about David. "But...but...." I was almost afraid to ask my next question. "Pedro, what purpose do you think they served?"

"Maybe for the energy or maybe...maybe only they know," Pedro answered, pointing once again to the sky.

I certainly had no answer. I was about to ask what he meant by "the energy," but the plane dipped so precariously I was thrown back in my seat – and glad to be there. Once we righted ourselves, a few other people had questions. Then, unfortunately for me, but fortunately for our pale-faced group, we soon landed, and the next group went up.

When the final group came down, I tried to catch Pedro and talk more to him, but clearly he was a man with places to go. I watched him shoot back up in the air and swerve off in another direction. There was probably another group of gawking tourists waiting in a different location. I wondered if he ever got into longer discussions with any of them – and if he knew more than he was saying.

On the third day, we flew to Trujillo, a beautiful city north of Lima surrounded by the rich Moche Valley. From there, we went by bus two and a half miles out to the ruins of Chan Chan. It was the once capitol of the ancient civilization which ruled Peru long before the Inca. As we walked around the area, our local guide pointed out the different temple structures and explained their significance, but I could hardly concentrate on what he was saying. I kept thinking, *Tomorrow we meet David. Thank god!*

Just before noon, I noticed two men, dressed in dark city clothing, who seemed to be following us. They were certainly not natives and did not look like your average tourists. Wherever our guide led us, around corners and up into intricate parts of the ruins, I would spot them. There was no one else around – only our group and the two of them. Although I couldn't have said why, I had a very uncomfortable feeling about them.

When they turned up at the next two sites as well, I gave them more attention, but I rationalized my concerns away. *What else do tourists do out here but visit the sites? They're probably too shy to ask about joining our group. Or maybe they're just loaners, content to follow us around and see what our guide is pointing out.* Besides, my thoughts were of the following day. We were going to meet David at Cuzco.

CHAPTER 31

Rebecca and I were roommates, and we usually reviewed the next days' itinerary in the evening and again in the morning as we dressed. Before our journey to Cuzco I couldn't stop myself from plying her with questions. "I've already told you everything…I can't tell you anymore," Rebecca impatiently exclaimed. "We're supposed to meet David and his group at our hotel. We're working with the same tour company. He knows when we're scheduled to arrive and will leave a message telling us what time to expect him. What's with you anyway? You've got a bug up your *you-know-what* about this stop."

Since I was not about to tell Rebecca anything about David or the diary, I had to button up my excitement and act like it was just another day. But of course, it wasn't. And to make matters worse, our early morning plane to Cuzco, "The City of the Sun," and once capital of the powerful Inca Empire, was delayed. Then, when we finally did arrive in Cuzco, the bus scheduled to take us to our hotel was also delayed.

I was restless and impatient and thought a quick walk would help pass the time. Rebecca wanted to keep all the troops, as she referred to our group, together, but I reassured her, saying, "Don't worry, I won't be long, and I'll keep a lookout for the bus." I set out for a fast walk around the all-purpose air terminal building. As I rounded the third corner of the building, I saw the two men in dark clothing who had seemed to follow us the day before. Now, a third man was conferring with the first two. I quickly backed away and returned to the group.

I kept an eye on the building, and, very shortly, the third man came around the corner and walked up to Rebecca.

"May I speak with you privately for a moment?" he asked her. They stepped away and exchanged a few words. *Why does he look so familiar?* Then it dawned on me. It was John, our tour liaison from Egypt. *What in the world is he doing here and who were the other two men?* But there was no time to question Rebecca. The bus rolled up, and she was busy boarding her troops and their tons of luggage.

Once the bus got going Rebecca stood up and called for everyone's attention. "Okay folks, listen up. There has been a slight change of plans. We were supposed to meet another group today for a visit to the remains of the Coriconcha, the ancient Inca temple to the Sun God, but they have been delayed. Their leader is an expert not only on sacred sites but on the incredible stonework from which the temple is made, so we definitely want to wait and tour the ruins with him.

"In a way, their delay works well for us," she continued. "After all, we are 11,500 feet up in the Andes Mountains, and as you've probably discovered just standing around waiting for the bus, the air is pretty thin up here. Even sitting still can make you lightheaded. So we're going to stay close to our hotel this afternoon and let ourselves adjust to the altitude. Anyone who is up to it can take a stroll through the Cuzco Indian Market. It's a very short walk, and they have great buys on local native clothing and other handcrafts. We will be meeting up with the other group tomorrow morning and then traveling with them for most of the rest of the trip."

My mind drifted back to what I had just seen. *Hmm, it's odd that John would be here.* Something about him, his mannerisms, seemed very different than before. His associates, if that's what they were, seemed a bit off, too! People had questions for Rebecca, and I had to suffer in silence until I could pull her aside and begin my own avalanche of questions.

"Was that John from the Egypt trip you were talking to before we got on the bus?"

"Yes. Apparently he works with this tour company as well. He wanted to tell me about David's change of plans."

"That's weird…I…don't know if you noticed," I said, a little breathy, "but two guys were following us around yesterday. They're here again. I just saw them behind the terminal when I took my walk. John was talking with them before he came up to talk to you."

"Really, I…." Rebecca's attention was pulled elsewhere. Someone was telling her a member of the group was feeling very lightheaded. "Um…I'll talk to you later. I've got to take care of this." But that evening Rebecca wasn't feeling well herself, so I didn't have the chance to express my concern.

By breakfast the following morning, the troops were feeling much better, but we hadn't yet heard from David. Rebecca made an executive decision to begin our visit to the ruins anyway, saying, "I was told yesterday that he would be here this morning, so I'm sure he will catch up with us at the site." We walked to the Church of Santo Domingo, which is built atop the remains of the Coriconcha. From the street, you see a wall, some four feet high, which was part of the old temple complex.

"David should be here shortly," said Rebecca. "Go ahead and wonder around but stay within earshot." My eyes were drawn to the old wall of the Coriconcha. It was composed of large stone bricks so precisely cut and laid that even a razor blade could not fit between them. The diary had talked about this kind of stone cutting. It said the Atlanteans had used crystals to cut stones that were this exact. The stones that made up this wall looked like they had been cut by a laser. *I thought it was all just a story, but now I'm not so sure. It seems like I might actually be seeing the same thing!*

I studied the wall for a while, then began to feel edgy. My eyes scanned the church, looking for someone who fit the description of David – someone who looked like the man I had seen in the Old City in Jerusalem. Someone with the face I had seen at the travel agency in Los Angeles. *I want to give him the diary but now…now I'm curious to hear what he has to say about the stones, as well.*

An hour passed and David still had not come. To fill the time Rebecca asked me to take a group shot in front of the old church. Of course, I knew that photographing the sights would be a piece of cake, but my new passion for hand-painting my black and white images had added a little complexity. I always took two cameras with me. It was professional insurance. However, my plan now was to keep one camera loaded with black and white film for what might later become hand-painted pictures. That left only one camera available for the color slide film for Rebecca. Ordinarily that would be fine – but not this time.

While waiting for Rebecca to organize the group, I climbed up on a low stone wall to get a wider vista for one of my black and white photographs. My other camera, loaded with color film, was slung over my shoulder. I had just framed the shot when I was startled by a noise behind me. I whipped around to find John standing directly behind me.

"Oh my god, John," I said, tottering on the wall as I fought to keep my balance. I regained my footing, but as I did, the camera with the color film tumbled to the ground. I was horrified.

I quickly jumped down from the wall, my eyes riveted on "my baby" now lying at my feet.

"You scared me to death!" My hands were shaking as I kneeled down to examine the camera. There was a pronounced dent above the viewfinder. *That's great! Is this going to ruin all of my pictures for the rest of the trip?*

"Is there anything I can do, Cassandra?" asked John, his voice excruciatingly kind. He leaned down and gently picked up the lens cap and handed it to me. Resting his hand on my shoulder in a reassuring way, he said, "I didn't mean to frighten you. Are you alright?"

"No, I am not alright…and neither is my camera! That was a stupid thing to do!" Then I recanted, "Forgive me, but you really frightened me," I answered, still absorbed in checking out the dent. I ran my fingers nervously through my hair. "I can't tell if my camera is totally wrecked or not."

"If anything is wrong, I'll be glad to pay for it."

"That's not it. The problem is I can't tell if anything is wrong, and I won't know until I get home and develop the film. Please I…I need a few minutes alone to figure out what to do."

He smiled sympathetically. "Yes, of course. I have to speak with Rebecca anyway. And your camera…I'm so terribly sorry. I do hope it is all right. But despite the unfortunate circumstances, it's a wonderful surprise to see you again. I hope we'll have a chance to talk later," he said, as he took his dazzling smile and walked off.

I checked the camera out every way I could think of and everything seemed to be working fine, but I certainly wasn't happy about the dent. I could just use the other camera and alternate between color and black and white film. *Nope! That won't work. I'll never have the right film in the camera at the right time.*

And, if I was busy changing film, I would miss important shots.

When I looked up, I saw John standing next to Rebecca. He handed her a piece of paper, and she frowned as she read it. She appeared to have asked him a question and didn't like the answer. She pursed her lips, folded the paper, put it in her pocket and signaled me that the group was ready for their picture. And so they were. Ruffled as I was, I still could barely keep from laughing. There stood twelve little Indians, with Rebecca on one end and a local Peruvian guide on the other. Each one of our group was wearing some piece of native clothing, a scarf or hat or poncho they had picked up at the bazaar the day before.

There was absolutely no time to debate the issue of whether or not the camera would work and certainly no time to unload the black and white film from the other camera and replace it with a roll of color film. So, without giving it any more thought, I jumped right in and began shooting.

Soon we moved on to the inside of the Coriconcha. However, in the few short moments it took us to go inside the old temple, I drove myself crazy running all the worst-case scenarios I could think of about my camera – and the film inside it. A horrible knot of fear grew in my belly, but there was nothing else to do, so I took a deep breath and forced myself to take a positive approach. *Whatever is going to happen to the film will happen, but at least I'll be seeing David later today...and giving him back the diary.*

The inside of the Coriconcha was dark and musty. Rebecca pulled out the piece of paper John had just given her, unfolded it and struggled, rather woodenly, to read it aloud. "This site marks a major energy node point on the planet. In fact, at one time, forty one different lines of power, emanating from three hundred and twenty eight different power centers, converged on this very spot."

Then she looked up and pointed to the stone wall behind us. It was exactly like the one I had seen outside. "If you look carefully at this wall, you will see that the stones are very smooth and look like they have been cut by lasers. They fit together so perfectly that no mortar was needed to hold them together. You will also notice that the wall slants inward. This is not an optical illusion, it does really slant in. It would seem that the original builders knew something that we still don't understand today...how to build brick walls that are earthquake-proof. In point of fact, numerous earthquakes have hit this area, and while newer structures were demolished, the more ancient structures, like this wall, have stayed perfectly intact. And," she said, looking around at the group, "we will see more of this as we continue our tour and visit some of the sites which still stand along the lines of power that I just mentioned."

Rebecca glanced at her watch. "It's a good time for everyone to look around on your own for a bit. There is something I need to take care of, then we'll talk about what we are going to do next."

As Rebecca headed for the street I caught up with her.

"What's going on? Where's David?"

"I don't know," she groaned. "John said he had been *slightly* delayed and would be here in the afternoon, but that's not good enough. I'm going back to the hotel to call the tour company. Could you just keep an eye on everyone while I'm gone and make sure no one wanders off too far...." She kind of trailed off, frustration showing in her every movement.

"Don't worry," I reassured her. "I'm certain everything will be fine. You go check things out, and I'll keep track of the troops."

But of course, that wasn't true – I didn't feel at all sure that everything would be fine. I looked around for John but didn't see him.

CHAPTER 32

Rebecca returned about ten minutes later. I could see her looking over the group and counting heads.

"Okay everybody listen up. There's a slight change in plans. We will not meet up with the other group until tomorrow, but we have a wonderful native guide, Manco," she said, indicating the little man standing beside her. He was dressed in jeans and a native embroidered shirt. "In the local language, *Manco* means 'king,' so I think we are in good hands," she continued with a self-conscious little giggle. Manco smiled broadly, revealing a few missing teeth.

After a quick lunch, we boarded the bus for an afternoon of touring. Manco, in his broken English, announced we would be going first to the "very mystery" site, Ollantaytambo. He kept a running conversation about things we passed as we drove through the countryside. Everyone was looking out of the windows and seemed to be enjoying the view.

Rebecca was sitting in the back of the bus madly leafing through some papers she had pulled from her briefcase. I went back and sat beside her.

"Okay," I said. "So what is going on now? Where did Manco come from?"

"Don't look a gift horse in the mouth!"

"Okay! Okay! But why aren't we meeting up with David?"

"I have no idea," she answered, distractedly. "Apparently there was some kind of miscommunication. David and his group are traveling through the Rimac and Lurin Valleys and visiting the ancient holy city of Pachamamac on their way here."

"But didn't John tell you David was just *slightly* delayed?" *Damn! I have to get this diary to him!*

"He did, and he gave me the sheet of paper I read with the information about the Coriconcha," said Rebecca, shuffling back through her papers. "David had faxed it so that we could get started without him. I wanted John to call the tour company with me, but I couldn't find him anywhere in the hotel. By the time I finally reached a live person at the company, not only couldn't he tell me where David was, he had never even heard of John. He said John must be with their other office and promised to make some calls and straighten it all out. But he did fax me some information about the sites we'll visit this afternoon.

"I just don't get it," she continued, "...maybe it's a language problem. I could hardly understand a word the guy said.... I'm not sure I would have scheduled this trip if it hadn't been for David. I sure hope Manco knows his stuff!"

"Don't worry. I know some things about the stone sites. Let me see the information you were faxed." I didn't want to add to Rebecca's concerns, so I kept my thoughts to myself. *Something fishy is going on here – I can almost smell it!*

Rebecca handed me four typewritten pages printed on very bad paper. The spelling was atrocious and the print very light. It was the old type of fax paper that was highly light sensitive and must have been exposed to a lot of light, because it was already brown around the edges. She was chewing on a nail and looking very doubtful. I put my arm around her.

"Where did you learn about the stone sites?" Rebecca asked, coming back into focus.

"It's a long story. I read this book…."

When we arrived at the first site, Ollantaytambo, everyone was amazed. There was a living city in and amongst the ancient stonework – stonework that was very similar to the old walls we had just seen in Cuzco. I read the faxed sheets to the group. It was all very informative, but when Manco began his talk, it was both informative and interesting. However, the last few pieces of information blew me away.

"Ollantaytambo," he said, gesturing broadly with both arms trying to encompass the entire site. "Nobody know who build her, but it was long time ago, long before even the Inca. See the large staircase? She used to lead up to a circular tower. Now is only archway…archway open to nothing but wonderful view. We go up soon but first, follow me please.

"The most mystery is this wall," he continued, as he walked with us over to a wall at the base of the site. He pointed to six gigantic polished stone slabs. "These great stones, they weighing over five hundred tons each."

He invited us to look more closely at the huge slabs. Once he made sure he had everyone's attention, he continued. "No one know how these very giant rocks got here since the place they came from makes more than two mountains and two deep river canyon away, near Rio Urubamba."

The group began to talk amongst themselves, their eyes searching the vastness of the sight. Then, unable to stop myself, I asked, "How do you think they got here, Manco?"

"Me…?" he responded. "Manco think the giant stones were levitated." He nodded, as if agreeing with himself. "Some say very ancient people were special wise. They knew things nobody knows today…they knew the ancient magic of the *curanderos,* and they knew the magic of the sounds. That's what I think. I think they knew the magic of the sounds to move things through the air."

Whew! Another thing that's in the diary! I remembered reading that great boulders were levitated long distances using some kind of sounds. The diary had even said that was how the first stones were moved into Stonehenge!

Almost as an afterthought, Manco added, "And maybe they get help from the people of the flying discs."

I can't believe it. Two times in two days local guides talking about "flying disks" as though they were some kind of common occurrence. And the diary…. I needed to talk to Manco alone.

While Rebecca led the group up the curving stairs toward one of the tower remains, I went in search of Manco. I found him sitting on a rock not far from the giant stone slabs. He had pulled a reed flute from his backpack and was playing a simple melody.

"Can you tell me more about the flying discs?" I asked. "The pilot who flew us over the Nazca Lines yesterday talked about them, and here you are talking about them again today."

He looked up at me, resting the flute in his lap. "Funny thing," he said with a wry smile. "All the tourists so surprised when Manco talk about the discs…lots of people, they don't believe me. I guess you don't have them where you live. But here, especially in the mountains…we see the flying discs all the time." His expression soon grew serious – almost intense. "You seem like a smart lady. Would you like Manco to show them to you?"

I was so surprised by his offer, it took me a moment to respond. "Really… you really see flying disks? Yes, of course! I definitely want to see them."

"Well, if Rebecca have me stay with you until Machu Picchu, I show you."

I hope so, I thought. *What an exciting turn of events! I wonder if he can really…? Don't count on it,* I told myself. But I was counting on it – big time. And I could barely contain my excitement.

Manco went back to his flute, and I hurried to join the group. I climbed the stairs to the tower, stopping frequently to absorb the beautiful views. I was surprised to see the same two men dressed in dark clothing in the distance. At the very moment I saw them, they froze – as if aware of my gaze. Then they turned around and walked in another direction.

This is getting spooky. Now I'm absolutely certain they are following us, but why?

CHAPTER 33

L ate that afternoon we traveled back toward Cuzco, riding the crest of the Sacred Valley of the Urubamba River. It was a breath-taking vista comprised of snow-capped mountains, terraced hills and deep canyons. We stopped briefly in the little town of Pisac, where many people still spoke the ancient Quecha language. Manco did a great job at showing us around. Everything was beautiful and interesting, but I couldn't stop thinking about David. *Something just doesn't feel right. If David made a commitment to Rebecca, he would have kept it. I wonder what's really going on. I hope he's okay.* I felt like a radio caught between two stations. One station was playing Manco's narrative and the other my questioning mind.

It was dark when we arrived back at the hotel. While the group went up to their rooms to rest and change for dinner, I went with Rebecca to the concierge's desk to check for messages from the travel agency – or David – or anyone. The eyes of the concierge were glued to a blaring television news program showing some kind of world health problem. Evidently people were fainting and having emotional breakdowns in their homes, at work – even in the street. The images were graphic and pretty intense.

"My god, Rebecca, I remember John and the doctor in Aman talking about some strange disease. I was too sick to listen to the details, but I remember hearing the words *fainting* and *crazy*. I hope it's not spreading, but it sounds like it might be."

"Well, we can't be worrying about that right now…we have enough on our plate." Rebecca finally got the concierge's attention, and he turned the volume down enough to hear us, but his answer was not what we wanted. He told us there were no new messages and turned his focus immediately back to the television.

Rebecca and I went up to our room, both of us frustrated, disappointed and angry. Rebecca had counted on having David lead her tour group, and I had counted on – well – something very different.

I awoke early the following morning with thoughts of the missing David. *This is ridiculous! I'm going to have to get to the bottom of things myself. I have to give the diary back to David.* Rebecca was still asleep, so after a quick check to make sure the diary was safely ensconced between my cameras, I dressed quietly, grabbed my camera case, took the tour company contact information and headed downstairs toward the front desk.

As I turned the corner to enter the lobby, the first person I spotted was John. It was as if he were waiting for me.

"Cassandra," he said, standing up. "I was hoping it would be you. I don't mean to be insulting, but I think you're more level-headed than Rebecca. We need to get to the bottom of this David thing, don't we?"

I was taken aback by his frankness. "Yes," I answered, concealing my surprise. "We certainly do."

"Well, from what I can ascertain, there's been a major mix-up by the tour people, and since I already know and have traveled with you and Rebecca, I've taken it on as my personal responsibility to set things right. How does that sound?"

After seeing John talking to the two men in dark clothing behind the building the day before – men who appeared to be following us – and after the delays in meeting up with David, I wasn't too sure I trusted anything he was about to say. But I put my voice in neutral and replied, "Well John, what did you have in mind?"

"Rather than go through the tour company, I re-contacted David myself and reviewed both of your schedules. I think it would be best if you met up at Machu Picchu two days from now."

"Two days." I said, feeling my heart sink. "Why two days?"

"I think you should stick to your original schedule. It will give you a chance to visit the other sites around here, which are quite marvelous. And especially you, as a photographer, most definitely should not miss them. Your group can then take the train to the base of Machu Picchu and the mini bus up the mountain to the 'Lost City.' You will have the rest of the day to look around before meeting David the next morning."

"But I...I don't understand. Where is David now?" I was completely confused.

"Well, and it beats me how this could have happened, but for some reason his group has back-tracked and is flying over the Nazca Lines today."

"But that's all the way back near Lima! Yesterday, you told us he was *slightly* delayed and would be here by afternoon. What's going on?"

"It's a mess, and I can't tell you how it all happened, but someone really screwed up!"

For a moment I was so caught up in John's spell of reassurance that I believed him. Then I remembered the two men. I looked him squarely in the face, and keeping all emotion out of my voice said, "John, yesterday when we landed in Cuzco and were about to board the bus, you had a conversation with two men in the back of the air terminal. Right after that, you went up to Rebecca to tell her about David's delay. Who were those men and do they have anything to do with David's not being here?"

"What two men?" he asked, seeming genuinely surprised.

"The two men in dark clothing! I've seen them several times now. How many people do you think are here walking around the sites wearing dark city clothes? That's not how the natives dress, and it's not how tourists dress either."

He looked right back at me, a confused expression on his face. "I have no idea what you are talking about."

My heart pounded in my chest. *The son-of-a-bitch is lying to me, and there's nothing I can do about it.* "Okay," I said, turning on my heels. "We'll talk about it when your memory is better!"

I went up to the room and found Rebecca getting dressed. I relayed everything that John had said. I also told her about the two men. She hadn't seen them and had no idea what I was talking about. "Are you sure you're not exaggerating things?" she asked, buttoning her shirt and looking in the mirror. "After all, John's our tour liaison, and he knows lots of people around here."

"I'm positive, but speaking of liaison, what do you think of John?" I asked, sitting on the edge of the bed.

"I think he's very nice. And very helpful," she added, grabbing a sweater.

"But don't you think he's a bit…strange?"

Rebecca looked at me and shrugged her shoulders. "Why? Do you?"

"Yes, I think he's very strange. He was very nice and helpful in Egypt, but something else entirely is going on here. I'm not sure why, but I think he is lying to us. Don't you find it odd just how mixed up our plan to meet David has gotten? And don't you find it even more odd that the tour company didn't know who he was?"

"They said he was from their other office," she answered, with a kind of blank look in her eyes. "What more do we need?"

It was clear Rebecca and I were not on the same page, or else I was losing my mind. I decided to drop the subject and we talked about the object of our common anxiety – David.

"Didn't David give you some way to contact him in case something came up, a change of plans or…well…something?"

"No, unfortunately," she answered. "We were both working with the same tour company, so I just assumed they would act as a liaison between us."

"Well, so far that assumption hasn't worked out too well. I guess we'll have to wait and see what happens at Machu Picchu."

Rebecca's priority was to do whatever it took to keep the pace of the group happily moving forward. And from her perspective, she was absolutely correct. So we agreed to follow John's suggestion and wait until Machu Picchu to meet up with David. *As though we have any other option here!*

It was time to have a silent conversation with myself. I decided not to increase the pressure on Rebecca by voicing my concerns anymore. It was up to me to do whatever it took to uncover what was going on with John and those two men. And, it was possible we would end up meeting with David at Machu Picchu and everything would turn out fine. With every fiber of my being, I wanted to believe that – but the knot in my stomach told me there wasn't a chance in hell it would happen. *David, I hope you are really out there and that somehow this whole thing will just un-complicate itself on its own.*

"Look how time flies when you're busy being aggravated!" Rebecca said, grabbing the rest of her things. "If we don't hurry, we'll miss breakfast." I told her to go on down and I would join her in a few minutes. I needed a little privacy.

I reached for my camera case and sat down on the bed. Taking out the diary, I slowly thumbed through the soft leather-bound book. *How can I be so stupid – there is nothing simple about any of this!* I wished I could just wash my hands of the whole damn thing but, deep in my heart, I knew it simply wasn't possible. *Apparently I'm in this as far as anyone can be and I probably have been since the moment I found the diary – or perhaps even before that. And now I've got these two strange men to worry about. Damn!* I shoved the diary back in with my cameras, took a deep breath and walked out to join the Rebecca and the group.

By the time I reached the dining room, Rebecca had come up with a brilliant move. She had arranged for Manco to continue as our guide for the next two days. "By then we'll be at Machu Picchu," she said. It's sort of insurance… at least until David shows up."

"What a great idea," I exclaimed. "He'll be a real asset." *Now I'll get to see the flying disks.*

We had arranged for the kitchen to prepare lunches, and once again John had provided Rebecca with information. This time he claimed David had faxed it to the tour company, and they had faxed it on to him. I didn't, even vaguely, believe in the faxing business. I looked around anxiously for the two men and was very happy to see they were nowhere in sight.

The group boarded the bus and took off to tour several sites along the energy lines that emerge from the Coriconcha like the spokes of a wheel. The sites were varied and continued to provide proof that what the diary said was true. At one site, Sacsayhuamanm, Manco told us, "...very large site...over on hundred thousand stones. Big stone blocks maybe eighteen feet high...each weigh maybe three hundred tons."

He pointed out the intricate jigsaw pattern of the cut stones and one stone in particular that had thirty-two angles cut into it. "Here we see more stones come from so far. And so long ago...how could they cut stone like this? With what? They had no stone-cutting machine...no nothing. No one knows!" He looked at me and winked.

It turned out that Manco was so informative, we didn't even need David's fax – at least not that day. And I was beginning to think I might be the only one on the trip who actually knew how to answer Manco's questions! The question I didn't have an answer to was when we would meet David so I could give him his diary. I wanted to get on to Machu Picchu and see if he would really show up.

Manco was peppered with questions as we made our way back to our bus and throughout the day. We stopped at Kenko, an amphitheater with unusual stone carvings, then at Puca Pucara, a small fort with terraces and stairways dominating two valleys. Our last stop was Tambomachay, where water cascaded over stone walls into what were once cleansing baths belonging to the Inca royalty and their priestesses.

As the end of the day approached, we headed back to the hotel to rest, eat dinner and pack our bags for the early morning train ride to Machu Picchu. Manco's colorful antidotes had made the time pass quickly, but the following day would be our seventh day in Peru. *We are more than halfway through the trip and I have no idea whether or not David will ever show up.* But I was certainly grateful for one thing – the men in dark clothing had not put in an appearance that day.

CHAPTER 34

Machu Picchu is an ancient city located high in the Andes Mountains. We arrived at the base of the mountain of Machu Picchu around mid-day. When we got off the train to board the mini-busses, I thought I caught a quick glimpse of my "favorite" two men. Before I could follow my line of sight, we were hurried onto the mini-busses. The weather at the base of the mountain was ominous and raining, which made things look a bit blurry. It was possible I could have been mistaken, though I doubted it. *They weren't following us yesterday, at least I didn't see them, so why are they back today?*

My mind would just not let it go. For some reason, I found myself wondering if it could have something to do with the diary. *No, that's ridiculous! Nobody even knows I have it. Besides, who would want it? I'm just becoming paranoid!* Our mini-bus took off with a jolt, and I shifted my focus to our expedition up the steep mountainside.

The bus snaked its way so tightly around the mountain that sometimes it seemed as though we were almost vertical. Then we would right ourselves and everyone would exhale. It was a daunting journey and it seemed to take forever to reach our destination that was nine thousand feet up in the Andes. But once we arrived, everything changed. It was like arriving in heaven!

The dark sky vanished, and my gloomy thoughts with it, as I stared out the window of the mini-bus, captivated by my first look at the dazzling, sun-lit Lost City of Machu Picchu. My gaze was held, as if in trance, by the perfectly formed stone city that lay nestled within a deep valley between the twin peaks of Huayna Picchu and Machu Picchu. Its location had kept it completely hidden until we rounded the last curve. Then it unexpectedly appeared, fresh and radiant, like a well-loved infant held in the large caring hands of its parent. Since the stones that comprised the city were light in color, they didn't seem to absorb any light at all. The sun reflected off each one and the ancient site positively glowed.

I couldn't wait to get off the bus and onto the site, but I knew that being on a tour meant staying with your group, and of course, I was the photographer. Rebecca had planned lunch for us before beginning our exploration of the site. I was fidgety as we checked into the lodge-like hotel adjacent to the site, dropped off our luggage and met in the dining room. It was agony waiting for the last person to finish their meal. I felt like a caged bird.

It seemed an eternity, but once everyone was ready, we eagerly followed Manco out of the hotel, through the gate and into the Lost City. It was even more awe-inspiring to be right inside the ancient city. My gaze flew over the site. Terrace after terrace filled with stone ruins stretched up and out as far as the eye could see. Manco explained that the city was about five square miles and "too much to see…but I try." He told us that most likely the Inca had used the area as a secret ceremonial center in the early 1400s. Pausing for a moment, he added almost conspiratorially, "They here but this place, it much, *much* older than Inca!"

As we walked, Manco began the task of showing us the intact remains of temples, altars, ceremonial baths, and dwellings of the common people, as well as those of the priests and nobility. He said the entire site was served by natural springs and showed us waterways carved into the hard living rock. "This bring water right to homes of noble peoples and priests, and to ritual baths.

"But most important," he continued proudly, "this city built right into center of high mountains, so the peoples had to grow all their food right up here on these terraces." As we hiked the terraces, Manco pointed out how the waterways were used to irrigate the crops. "…and still working today even! You see," he said, looking down on the city and making a sweeping gesture with one arm. "Here, a whole city built into mountain and complete self-sustaining. This most amazing thing!"

And of course, all of it was a photographer's dream – an architectural, aesthetic wonder – a stone city cut into the grey granite rock, surrounded by high mountains with billowing clouds. After shooting pictures of the group here and there, I shot roll after roll of film for myself in both black and white and color. It was the most breathtaking place I had ever seen. I was so in awe, I almost completely forgot about my dented camera, the men in black and the fact that the clock was ticking away the days of our trip.

My blissful mood did not last long. As we returned to the hotel, thoughts of David returned as well. *I need to get this diary back to him!* Rebecca and I went up to our room and were met with quite a surprise. Someone had emptied the contents of my suitcase onto one of the beds – and there was not the slightest question in my mind just who that "someone" might have been. *It's no coincidence I saw those two men in dark clothing at the bottom of the mountain. They must have waited until we walked out into the ancient city before they made their move.*

Before I could utter a word, Rebecca was at my side. "Oh my god, Cassie, what…? Is everything here…did they take anything?" She was beside herself with fear and anger. I was just sick to my stomach as I walked over and slowly began to pick up and look through my private possessions.

"Wait…wait a minute! They didn't touch anything of mine! Why…why didn't they? Cassie, why were they only looking in your suitcase?"

I couldn't answer. I couldn't speak. I numbly shook my head.

"Maybe they just didn't get to my case," Rebecca said to herself, wrinkling her forehead. "Or… or maybe they heard a noise or something. I'd better check to see if anyone else has had visitors. I'll be right back. Will you be okay…?"

I nodded. "Are you're sure?" I nodded again.

"I'll just do a quick check and report it to the front desk. I'll be as fast as I can. Then we'll go over your things and see if anything's missing. I just can't believe this has happened," she said, shaking her head as she ran frantically out the door.

I knew, even without looking, that nothing would be missing. I sat down on the bed, and my body began to shake all over. *Those bastards!* Now I understood why they'd been following us and what they were looking for. *Thank god I've kept the diary in my camera case and I've always had that with me. There's no way in hell they're going to get their hands on this diary.* I might not have known who the two men were, but there was no doubt in my mind that John was behind it.

Rebecca checked with everyone on our tour. No one else had had their luggage tampered with, but the hotel management told her that one other room had been broken into. "How weird is that!" she said. "I wonder how they chose which rooms to attack?"

I shrugged my shoulders vacantly but my mind was raging. *No big mystery there! They broke into the other room just to throw everyone off track. They wanted to make their rifling through my stuff look like just a random burglary. Well, they damn sure did not fool me. They didn't go through Rebecca's things!*

"Cassie! Cassie! Are you all right? I think you'd better sit down...." Rebecca's voice rammed its way into my thoughts.

"I'm fine, just a little shaken...what were you saying?"

"I was just telling you the Hotel Manager was very apologetic and reminded me that there's a vault if anyone has valuables they want to keep safe."

Fat chance! I would never trust the diary in their safe. A night watchman could be very cooperative for a little extra money. *What in the world would John want the diary for...and what is he willing to do to get it? I guess I'll just have to be very sure I'm never alone.*

"Is anything missing?"

"What...? No...no...nothing is missing."

"Are you sure? You're looking a little pale. Let me help you go through your things again."

"No...really! Nothing was taken. I didn't bring anything of value except my cameras, and there're right here" I said, hugging my camera case close to my breast. "I'm really alright. It was just a shock, that's all." I wondered how David was. Had they been harassing him, too?

Just to be sure, I slept with the diary under my pillow. And it was no big surprise that, when we went to the front desk in the morning, there was neither hide nor hair of David as John had promised – or, for that matter, John. We called the tour company to inquire, once again, about our two "missing persons." The language problem seemed worse than ever, so we put the concierge on the phone to ask our questions. The tour company still didn't know who John was or when David would be arriving – and they seemed clueless as to why we were so upset. Rebecca was furious.

"I just don't get it!" muttered Rebecca, as we settled into a little table in the hotel coffee shop. I don't understand how everything could have gotten to be such a wreck. I guess we're just not going to ever meet David," she said, glancing at me with a look of despair. I nodded, hiding my own anxiety. Rebecca was biting her lip, but I could see her mind beginning to work.

She rifled through her papers, pulled out the trip itinerary and turned to the second page. After a quick review she said, "I guess the thing to do is to see if I can keep Manco for today…or even better, until we get to Puno, tomorrow night. Then we go across Late Titicaca and into Bolivia…." she said, trailing off, not moving and still looking a bit dazed. I wasn't moving either – but fortunately, I was thinking.

"Let me look at the itinerary," I asked.

"Please, be my guest," Rebecca replied, handing it over. "Work any miracle you can."

"Hmm…." I mused, looking over the paperwork. "It's not so bad. Keeping Manco is a good idea. Tomorrow morning we take the train to Puno. That takes the whole day, and Manco can keep us informed on what we're seeing. Okay, now let's see. The following morning we take the hydrofoil from Puno across Lake Titicaca and into Bolivia. We already have a mini-bus to take us to our hotel in La Paz. That's almost another whole day and the hydrofoil has its own guide.

"The only thing we need, since we don't have David, is a guide to take us to Tiahuanaco, the last site on the trip. The morning following that, we just get up, have breakfast, go to the airport and fly home. And we already have transportation back and forth from the hotel in La Paz to Tiahuanaco and to the airport."

"Well, it might be doable," sighed Rebecca, looking slightly more relaxed.

"I definitely think it is. Now, here's the plan…while you check with Manco, I'll call the hotel in La Paz and arrange for a guide."

"Thank you, Cassie! You have been just wonderful!" She leaned over and gave me a hug. "Honestly, I couldn't have done it without you. I have no idea how everything got so mixed up. Maybe it was John…it has just been so crazy.

But Cassie, you've been…you've been…!"

"I know! I know, thank you. Now you get moving and let's get this thing back on track!" Rebecca stood up, hugged me, smiled and took off. She had literally come back to life with our new plan. I started to go up to our room, but a jolt of memory put a stop to that. *Do not go anywhere alone!* A quick but thorough search of the lobby revealed no unwanted sightings. I went back to the concierge who called La Paz and arranged for the guide we needed. And I stayed close as people started gathering for breakfast.

I couldn't help but notice the small television located on a file cabinet right behind the Concierge's station. I could tell it was talking about and showing pictures of the same terrible disease I had seen on the television in Cuzco. It seemed to be getting worse. A few people had literally gone insane, and many doctors believed that insanity was a natural progression of the ailment. A cold shiver ran down my spine. *How horrible….*

CHAPTER 35

The group reconvened after breakfast and spent another inspiring day touring with Manco. Once more he ran a constant and fascinating monologue. He explained that the name *Machu Picchu*, also the name of one of the mountains that cradle the ancient city, meant "old peak." The other mountain, called *Huayna Picchu* meant "new peak."

There was one "…most special place," that Manco wanted to show us. It was called the *Intihuana*, or The Hitching Post of the Sun. It was a large stone slab with an upright stone pillar growing out of its center. He told us the word *inti* meant "sun" and that the Intihuana had probably served as an astronomical calendar or clock.

"At time of equinoxes," Manco further explained, "sun in the sky appear to sit on pillar…like it tied to the rock. And while he there, the sun, he cast no shadow. Used to be many of most special stones in different places, but when Spaniards come, they break them all, because they think stones something like idols for Inca peoples. So down come all the stones…all broken. This is only one left in all Peru, because Machu Picchu is Hidden City. Thanks god, Spaniards never find it! Make this stone most very special."

After Manco showed us many more amazing places on the site, we were free to walk around for a bit on our own. Although a few hardy souls decided to hike up the path toward the top of Huayna Picchu, I was content to just take photographs of the magical place. I had finished a series of shots when Manco ambled over to me and in a low voice asked, "Still want to see the flying disks?"

"Absolutely," I answered excitedly.

"Good! When we go back to hotel and peoples go to rooms, you stay down…." Someone came up to ask Manco a question and that was the end of our conversation.

The day passed swiftly, and when we arrived back at the hotel Manco announced he had had a surprise planned for the evening. He encouraged everyone to "wash the face and eat the early dinner." We would all meet at the gate to the site at nine in the evening.

I took a minute to tell Rebecca that I was going to stay outside for a while, then joined Manco on the veranda. "Come with Manco," he said, taking my arm as we walked out of the hotel and back to the site. The ancient city glowed golden in the late afternoon sun. Manco led me this way and that before heading up one of the many sets of stairways carved from solid rock. We climbed up and up and up, over the un-mortared terraces, passing temples and altars until he found exactly the spot he was looking for.

We had walked in an easterly direction, away from the sun. It seemed to take forever. Finally he stopped and pointed toward one of the mountains. There, glittering in the reflection of the late afternoon sun, I could make out several oval-shaped objects hovering in the sky above Huayna Picchu. I watched in awe as they floated in suspended animation for nearly five minutes. Then, in unison, they quickly dropped behind the high peak and vanished.

I started to speak, but Manco put his finger over my lips. "Just watch," he whispered. It was an awe-inspiring sight for which I had no frame of reference. "Look," he said. In that moment I saw two more oval-shaped discs shoot straight up from behind the peak of Machu Picchu and head right toward us. When they were directly overhead, they stopped and hovered in mid-air. I had a strange feeling of disorientation and thought I saw a flash of light – inside my head. Reflexively I reached for Manco's shoulder to steady myself. Then the "disks" made a sharp right turn and darted out of sight. *That flash of light… I've felt it before! Where…?*

Manco gave me a reassuring smile, having no idea what I had just experienced. He silently took my hand and led me down the terraced steps and back to the hotel. My mind was awhirl with questions. *Has Manco ever seen…or met…any of the "beings" from the flying discs? Have other people? How often do they come?* I tried repeatedly to get answers to my questions but Manco would only say, "later…later." I tried again when we reached the hotel, but all he said this time was, "I think it better you not tell your friend." *He didn't need to worry – Rebecca would never understand.*

What I couldn't understand, though, was what I was going to do with the diary. It had been an amazing day, but I had not stopped thinking about David. *What if he does need the diary? What if he can't do his important work without it?*

After dinner, a few other people who were staying at the lodge joined our group for Manco's evening "treat." As promised, Manco took us back onto the site. Under a navy-blue sky brilliant with stars, he led us through an ancient ritual, a prayer of thanks to the gods who watched over the site. It was magical, and despite the craziness of the trip and not finding David, a wave of appreciation washed over my body. *Aside from Manco, I'm probably the only one here who knows who those "gods" might be.*

I had hoped to talk to Manco privately, but unfortunately, he had other ideas. "Is to experience…not to talk," he said earnestly. "I say good night now. Tomorrow you have another busy day. Go take train through Andes, across Continental Divide. Is very, very beautiful!" Then he, along with most of the group, retired to their rooms.

I had promised myself to not be alone but it was much too beautiful a night for me to be indoors. *There are still a few stargazers out here* I rationalized, seeing the silhouettes of a couple of people not too far from the lodge. *I'll just stay for a minute or two.* I settled into one of the comfortable chairs lining the veranda and silently looked out at the night sky. My mind drifted. David...*flying disks...the diary...Machu Picchu....*

"Mind if I join you?" Rebecca asked, standing in the doorway, "Or is this a private party?"

"Well, if it is, you're welcome to crash it," I replied. *You have no idea just how welcome you are!* Rebecca sat down in the chair next to me and we both gazed silently up at the sky.

"I really appreciate your help this morning," said Rebecca, her voice puncturing my thoughts. "For the life of me, I still cannot figure out why this has all gone so wrong. David, John, your luggage! It just doesn't make any sense," she lamented.

"Rebecca, we can't keep going over the past ...we just have to move forward. You have a group to lead and I have pictures to take." I patted my ever-present camera case. "Thank goodness for Manco. He's been a real godsend. Can we keep him until we get to Puno?"

"*Yes, thanks god!* This morning he wasn't sure, but just before dinner he told me, 'I love to be staying with you!'" We both laughed at Rebecca's Manco-isms. "I may not be able to control anything else about this trip, but I've managed to keep Manco."

We talked for a few more minutes before Rebecca said she was tired and ready for bed. *Damn! Tired or not, that means I have to go in, too!* Just as she was getting up, a few people stepped out onto the veranda. "We decided the night's too beautiful to sleep through," one of them said. "Brilliant minds think alike," I replied, as Rebecca disappeared inside. *Fantastic! Now I can stay out a little longer and be safe.*

The people wondered out onto a grassy patch of lawn about twenty yards away. They moved some lounge chairs into a circle and settled in to enjoy the starlit evening. I leaned back in my own chair, took some deep breaths and tried to relax. All of a sudden I heard a rustling sound and snapped to attention. My eyes searched the darkness. Nothing! Then I heard it again.

I stood up and gingerly walked to the far edge of the veranda, my eyes following the sound. John immediately emerged out of the shadows and began walking toward me. I glanced at the circle of people, than back at John. "You can't just jump out of nowhere and scare people like that," I hissed, wishing I could make myself – and my camera case – vanish right before his prying eyes.

"Will you please lower your voice, Cassandra. I'm sorry...I didn't mean to scare you," he said in a hushed tone.

I was fuming.

He walked quickly up the stairs and came close – far too close – to me and to my camera case. "You're quite beautiful, you know," he said, reaching his hand out toward my face. I literally jumped backward to escape his touch.

"Don't be afraid, Cassandra, I just want to be your friend. You were sitting there looking so lost...so alone," he purred.

I shot a look at the people chatting away on the lawn. *He won't try anything with them so close. But I have to get away from him, now!*

"I need to go in John," I said curtly. "Good night."

His shirt sleeves were rolled up and for the first time since Egypt, I noticed the tattoo on the back of his wrist. It was small but distinct – a black Celtic cross with an open circle in its center and a black slash of lightning running across it. I had no idea what it meant, nonetheless I cringed involuntarily. John saw me looking at it and immediately pulled his arm away. I turned and headed for the entrance of the Lodge.

"Cassandra, everything is going to be just fine. As I said before, it's just been a major screw-up by the tour company, and I'm doing everything in my power to fix it. David will catch up with you, I promise. I just need your patience."

He is absolutely crazy...we are leaving in four days! I did not turn around.

"Look, Cassandra, I'm on your side," he continued.

He's a maniac! I had reached the door to the lodge and had my hand on the door handle. I pushed down on the latch but the door wouldn't budge. *Dear god, please let it be open!* I could feel John closing in on me, and I began to jiggle the handle frantically up and down.

Abruptly the latch engaged, the door swung inward, and I was inside. I slammed it behind me and luckily, he didn't follow. I heaved a sigh of relief as I hurried up the stairs and into my room. But the image of the tattoo stayed in my mind. *Why does it seem so familiar?*

I entered our room to find Rebecca stretched out on her bed reading a book. It was about the most ordinary and therefore the most comforting sight I could have wished for. "The bathroom's all yours," she called out. "And don't worry about keeping me up. I'm at an exciting part here," she said, holding up her book.

My eyes latched onto Rebecca's book. *Book! The diary! I remember now.* I had noticed a tattoo on the back of John's wrist in Jordan when he brought the doctor to my hotel room. But I never saw it close up, and I couldn't focus on it because I was too sick. Seems to me there was a description of a tattoo in the diary. I've got to check!

I slipped into the bathroom and locked the door behind me. My heart was racing as I sat on the lid of the toilet, opened my camera case and pulled out the diary. I opened it to a place that talked about genetic engineering and quickly skimmed it. Then, not letting myself be diverted, I searched for the part about Atlantis. I found the section in time where the Forces of Darkness were beginning their rise to power. There it was, a perfect description of the tattoo I had just seen. "It was small but distinct – a black Celtic cross with an open circle in its center and a black slash of lightening running across it." But in the diary, the people who had that tattoo were the ones who were following the Forces of Darkness.

My night was filled with disturbing images – the break-in, the tattoo and John coming at me out of the darkness. My head stayed on the pillow, but each of these things wrenched me from the depths of sleep and left me panting, eyes wide open, staring fearfully into the darkness. Finally, my mind let go and succumbed to a restless sleep.

Only the promise of a beautiful day's journey helped me drag my exhausted body out of bed in the morning.

CHAPTER 36

Manco was right. The train journey the next day was amazing. It took us through some of the most breathtaking expanses of the Andes. My eyes were very busy taking in the scenery and being on the lookout for John and his friends. And my mind – my mind just couldn't let go. *Would they follow us? Would they try again to get the diary? Was I at risk? Stop! Stop obsessing about it! Just keep your eyes open and stay with the group.*

And I did just that. I didn't even go to the bathroom by myself.

It was almost evening before we reached our hotel in Puno. As was our ritual, Rebecca and I went directly to the concierge to see if there were any messages awaiting us, and, as usual, there were none.

The following morning, we reluctantly said our goodbyes to Manco and traveled by hydrofoil over the turquoise waters of Lake Titicaca. The guide on the hydrofoil, a Peruvian archeology student, told us, "Lake Titicaca, at a little over twelve thousand feet, is the highest navigable lake in the world. An even more fascinating fact is that many experts believe Lake Titicaca was once a part of the Southern Pacific Ocean. The saltwater content of parts of the lake, as well as its fossil remains, is a testimony to its geological evolution."

I knew about testimony, alright. My stiff neck was testimony to my ever-present vigilance– always on the lookout for John and his friends. The guide was informative, but I felt a sense of loss without Manco. The funny, wise little man had become my friend, and his presence was, somehow, reassuring.

We arrived at our hotel in La Paz, Bolivia, the world's highest capitol, just as the sun was setting on the towering white peaks of Mount Illimani. And, wonder of wonders, this time there actually was a fax waiting for us. We waited impatiently as the concierge pulled out a non-descript white envelope addressed to Rebecca.

"So sorry," he said, handing her the envelope. "Three pages came through the fax, but the first and last were blank. Nothing! We've checked our machine and it's working perfectly. I'm very sorry."

Rebecca and I looked at each other in disbelief. "Why am I not surprised?" Rebecca growled. "Everything about this trip has been a mess. So of course, the last day we finally get something, and the damn fax machine messes up. Can you believe it?"

Of course I can! At this point absolutely nothing surprises me…but I can't wait to see what's in the fax. As soon as the group had dispersed to their various rooms to settle in and freshen up for dinner, Rebecca and I hurried out onto the privacy of the veranda. The light was quickly vanishing, and in the crisp dark mountain night the lights of the city flickered like a million stars.

Rebecca tore open the envelope and pulled out a single sheet of hand-written information. I recognized the distinctive script immediately. It was exactly the same as in the diary. It was definitely David's writing. My heart began to race, and I started to shake – both inside and out.

There was no greeting. It simply began, "Tomorrow you are going to visit Tiahuanaco, an ancient sacred city that lies over two miles above sea level. The city is almost entirely in ruins, but the site is important because what remains is a part of what is thought to possibly be the most ancient city in the world. It is more than seventeen thousand years old and lies upon some of earth's most prominent grid points.

"While this dating of the site is not accepted or acknowledged by the archeological community, it is astronomically verifiable. The sophisticated sacred city of Tiahuanaco is not only older, but very unlike any other city in the Andes. In fact, the city is the origin for all the creation myths throughout the entire region. The city was built under the direction of those not originally from this planet and was used for, among other things, genetic engineering."

Rebecca looked up, her eyes like a deer stunned by the headlights of an oncoming car. "Built under the direction of those not originally from this planet? Used for genetic engineering? What does that mean? Is this from David? Is he some kind of nut?" she exclaimed, her voice reduced to a loud whisper.

Genetic engineering! Crazy! I don't think so! "May I see it?" I asked, controlling the quiver in my voice.

"Sure, help yourself," she replied, handing me the letter and groaning again in disgust. "Imagine! All this time, and this is what we get? Where has he been? Where was he when we needed him?"

I held the single sheet of paper in my shaking hands. I almost lost it. A guttural sound formed in my throat, but I caught myself. *I can't say anything about the handwriting…or the diary!* So I acted like I was elated we had actually gotten something – anything.

The letter contained three more paragraphs telling about what we would see the next day. I read them aloud. The last paragraph described a courtyard. "Below the steps of the Kalayasa Temple is the semi-subterranean temple courtyard. You will notice that set into the walls of this sunken temple are carved heads that represent all of the races on earth and then some…."

"Well, go on," said Rebecca impatiently.

"That's it," I replied, "the letter just stops there."

Rebecca stared at me, her mouth slightly ajar. "I don't get it. It doesn't make any sense. Do you think the letter just stopped like that? Do you think David really wrote it?" I gave a noncommittal shrug. Each of us pondered the letter in our own way as we went up to our room, changed our clothes and met the group for dinner. Neither one of us mentioned the letter again, but I could not forget the sight of David's handwriting – or David, period.

The following morning we met Ernesto, the Bolivian guide I had arranged for. He turned out to be an extremely fortunate choice. He was educated on many different levels, and he started out by saying, "I, myself, go to University for studying archeology, and yet, I know there are many things here at Tiahuanaco that do not make sense in the timetable we were taught about this place.

"Our books say this site was built and used between 500 and 900 BC. However, both local mythology and what you might call alternative science support the idea of an ancient flood and catastrophe in this area some twelve thousand years ago. A few scholars believe that the human remains, as well as artifacts such as tools found here, clearly show that this place was used prior to that flooding. In fact, it's highly possible that this site goes back seventeen thousand years, but this not taught in university…this my own researches."

To prove his point, he told us that in the language of the local indigenous Aymara Indians, the name *Tiahuanaco* translated as "the place that was already here." My pulse quickened. *That's what David's letter was talking about! This is going to be interesting.*

Ernesto continued, "One thing many scholars do agree on is that at one time very long ago, before the earth went through many changes, Tiahuanaco City sat at very shore of Lake Titicaca. Some ancient stories even say the same earth changes that created the Andes Mountains raised this entire area intact."

Ernesto's speech patterns were very interesting as well. He spoke excellent English, but when he got excited about what he was talking about he would occasionally lapse into broken English. Ernesto said the excavated part of Tiahuanaco was very small. "There are not much left, because over a so long a time period, very much was taken away…stolen. But still, amazing things I have to show you."

He took us to explore many of the ruins of Tiahuanaco, but the most remarkable was the remains of the Kalasasaya temple complex, which was also the most intact part of the site. We spent the rest of the day at the temple complex with its sunken courtyard and monolithic stones. It was a strange place. It wasn't beautiful like Machu Picchu. It was ancient, but very different from the other sites we had been to.

Rebecca wanted me to read David's information to the group, "…but leave out the crazy stuff about genetic engineering and extraterrestrials," she whispered, as she handed me the handwritten sheet.

I stifled a laugh as I watched Rebecca walk away shaking her head and throwing her arms in the air. She had no idea what it all meant, but of course I did – maybe! At least I knew what the diary had said about extraterrestrials, or Star Beings, adding their own genes to that of evolving human race. And although I would have loved to talk about it, under the circumstances, I zipped my mouth and went to the safer parts of David's letter.

I stood with the group at the base of the temple and read part of David's fax. We climbed the steps of the now mostly destroyed temple and marveled as Ernesto pointed out the twenty-foot high sandstone megaliths and a twelve-foot sandstone statue dedicated to Virracocha, which translated to God of The Power of Creation. Then I took the group down two sets of steps into the subterranean courtyard and continued reading.

"You will notice that set into the walls of the sunken temple are carved heads that represent all of the races on earth and then some." Ernesto had walked down into the sunken courtyard with us. "Myths and legends describe the god Virracocha, the huge statue we just saw upstairs, as a tall, light-skinned man with blue eyes." He pointed out two tall, carved-stone statues of bearded non-Andean men standing not far from us. "You can see these two statues look nothing like the local people either. We don't know…were the peoples of these three statues family to each other?" He shrugged. "Bigger question is…who were these people?"

He answered some questions then mentioned, almost off-handedly, that one of the legends surrounding the site told of a tribe of red-haired people who had once occupied the area. I was still thinking about his reference to "a light-skinned man with blue eyes," and it took a moment for "…a tribe of red-haired people living in the Andes" to enter my brain. But when it did, I snapped to attention.

I know there's something in the diary about red-haired people. I have to….

I looked around cautiously, but there was no sign of John or his cohorts, so I decided to renege on my vow to stay with the group and take a chance to explore the site on my own. I left the troops to Ernesto and Rebecca, and climbed up the stairs and out of the sunken courtyard. I climbed the second set of stairs and entered the Kalasasaya temple. I sat down behind the statue of Virracocha, where I hoped I would be somewhat hidden, and pulled the diary out of my camera case to look for the part about Atlantis. By now, I had looked through the diary enough to have some idea of where things were.

Sure enough, it was in David's first description of Atlantis, when he wrote, "I noticed that the greatest number of Atlanteans had light skin and red hair." *Wow! So Atlanteans were here and they had something to do with this site. And clearly there were also extraterrestrials, Star Beings.* It sounded like they not only built the place, they did some kind of genetic engineering here. This whole trip has been nothing less than a verification of so much of the information in the diary. I closed my eyes, trying to absorb it all.

I had no idea how long I'd been sitting there, but I was startled by the sound of laughter from the group. I stuffed the diary into my camera case and struggled to my feet. Knowing that time was limited, I began to explore the site on my own. I went back down to the sunken courtyard and looked, really looked, at the carved heads set into the stone-block. I was mesmerized. After studying it for some time, I was able to make out "all of the races on earth and then some," exactly as David had written.

Over and above what we had learned from David's note and the intriguing implications of Ernesto's talk, there was something else about the site – something I couldn't put my finger on. The place held a kind of spellbinding energy that was more than just ancient – it was otherworldly. In fact, this was the most mysterious place I had been to yet. The energy was so elusive, yet palpable, I could almost touch it. And even though I did not really understand what I was looking for, I knew I had to capture that elusive energy on film.

I took picture after picture, as though I could not possibly soak up enough of the place. By the end of the day, I had taken more pictures there than I had during the entire rest of the trip. This was the one and only time when I became so lost in what I was doing I almost forgot about John and the two men in black. Almost – but not entirely. I was never too absorbed to lower my vigilance. And of course, my mind kept going back to David. *Is it possible he was here all the time, yet we never met up with him? If he was here, it cannot have been David's doing that we never connected. It had to be John's…but why?*

We spent the night in La Paz before leaving the following morning to fly back to California. I was relieved I hadn't seen any more of John or his friends. But crazy as it was, a part of me still kept looking for – and hoping to see – David, until the very moment I stepped onto the plane bound for home.

CHAPTER 37

On the long plane ride back, I tried to digest everything that had happened in Peru – why David had never showed up and why John and the men in black had. There were plenty of questions, but no answers. I closed my eyes and tried to sleep, but it was impossible. Then a new stream of my geometric doodles began to appear. I quickly pulled my film notepad out of my camera case and drew the three images I could remember. I looked back at the other three drawings that were at the beginning of my pad. *They all look related…but what are they for?* I managed to doze a bit as we continued to fly through the skies, but even when I was awake, I felt like I was still in a dream.

My friend Tina was waiting for me as I emerged from customs. She wanted to hear about everything, but I didn't want to talk about anything. I gave her generalities about the sites, the people and the food, and then drew the line.

"Tina, I'm too tired to go into detail now, but I took a ton of pictures, and I'll tell you all about it when I show them to you. Trust me! It will be much better, I promise."

Tina took me home and helped me with my luggage. I hid my apprehension as I entered my apartment. *I hope John or his men haven't been here, too.* There was nothing unusual – just my roommate's usual clutter lying around. Under the circumstances, it was a welcome sight. I thanked Tina, told her I desperately needed to take a nap and ushered her to the door. But the moment it was closed, I raced to my desk and searched for the key to my safety-deposit box. My heart was pounding, but I quickly found the key, put the diary in my purse and headed out to my car.

It was the middle of the day and there was practically no traffic – and nobody following me. I heaved a sigh of relief. I couldn't wait to get the diary safely into the vault. David might have written something in here that John wanted. I couldn't begin to imagine what it might be, but I knew for sure the diary was what they were after in Peru. Now at least, they wouldn't be able to get at it.

I pulled into the first available space in the bank parking lot and got out of the car. Nonchalantly, as if I were carrying the crown jewels of England, I walked inside. But once the diary was safe in the bank's vault, I really did go home and straight to sleep.

The next morning, I mustered my confidence and dropped off my film at the lab that processes my color work, but the cold, harsh reality hit when I went back to pick it up. In spite of my earlier decision, I was a nervous wreck, reprimanding myself for using the obviously damaged camera. I am often anxious right before viewing the long strips of film over the light box, but that day I could hardly breathe. As long as I live, I will never forget the look on the lab owner's face. He was a long time friend, and I usually got very prompt service, but this time the wait seemed to take forever. Finally he returned with my file, pulled out the strips of film and briefly glanced at them. I watched his cheery smile vanish.

"I'm so sorry," he said. His face held the expression of a doctor about to delivery very bad news. "I think there was something wrong with your camera." I felt the blood drain out of my face.

"Oh no," I gasped, unwilling to believe I was hearing my deepest fears confirmed. With a horrible mechanical movement, I took the film from him and began to lay a few strips over the light box which was sitting on the counter. I held my breath as I gingerly flicked on the toggle switch and – it was incredible! I was looking at some of the most provocative images I had ever seen.

At the specific locations where I had the most profound, mind-altering experiences, the camera had indeed gone mad. It had created a series of impossibly beautiful time-lapse, multiple-image exposures. The way in which the sites had been captured on film paralleled my experiences in a way that I could never have consciously planned. There was a timeless, otherworldly quality to the images. Equally remarkable, there was still enough "normal" film to fulfill my obligation to Rebecca. In fact, the images were great. I was so relieved, I even thanked God, or "something," for what seemed, indeed, a miracle.

Later in the day, I looked at the multi-image filmstrips on my own light box at home. Because I saw their unique beauty, I had already cut the long strips at the places where it made sense, where one multi-image piece seemed to naturally end and another begin. I lined up the pieces of film by location, putting all of those from one site together on the slide box at a time. Then I noticed that when I looked at them this way, showing the sprocket and edge numbers along the side, it was almost as if I were seeing a code. I kept staring at one grouping after another, mesmerized, seeing things in the images that I had not even seen at the sites.

As I stared at the images of Tiahuanaco, something strange happened – a new connection began forming in my brain. It was not a conscious act, yet I could not pull my eyes away from the images. Then I saw a "pop" inside my head – it was like seeing a flash of lightning, but from the inside out. It was such a strange experience, I had absolutely no point of reference for it. I became light-headed and had to sit down. For a short while, everything around me looked brighter and more sharply defined. I experienced a moment of intense "awakeness" before the feeling slowly began to fade. *What the hell was that?*

When I recovered, I realized I had experienced that strange sensation before. I got up and walked around, testing my balance. I knew for sure I had a mini-version of the same sort of light flash when I was with Manco in Machu Picchu, and the flying disks had hovered above our heads.

Then I remembered a much bigger flash when I was in Greece. I had stayed behind in Athens while the rest of my group went on the Isle of Patmos. I was alone in my hotel room reading the diary when exactly the same sensation had hit me. It had made me furious – but it also helped me remember an incident from my childhood. It's still frightening to think about it, but I guess I have to. I was ten years old and showing off a bit. I had made a pencil lift into the air just by thinking about it. Later, many of the children circled me in the schoolyard, yelling, "freak!" A teacher had come out, taken me to her office and called my mother. I was still sobbing when my mother came to pick me up.

While driving home, my mother was very angry with me. She made me promise I would never again do anything like that. She also told me it was not true that the beautiful lady had visited me at night – but I knew she had. The whole episode with my mother had been terrifying. She was like a stranger – someone I had never known. We drove home in silence and no one ever spoke of it again. But I spent a week sleeping on the window seat in my parent's bedroom, and whenever I was in my own room, the door always had to be left open. From that time on, I was a different person. My main objective in life became to not be different, but rather to fit in and be like everyone else.

CHAPTER 38

That night I had a very disturbing dream. In it I saw Atlantis as it was portrayed in the diary. I saw the dark Priest Carmac speaking to the people, riling them up and telling them how he and the other errant priests would save them from the creatures called the *Things*. He encouraged people's fear that the Things would take over the island-continent, but told them they would be protected if they put their faith in the New Order. Then I saw the scene where David, the Prince-Priest A-Ta, and young Priestess A-Lan were thrown from atop the Great Pyramid of Atlantis, A-lan's broken body claimed by Carmac. As if I were watching a movie, the camera zoomed in on the tattoo on Carmac's wrist. When it zoomed out again, it was the face of John that I saw.

I woke up with my jaw and fingers clenched, and my neck so tight I cried out in pain. My brain was foggy, yet my head spun with questions. *Carmac and John...what's the connection? Carmac is evil...is John evil too?*

I lay silently in my bed for a long while, massaging the knot in my neck. This was probably just a bad dream – a very bad dream. Looking at the pictures yesterday must have stirred something up. It was a long time before I could fall back asleep.

CHAPTER 39

Now that I was back in California, I had to reassess my situation, see where I stood and figure out what to do next. More than anything, I wanted to find David – needed to find him. I couldn't get past the feeling that I had to get the diary back to him, that there was something in it he needed to know, or to remember, in order to do his work – in order to save the world.

Since I was no closer to my goal of finding David than the day the diary had appeared, I decided to try an objective technique. I got out a pen and a piece of paper, and drew a line down the center of the sheet. On one side I wrote, *What I know.* On the other side, *What I don't know.* I toyed with the pen. This seemed ridiculous, but I had to begin somewhere. Okay! What I knew was that David was a real person. I saw his handwriting.

I also knew that at least some of the diary was true, especially the part about gigantic stones being transported over great distances by means of some mysterious technology. I'd seen evidence of it. I also knew, as weird as it was to admit, that extraterrestrials had visited and were currently visiting earth – at least in Peru!

How is this going to help? I sat staring at my piece of paper, fingers drumming on the table, then got up and paced the room. *I can't walk away from this…I'm much too invested in the whole mystery. I feel like I was propelled into this thing, and now I'm compelled to follow it through.* Too many things had happened in Peru and Egypt – too many coincidences to be a coincidence – and way too many things that were personal!

I had to be connected to the diary in some way or it would never have come to me in the first place. I would never have seen David in the Old City in Jerusalem and I certainly wouldn't have seen his face at the travel agency – before I even committed to going on the trip!

Sighing in frustration, I went back to my desk and stared at my list. I added John and the two guys who were following our group to the *What I know* side. But then I had to add them to the *What I don't know* side, as well. I simply had no idea what the hell they were doing or why. I balled up the piece of paper and slam-dunked it into the wastebasket.

I was still at ground zero and the big question remained where to go from there? Other than what I had read in the diary, I knew absolutely nothing about Atlantis. That was probably where I should start. It might give me a clue as to why the diary had come to me and what I was supposed to do with it. Or perhaps, somehow, it would give me a clue on how to find David. I knew I was reaching but, under the circumstances, doing something was better than nothing.

Late afternoon found me in a very out-of-the-way place – a dusty old antiquarian bookstore near Japan Town. My friend Peter, who was considered a crackpot by everyone except me, had said the bookstore was a real find when it came to arcane subject matter. A small, roundish, possibly Asian grey-haired man with wire-rimmed glasses and a goatee sat behind the front counter. He didn't even bat an eyelash when I asked if he had any books on Atlantis. He simply pointed toward the back wall without so much as looking up from the book he was reading – or the noodles he was eating. *He's so nonchalant about Atlantis. Maybe it's a good sign.*

I followed his finger to a wall of shelves lined with books from floor to ceiling. They did not seem to be in any particular order, or perhaps they were in an order that only he understood. Some of the books were even lying on their sides atop one another. Fortunately, there was a ladder. I started at the top and worked my way down and across. At about nine o'clock in the evening, smack in the middle of the bottom shelf, I hit pay-dirt – three books with Atlantis in the title. Skimming only the indexes, I decided to buy all three books.

Once back home, I settled in to read and read and read. There was certainly a lot of information. Much of it had a great similarity to the diary, but a lot of it was very mathematical and way over my head. However, one of the books focused on *ley lines,* or lines of energy, described in such great detail in the diary. It said they were everywhere on the planet. There seemed to be an inordinate number of references to books written by British authors, who referred to these lines as "The Old Straight Track."

One book in particular snagged my interest. It was entitled *The New View*

Over Atlantis. and it described the science behind the ancient stones as belonging to "Druid magic." The author, John Michell, delineated the great number of ancient stone sites that still stood in the British Isles. He painstakingly related that some of the old sites had been co-opted by Christianity and that churches had been built where once only stones had stood. However, no matter what was built on the sites, they still marked off the lines of energy – the ley lines.

Maybe I'm really onto something. In essence the book said, "…the further back one traces the old tradition, the higher and more universal appears to have been the knowledge behind it. Thus, finally one is impelled to take seriously the legend of a former world-order of which the Druids and other initiate orders were the fragmented survivors." Then it quoted a Mr. Lewis-Spence, "I have come to the conclusion that Atlantis was not only a great territory between America and the West Coast of Africa, but the cradle of all our civilization as well."

The wheels of my mind begin to click into gear. *Stone Sites marking off the lines of energy…Atlantis…the cradle of all our civilization…. Pretty powerful stuff!* Not only did many scholars connect the stone sites in Great Britain to Atlantis, but much of the information itself came from experts in the British Isles. In addition, the diary had talked about the Druids carrying fragments of the ancient mystery tradition that originated in Atlantis and was known only to the Great Brotherhood of Light.

I felt like I had just seen a ray of light myself. I was definitely getting the feeling I needed to see some of the stone sites in the Great Britain. It was just possible I could meet someone or find some clue to give me the next pieces to the whole crazy puzzle.

CHAPTER 40

I heard a phone ringing far off in the distance and instinctively reached for the pillow to block out the sound but, instead of the pillow I felt something hard. I pushed it aside and heard it thump to the floor. The phone was still ringing. Damn! Who could be calling so early in the morning? I rubbed my eyes, blinked them open and discovered that I was still in my jeans lying on the sofa with two books sitting open on my lap. I stumbled over and picked up the persistent and very loud phone.

"Hello," I mumbled.

"Cassie, is that you?" asked a familiar sounding voice on the other end.

"Mmmm hmm," I answered.

"Hello, luv, it's Tina. You're sleeping awfully late."

"Late? What time is it?"

"It's past noon. That's not like you."

I looked around at the living room before answering. "I guess I fell asleep on the couch. I must have been up reading all night." I yawned.

"Reading what?"

"Some old books I found about sacred sites in England and Scotland and…other places in Europe…I think."

"You're taking this sacred site stuff pretty seriously, aren't you?"

"Actually, I think it's taking me pretty seriously," I said, muffling another yawn.

"Well, in a way, that's good," said Tina, "because I'm about to make you an offer, and now I think you might say yes."

"You do?" I asked, making my way to the kitchen and putting on a pot of coffee.

"What kind of offer?"

"Well, you know I've been thinking for a while about popping over to England and visiting me mum and dad, but I'm not all that keen on it. So I thought you might like to come along, and then we could rent a car and take a little road trip together. You could photograph some of the old stone sites and…well…I could learn about them. And you'd be my excuse, so I don't have to stay too long with my folks. What do you think?"

"Sounds great," I answered, putting some bread in the toaster. "I only have one problem…money."

"Don't worry about it…I've got a ton of airline miles racked up."

"You're kidding!"

"No, why would I be kidding? Besides, little inns in the countryside are really cheap. In fact, everything's cheap in the countryside, and we'll be staying with me mum and dad in Kent. I'm not sure of the date yet, but it will need to be soon. I have a window of time in about two weeks when I can get away from work before I have to set up this huge conference. After that it gets freezing cold up there anyway."

My head was ablaze and my heart thumping. It was one of those times again! I was speechless. *How can things be happening this easily for me? This never used to happen and now it's happening all the time. I barely have time to think of something and it happens…at least it happens if it has anything to do with the diary!*

"Hello! Are you still there, luv?"

"Yes, I'm still here…I don't know what to say."

"Well then, don't think about it, just say yes"

"Okay then…yes, but what about your parents?"

"Don't worry, they'll be fine with it! All you need to know is me mum will try to feed you every chance she gets and constantly tell you that you are much too thin."

"Okay, I can handle that. What about your dad?"

"Well, me dad, he's a bit different."

"What do you mean?"

"Ah, he's a bit hard to describe. Sometimes he's very quiet. If fact, sometimes he'll barely say a word for days, but when he talks he's loud and has lots to say. It's a bit jarring, but he's not manic or depressed or anything like that. It's just the way he is, but don't let him near your cameras. He breaks everything he touches."

"He doesn't sound so bad, especially now that you've given me a warning. What kind of work does he do?"

"Well, that's where the quiet comes in. He gets a pension from the Navy, but we don't exactly know what he does now. He goes to work every morning, but his office is in the house, and we never actually see any 'work.' Oh… and sometimes he just disappears for a few days. He never says where he's been, and we joke that he's gone round to see his other family."

"He sounds…interesting."

"That he is! Everyone says so. Of course to me, he's only me dad. And, there's just one more little thing. He is very conservative, so don't tell him too many of your…well… esoteric ideas. But he does love to talk about his time in the Navy and his travels."

"Don't worry," I laughed, "I'll be good, so they won't think you're best friend is a weirdo! I better get going now. Talk to you later."

I jumped into the shower, frantically sorting out what to do first. As I stepped out, the answering machine was clicking off. *It's probably Tina…bet she's already talked to her folks.* I threw on a robe and, towel-drying my hair, hurried to the answering machine and pressed the play button.

"Hey, Cassandra, this is Chase, Kayla's friend. You did some headshots for me a month or so ago. Well, a couple of my buddies need some too and one wants a hand-painted picture like you did for Kayla's mom. Can we talk? Call me."

Can we talk! I think so! Now I'll be able to pay all my bills and still have money for the trip. Very strange…

My "charmed life" got even better once they saw my portfolio. They not only wanted the headshots, but full-length shots as well. The one who had wanted the hand-painted piece decided on a full-length shot of himself in a forties, double-breasted suit and hat, blown up and hand-painted. I didn't think I could finish it before the trip, but he said, "No problem! Chase showed me your work, and I'm sure it will be worth the wait."

Even though it was one busy time, I found myself thinking about David, the diary, and now – Atlantis! I scheduled the photo shoots and jammed in dozens of essential errands. I took the dented camera in for repair. Then, looking at the hand-painted picture of the pyramids on my bedroom wall, I decided to bring three of my multi-image strips of film into my color lab. I wanted them blown up really large, so they would be ready to frame by the time I returned. *I'm beginning to feel like a real artist!*

The headshots for Chase's friends turned out great, and everyone paid their bill immediately. The guy with the hand-painted request put fifty percent down upfront. They were thrilled and I – I was ecstatic.

CHAPTER 41

Exactly two and a half whirlwind weeks later, Tina and I boarded a plane headed for England. In my hectic schedule prior to our departure, I had found myself "seeing" three more of my geometric doodles. The first one just seemed to pop up. I was at home cleaning my camera lenses and prepping to do the shoot with the first of Chase's friends. I was focused on selecting a location and framing the shot in my mind when *boom*, there it was dancing before my closed eyes. About forty seconds later, a second one appeared, followed by a third.

I hurriedly drew them on the note pad that was always in my camera case and looked back over the earlier drawings. Combined with the three newest ones, they totaled nine. I was fascinated. They all seemed related, but I had no idea what they meant. And I certainly couldn't think about them now – I had pictures to take and research to do.

Even though I made several attempts, I only had time to learn a little about the main sites mentioned in the books I had found in the funky bookstore. In general, I knew I wanted to go to Stonehenge, Avebury and the Salisbury Plain, but there seemed to be dozens of sites going from the southern tip of England all the way up into Scotland that looked promising. I had no idea where to begin.

Once on the plane, I pulled out a couple of maps I had bought at a British bookstore but had only looked at briefly. "Okay Tina, we have lots of options but you only have a week before you have to get the train back to your folks."

"I wish I could travel with you the second week too, Tina moaned, "but me mum would kill me."

"Don't worry, we can do a lot in one week. We'll have tons of fun. Have you ever been to Stonehenge?" I asked.

"Yeah, with me mum and dad," she answered. "Can we go someplace else? You can see Stonehenge on your own."

"Sure. How about Scotland? Ever been there?"

"No, I haven't. I've always wanted to, but I never made it."

"Great! I've read about several sites up there, so Scotland it is! Now... we just have to figure out where we want to stop on the way."

As the airplane carried us over the Atlantic Ocean, we began to plot a course for our adventure. I started with the sites that seemed close to where we would begin our trip while at the same time heading us in a northerly direction. "Which sounds good, the Isle of Lewis in the North Atlantic or the Orkney Islands in the North Sea?"

"Both," Tina said with delight. "You're the expert on the sites, and I'm the expert on driving on the wrong side of the road."

"A fair division of labor," I replied, with a sigh of relief. "Driving on the wrong side of the road is not my idea of a relaxing time."

Our plane landed as scheduled, and Tina's parents picked us up from Gatwick Airport and took us to their home in Kent. Tina's description of her parents was totally accurate. Her mother never stopped trying to feed me, and her dad didn't say a word after "hello" and "welcome." However, sitting at the dinner table two nights later, her father, a large man with wire-rimmed glasses and a mane of black hair, spoke up with a thundering voice. "So, my Tina says you're interested in The Old Straight Track, and all the stones and churches that stand upon her."

Tina shot me a look of surprise. Her father had not spoken to me in the entire two days I had been there. Now, his direct question about this esoteric and "forbidden" subject, as well as his booming voice, set me off on a coughing jag. Food caught in my windpipe and it took a full minute before I could squeak back yes.

"I'm somewhat of a buff as well," he said, winking at me. "Did a bit of traveling myself when I was in the Navy and learned some mighty interesting things about this old world of ours. I can tell you one thing...there's more mysteries going on than you can shake a stick at, and that's the truth." I snuck a glance at Tina who was holding a napkin in front of her face to hide her laughter.

After dinner, as I was helping Tina and her mother with the dishes, I heard her father's heavy footsteps in the hallway. A moment later he was in the kitchen, waving something in his large hand. "I thought I'd show yer friend here some snapshots from my travels."

"But dad," Tina called out exasperated, "were going to visit the neighbors down the block. I haven't seen them in years, and I know they'd love to meet Cassie."

"Hogwash! She doesn't need to meet any old neighbors. She'd be much more entertained looking at pictures from me travels."

Tina looked at me, rolling her eyes. "But dad...."

"No, it's fine," I said, giving her a reassuring look. You two go have a good time. I'm interested in whatever your dad has to say."

After we finished the dishes, Tina and her mum left to go on their visit, and I followed her father into his office. It was a small room with large stacks of books in every corner and papers strewn about. He quietly closed the door.

"I've been waiting for the chance to talk with you alone," he said, in a low voice – a voice that didn't sound at all like him. "I have some things I want to show you, but this is just between you and me. I know Tina's yer friend and all, but I don't want my little girl thinking her old dad's gone round the bend," he said, looking directly at me and winking again.

"Absolutely," I said, hiding my surprise. Tina told me he was a bit different but...!

Her dad seemed reassured. He turned and walked over to a massive bookcase lining one of the walls. He kneeled down and removed some books that were crowded onto a fairly low bookshelf. After pulling a keychain from around his neck, he leaned in toward the empty shelf and fumbled with a lock. His groans mingled with the sound of the lock opening. Then he straightened himself, reached up to a higher shelf and pushed the books aside. I heard the clicking of another lock being turned and tumblers falling gently into place. He pulled a lever behind one of the books and stood back. The entire bookcase slid to the side revealing another hidden bookcase behind it, identical to the one in front. It was an extraordinary sight.

"Ha! Remarkable isn't it? Put it in myself," he exclaimed, his booming voice normal once again.

He pulled out some charts, yellowing around the edges, and spread them out on top of the papers on his desk. They showed the outlines of England, Ireland and Scotland. The charts were covered with straight lines, and small circles were located here and there along the lines. In some cases two lines crossed, and there was a larger circle at the point of intersection.

I leaned over the desk to get a closer look at the charts. I was shocked! These maps look exactly like the description of the maps in the diary – the ones David and the Atlantean priests used to plot the energy points of the planet. I looked up startled, but before I could formulate a question his voice boomed out again.

"Yup! Pretty much tells the whole story, then, doesn't it! Shows you all the energy lines. And the circles, well, that's where the stone markers and churches are. Now I've got something else you need to see," he said, abruptly turning back to the hidden bookcase.

He quickly pulled out a stack of three very thick books, plopped them on the desk next to the charts and stared at them. "Ah, here she is," he said, pulling out the middle book as the top one slid to the floor. It was an obviously old book, its worn leather cover cracked and lined. "I can tell you one thing for sure," he said, holding the book in one hand while knocking on it with the knuckles of the other, "This book here…this is a treasure. This fellow's really onto something!"

This is very weird, but exciting! Tina's father was overjoyed to have an enthusiastic audience.

"Now, Tina's told me you've been to Egypt. Is that true?"

I hesitated before answering, unable to imagine where his train of thought was going. "Yes, just a few months ago."

"Aha," he exclaimed as if he had just solved a difficult math problem. "Well then, this just may interest you. It's a known fact to a very few people, but certainly to the author of this book and, of course, to those such as myself…." He paused, brought the thick book closer to me and tapped it again with his knuckles. Whatever the title was, it had long since been worn away.

"As I was saying," he continued, pushing his glasses back to the bridge of his prominent nose, "those who are informed about such things agree that the Great Pyramid of Egypt was not just an object of visual perfection, it served a very a practical purpose as well."

Practical purpose! Where is he going with this? His comment was so out of the blue that I couldn't hide my look of surprise. He had paused, looking for a reaction from me – and he got it.

"All right then," he continued, "I can see I have your full attention. Right! Now where was I? Ah, yes! The marriage of heaven and earth! That was the practical...but secret...purpose it served. Within the Great Pyramid occurred all manner of High Magic. That is where the energy from the earth, held within the massive stones that form the Pyramid itself, merges with the Heavenly energy brought down through the top of the Pyramid. But what is more to the point is that this mix of energy was finally brought right down into the ground to join with the flow of earthly currents to keep the land and the people who tended her healthy and vigorous."

How can he know that? It's what the diary said! I was so surprised, I stumbled against a chair and sat down. "How...?"

"I know. We know."

"What you've just said," I managed to say almost in a whisper, "does any of it have anything to do with Atlantis?"

"Ah, I'm getting to that. I thought you might be wondering why I am explaining all of this to a world traveler like yourself? Well, before starting out on your journey here it is important for you to understand that the same principle, the union of heaven and earth, underlies all of our ancient stone sites right here in Britain. It is all a sort of a *sacred engineering* that has been practiced all over the world and was laid out at the time before the sinking of Atlantis.

"Those Old Ones, they really knew how to control the earth, the weather and all manner of things for the common good." More to himself than to me, he said, "It's a real pity the old knowledge has all but died out." He stopped himself and seemed to reconsider what he had just said. "But you mark my words, it's all coming back. What goes around comes around, and those who try to stop it shall pay dearly." He nodded several times, looking proud of himself for adding that last piece.

He tapped the book one more time before returning it, along with the other two books and the old charts, to the shelf of the hidden bookcase. After that he slid the huge front bookcase back into place and relocked the various locks.

Who is he locking the book away from…certainly not from Tina or his wife?

"Just to be safe," he said, patting the bookcase. "Now remember, not a word to my daughter! Tina is very conservative in her thinking, and we don't want her worrying about her old dad who's gone round the bend, now do we? I'll make sure to give you some lists and maps in the morning, private-like, before you leave. They will mark out the most important sites I think you should see. And yes, they're all related to Atlantis. Just don't you tell Tina where you got these maps! Agreed?"

"Agreed," I answered, following his conspiratorial tone. "But can you tell me something about Atlantis?"

"What I can tell you won't be nearly as good as what you can experience for yourself at the sites." Then, opening the office door, he led me into the sitting room. "Make yourself comfortable," he said, motioning to a large armchair by the fireplace. He walked over to a bookcase on the other side of the room and selected a magazine. "Tina and the little woman should be back in a few minutes. This will keep you interested in the meantime. Some scientists have recently discovered three buried pyramids in Bosnia. They are bigger than the ones you saw in Egypt. Of course, there are those who don't want this information to get out," he said, shaking the magazine, "but you can see, it has." He dropped the magazine in my lap and disappeared back into his office. I heard him whistling as he closed the door.

After I got comfortable in the huge chair, I opened the magazine, looked at the pictures and started to read the article. He was right! Although scientists had clearly concluded that these were man-made structures hidden under mountains of earth, there were other people who firmly declared they were natural mounds. *That's ridiculous!* I looked at the pictures again. Anybody can see they're not natural. I read a bit more but couldn't concentrate. I closed the magazine, put it on the coffee table and curled up in the old chair. My mind was buzzing. *How could her father know all of those things straight out of the diary? Where could he have gotten those old maps? And, how in the world did he know I was, specifically, interested in Atlantis?*

Of course, I had no answers to those questions, but Tina was certainly right about her father, he was a character! She would have been shocked – but a promise was a promise. If that was the way he wanted it, then that was the way would be. *But I'm sure glad he's going to give me some maps and a list of sites in the morning. Guess I don't have to worry now about not having had time to do my own "proper" research. What he's going to give me will be much better than anything I could have found myself.* I closed my eyes, still marveling at our conversation. A few moments later, true to her father's words, Tina and her mother came in chattering about the neighbors. I joined them for tea and biscuits, and then we were off to bed.

* * * * * * * * * * * *

In the morning, while Tina and her mum were in the kitchen cleaning up from breakfast, her father pulled me aside. After making sure no one could see us, he pulled out a manila envelope from under his vest and handed it to me. "Here's the lists I promised you, but remember…."

"Don't worry," I replied, as I took it from him and put it in my tote bag along with the many snacks from Tina's mother.

"Well, I guess we're ready to go," Tina called, emerging from the kitchen. "Want to go over our maps one last time?"

"Come on ladies, time's a wasting," called out her father's booming voice. We need to pick up the rental car before they give it away to someone else."

"But Dad," we're just going over our itinerary," Tina called back.

"You can do that once you have the car. I promised the kind gentleman at the car rental agency that I'd have you there by ten o'clock sharp, and it's already ten thirty," he said, knocking something over as his great body moved through the narrow hallway. Tina rolled her eyes as she always did in certain situations, especially those involving her father.

"Okay," she said reluctantly, knowing she didn't have a chance of convincing him of anything once he'd made up his mind.

So off we went, Tina and I in the back seat, her mum and dad in the front. Once we arrived, her father insisted on paying for our rental car. The paperwork was handled quickly, and we went out to the yard to select our car. Tina and I gathered our luggage while her dad went inside with the agent to get the car keys.

"Do you think I should get more maps?" asked Tina.

"Absolutely! Local maps have more detail." Tina went back to the office while her mum and I finished organizing the car. She and her dad were back in a matter of moments with the rental papers, maps and car keys. We said our thanks and goodbyes. I gave her mum a big hug and thanked her again. "Now Tina," she called out over my head, "You make sure this one eats those snacks I packed. The two of you are much too skinny."

"Don't worry, I will," Tina said, laughing. As we pulled out of the rental agency, Tina at the wheel, I turned to wave one more time. Tina's father shouted, "Cheerio," and winked at me. I waved again – then froze. In and amongst the trees behind Tina's father's waving arms I saw the tall shadow of a man dressed in dark clothing walking through the woodland area. *Dear God... please don't let it be John!* I grabbed instinctively for my camera case then remembered that I didn't have the diary with me anymore.

A moment later the man cleared the trees, and I saw a flash of his face. *Is it John?* I couldn't be sure. I felt completely immobilized. I careened around to get a better look, but the man had already turned and was walking in the opposite direction.

If the man I'd seen was John, then it would make sense that Tina's father had hidden and locked away all of his "special" books and maps. Her father became more mysterious than ever. He knew information straight out of the diary, had the same maps as the Atlantean priests, knew I was looking for information on Atlantis – and he might also have known about John.

CHAPTER 42

As Tina drove toward our first destination, I pulled myself together. *There's no point in freaking Tina out...and absolutely no point in freaking myself out either!* I put my mind elsewhere, and reached for one of the books I had brought and a spiral notepad containing some hastily scribbled information. I slid the manila envelope from her father under the small pile on my lap. I briefly read my notes, looked at a few pages in the book then opened the envelope. It was not at all what I expected. There was one page that looked like a Xerox of the sheet with all of the lines and circles placed over the whole of the British Isles, but it had been so reduced in size from the original that the writing on it was illegible. All of Ireland was so blocked up I couldn't make out any of it.

I pulled out the second page, which was just a long list, in alphabetical order, of names of various sites in the British Isles along with their locations. It started with *Avebury,* and ended with *Stonehenge.* Next to some of the names was a short description of the site. That was it. *What a disappointment! How odd!* I went back to my spiral pad, noting that most of the names on her father's list were also on mine. *Hmmm.*

"What's the matter?" asked Tina, noticing my expression.

"Nothing! I just hate looking at maps."

This is ridiculous! He didn't tell me anything new. With all his knowledge, I thought her father would be more helpful. I should have done my homework. How was this possibly going to help me to find out anything about Atlantis – or David?

I put on a good face and we headed north.

The countryside was beautiful, and Tina was driving, so I tried to decipher more of my notes and the maps. In my brief research I had discovered that there were over five hundred stone rings in the British Isles and that they were called "rings" not "circles," because very few of them were true circles. By late afternoon we reached the first site, Swinside, in the county of Cumbria, which was also on her father's list. Although we had asked for directions to the site we still had to hike around a bit to find it, but once we spotted it we were delighted.

Located in the middle of nowhere, Swinside was a small, charming, well-preserved stone ring surrounded by farmland. Since this was the first ring I had ever seen, I had nothing to compare it with. All I could think of was that it seemed very tranquil. Inside of the ring were three sheep. One appeared to be napping and the other two grazing. Tina and I shooed them out so I could get a pristine shot of the ring surrounded by the lush countryside and billowing clouds.

"Let's go inside and see what it feels like," suggested Tina, as I began sorting through my camera bag. I put my equipment down and we walked in through one of the two entrances formed where stones had fallen down. "It's a little different…kinda quiet and peaceful in here," she said standing next to me. I nodded. Then I noticed something strange – a little bump.

"Did you feel that?" I asked.

"Feel what?"

"Nothing, it was probably just my imagination. I guess I should set up and take a few shots," I sighed, strangely uninspired.

I put the camera on a tripod and took a few shots. The site was storybook beautiful, but I wondered why her father thought I should see this particular site.

"Cassie, is this the kind of place you would do a ritual?"

"Well…yes, I think it could be."

"Great! Can we do one…or could you? I mean, you know more about all this than I do."

"Absolutely," I answered, and we both stepped back inside the ring. I was a bit self-conscious, but I took her hands in mine. "Let's see…. Okay, I think we should both close our eyes and take a few deep slow breaths." Thinking of the diary – and Tina's father's maps – I said, "Imagine that we are standing on a spot where two lines of energy cross. Imagine those lines spreading out across the countryside and see the grass becoming even more green, more healthy." I felt another bump and my eyes flew open. I shot a glance at Tina, but her eyes were still closed and a slight smile curled at the corners of her lips.

Obviously she hadn't noticed anything unusual. I shut my eyes again. This time I saw the lines spreading out from under us. But instead of smooth, straight lines, I saw thin, tight, little lines that looked like they were about to crack and wither away. Then a few images flew madly before my closed eyes. The last was awful. It was that of a mother standing fear-stricken as a mud-streaked soldier with a semi-automatic rifle ripped a screaming child from her arms. Again my eyes flew open, but all I saw was beautiful lush countryside surrounding us.

Tina must have felt my body jerk, because she opened her eyes as well.

"What's the matter?" she asked.

My heart was pounding. "I'm not sure. I saw something very strange."

"What do you mean, *strange?*" That was Tina, always full of questions – always wanting answers.

"I'm not sure, but I think I'd like to leave."

"You do? I thought we could have a little picnic here. I'm starving and me Mum gave us an enourmous basket of snacks. She thinks you're much too thin. Big surprise!"

"If you don't mind, I'd like to go. We can picnic at the next place. It's not too far away."

"Okay," she said, looking longingly at the ground. I could tell she was ready to sit right down and eat exactly where we were.

"Yes...I'd really like to go. The next place is very close."

As we began to leave the site, I saw a small patch of very brown grass. *I didn't notice that before.* Then I saw something lying on the dying grass, glinting mirror-like in the sun. I walked over and picked it up. It was a thin piece of some kind of metal, rectangular in shape. And it was hot – much hotter than it would have been from just sitting in the sun. The side that had been lying face-up on the grass looked like mirror-glass. I turned it over and my breath caught in my throat. The other side was engraved with exactly the same image as John's tattoo. It was small, but distinct – a black Celtic cross with an open circle in its center and a black slash of lightning running across it.

He's been here! I spun around, ready for a fight but praying I wouldn't see him. He was not there but the object was still locked in my hand – and pulsating.

My heart beat even faster, and fear began to moisten my forehead and upper lip. I dropped the thing and watched as it scorched the green grass where it landed. I was panting and wiped my brow with the back of my hand. *What should I do? What can I do?*

Then I remembered what had been written in the diary about choice, "We always have a choice." I slowed my breathing. *If we are all connected the way the diary says we are, it's possible I've found this thing for a reason. Besides, if I go into fear and panic, I am helping to spread fear just by feeling it.* I certainly didn't want to do that – it would just empower the Forces of Darkness. I calmed down, but the question remained, *What...what should I do? I have no idea how this thing works. If I leave it here it might destroy the place and this entire part of the grid. If I take it with me, it could blow up and kill us!*

Suddenly a snippet of memory flashed through my mind – something so minute that I had only seen it out of the corner of my eye. It was in Egypt the second day of the trip, when we were at Karnak Temple in Luxor. I was following Gabriel and the group when I saw him reach down for something sparkling in the sun. He picked it up, examined it, frowned deeply, then wrapped it in a cotton handkerchief and put it in a metal container. The only reason I remembered it was because I'm always keeping an eye open for special things, like beautiful shells or stones. I looked around but hadn't seen anything worth picking up. But he could have found one of the same strange objects and known how to block the power of whatever it was.

"Tina, do you have your Wipe-Its with you?"" I called out, sounding much more urgent than I had meant to.

Still inside the stone ring, she looked up startled. "Why? Did you cut yourself?"

"No...um...it's just something that I need."

"I have them in here somewhere," she answered, walking toward me while searching in her backpack. "Here you go," she said, handing me a square of moistened towel.

"Thanks, that'll do it. I'll take two." She handed me another one. I doubled them over and used them to pick up the object. "That's great! You wouldn't happen to have an almost empty mint tin, would you?"

"Of course I do. I so love those mints. They keep my breath fresh," she laughed, giving out a particularly long exhale. She dropped the remaining mints in her mouth and handed me the tin.

I laughed with her – and with relief – as I put the object wrapped in Wipe-Its in the tin, and the tin in my camera case. I felt reassured, though I had no idea if my little scheme would protect me from anything. And I couldn't even begin to guess what that *anything* might be.

I quickly packed up my camera gear and we left the site.

"Tina, I have a great idea" I said, as we walked to the car. "I think we should find a nice inn for the evening, and I'll treat for dinner!"

"No! I think you should save your money. I'll pay for myself."

"No, I insist!"

CHAPTER 43

The next morning dawned bright and sunny, but it seemed to have turned to fall over night and there was a definite chill in the air. After a hearty breakfast, we were on our way to Castlerigg, thought to be one of the oldest stone rings in Great Britain. I had taken the little mint tin holding the object I had found and put it in the trunk of the car, or as Tina called it, the *boot*.

Who knew what effect that thing might have on my cameras or film – or on us, for that matter. *But, I refuse to worry about it. That's just what John would want me to do...worry about it.*

We drove a few short miles before coming upon a small sign that read *Castlerigg*. It was easily accessible from the road, so there was no tromping around in deep grasses this time. Once we got out of the car and moved closer, I could see that the ring was oval in shape and had an entrance marked by two slightly larger stones. The scene was beautiful, with puffy clouds hanging over us like spun cotton candy and the mountains of the Lake District in the background.

As we approached the site, my eyes searched the ground, going back and forth like windshield wipers. I was on the lookout for anything unusual, most particularly for anything shiny. I was very relieved when I did not find anything but green-green grass spreading out for what seemed like miles. I walked the perimeter of the site looking carefully for brown patches or any kind of disruption. Everything looked – and felt – wonderful.

I put my camera gear on the soft lush grass and entered the ring. A slight breeze blew against my neck, and I could almost hear the silence. I looked around for Tina and saw her bending over and picking something up. My heart began to race.

"What is it Tina? What have you found?" I called out anxiously.

She straightened up and started to move toward me. "It's a tiny, tiny wildflower...I don't think I've ever seen one quite like it." She walked inside the circle and held it out to me. "See!"

"Yes, it's lovely," I said, my heartbeat returning to normal. *This place looks so peaceful...so pure. I may not be learning anything about Atlantis, but the last two days have showed me that I don't want to live my life in fear. I've done that long enough.* "Tina, let's do another ritual...in honor of all things small and beautiful."

"I'd love to," she answered, almost dancing in place. I had never been as aware of Tina's childlike quality as I was on this trip. She was so successful and productive in her business life, yet she managed to retain a childlike sense of wonder. *I don't remember ever being that free.* And certainly, with everything I had been going through, I felt more responsibility every day. But strangely enough, for the first time in my life, I really did feel in charge. Not the way I used to – not in charge of the outside world. The change was in my inside world – how I felt. And I realized how empowering that new feeling was. I had something else that was new – a sense of foreknowledge. I didn't know when – or how – but I absolutely knew I would find David!

I reached for Tina's hands and we both closed our eyes. This time I easily saw the lines running underneath where we stood, and they were strong and pulsating with life. I had the strangest sensation, as if we were standing atop the veins of the planet and making them stronger just by standing there. *Is it possible?*

We opened our eyes at the same time. "Mmmm, Cassie, that was really wonderful." I agreed and we stood together, hand and hand, relishing the moment – and the mood. A flock of squawking birds broke the spell, and I got busy setting up my shot. It only took a few clicks, nothing fancy, and I was done.

We were silent as we walked toward the car. Tina started the engine while I pulled out the map and my various notes. "Okay, on to Scotland! Our next site is only about half an hour away." I showed her the map with the next spot clearly marked, and she began to drive.

I continued to study the map and my notes, along with the pages from her father. It appeared that after our next stop we would be driving all the way up to Inverness in the far north of Scotland. From there, we could fly to the Orkney Islands, come back, and then go to the Isle of Lewis in the Outer Hebrides. *Why did her father pick these particular sites. There are so many to choose from, and I just don't get how all of this relates to Atlantis.* I sighed as I remembered my "foreknowledge" and the object I'd found stuffed into Tina's mint case. I wondered what, if anything, I should do with it. For all I knew, it was a time bomb waiting to go off at any moment. Or, maybe I was just making a big deal about nothing!

Thirty-five minutes later we were at our next destination, Croft Moraig. This stone ring site was just off the road on what seemed to be private land. We walked through a little gate, making sure to close it behind us. We could see a house very close by and realized that we could be trespassing and might even be asked to leave, so we decided to move fast.

Croft Moraig was a very different sort of place than the two stone rings we had already visited. It was older, rougher and much more elemental. "Here's the information I have," I said, reading from one of my books, "The original ring, perhaps five thousand years ago, consisted of fourteen wooden posts set in an egg-shape. Later the posts were replaced by eight stones of graded height…." I looked around. *This is ridiculous…who cares!* I closed the book.

"Well, now there seems to be twelve stones, and it looks like it's on a raised platform. My notes don't tell us much. I think we should just be quiet and see how it feels."

We each took our turn around and inside the ring. Of course, I kept my eyes open for anomalies, like metal objects – and John. Fortunately there were none, but as I stood in the ring's center, I experienced a distinct sense of power. I had the sensation of seeing a lightening flash from the inside out – just like I had when looking at the filmstrips from Tiahuanaco. It was the same, but milder, and passed more quickly.

Neither Tina nor I spoke, but we indicated to each other that we'd had enough. It never occurred to me to do any kind of ritual, and I guess the same was true for Tina. The site lacked the coherence of the earlier rings, so it was not an easy place to photograph. I had to shuffle around, here and there, until I found an angle I thought captured the energy of the place. I took the pictures and we hurried to the car.

"That was kind of a strange place," Tina said in a somber voice.

"What do you mean?" I asked. I knew what I had sensed, but I was curious to hear what she had to say.

"Well, I don't know exactly, kind of rough and ancient feeling. And besides, I'm freezing."

"Yeah, me too," I said. "It's odd, but each of these places has a feel and a mood all its own. And they're all so different than any of the sites in Peru and Bolivia, or Egypt, for that matter."

"Do you think it's because the land in different parts of the world is so different? I mean, if the landscape is so different, I guess the energy must be different, too."

"By George, I think you've hit on something, my girl," I said with exaggeration, wanting to lighten the mood. As soon as we got to the car, Tina opened the trunk so we could get at our suitcases – and some warmer clothes.

CHAPTER 44

We spent the next two days glued to the seats of our car, continually heading north toward Inverness. Although it seemed to get a little colder with each passing mile, the scenery was beautiful. There were green rolling hills, rocky crags and many lakes. Aside from a couple of quick meals, we only made two stops. The first was at a castle Tina wanted to see. The second was at Edinburgh where we spent a couple of hours wandering around the old city.

It was probably the most beautiful city I had ever been in. The streets were steeped in history, it had a thriving cultural scene, and, of course, Scotland's most famous castle dominated the skyline. Tina insisted we take the tour of this castle as well. The high point for me, however, was finding a small trendy restaurant that served great cappuccinos. It was the first real coffee I'd had on the trip. I drank it slowly, savoring each drop, but I also kept looking closely at every face. *There's no way to know where I'll find David.* Then I thought, with some distraction – or John.

Toward the end of the second afternoon, it began to drizzle. It was so cold that both of us had on every layer of clothing we had brought. When we got out of the car to stretch our legs, we had to put on our foul weather gear.

"Gosh," Tina remarked, "I had no idea the weather up here got so bad this early in the year." And that pretty much summed it up – it was cold and wet, and we had not brought warm enough clothing.

We made it to Inverness by late afternoon and got out to look at Loch Ness. We didn't see any monster and hurried back into the car. While we were searching for lodgings, we came upon a quaint little general store and we each bought an extra large down vest to put over our California-weight parkas. Before long, we found a small hotel, had a warm dinner, kept on our long underwear and went to bed chilled to the bone.

During the night, I had an intense dream that was similar to the one I'd had after my return from Peru. It was like tuning into a very bad news program, seeing one disaster scene after another. There were bombings, murder, rape –

just about every inhumane act one person or group could do to another. I also saw scenes that looked remarkably like what had happened in Tiberias, when the man fell down and the ambulances came, only now it was happening all over the world and people were raving mad.

I tossed and turned, helpless to do anything but watch the scenes unfold. Just before I awoke, I saw David's face flash by and I called out for help. Then I saw an image of John. He was laughing, and his distorted face grew wildly larger until I was afraid it would smother me. When I woke up, the words, *See how you like what comes next,* were ringing in my ears.

Just as after my earlier dream, and despite the freezing-cold room, I found myself drenched in sweat. Okay, so what was it with John and all of those horrible events? I kept dreaming, and feeling, that he was in some way connected to them. *Is he somehow responsible for those awful things in the world or this illness that was making people mentally deranged? What could he have meant by "See how you like what comes next?"* I thought back to the diary. It would have been helpful to have it here to refer to, but I was so glad it was someplace where he couldn't get at it.

I just wish I could find David. It looks like John and his men are winning... something. I felt frustrated and alone.

I looked at Tina, but she was still sleeping, her long blond hair fanning out from her face like little angel wings. Good! I didn't want her to question me about anything. Then I thought about the "thing" I stuffed into her mint tin. *I will not be a victim here! There have to be answers, and I need to find them!* I got up feeling a bit worn but determined, took a not-very-warm shower and dressed.

Gradually Tina began to stir. "You're awake," she said, leaning on one elbow and yawning.

"Yeah, I didn't sleep very well."

"Is anything the matter?" she asked, stretching. "You look awful!"

"Thanks a lot," I said, trying to smile. "I'm just tired...and cold."

"Me, too, it's *freeeezing* in here," she said, pulling the blankets tightly around her.

"I hate to say it, but if we're going to do this, we have to get to the tourist office early."

About half an hour later, over hot porridge and lukewarm tea, Tina and I talked about our plans. "You know," Tina said tentatively, "I never expected it to be so cold."

"Neither did I."

"I don't think I can make it to both the Orkney Islands and the Isle of Lewis. It's just too cold."

"I was kind of thinking the same thing," I said with a shiver. I pulled out all of my notes and selected my original note pad. "I guess the best choice would be to go to the Orkney Islands. I think they're closer, and it looks like they have at least three ancient sites. The Ring of Brodgar, the Standing Stones of Stennes and a chambered tomb, Maes Howe, are all on Orkney. Are you up to it?"

"Well I…I guess I am if you are. I mean, we're already here. It would be a shame to have tortured ourselves for nothing."

"It sure would!" I pulled out the sheets from her father and saw that the Orkney Islands were not even on his list. *That's weird, I'm sure they were on this list when I looked at it before.*

After breakfast, I gathered my information and we headed for the car. Tina was walking unusually slowly, and I noticed that she was not looking too well, herself. Her eyes were glazed and her body was beginning to shake. "Are you alright?" I asked, as we settled into the car.

"Well, I'm not sure. I just can't seem to warm up, even with this new vest," she said, turning on the ignition.

I leaned over and touched her forehead. It was very warm. "I think you're running a fever. Do you feel like you might be?"

"I'm too cold to tell," she answered, sounding a bit wan.

"Tina, you need to be honest with me. Should we put you on a train back to your parent's house? I can do this alone. It's just some silly photographs."

"Give me a few minutes. Let's get over to the tourist office. When I warm up, I'll probably be fine. And your photographs are not silly, they're wonderful," she said, with the best smile she could pull off. In that moment I knew exactly why she was my best friend.

The rain had started up again, but once inside the tourist office, I was relieved about one thing. I would be able to get a detailed map to the three sites we want to go to. I looked at the part of the bulletin board that listed transportation to both places but didn't see anything listed for that day.

I went up to the counter. "I think we would like to fly to the Orkney Islands today, however I didn't see anything listed."

"Sorry, lass. No flights until tomorrow."

Tina groaned.

"What about the Isle of Lewis?" I asked.

"Well now," said the man. "The Isle of Lewis....Yep, you could take the four o'clock ferry from Ullapool. It's quite a drive and the weather doesn't look like it's going to get any better, but if you leave soon, you could just make it. You can buy your ferry ticket from me and use the phone over there," he said, pointing to the opposite wall. "It's for making your reservations. You can book your hotel in Stornaway."

"Stornaway?"

"Aye, that's the little town you'll be staying in on the Isle of Lewis. As a matter of fact, it's the only town there. 'Tis a wee island, you know."

"I'm...uh...give me a minute," I said, stepping away from the counter. I looked again at my notes. *He's right, it is the only town and there's only one site there,* The Standing Stones of Callanish. I scanned my notes for information on the site, but could not find any. I sat down and looked everything over again. *That's strange! I didn't notice it before, but Callanish is starred on Tina's father's list, and of course, Orkney isn't even there. Not my first choice, but I guess we're on our way to the Isle of Lewis.*

Tina sat huddled in a chair. Her teeth chattering and her face flushed. I went over and felt her forehead again. "Tina, I think it would be stupid for you to even try and go anyplace else, especially someplace that's even colder than where we are now. You need to go home and go to bed."

She looked at me, a mixture of misery and disappointment flooding her face. She nodded and whispered, "I'm so sorry...."

I hushed her, blew her a kiss and went back to the man at the ticket counter. "My friend here is not feeling too well and needs to go back to her family. Is there a train that goes to Kent?"

"There's a train that that goes from here to Edinburgh. She could change trains there and go directly to London. Her people could pick her up there."

I conferred with Tina who was looking sicker by the minute.

We called her parents and told them she had come down with a virus – nothing serious – but since it was so cold where we were, she was better off at home.

"Don't worry about me," I lied. "I'll be fine. It's not like I'm in some strange foreign country where I don't speak the language. Besides, what will make me the happiest is knowing you're warm and comfy and that your mum is taking care of you."

"Okay, but you can't wait for my train. You have to leave right now or you'll never make it."

Fortunately, the train to Edinburgh was scheduled to arrive within the hour. I made a sleeper car reservation for both that train and the connecting one. They were well coordinated with very little wait time in-between. When the man behind the counter realized how sick Tina was, he assured me he would personally see to it that both she and her luggage got on the train. *It's really the best thing to do. She'll get there faster by train then if I drove her myself…and she'll certainly be warmer.*

I was at the phone about to book my hotel in Stornaway when the man from the ticket counter tapped me on the shoulder. "It might be better, lass, if you waited until tomorrow. I just got a bulletin and the weather will only be getting worse in the direction you're heading."

"No," I snapped back. "I'm going!" Nothing was going to stop me! I was angry! Angry at John and my dream, angry that Tina was sick, angry at the weather – angry at the whole damn thing! I booked my lodgings in Stornaway, got my tickets, made an apology to the ticket man, said my good-byes to Tina and drove off into the pouring rain.

I tried to tell myself I was not afraid, but it wasn't true. Not only was it pouring and freezing, I was exhausted and had to drive on the goddamn "wrong side of the road." And I had no flipping idea where I was even going. *I bet John has something to do with all of this, even the weather, but I will not let him win!*

The drive was horrible and it took five hours, hours during which I tried very hard not to think, but my mind had a life of its own. Many times I had to pull to the side of the road – the wrong side – because sheets of water completely blocked my vision. I was amazed that I didn't have at least a dozen accidents.

I made it to Ullapool just in time to drive onto the waiting ferry. It was a bumpy two-hour ride. Several times I thought I would lose my lunch, except that I hadn't had any lunch. The lounge area was heated but stuffy and smelled of rancid food. Occasionally I would go outside for air, but the sharp wind and icicle-like rain pounded my face and body, and I was forced back inside. *I must be insane. I don't even know why I am going. This has nothing to do with Atlantis… nothing to do with David or anything else I am remotely interested in.* I had made the plans with Tina when we were both warm and in a playful mood. It had sounded like an exciting adventure for two friends to take, but now it makes no sense at all. *Why do I feel compelled to do it?*

Although it was dark and still raining, I was relieved when I finally arrived in Stornaway. Fortunately, the town was truly small, and I easily found the little old hotel. The check-in counter was located just opposite the front door, and an old radio was turned on to a news channel discussing the "horrible new disease" that appeared to be circling the world. *Thank god, Tina just has a simple virus, no nausea or vomiting.* As I walked through the hallway to my room, I passed the open doors of rooms that were vacant. The place was as basic as it could get, probably built for fishermen and sailors. The musty little room had a small chest, a straight-backed chair and a single twin bed. I went directly to bed wondering how I was going to take pictures of the site the next day. *Please… please let the rain stop by morning.*

CHAPTER 45

S till wearing my foul weather gear, water dripping off it onto the stone floor of a teashop, I stood in front of the large window and stared out at the giant standing stones of Callanish – and the pouring rain. My body was quiet, but my mind raced. *This is ridiculous! What if I had thought...? If only I had listened! But, thought of what? Listened to whom?* Even Tina's father and his lists were no help. He had said I would learn things about Atlantis, but I hadn't. *Now I'm in this god-forsaken place, it's pouring rain, and...*

"Welcome to the Isle of Lewis, dearie. And I must say, you do look a bit worse for the wear. Wouldn't you like to sit yourself down by the fire? You could take off those wet clothes. And I dare say you'd be wanting a nice hot cup of tea, now wouldn't you?"

The heavy Scottish brogue snapped me out of my reverie. I looked around and met the warm hazel eyes of a sturdy, round-faced woman busily drying her hands on a gingham apron. Her gray hair was pulled back in a tight bun at the nape of her neck, stray wisps brushing against her pink, apple-cheeked face.

"Come along now, lassie." I didn't protest. I followed as she gently led me over to a rocking chair beside a crackling fire. "You can take off those wet things and set them to dry while I fetch your tea." I plunked down my camera case and began pulling off my rain parka. In a moment she was back with a tray sporting a china teapot, two cups and some shortbread cookies.

"Me name is Mary and this is me teashop," she said cheerily, her eyes crinkling up in a smile.

"Um, thank you. I'm pleased to meet you. I'm Cassie, Cassandra actually," I said, absentmindedly shaking her extended hand.

I glanced down at the teapot then back out at the rain and heaved a deep involuntary sigh.

"Mind if I join you for a bit, lassie? It would do me good to sit myself down for a spell."

"No...I mean, yes, that would be lovely."

She looked at my camera case. "Spent a long time looking out the window at those standing stones didn't you? There's certainly is a lot of rain coming down on them. I see you've got your camera there. You're probably thinking you picked a terrible day for picture taking, aren't you?"

"I don't think it, I know it."

"Now, don't be fretting yourself. The sun may come out for a bit yet. It often does. But the stones do look quite remarkable, even in the rain, don't you think?"

"Yes, they certainly do. It's just that I've come so far and I have to leave in a few hours."

"I understand. We have a lot of rain around these parts, and sometimes this little shop is filled to the brim with folks from all parts of the world. They come here to see the sacred stones, to photograph them, and to learn from them. Some people even say the ancient stones speak, that they have a message they want to tell the world."

"A message?" I perked up at that bit of news. "For everyone?"

"Aye, they do. But not everyone will be getting it. Many folks only come to visit because this place is unique, famous you might say. Others come here looking for something, listening for something."

"Listening?"

"Yes indeed! Legend has it that those old stones lie dormant, waiting for just those special ones to come and carry their stories to the people." Then Mary leaned toward me, and even though there was no one else in the shop, she lowered her voice. "Between you and me, truth be told, I think the stones call out to those special ones."

This last comment took me completely off guard. My mind stopped drifting and I snapped to full attention. *Whatever does she mean by that? It sounds a bit like the diary.*

"Do you really believe that?" I asked, trying to keep my voice calm.

"Don't you?"

"I, well…I've never thought about stones in that way. But then, this is one of those days I'm not too sure about much of anything," I said, forcing a smile.

"Sometimes that's a good thing. Keeps you open-minded."

"Open-minded?" I had to laugh despite myself. "Are you saying that sometimes it's *better not to know?* That's certainly a different way of looking at things."

"Aye! And that's what most people need, a different way of looking at things. It opens them up to new ideas."

This was turning into an interesting conversation. I looked at the woman closely to see if she might be mocking me, but the kindness in her face was unmistakable. Then I noticed her eyes. They were warm with understanding, yet there was something else in them – something I could not quite put my finger on.

"So, me lassie, tell me what brought you here to our wee little island?"

"That's a very good question, but I can't say I have a good answer." I hesitated, not knowing where to begin. "It's a long story. Other people may come to see the stones for one reason or another, but the truth is, right now I have no idea why I'm here. It just sort of happened. I was traveling with a friend and photographing some of the old stone sites. She got sick, and this was the next place on the list so I just continued on by myself."

"Hmm, now why is that?"

There was something about this Mary, something so comforting that, although I did not mean to do it, I found myself telling her about Tina and our last four days. "Actually I didn't have much of a choice about coming here. We were either going to Orkney or here, but there was no flight to the Orkneys yesterday. So, without thinking about it, I decided to come here...because of the schedule. Sounds crazy doesn't it, coming all the way up here in such terrible weather for no particular reason."

"Ah, but that's where you're wrong, lassie. There always is a reason."

"There is?"

"Aye, there is and that reason is always in your service. It sounds to me that you've been guided here, and whether you knew it or not, you followed that guidance."

"Funny you should say that. My friend's father made me a list of sites to see in England and Scotland. He's a bit of a stone site aficionado." *And a little more than that,* I thought, remembering the hidden bookcase and just how much information he had given me. "Anyway, I was sure that both the Isle of Lewis and Orkney were on his list when I first read it. But when I looked again yesterday morning, Orkney wasn't even on his list, and this place had a star next to it. Kind of spooky! Do you think that's *guidance?* Trust me, stranger things than that have happened in my life lately!"

"Yes, dearie, I would definitely say you've been guided. There's so many people coming here looking for something. Some of them know what they're looking for, and some of them don't. It don't much matter what they know. They find it one way or another."

"They do?"

"You bet, dearie. And they've not been having the guidance in life you've had."

Now she really had my attention. "You just met me, yet you think I've been getting guidance in life?"

"Indeed, I do. And, that's why you're here. As a matter of fact, I've been waiting for you. Glad you finally made it, love."

What a bizarre statement!

Before I could put together a question, the bells on the door handle jangled, and two men, covered from head to toe in shiny yellow rain gear, walked in. One was tall, blond, bearded and appeared to be in his late forties or early fifties. The other was about average height with a medium build, shiny black hair and eyes, and seemed to be somewhat younger.

"Excuse me, love. I need to give a package to these nice gentlemen here."

Mary smiled and stood up to greet them.

"Carlos," she said, talking to the man with the black hair, "you and your friend take off your wet things and come warm yourselves by the fire. Meet me new friend, Cassandra. She's come to visit the stones."

"Is my pleasure, Señorita Cassandra," Carlos said, nodding to me, a twinkle in his eye. He turned back to Mary. "Ah María, *no hay tiempo,* we have no time this day," he said, taking off his gloves and grasping her hands, his heavy Spanish accent rolling over each word. "The others, they are waiting for us. But *un momento* by the fire *estaría muy bien. Hace mucho frío,* is very cold!"

"Alright, love. I'll be right back," Mary said, disappearing through a flower-curtained doorway, which must have led to the back of the teashop.

The blond man briefly nodded at me as he went over to the window and looked outside. Carlos walked to the fireplace. I could see the contours of his face softened in the firelight. His dark straight hair was pulled back into a short ponytail, and his skin was a burnished golden brown. He had a broad face with high cheekbones, but did not look like anybody I had ever seen before. He was certainly did not look like a local, but clearly he was not a tourist either. I was intrigued by face. He resembled a Mayan statue I had seen in a magazine.

Rubbing his hands together, he turned and looked at me. *"Una amiga de Señora María* is a friend to me also."

"Gracias. Carlos," I answered, smiling. *He's certainly charming.*

"Hablas Español?"

"Hablo un poco, a little bit," I said, forming a very small space between my forefinger and thumb.

Carlos laughed. He had a beautiful smile. "Well, *Señorita,* the weather, she seems to be changing. *Hace mucho frío pero es possible que el sol,* the sun, he may be out before the day is gone."

"That's wonderful news, Carlos. You have no idea how badly I need to hear some good news right now."

"Gracias Señorita," he said, making a small bow. "Always happy to be of service to such a beautiful woman."

He's flirting with me! I could feel my face redden, and my hand automatically reached up to smooth my hair. "Thank you," I said, a bit self-conscious.

The other man turned and looked at me, but I could not tell if he had been listening to our conversation or not.

Mary reappeared, a small parcel wrapped in brown paper and tied with a string in one hand, and a larger, heavier-looking shopping bag in the other.

"I've the package you're wanting Carlos," she called out, setting it on a small table by the front door and placing the larger bag on the floor beside it. "And I've packed up some nice cookies and a thermos of hot tea for the others."

"Ah, Señora María, *gracias. Símpatica* as always." Then looking back at me he said, "Señorita Cassandra, *mi hermana,* pleased to make your acquaintance. I hope you enjoy the rest of your trip." Both men walked toward the door. The blond man nodded again, caught my eye and bowed deeply. Carlos put on his gloves, collected his packages and both men were quickly out the door.

"What strange men. Carlos was very friendly, but the other one.... Even though he didn't say a word, he filled up the room in a way I can't explain. But why did Carlos call me *mi hermana,* 'my sister'?"

"You're right about the other man. I've known him for a long time, and no one can quite explain him, lassie. He is a most, most unusual person. As to why Carolos called you 'my sister,' I will explain that in a little while. We have so many things to talk about. But first, love, take a look outside. It's stopped raining!"

"It has?" I turned and looked out of the window. I was shocked. Only moments before it was gushing but now puffy white clouds filled a rich blue sky. "Yes!" was all I could say as I jumped into my parka and boots, grabbed my cameras and bolted out the door.

Once outside, I carefully made my way through puddles of muddy water. Set against the rugged terrain, the sanding stones were magnificent – and powerful. My breath caught in my throat as I approached them. I walked slowly amongst the weathered giants. The air bristled with a kind of electricity. I experienced a tingle of excitement and knew the magic and mystery of being in the presence of something much larger than my understanding. I stood motionless, needing a few moments to just "be" with the stones. After a time, the site begged to be photographed. I took some incredible shots. Then, as rapidly as the storm clouds had cleared, they reappeared.

The downpour resumed the moment I reached the covered porch of the teashop, but I was not ready to go inside. I still wanted to look at the standing stones. *I guess I am meant to be here – these are the most powerful standing stones I've felt yet. I wonder what they are trying to tell me?*

A cold shiver propelled me back inside, and I hurried to the comfort of the rocking chair and the roaring fire. I was in awe of what I had experienced, but I had not forgotten Mary's last line, "I've been waiting for you." I was still thinking about it all when she came back out from behind the curtains.

"You're right Mary, the stones are amazing, absolutely amazing. I could definitely feel them."

"Aye, and that's what keeps folks coming back here," she said, putting a warm shawl over my shoulders. "Thought you might like a bit of cozying up after taking your pictures."

"Thank you. That's very kind." I turned to face her. "Mary, what did you mean when you said you've been waiting for me?"

"Well dearie, as I said, we've lots to talk about. Let me just put my soup pot on the stove, and I'll be right back out." Then she patted me on the shoulders. "You just keep yourself warm and comfy for a few minutes."

CHAPTER 46

I settled back in the rocking chair and closed my eyes. Mary's words kept running through my mind. "There's so many people come here looking for something," she'd said. "Some of them know what there're looking for, and some of them don't. It doesn't matter what they know. They find it one way or another." But her most mysterious words were, "I've been waiting for you."

A strange excitement surged through my body. *Is it possible this woman might actually have some answers for me?* The heat of the fire made me drowsy. I fell into the midst of a bad dream. Flashing images of David awakened me. My eyes flew open. I was disorientated.

Mary had tiptoed in and was placing a tray on the side table. "Shhh, dearie," she said. "Everything is just fine."

"But I...have I been asleep?"

"Yes dearie, for about an hour. You needed the rest."

"But...."

"No buts," she said, handing me an old wooden tray laden with a steaming bowl of soup and some hot biscuits. "Eat this, love. It'll warm your bones."

"Um! It smells delicious." I took a few sips. "This is warming much more than my bones, Mary." I ate with zeal. I had not realized how hungry I was.

"Alright now," she said, sitting down in the rocking chair beside mine. "The question is where to begin?" She closed her eyes for a moment. "Okay, I see," she said to herself. Then she opened her eyes and looked directly into mine.

"You need to know, my dear Cassandra, the world has been waiting for you. You have a special mission here in this life, and it will affect everyone on earth. Everything up till now, right from the moment you were born, has had a purpose to it and has been leading to this mission." The tone of her voice had changed. It was still warm, but it was also very matter-of-fact. "The planet is in deep trouble, and you are the one who can save it."

"What! What are you talking about? I can't save the world."

"I know lassie, that's what you're thinking now. But truth be told, that's your destiny... it's what you were born to do."

Destiny! Born to do! Her words hung in the air. An odd feeling engulfed me and my body seemed to jump. *David! The diary! David was born to do something special, not me! I don't want any part of anything like that. I don't know if she's crazy or what, but I'm not going to hang around to find out.*

I painted a smile on my face and said, "Thank you so much for the soup, Mary. You've been very kind, but I do need to get going." As I got up, I reached for my parka and boots, quickly packed up my cameras and shot toward the door.

My hand had just touched the doorknob when I heard Mary say, "I know all about your childhood and about the beautiful lady who visited you at night."

I froze – rigid as the standing stones just a few feet outside the door.

"She told you that you were special, remember?"

My mind turned inward, searching for a faded memory. "I...I.... It wasn't real.... It didn't really...."

"That's not so, lassie. It wasn't a dream. It did happen."

How could she know that? This is too creepy. I've got to get myself out of here.

"Where are you going to run to get away from the truth?"

I turned slightly, my hand still on the doorknob. "Aren't you looking for some answers, dearie?" Mary asked. I gave a small nod. "Well then, why don't you come back in here and sit for a spell. I promise you can leave anytime you want to."

A part of me wanted to hear what Mary would say – but a bigger part of me didn't. *She's right, I do want answers. And if I leave now, I may never get them.* That tipped the scale, and I cautiously went back to the rocking chair in front of the still roaring fire.

"I'm proud of you, lassie. You've got spunk! Now, just how much do you remember about the beautiful lady?"

My mind raced backward, trying to recover what I had worked so hard to forget. It was all so vague.

"I know, love, you've spent your entire life pushing down all that's inside you, but you don't have to be doing that anymore. Truth is, you never should have had to in the first place, but it couldn't be helped. The timing wasn't right.

"The beautiful lady told you then that you had certain gifts and that you were special…and you are. But your mother was afraid for you. You see, dearie, your mother had her own special gifts as well, but they frightened her. So when she saw what you could do, like the time you were making that pencil move about in the schoolroom, she had to stop you. She was very harsh with you, dearie, shut you down, you might say. Both of your parents did. It was their way of trying to protect you. Like every parent, they thought they knew what was best for you. They wanted you to fit in with life and be successful. But they only knew the world by their standards, their definition. They had no idea who you really were or what you came here to do."

Images and conversations came rushing back. I heard Mary's words. They were words I had yearned for as a child. *But now, now…? I don't know if I want to hear these words now! As a child, all I wanted was to be understood – to be validated. But now I'm an adult. I've learned how to function and get along in the world. I don't want to stir up those old feelings and memories…*

it's too painful!

"How…how do you know all of this about me? Who are you?"

"Never you mind," Mary said, resting her hand gently on my arm. "We'll be getting to that later. We have more important things to discuss now. The reason Carlos called you mi hermana, his sister, is because in a way, you are. Surely you remember that you come from a mixed ancestry. One side of your family is Jewish and the other side Arab. But there is also Mayan that runs through those veins. Carlos knows that. However, and even more importantly dearie, you carry a very ancient lineage in your bloodline. This lineage goes back to the very beginnings of Mankind and will serve you well in the time to come."

There was a long pause. Finally, Mary leaned forward and said, "I must tell you now, love, that diary you found…the truth is…it found you. It was meant for you, and you are meant to be a part of its story. All of this is no accident."

I could see Mary's lips move, but I was hearing, "Miss, want camel ride… I show you…. My camel name Cal-E-Fornee-a…."

Mary touched my shoulder and I flinched. "Oh, uh…sorry. I was just remembering…."

"I understand. I know I've been telling you a lot but there's even more," she said gently. "You asked before about Carlos. Well, dearie, he is one of those that you read about in the diary, one of the Great Brotherhood who carry the ancient knowledge. He has chosen to live in Light and help transform our planet. But you…you were born with a different set of gifts and talents. You are one of those whose destiny it is to bring that Light into fruition."

"Me! How can you say that? All I've ever been is a photographer."

"Ah, lassie, that's what you've 'done,' *not who you are*. Truth be told, you are one of those the world has been waiting for. These are Dark Times we live in, and bad things are happening all over the planet. But it is also a time of great change, an opportunity for expansion this earth has never known before. The Light is very close. Mankind has the opportunity to change his ways and consciously evolve. That is, if he can make the choice to do so. And you have a part to play in this choice."

I was hoping to get answers about the diary, not be a part of it for god's sake! "Mary, if you would be so kind, could you please tell me how I'm supposed to help with something so huge?"

"Dearie, you'll be surprised. In fact, you've already begun. It's all about your relationship to energy. Didn't you feel something unusual when you were at one of the sites with your friend the other day?"

"Wa...what? You mean those funny bumps? But that was awful! And I saw terrible things."

"Aye lassie, you did, and it was bad. But right now, the important thing I want you to be knowing is that you can feel energy. It's something you have always been able to do, but what's essential now is for you to become aware of it. Your sensitivity to energy is one of your gifts. And it's one of the things you'll be needing in order to help Mankind with its choice. The more you're aware of this ability, the more it'll be growing. But the awareness, dearie, that's the beginning.

"And don't be forgetting how you could make that pencil move when you were just a wee child. As you remember who you truly are and open up to all your powers, well, new understandings will come to you all natural-like. Everything you need to know is right there stuffed down inside you. After a while, there'll be no end to what you can do."

"Mary, just because I have some kind of blood in my veins and could move a pencil when I was a kid and maybe...maybe I can feel some kind of energy, doesn't mean that I can solve all the problems of the world. What exactly is it that you think I'm supposed to do?"

"I'm getting to that." She faltered and stopped, as if caught up in an inner struggle. Then she sat for what seemed like a very long time, hands tightly folded in her lap. I looked deeply into her eyes. They were fathomless, but I sensed an edge of sadness in them. When she began to speak, her voice was unusually soft. "There are those who would like to take this dear planet away from us to use for their own purpose, but that purpose would serve only them. It would be very bad for everyone else. You already have some idea who our enemy is. You've seen that enemy in your dreams. You even have a sense of their power and suspect what they can do."

I was in shock, unable to utter a sound, almost unable to even think, yet I had taken in every word. Questions flew through my mind so quickly that I was hard pressed to pause long enough to catch even one. Finally I was able to blurt out the words, "John! Are you talking about John? Is he one of the enemy you're referring to?"

"Yes, he calls himself John now. That is one of his many names. He was called Carmac in the diary, in the time of Atlantis. But his agenda is still the same."

"You know about Atlantis…and David?"

"Yes dearie, I do."

"That's unbelievable! But what does it all have to do with me and where is David? Do I need to get the diary back to him? Will he remember what to do without it? How in the world am I supposed to stop John and the others? What can I…?"

"Wait a minute, slow down dearie. I knew you'd be having lots of questions. There is so much I would like to be telling you, but I simply can't because only you have the power to access those answers. In fact, that's all a part of your journey, your destiny. It's what you were born to do."

"I'm not convinced about that. But just for the sake of discussion, if I were to take on this…whatever this means, how can one person do such a thing? I mean, how can one person save the world?"

"Well, love, you won't be entirely alone. But as for your part, lassie, even if I had answers for you, it wouldn't be serving you. You need to be making that connection deep inside of yourself, becoming strong in that way. You have all of the answers right there inside of you."

That's crazy! All I have are questions inside me but she won't answer them. I have to try to get her to answer just one. I forced myself to organize my thoughts – to formulate them into one concise and intelligent question. I took a deep breath. "Mary, I want to make sure that I understand what you're telling me. Are you saying that John…that John was Carmac in Atlantis…and that he and his…associates are trying to take over the world, like they tried to do in

Atlantis?" I stopped and took another breath. "And are you saying that I have the ability to stop them?"

"Well, love, the short answer to that would be yes."

"And how exactly am I supposed to do that?"

"That's what you're going to have to uncover. All I know is, you have the power within you to do it. But, it will take a mighty focus and discipline to go inside and find that power. And it will call upon every fiber of your being to stay the course. You will have to open your mind and listen to your heart. When you do that, you will find the next clue, and the next and the next.

"Truth be told, you've already begun. In fact, you've done a mighty good job with your growing so far. You were a little slow at first, but look, you made it all the way up here to me to learn about yourself. But in the end, dearie, it's up to you. You need to be deciding whether or not you will take this on. Destiny or no destiny, we live in a free will universe, and it is you who must do the choosing."

"I...I don't know.... I can't imagine...."

"It's not in your head, lassie, it's in your knowing. If you look back, you'll discover that you've been truly led, and you always will be, because like I said, it's your destiny. Your job right now is to make the commitment, then go within and follow the clues, follow your heart, your intuition. The commitment itself will guide you, and your journey will unfold."

"Whew! That's a pretty vague answer...and a pretty big job." I said, rubbing my neck and remembering the dream about John I had two nights earlier.

"Yes dearie, it is. Just remember, it's within you to do it. If you make the choice to go forward, I can give you some starting points. But it's you, love, that has to do the work, to experience it...to become it. Why don't you just sit a spell by yourself and think on my words." Mary pulled herself up from the rocking chair, reached for the old wooden tray and walked through the curtains and into the back of the teashop.

CHAPTER 47

I sat gazing at the fire, watching the wood turn into flames and the flames dance before my eyes. Many things passed through my mind – how I had chosen to become a photographer in the first place, how I spontaneously decided to move to Los Angeles and how I had managed to get the money for the trips to Peru and England. I also remembered Jean Luc calling me about the Egyptian trip with Gabriel. I had certainly not wanted to go, but then I found the diary. Reading it, along with listening to Gabriel's lessons, had acted upon my very soul. *And David! Dear David!* I couldn't deny my heartfelt connection to him – since the moment I first saw his face that day at the travel agency.

Leaning back in the rocking chair, I remembered the dream I'd had in Egypt, the same dream that David had. In that dream I made a choice. David had made the same choice in his dream. Even then, I knew it was a choice to lead a different kind of life – a non-ordinary one. I sat bolt-upright. *She's right! I am already a part of this story!*

The diary was clear about Mankind needing to evolve – to make the choice to live in love and interconnection. So many terrible things were happening in the world, the constant wars, greed, poisoning of the planet and the food supply, and now the spread of this new and horrible disease. It felt as though the world was falling apart. Somebody had to do something! If John and his henchmen were in some way responsible, and if I truly had the power to stop them, I had to do – I didn't know what – but something. I owed it to myself, to the rest of the world, and to the evolutionary process itself, to say yes.

Mary must have somehow realized that I had made my decision, because she chose that moment to come back in through the curtains.

"I guess you know I've already decided to do it."

"That I do, lassie. So now I'll be giving you some tips to help you get started. First you need to understand that, as you move along on your path, there will be things that will make you question yourself, even deny who you are, but that's just a part of the journey. In fact, it's precisely what John will be wanting you to do – doubt yourself and become immobilized. But time is critical, and you can't be wasting it on foolish doubts. There's too much at stake.

"Now, do you remember the way the beautiful lady taught you to slow yourself down and focus your mind so that you could move small objects about?"

"Yes, I remember, more or less."

"Well, that's exactly what you're being called on to do. The only difference is that now it has to become a way of life. In order to access your true power, you have to be in charge of time. And to do that, you need to be in charge of your thoughts, to slow your thoughts way down. That's so you can pick the thoughts that serve you and toss the others away. You must slow things down so much that you move into the real rhythm of life…the cosmic rhythm. Once you do that you will see things that other people can't. That's how you spotted the *talisman* when you were at the stone site with your friend."

"The *what?*"

"The talisman you have in the tin box in the back of your car."

"That metal thing! Is that what you call it?"

"Yes. While you were doing your ritual, your mind slowed down and you were able to see it plain as day. In order to do that all the time, you need to develop a consciousness about your breathing that is so automatic that even when you're under great stress your breathing stays slow and deep. It's what will help to keep you planted in the present. That's where you have to be, dearie, because that's the only place you have any power…in the present. When you're in the present, you start to notice little things that give you clues about what to do next.

"Why don't you go out and get your tin? Go now, while the rain's not coming down quite so hard."

I tossed my rain parka over my head, ran out and was back in no time. I was so relieved to give the talisman to Mary. "I've been concerned about this thing since I found it. In fact, this talisman, had already turned a patch of grass completely brown. And while I was doing my ritual with Tina, I could see the lines beneath the site withering. Do you think it did some real damage?"

"It might have. That's what makes your job so important." Mary took the talisman out of the tin, unwrapped it and turned it over a few times in her hand. "You see, love," said Mary with a laugh, "John never should have left this behind. It's just the kind of thing that will foul him up. He's arrogant! They all are. That's their weakness. It makes them take foolish chances and make sloppy choices. They are that way because they're operating from their egos. That's all they have, lassie.

"You however realize, or you'll be coming to realize, that you're connected to everyone and everything. That's the source of your power, and a great power it is. Carmac, or John as he now calls himself, doesn't have that. He's long since forgotten his connection. All he and his people understand is 'power over,' and that's not nearly as strong. It's artificial power. It only works by intimidation and stealing away other people's power. He does have his mind, which is not to be underestimated. He's harnessed that greatly. But, nonetheless, that's all he has. A highly developed intellect gives him, and others like him, a false sense of power, it does. But it's a limited power.

"He left the talisman on the grass to frighten you, but he didn't take into account the resources you already have. In spite of all the odds, you pulled yourself together, stepped right over the obstacles he put in your way and came up here all on your own. You know dearie, he never expected that," she said, with a kind of pride. "His arrogance made him underestimate you, but you can use it to your advantage. Now that we have his talisman, we can use it against him. Come with me."

Fascinated, I followed her through the flower-print curtains and found myself in a beautifully kept, old-fashioned kitchen with a lovely wooden dining set. A pot-bellied stove warmed the room. Mary placed the talisman on the table and went over to an antique cupboard that still bore traces of hand-painted flowers.

"What a beautiful cabinet."

"Thank you," she said, touching the hand-painted flowers lovingly, "It was me great-grandmother's. We don't throw things away like you do in the States. We pass them down through the family. Now it's me turn."

"If more people did things this way, our planet wouldn't be in such a mess."

"Aye lassie," Mary sighed, "it's true." She opened the cabinet doors and pulled out a crystal that she called a "wand," because of its elongated shape. It was as long as my hand, about an inch around, and was pointed on one of its ends.

"This crystal is an activator crystal and can be programmed by thought. It's a very handy little tool. Now look closely and watch what I'm about to do."

She made a few passes over the talisman with the point of the crystal. Her eyes were closed and her lips moved slowly, though I couldn't hear the words she said. Finally, a small wisp of smoke rose from the talisman.

"Done," she said.

"What did you do?" I asked, feeling like a child at a magic show.

"I used my thoughts to deactivate and reprogram it. Since it already had his energy signature, you'll now be able to see John and track his movements anytime you need to."

She pulled out a dining chair and told me to sit down and make myself comfortable. Then she told me to close my eyes and keep them closed until I had slowed my breath and heartbeat way down. It took a few minutes. Once I felt relaxed enough, I opened my eyes. Mary was holding the little talisman before me, the side with the engraving of John's tattoo staring me in the face. When she turned it over, I could see that the other side, the side that had looked like mirror-glass, now looked like a small television set. John's image appeared. I couldn't tell where he was, but I distinctly saw him sitting at a counter drinking a mug of beer. Mary said, "Off!" and the image vanished.

"It's for you to use, but you have to tell it what you want."

I looked at her, not understanding what she meant. "When you're wanting to see John," Mary explained, "ask to see him. If you want to see him more clearly, say *closer*. If you want to see what's going on around him, say *further*. Tell it what you want, but do it forcefully and really mean it. Here, you do it."

"I want to see John!" His image immediately appeared. "Further!" Sure enough, like a camera pulling back, I could see John sitting in a bar with men on either side of him. "Closer! Closer!" I said in my most commanding voice. The image moved in so close, I could see he pores on his face.

"You can also say, *go left or go right*, which means to your left or your right," she said, walking back to her cupboard and reaching up high for a wicker basket. She pulled out a small pouch with a drawstring top and narrow leather cord, and replaced the basket.

Mary said, "Off!" and the image disappeared. She put the talisman into the small pouch and gently placed the cord around my neck. With a note of warning in her voice she said, "Don't be using it to check on John every five minutes. That would be abusing it, and it'll stop working. Use it only when you absolutely need to. And…always keep it close to you. It'll protect you, you'll see!"

I was excited but apprehensive as I tentatively reached up and touched it. "And for Lord's sake, don't be nervous, it's just a tool," she chuckled.

"Mary, what did you say when you closed your eyes?"

"You don't need to know that now. You'll be learning all those things when it's your time to."

"You sure you're not a witch?" I asked, only half jokingly.

"Dearie, what I am would take far too long to explain, and it isn't the right time for that" anyway. She took my arm as she led me out through the curtains and back into the teashop. "My goodness! Look how the time has flown! You'd be needing to rush to make the late ferry, so why don't you just spend the night here. I've plenty of room and I'd love the company. Besides… look," she said, pointing to the window, "your sun is out again. Wouldn't you rather be spending your time with the stones?" It didn't take much persuasion for me to agree to stay.

For the second time that day, the view through the window took my breath away. In a moment, I was back outdoors looking at the magnificent site through the lens of my camera – only this time it was completely different. The way the light diffused through the clouds almost made it look like a completely different place. I snapped away, unable to believe what an extraordinary photographic opportunity I was being given. Within the span of a few short hours, I had captured many days worth of images – images so diverse and magnificent I was awed.

Suddenly I felt a blast of energy and experienced the familiar flash of lightening from the inside out. This time I was not afraid or surprised – I understood. My body and mind opened to it. I absolutely knew it was the energy of the site acting directly upon me. It was as though I could, literally, see it altering my DNA. My body grew taller, my entire self grew larger, and my will grew stronger. I was fortified and fed. It was a magnificent moment, and I savored every second of it.

I wanted to stay there longer, but the rain soon returned, and I made a hasty retreat. Back inside, feeling warm and cozy once again, I sat staring at the fire and thinking about the stones – and about what Mary had said about John only a few minutes earlier.

Mary came back through the curtains and sat down beside me. "Mary, I'm so glad you're here. Just now, while I was out there among the stones, I felt something strange. It's happened a few times before. The first time it scared me to death, but this time it felt great. It's hard to describe, but it's like seeing lightening from the inside out. What exactly is happening to me?"

"You're being activated, dearie. It's a good thing, and your job right now is to allow yourself to be guided to the next place you need to be for it to happen again. And you'll be getting more powerful all the time, now that you're connecting with the energy of the sacred sites. Each time it happens, you will get a new piece of the puzzle. In time, all the information will come together and make sense, and you'll know exactly what you need to do and how you need to do it."

I couldn't resist. "Do I need to find David? Is the diary true?"

"You'll be finding out all about David when it's your time, but if you keep obsessing about him now, you won't be able to experience what you need to experience. As for the diary, yes love, it's true…and that's all the discussing for today. It's getting late, and I best be getting supper on. I've plenty of leftovers just waiting to be warmed up, so don't you worry about helping me. You just sit a spell, and I'll call you when everything's ready."

I leaned back in the rocking chair and closed my eyes, replaying images of the standing stones in the various lights. I must have drifted off, because I was startled when I heard Mary's voice calling, "Come on back, supper's on."

The little kitchen was warm and inviting. A flowered cloth covered the table and candles sparkled in copper candlesticks. Steam was coming from big bowls of delicious-smelling stew, and crusty fresh bread had come right out of the oven.

"Mary, thank you so…"

"No, no," she interrupted, "it's me should be thanking you. I would be eating me dinner alone otherwise."

Although I couldn't get Mary to say another word about my "mission," she kept me laughing with stories about people who had come into her little teashop through the years. "Yes indeed, there's been a lot of rain dripping on this floor, lassie, there has," she chuckled. "My word! Look at the time. You're such good company, you are, but I'd best be getting my tired old bones to bed. I have to be up early for me baking. Come on, dearie, I'll show you to your room."

Mary led me up the narrow stairway and into a small cozy room with a peaked ceiling and a dormer window. An old sewing-machine table was used as a nightstand, and twin beds were piled high with quilts. "I'm sure you'll be warm enough, dearie, and the bathroom's right across the hall. I'll leave the light on for you. It's always nice to be able to see where you're going in a strange house. Do you need anything before I go?"

"No, everything looks perfect. I can't thank you enough."

"It's nothing, love. And you sleep in as long as you want. You've a lot of driving to do. Don't be getting up just because you hear me. Night now, love."

"Good night, Mary. See you in the morning." The last thing I remembered as I snuggled under the down comforters was a sudden flash of lighting – real lightening – followed by a long rumble of thunder.

* * * * * * * * * * *

I awoke to the aroma of coffee, freshly baked goodies – and sunshine. The heat from downstairs had moved up and made taking a shower a pleasure. The wonderful smells increased as I put on my clothes and hurried downstairs.

"I remembered how much you Americans like your coffee, so I uncovered a tin I had hidden away and made this just for you," Mary said, putting a coffeepot and a mug on the dining table. "Sit yourself down and have your coffee while I finish me baking."

"That's so thoughtful Mary," I said, sitting down, pouring the coffee and savoring the taste.

"What will you be having with your coffee, dearie?"

"Well Mary, you know I still have more questions, like *will I ever meet David* and…but I guess answers aren't on the menu this morning, are they?"

"No love, they're not," said Mary, chuckling, "but that was a good try. How about a nice blueberry muffin instead? Just help yourself. I have an almond coffee cake and some orange muffins, too. They're my favorite."

"Then that's what I'll have," I said, walking to the counter covered with trays of cookies, muffins and tarts. "Mmmm, it's hard to choose, but I think I'll stick with your favorite." Mary was right. The muffin was light, flavorful and thoroughly delicious.

"Thank you! This is the best muffin I've ever tasted. Do you make this much every day?"

"My goodness no, but today's going to be a busy day! It's the first clear one we've had all week, so there's going to be lots of tourists coming through that door, don't you know. That's why I love this old stove," she said, "it's got two big ovens, and I can keep them busy when I need to."

The bells on the door of the teashop jangled, and we could hear a group of people enter. Mary quickly pulled the coffee cake and last batch of muffins from the oven and put them on the counter to cool. "Excuse me, dearie, I need to get these finished trays out for me new customers." Mary picked up two trays and started out through the flowered curtains to greet the newcomers.

"Let me help you," I said, as I picked up two more and followed her into the teashop.

"Thank you, dearie. I'm glad for that bit of help, but you'd best be getting on your way. You've a lot of miles to travel and don't be forgetting that ferry schedule."

I was reluctant to go, but now that I understood what I needed to do, resolve pushed me forward. I headed upstairs, gathered my belongings and was soon back down in the teashop. "Mary, I'm going to put my things in the car and spend a few minutes with the stones before I go."

"You do that, love. I'll make you up a packet of goodies to take on the road as soon as I've helped these people."

On my way outside, I passed Mary's new customers and heard one of them say, "The last time I was here, I was lucky enough to see the rising of the Pleiades right over those stones."

The Pleiades! Where had I heard that name before? Of course, in the diary! It was the place where some of the Galactic Visitors, including David's teacher, were from. *I almost feel like I've been living in the diary and now, in some ways, I guess I am!* I put my things into the "boot" of the car and once more became mesmerized by the power of the giant standing stones.

I had no idea how much time I'd spent with the stones before Mary called out to me. As promised, she was carrying a large bag of pastries. "Mary, I hate to leave. It seems like I've known you forever." I looked at her pink, apple-cheeked face framed by stray wisps of gray hair. The warmth and kindness were still there, but there was something else – something in her eyes – something familiar. "Mary, how am I going…?"

"I'll be with you lassie, don't you know. All you have to do is think of old Mary, and I'll be there. And they'll be others along the way that will be helping you as well, like your friend's father. He's one of the Brotherhood, too! His 'appearing' and 'disappearing' directions helped make sure you'd get here." Mary chucked. "See, I told you that you've been guided. And love, you always will be, because what you're doing, it's needed. It's your destiny.

"The most important thing for you to do is to remember that, no matter how impossible things seem, you have a mighty powerful power. And it will be growing all the time. I suspect you're still not sure how to summon it, but just knowing that it's there gives you a place to start.

"But, I'll tell you this, dearie, when in doubt, open your mind and listen to your heart. It will always steer you in the right direction and…." Stopping in mid-sentence, she groaned, "Wouldn't you just know it, there's even more people a-coming."

"Mary, before I leave I really need to find out how you've learned all these things about me...and the diary...and what I have to do...and everything."

"Let's just say I have my own connections to the Brotherhood, love. And that's it for now!" Then with hugs and goodbyes, I left Mary and the little teashop and headed off in my rental car, her words ringing in my ears, "I have my own connection to the Brotherhood...."

I headed toward Stornaway where I would catch the early afternoon ferry back to the mainland. So much had shifted inside of me, it was hard to believe that I had only met Mary Yesterday morning.

CHAPTER 48

I spent the first part of the ferry ride sitting quietly, allowing everything to sink in. The rain had stopped and it wasn't quite so cold, but the water was dark and choppy and the waves as hypnotic as the fire had been. I was changed in a way that was hard to describe. Something in me had settled down – settled *in*. I felt a deep connection with that child I had been before my parents had "shut me down" as Mary had put it. And although it was still a bit unclear, that inner relationship gave me a new sense of certainty – of power. I also understood that, for now at least, I could let go of my need to find David.

About half way along, I pulled out my materials. I looked back and forth between my notes, the list of sites and the maps, trying to plot a course that covered everything, but I was just making myself crazy. Then I remembered what Mary had said about being in charge of my thoughts, of slowing them down so that I could feel what I needed to do. It wasn't easy, but by the time we reached the mainland, I could sense the next places calling. I was going back to England, first to Glastonbury then on to Stonehenge. *I can't tell why I'm supposed to go to Glastonbury, but I'm sure there's a reason. Perhaps I'm going to be activated.* As for Stonehenge – well, I needed to be with those stones!

CHAPTER 49

It took almost three days of driving, on the wrong side of the road, to reach Glastonbury. Although the scenery was beautiful, the drive was slow. It had taken longer than expected, and I became anxious. From time to time, my hand reached up to touch the talisman.

I made a few stops, but I could easily tell that none of them were "my spots." I had made a reservation at a bed and breakfast in Glastonbury and easily found it. The owners were a couple by the name of Moseley. It was the wife, Kathryn, who greeted me warmly and showed me to my room.

There was a quality to the light in Glastonbury that lent an aura of mystery and magic to the place, so even though it was already late afternoon and I was tired, I decided to roam around the town a bit. I especially wanted to see the ruins of Glastonbury Abbey because all three of my books had mentioned it. The Abbey was very old and legends abound that tell of its colorful history.

One of the books said the real King Arthur was buried there. It also said there was a line of energy that ran from the Abby directly to Stonehenge. By the time I reached the Abbey, the sky was awash with the pinkish gold that precedes sunset. I was sorry I hadn't thought to bring my camera. Although it was not one of the ancient stone sites that held my fascination, it was nonetheless quite awe-inspiring.

I wonder if I can find the line to Stonehenge? Standing directly in front of the Abby, I took a long breath and slowed my breathing. I went deep inside and focused on feeling the energy. My mind kept wandering, but I kept bringing it back. Time and again, I focused on the energy, but I still couldn't feel anything.

I remembered the general direction of Stonehenge, so I slowly crossed the Abbey grounds and positioned myself in that area. *Nothing!* I moved to the right – *nothing. This is ridiculous! I can't...!* But I was determined, so I moved a little more to the right. Still nothing!

Wait a minute, if I could do those "tricks" as a kid, if I had that power then, I should certainly be able to do this now. I took several big steps to the left and – *was that something?* I thought I felt a slight pulsation beneath one foot. I took another small step to the left. Nothing! I stepped back and felt it again. Tentatively, I walked a few steps forward – it was still there. A bit more confident, I walked a little further. The pulsation was stronger – undeniably stronger. *That's it! I can't believe it! I've found the line. Mary was right, I do have a gift.* I had no idea what I was going to do with it, but I now believed what she'd told me.

My stomach started to growl, and I realized I hadn't eaten in hours. Kathryn had told me there was a vegetarian restaurant nearby, and the town was so small I had no trouble finding it. I chose something simple and quick to prepare, however it seemed to take forever. I leaned back in the chair at my little corner table and let fatigue overtake me.

"Veggie garden burger?" I heard the young waitress call out. She looked as frazzled as I had been earlier dealing with the right hand driving.

"Over here," I called back, waving my hand.

"Oh, I say," she said, carefully putting my plate in the center of the check-ered placemat, "Sorry it took so long. The cook's new and it's only my second night so things have gotten frightfully backed up."

"That's alright."

"You American, then?"

"Yes, yes I am."

"Ah, just visiting, then?"

"Yes."

"You'll have a smashing time figuring out all of the legends."

"Well, that's not why I'm here. I have been photographing some of the old stone sites, all the way up to Scotland, and now I'm heading back down again toward Cornwall. Do you have any idea how far it is to Stonehenge?"

"Not far. Why, are you planning to photograph there as well?"

"Yes, I am."

"Through the chain-link enclosure?"

"What chain-link enclosure?" Now I was fully awake and alert.

"You don't know about it then, do you?"

"No! A fence? Around Stonehenge? How could…?"

"Can't say...they just did it. You see the English Heritage was quite worried that the stones might come loose, due to the rock concerts and all."

"What rock concerts?"

"Well, the hippies in the seventies and then others, even up until...well... not so long ago, had rock concerts there. Lots of people dancing and such! The Heritage was quite afraid the stones might come loose with all the pounding, so they put a fence around it. Now you have to view it through the fence, and it's only open to tourists at certain hours of the day. And not every day, to be sure."

"Oh, no!"

"Oh, yes, I'm afraid so. Oops, I'd better get back to the kitchen before things start piling up again!"

I sat there in a bit of a quandary, staring at my veggie gardenburger and green salad. I decided to have it packed to go. I had some thinking to do.

Okay so what am I going to do now? I have to get inside! I need to be right in amongst the stones...to feel them. I had to photograph them as well, and there was no way I could do either of those things through a chain-link fence.

I made my way back to the Bed and Breakfast, went directly up the stairs into my little room and shut the door. Too tired to unpack, or even undress, I crawled onto the bed, stretched out flat on my back and closed my eyes. I must have lain like that for hours, not quite awake, but not really asleep either.

Somewhere in those hours, I felt a realignment take place inside of me and knew I would get inside the fence. I had no idea how it would come to pass – only that it would. The image of myself inside the enclosure at Stonehenge, being with the stones and photographing away, floated across the screen of my consciousness. It was so real I dropped down into a deep and dreamless sleep, a smile curling at the corners of my lips.

The next morning, I awoke feeling amazingly energetic. I washed and dressed quickly so as not to miss breakfast. Midway down the stairs I remembered the conversation with the waitress and felt myself begin to sink. *Wait! I know better! I absolutely cannot give into doubt and fear.* I decided to spare myself the drama and "chose" to trust. Good girl, I thought as I happily continued down the stairs and into the dining room.

Seven or eight people were sitting at a long wooden table in the brightly lit room. There was a cacophony of sound. American English, British English, as well as German and another language I could not quite make out, all mingled together with the pinging of forks and knives against china plates and the clinking of teacups as they touched down on their saucers. It was a very lively scene. I helped myself to some tea and scones off the sidebar and sat down in the empty seat toward one end of the table.

"Hi, I'm Jeff from Portland, Oregon, good old U.S. of A.," said the cheery-faced sandy-haired young man on my left. "And this is Helga and Peter from Munich," he continued, pointing to the older couple across the table from me. They nodded. "And this is Karin from Sweden," he said, indicating the woman on his left. "Now, let's see," he said, pointing across the table again to the women seated next to the German couple. "Over there, we have Janette and Anne from Liverpool. Or is it Anne and Janette?" They all laughed. "And I'm sorry, I must have forgotten your name," he said, looking at the man next to Karin.

"He's joking with you. I'm his uncle George and this is my daughter Mary Louise," he said, indicating the teenage girl at the foot of the table. "We're both from Oxford," he said, in clipped tones.

"Well, I'm Cassandra, but you can just call me Cassie. I'm very happy to meet all of you, but I'm afraid I'll never remember your names."

"Not to worry Cassie," said Jeff. "I was just practicing to see if I did. I didn't mean to overwhelm you. I do that sometimes."

"No, that's alright. I'm terrible at names. Faces I'm great at, but names, forget it!"

"You're American," said Jeff, "I'm glad. I get so bloody tired of all these accents."

"Jeff doesn't seem to realize that he's one of the people with an accent here," said his Uncle George. "You're in England now Jeff, remember?"

Jeff laughed, looked at me and said, "I bet I can guess exactly where you're from!"

"Young Jeff here is our local psychic," said George, shaking his head.

"You're from California, aren't you?" asked Jeff.

"Yes, I am."

"Los Angeles, California?"

"Is it that obvious?" I garbled with food in my mouth. "I'm from West Hollywood, but that's close enough. I'm impressed."

"I knew it, didn't I George? I was just saying that what we need at this table is someone from Los Angeles, home of fruits and nuts!"

"I guess I qualify as nuts," I said, washing down my bite of scone with a sip of tea and trying not to choke with laughter.

"See, I told you, Jeff is our local psychic," said George.

"I'm sorry. I can be a bit much at times," Jeff confided, but I've been here the longest, so I've taken to introducing the new people as they arrive. I guess I've become the official 'meeter and greeter.' I'm chatty, but harmless."

"No, it's fine. It was just a lot all at once."

Jeff and I talked throughout breakfast. He almost had me rolling on the floor with his dry sense of humor. He told me that, "seriously," he was in England trying to research his family's lineage. He had traced them to a small town in the North of England where they had resided for generations. In fact, he still had distant relatives there on his father's side. George, it turned out, was his uncle on his mother's side.

"We even have a coat of arms," he stated, with some pride. "But that's enough about me. What are you doing here?"

"Well, that's a tender subject at the moment," I said, taking a deep breath. "I've been traveling around photographing some of the old stone sites. I had planned to go from here to the Salisbury Plain and photograph Stonehenge, and then on to some of the other sites. But, I found out last night that they've built a chain-link fence around Stonehenge. That's sure going to make for some pretty crumby shots."

"Gee, that's too bad. Can't you get permission or something to go inside?"

"Your guess is as good as mine. I'd have no idea who to get permission from."

Our conversation was interrupted when our hostess came in to make an announcement. "Excuse me, ladies and gentlemen. This morning our own local scholar, Bradley Jamison, will lead a tour of the ancient mystical places in and around Glastonbury. He is the owner of one of our local bookstores that specializes in books related to the area. The tour will leave at ten o'clock, which is in about forty-five minutes. If anyone is interested, come see me in the front parlor at the end of the hall."

A tour of old mystical places…! Hmm…he just might have some information for me. "Want to go?" I asked Jeff.

"Thanks, but I've already been, and I have some calls I need to make."

"I think I'll go. I need something to take my mind off of that god-awful fence. I refuse to stress out over photographing one more sacred site…even if it is Stonehenge."

"Good idea," said Jeff. "You will probably enjoy the tour."

"I think you're right," I said, as I turned and shook his hand. "I've enjoyed this morning. It was great fun talking with you. I'll see you later." At last, with goodbyes to the group, I got up and headed off in search of our hostess.

CHAPTER 50

Bradley Jamison was a fascinating, erudite tour guide who held us enthralled with tales of earth magic and fairy kings. In a few short hours he managed to weave together many of the myths and legends surrounding ancient Glastonbury. Although the Glastonbury area did not have stone sites, it had clearly been experienced – since time immemorial – as a sacred landscape.

One of the most intriguing places we visited was Glastonbury Tor, a conical hill with a mediaeval tower on top. Over time, the Tor had been honored as a place of great power and mystery. Although it was a natural hill, at some point in its misty past, a winding labyrinth had been carved into its earthen sides, spiraling all the way up from base to peak.

Bradley explained that the labyrinth followed two lines of earth energy – one that had been perceived as masculine and the other as feminine – until they met and interpenetrated, or mated, at the summit. The top of the hill was thought to pull in energy from the heavens, and at one time a stone ring or single standing stone may have stood atop it. But those stones had ceased to exist long before the building of the church, whose tower still stood in relatively good condition. Walking the Tor's snaking labyrinth, a pilgrim would come into a deep attunement with the energies, both terrestrial and celestial, that it held.

Our guide told us that in ancient times parts of the area adjacent to Glastonbury were covered by an inland sea. That would have made the Tor and other hills around it islands. He painted a picture of pilgrims tying their boats at the shore of the Tor before ascending its height. He also said that visitors, to this day, related stories of seeing balls of light surrounding the Tor at night.

Bradley went more deeply into the Arthurian legends, and the story of Joseph of Arimathea and the Holy Grail, things I had read about in one of my books. It was a very fulfilling – and confirming – four hours. By the time the tour ended, Bradley had created a spirit of enchantment that was as palpable and alive as the air I breathed or the beating of my own heart.

When I arrived back at the Mosley's in the afternoon, I was greeted by our host, Gerald Moseley.

"Are you the photographer from the U.S.?"

"Yes."

"Would you mind stepping into my study for a moment?"

"No, of course not." *What in the world could he want?*

I followed him into the wood paneled study. He led me toward an overstuffed leather guest chair and took his place behind a large antique desk.

"I understand you are a well known photographer in the U.S. and are presently writing a book about the sacred sites of England and Scotland. Additionally, it has come to my attention that you need permission to go inside the enclosure at Stonehenge in order to obtain your photographs."

"Well, I...."

"No, no, you needn't worry yourself about it. Jeffrey told me about your little problem. He said that you were unaware of the necessity of making proper arrangements. I hope you won't mind, but I've taken it upon myself to contact the English Heritage, and they've given permission for you to enter the site tomorrow morning. However, you must be out of there before eight thirty when it opens to the public. If you need more time, you can return to the site after it officially closes at five thirty. Now, Jeffrey tells me he will be accompanying you as your assistant. Is that correct?"

"Well, I...yes, that's correct." I had to work hard to keep from bursting into laughter.

Mr. Moseley reached for a piece of paper. He jotted a note and handed it to me. "Here is the name of the gentleman at the Heritage," he said, pushing back horn-rimmed glasses. "Your name should be at the gate, but if you have any problems just tell them to ring up this number. Now, is there anything else I can do for you?"

"Not a thing. I'm very grateful. Thank you so much," I said, trying to sound like someone important – someone used to receiving this kind of attention.

Mr. Moseley walked me to the door of his office. "Thank you again Mr. Mo...."

"No, please call me Gerald, and it was my pleasure," he said, extending his hand.

I shook it and, with as much grace as I could muster, turned and left the study. I could hardly wait to get to the privacy of my own room. As I approached the stairway, I heard a soft "psssst" from above. I looked up and saw Jeff at the top of the stairs. I almost ran up the steps to meet him.

"Ready to go to Stonehenge tomorrow morning?" he asked, a sheepish grin on his face.

"Jeff, how in the world...?"

"Say not another word," he said chuckling, his smile wide and wonderful. "I know a damsel in distress when I see one. Besides, I've always wanted to go inside Stonehenge, so I think that it is I who must thank you."

"Okay, so we get to thank each other!"

"Jolly good. Now that that's settled, let's go out for a walk," Jeff said, taking my arm. "I'll show you the local pub and we can have 'a spot of tea,' as the Brits say."

"Let me get my jacket, and I'll meet you out front."

Moments later, we were headed down the High Street to the pub. We sat down and Jeff ordered the usual round of tea and biscuits, which I finally understood to mean not a biscuit at all, but any type of cookies or little cakes.

I shook my head. "I still can't believe you managed to get Mr. Moseley to call the English Heritage for me."

"Are you referring to the selfish bit of maneuvering I performed this morning?"

"Whatever you choose to call it, I have to tell you, it was pure magic to me. You're one more example for my thick head to understand…it's true that life can be easy! I haven't always believed that."

"Hmm! Did you used to think things had to be all that difficult?"

"Absolutely!"

"What changed your mind?"

"Well, my friend. As the saying goes…it's a long story."

"Great! I have no place to be," Jeff said, with a glint in his eye. "But seriously, I've learned that things can be as easy or as difficult as we imagine them to be. I think it's a choice. It might sound simplistic," he continued, pouring us both more tea, "but I believe we create how our life is by the way we think about it. I mean our thoughts do matter."

"Hmmm…I think you're absolutely right." *That's exactly what I did at the Abbey last night. When I changed my thoughts about what I could do, and I found the line of energy.*

"In that case, are you ready to hear the next important thing I've learned?"

"I certainly am."

"Well, now this may sound silly, but I've found that when we're ready to learn something the opportunity appears right in front of our nose…if we're paying attention, that is!"

"You know, I've been learning that, too." *And you wouldn't believe what else I've been learning lately!* I couldn't talk about it, but it was good to be with a kindred spirit.

"By the way, did you enjoy the tour today?"

I relaxed back in my chair. "I loved it! I'm more familiar with the stone sites so this was something new for me. I especially loved the Tor and the stories surrounding it! It was clear from what Bradley said that the people who carved the labyrinth understood the energies of the earth and the way they circled up and around the Tor."

"That reminds me of something I read recently," said Jeff, leaning forward into a thinking position, elbows on the table and chin in his palms. "Let's see...." He closed his eyes and I could almost see his brain working. "Ah!" he said, leaning back in his chair, eyes wide open and shining brightly. "Now this is an exact quote: 'We are a civilization suffering from amnesia.' I think that's really true. Anyway, that's the way I felt when I was walking the labyrinth at the Tor. The very existence of the labyrinth is proof positive that in prehistoric times we were connected with the earth in ways we've now totally forgotten. I wonder what else we've forgotten?"

"Lots!" I answered, with a deep sigh. *You have no idea what a good question that is but it's not the time or place to go deeply into it.* "I think we've lost a sense of connection not only to the earth, but to the natural cycles and rhythms of life itself and that...that has altered our connection with other people...and even ourselves."

"Hmm, you're right! I guess all of those things are interrelated," said Jeff thoughtfully.

Just then the music that had been playing in the background of the pub seemed to get louder. "I can't give you anything but love, baby. That's the only thing I've plenty of, baby...." I recognized the old American standard and tried to remember who was singing it.

Jeff had stopped speaking and was listening to the music as well.

"How about a dance?" he asked, glinting again.

"Oh, Jeff," I said, laughing.

Before I knew it, he had me up on my feet and was twirling me around the pub. It happened so fast that it took my full attention to stay upright and not trip.

"Jeff, wait!"

"Why? We're the only ones here, so who cares?"

We twirled and glided around until the song ended. Still holding my hand, Jeff made a proper English bow and escorted my back to my seat.

Still holding my hand, he looked deeply into my eyes and said, "What do you think about love? I mean, as long as we're plumbing the depths here…."

"Love?" I asked, with some surprise, pulling my hand back. *Is he talking about him and me? We've only just met!*

He stared at me for a second then burst out laughing. "Now don't get nervous, I meant 'love' as a way of life."

In spite of myself, I blushed with embarrassment. "I'm not quite sure how to answer that. What exactly do you mean?"

"It's just something I've been playing with. We were talking about how we have a choice in our way of thinking and therefore, in how our life turns out. I believe it's the same way with love. It's a frequency, an energy field, and we can choose to live in it or not.

"Did you know that the opposite of love isn't hate, its fear? I think that fear is a frequency, too, and either one can become a habit…an unconscious pattern we live in. So in the end, it's all about making a conscious choice…love or fear…fear or love. It's as simple as that! I believe that as long as I'm here in this life, it's a part of my job as a human to choose to come from love. Well," he said, looking slightly embarrassed, "at least to the best of my ability."

My eyes locked on Jeff's, and I felt a deep sense of connection. In some ways it was like looking in the mirror – his eyes reminded me of my own. *Choosing love over fear! The diary was right. There are people consciously choosing to live in love…and one is sitting right in front of me. I just hope there are enough of them to heal the world.*

"Thank you," I said quietly.

"For what?" he asked, looking genuinely surprised.

"Just for being here and for being who you are."

"Well, I might say the same to you."

We both smiled, sipping our tea in silent contemplation.

"Well, young lady," he said, hesitant to break the silence. "I believe that sunrise is at about six thirty in the morning so I'm going to grab a bite of dinner here. Care to join me?"

"No, I think I'll just get a sandwich and take it back to my room. I'm pretty sure I'm going to want to go back to Stonehenge after it closes, because the light will be very different at sunset. I might as well look at my maps and plan an interesting day for us."

"Sounds good to me! I'll arrange for Mrs. Moseley to pack us a picnic lunch. And, I'll even do the driving."

"Great! Driving on the wrong side of the road makes me nuts."

"Always glad to be of service," he said, with a smart salute. I'll meet you at the bottom of the stairs at five. But you're buying the cappuccinos…and I know just the place."

CHAPTER 51

The sky was pitch black when Jeff and I got in the car and headed for Stonehenge. We drove in silence, slowly sipping our cappuccinos, my first one since Edinburgh. I closed my eyes and leaned my head back. I thought about what Jeff had said the evening before. *How often does "love as a way of life" come up in general conversation?* I thought about what Mary had said about the diary – and about me. *Egypt seems like a lifetime ago. I wonder where David is now and what he's doing. Does he know I'm here – that in some way we're connected?*

"A penny for your thoughts," said Jeff, breaking the silence.

"I wasn't thinking much, just pondering life's deeper mysteries," I said wistfully.

Then before either of us could say another word or think another thought, there was Stonehenge silhouetted in the earliest blush of morning light. It was magnificent! Jeff stopped the car and we just sat there, awestruck. After a few moments, as if on cue, we got out, divided my camera gear between us and walked toward the gate. With a mere nod from the attendant, the gate on the chain-link fence swung open, and Jeff and I were inside.

There I was, just after dawn, standing within the protective circle of the giant Megalith of Stonehenge. It was exactly as I had imagined. The energy of the place coursed through my body. I closed my eyes and felt the now-familiar lightening flash. *Oh my god! I'm being activated!*

There was a sudden moment of clarity and everything seemed completely organic – the trips to Egypt, Peru, Bolivia and Callanish, meeting Mary and now Jeff, my being inside of Stonehenge – and of course, David and the diary. I experienced my connection, not only to my life but also to life itself. In that flash I knew exactly what I was doing. Over and above everything Mary had said, I was "on assignment"– and it was not about taking photographs.

Simply by my presence, I am working with the planetary energies. As I travel from sacred site to sacred site, I am cross-pollinating the energy and help-ing to prepare the way for David. I am clearing and reconnecting the planet's Crystal Grid System. Amongst everything else, I am an "Earthweaver." As if in confirmation, I saw lines of energy instantly shoot out in various directions like lightning bolts racing across and beneath the surface of the ground. I could al-most see them stretching for miles and miles. It was extraordinary!

The moment passed and the photographer in me went to work capturing the magic of Stonehenge from every possible angle. Jeff, in silent meditation, made it his job to avoid the probing eye of my camera's lens. All too soon the guard signaled it was time to go. Jeff packed my gear while I marked the film. We saw the first tourists of the day begin to peer in at the site through the chain-link enclosure. A few pointed at us. I could almost hear their comments, "I wonder who they are? They must be important." Jeff leaned over to me and whispered, "Smile, you're a celebrity." I glanced at him with a conspira-torial grin.

The guard was waiting for us, so we hurried toward the gate. I thanked him profusely. "Will you be coming back this evening?" he asked.

"Definitely," I answered, as we made a hasty, but happy retreat.

"That was remarkable!" Jeff exclaimed, as we exited the gate.

"There are no words," I replied. *If you only knew!* "Jeff, I've been so busy shooting, I think I need a few minutes alone before we move on. Do you mind if I take a little walk."

"Of course not! I was numb in there. I have no idea how you could focus on all those pictures. Take all the time you need."

"Thanks. I won't be long...I just want...." I wandered away from the standing stones, allowing the experience to integrate inside me. I don't have to look at them. I just felt them – and so much more.

When I returned, Jeff was leaning against the fence, eyes still riveted on the giant stones. "Still amazing?" I asked.

"Yep, still amazing! And you know what else is still amazing? Some people walk up and look for thirty-six...maybe forty-two seconds, think they've seen it all and walk away. They may see the stones, but they don't experience them."

"Not everyone is as sensitive as you, my friend." I took Jeff's arm as we walked back to the car. "I'm ready for our next adventure, how about you?"

"Ready and willing...to drive that is," Jeff laughingly quipped.

The next place I wanted to visit was nearby Silbury Hill. At first glance, the site appeared to be a rather ordinary, conical shaped, large grassy hill on an otherwise completely flat plain. As at Stonehenge, there was a chain link enclosure. "I can't imagine why this hill is considered to be so special that they had to put a fence around it," questioned Jeff. "Hey look, I think there's a tour going on over there. Let's see if we can find out what this place is all about."

The guide was happy to include us, and we soon learned that Silbury Hill was Europe's largest man-made mound. It covered over five acres and was one hundred and thirty feet high. Its volume rivaled the Great Pyramids of Egypt. Legend had it that the mound was the burial site of some ancient king, however thorough excavation had never turned up a tomb. To this day, absolutely no one had any idea why Silbury Hill was created or what function it served.

After the tour, we wandered around on our own. "So," said Jeff, "in a way this hill is even more mysterious than Glastonbury Tor. That was a natural mound, this one's man-made. They had to have had some really good reason for altering the landscape so dramatically."

"I'm sure they did," I responded, taking out my camera and shooting a few frames.

"Look how high it is," Jeff marveled. "It must have been quite an observatory in its day. Imagine what you could see standing on top of it. I bet it served an important purpose. And it wasn't created overnight, either. It's gigantic."

I finished shooting and stopped to look more closely at the mound, appreciating its size. I walked a few yards to my right and felt a slight lurch in the ground beneath my feet. It was coming from the direction of Stonehenge and heading right for the mound. *I can feel the line of energy running straight through this mound. I must be standing directly on a ley line.*

Filled with unanswered questions, we drove to Avebury, a stone site about a mile away from Silbury Hill. At first glance, it too was a huge disappointment. Avebury had been largely destroyed through the centuries. The massive stones that remained stood at such a distance from one another that the site simply looked like a scattering of rocks, one giant stone here and there, with no rhyme or reason. But once we got out of the car, I felt something – something very powerful.

"Want to know what I think about this site?" Jeff asked, in his serious voice. I looked up expectantly. "I think that it looks like the perfect place for our picnic lunch. Some stone-ground crackers and a bit of cheese perhaps?"

"You funny man," I laughed, poking him in the ribs. "Sounds yummy… I'm starving!" After we finished eating, Jeff's curiosity about the place got the best of him and he went off in search of information. Before long he returned with a small booklet.

"Boy, there's a lot to learn!" Jeff mumbled, looked down at the booklet. "Do you realize that there is an entire village enclosed within the boundaries of this place?" he asked, incredulously. "I'd like to look around. Are you up for a walk?"

We followed the perimeter for some time before finally stopping to rest in the shade of a tree. I leaned my head against the rough bark and closed my eyes while Jeff's went back to his booklet.

"Wow, the whole of this site encompasses twenty-eight acres. It was originally composed of about one hundred stones, but only twenty-seven of them are still standing. That's why it's so disconnected looking. Back in the fourteenth century, Christians, wanting to 'de-paganize' the site, toppled many of them. A couple of centuries later, when the village of Avebury was growing inside the site, people broke up many of the stones to build homes. It's amazing that there's anything left."

As Jeff read on, his booklet making it clear that the formations would make sense in an aerial view, my mind wandered back to the diary. I could almost see the Galactic Visitors and Atlantean priests as they moved their hands over giant maps, feeling the energetic frequencies of the land. They had marked the vortex points, just as I had seen on Tina's father's map, so that later stones could be placed there to augment the earth's energy. And these were those stones.

Suddenly I felt lifted up in space – and back in time. I was looking down on the site, seeing it as it must have once looked from the air. Comprised of both stone and earth, the site was a gigantic formation in the shape of a great snake, which moved in one side of a large mound and out the other.

Jeff was still reading when I finally opened my eyes. "Is there a drawing of what this place might have looked like?"

"As a matter of fact, there's one in the back. I don't know how they figured it out, but here it is," he said, handing me the booklet opened to the back page. To my amazement, it was almost exactly like what I had just seen in my inner vision. It had been drawn in the early 1700s by a man named Dr. William Stuckeley, who was a student of sacred history. A note on the bottom of the page read, "…Dr. Stuckeley noticed in the ground plan of many ancient sacred sites, and specifically at Avebury, the reoccurring symbols of the serpent and the winged circle. He identified these as the ancient symbols of alchemical fusion."

Alchemical fusion…ancient sacred sites…! So this Dr. Stuckeley understood that this was a place of earth magic, like Glastonbury Tor.

My brain grappled with the deeper connection. Tina's father had talked about the marriage of heaven and earth – and Mary had said he was a member of The Brotherhood. This must all be related to the knowledge that came out of Atlantis. *We might be a civilization with amnesia, but the ancient wisdom is all around us, written in earth and stone, just waiting to be rediscovered!*

I stood up and gazed across what once must have been an amazing sight. My eyes closed and I focused on the energy as it coursed through my body, merging with the energies from the other sites I had visited. The power of the place was intense. It was clear just how the lines of energy tied this site together with the other sites throughout Great Britain. *It's strange…there really isn't anything much to see here…yet this is possibly the most powerful site of all.*

All too soon, the afternoon was all but over. We got in the car and headed back to Stonehenge so that I could take more photographs. The sun was just beginning to set when we arrived. As it dropped lower and lower in the sky, the red–gold evening light snaked its way down the ancient stones before setting behind the giant henge. It was breathtaking. I put my camera down, and Jeff and I shared the sun's final burst of light. The purple afterglow seemed to last forever – reluctant as we were to end the day.

The sky was still a magnificent nighttime blue when Jeff and I tore ourselves away and headed back toward Glastonbury. He had enjoyed himself so much he decided to accompany me the next day to Cornwall, where there were a few more sites I wanted to photograph.

CHAPTER 52

It had been a long day, and it was late when Jeff and I arrived back at the Bed and Breakfast. We were both exhausted and exhilarated by the experiences we had shared. But all of that changed the moment we opened the front door. The usually quiet little inn was ablaze with light and activity. Jeff's uncle must have heard us, because he rushed out of Mr. Moseley's study and greeted us with, "Have you heard the news?"

"No, what news?" asked Jeff.

"The most remarkable events have been going on around the world... especially in Africa. You must see for yourself," he said, reaching out to grab both of us by the hand. We put down my camera gear and followed him into the study where all of the guests were gathered around the television set. They sat in rapt attention on the piano bench, dining room chairs and edge of the desk.

"As we said earlier, at approximately 7:15 a.m. London time, a giant electrification project in the Sudan in Africa, which has been stymied in red tape and economic difficulties, unexpectedly came on line, bringing light and electric power into villages and townships. The most remarkable and unexplainable subject of today's events is that the project was far from finished. Experts in the area have no explanation as to why, or even how, today's miracle...yes, even they are calling it a *miracle*...could have happened.

"Now we will go to Bill Phillips at CNN who has Drs. Amherst and Manjubu on the line with us to discuss what has...and still is...going on."

"Doctors, this is Bill Phillips. Can you hear me?" There was some static, and then the image of a heavy-set man with glasses appeared on the other side of the split screen.

There was more static, then, "Yes, Bill, we can hear you."

"Before we begin, will you please identify yourselves for our viewers."

"Yes, of course. I am Dr. Amherst and this is Doctor Manjubu." The camera panned to reveal a slender black man in a lab coat. Both men were wearing hardhats.

"Thank you, gentlemen. Now, if you will, please share with our viewing audience, what you two make of today's events?"

"Well, it's very puzzling, Bill," answered the Sudanese doctor. We have no explanation. The project was nowhere near completion. Scientifically it makes absolutely no sense that the electrical plant should be working."

That side of the screen broke up and began to tile. It was soon replaced by the interior of a village hospital. We saw doctors, patients and large number of children all smiling and waving at the camera.

The reporter resumed speaking. "So folks, you've heard it with your own ears and seen it with your own eyes. It would appear that today a miracle has taken place, a miracle that even science cannot explain. This is Bill Phillips reporting live at CNN. We will now return you to your local television stations, which have their own reporters covering this astonishing event, as well as the number of spontaneous healings that also took place in the Sudan today. As we mentioned earlier, the sheer number of these healings for people…people with 'certain death' written on their medical records…far exceeds random chance."

A local British commentator came back on the air, and Mr. Moseley turned down the sound. "What do you make of it?" he asked the group. Everyone started talking at once. Jeff had a strange expression on his face as he said, "I have no idea, but you'll have to excuse us. We've had a very long day and another early start tomorrow. I think both Cassie and I need to grab a bite to eat and get some sleep. We'll leave it to you to figure out and catch up with you in the morning."

We went out into the foyer, picked up my equipment and made our way up the stairs. I opened the door to my room, and we deposited everything on my bed. Once in the privacy of my room, Jeff stared at me with a quizzical look. "You realize that the event we just witnessed happened at the exact time we were inside Stonehenge, don't you?"

I nodded, wondering where this was leading.

"Well," he said, "I saw a little bit of what you were doing there."

"Doing?"

"Um hum…doing! My uncle George was only half kidding when he said I was psychic. I'm not saying I'm really psychic, but sometimes I just know things. Usually small and unimportant things, like the next guest at the inn would be from California. And occasionally, very occasionally, I see things. Don't worry, I'm not exactly planning on getting a crystal ball and hanging up my shingle," he laughed. "This thing just kind of comes and goes. But today, at Stonehenge, I knew you were doing something. It was like lightening sparks were flying off of you, and for a moment the whole henge lit up like a light bulb."

I started to say something, but Jeff shushed me.

"I'm sure no one else could see it. I can tell when I'm seeing things other people can't. The moment we met, I sensed you were not just a photographer. Something else was going on, I just didn't know what. I wasn't going to say anything, but now this has happened…."

We were interrupted by Jeff's uncle's voice calling excitedly up to us. "Hurry down! You have got to see this! It's all ended! Whatever it was, it's all over!"

We scrambled down the steps and into the study. The broadcaster from CNN was on again. "So folks, just as mysteriously as it all began, it seems to have ended. Experts have no clue how or why it began, and now they are just as stymied as you and I as to how and why it's over. But the fact is, all of the villages and townships are back in darkness. The electrification project remains unfinished, and once again the people of the Sudan are living in primitive conditions."

The reporter began calling on some other expert witnesses. *This is too much!* I turned to Jeff and whispered, "I can't take anymore. Can we finish our discussion tomorrow?"

I must have looked as badly as I felt, because Jeff was concerned.

"Don't you want something to eat?"

"No, I'm too tired. I have an energy bar upstairs that'll do just fine. I need to go to bed."

"Do you want me to walk you up?"

"No, really, I just need to get into bed. We'll talk in the morning."

It was all I could do to drag my body up the stairs and into my room. I undressed, ate my energy bar, got into bed and turned off the lamp. I lay in the dark breathing slowly, trying to make sense of what I'd just seen. Then I closed my eyes and went down deep inside myself.

I remembered – and almost felt – the energy that had coursed through my body at Stonehenge. That was why the lights had come on. *It was the grid… the blast of energy that shot out across the grid when I was activated.* I had seen it with my very own eyes — or with my inner vision. While it was too new to understand how I had seen it, what I did comprehend was that some kind of real energy event had transpired. However, I had never imagined it would show up on such a large, definable scale.

The big question was not why the power plant in the Sudan had begun working, but once it did, why would it reverse itself? *I am in such new territory that, no matter how deeply inside of myself I go, I can't come up with an answer. At least not yet!*

I was only beginning to truly understand the magnitude of what I was involved in. A wave of excitement – and uncertainty – washed over me. The only thing I could do, as Jeff had so succinctly put it, was to "choose" to trust.

With that peaceful thought in mind, I drifted off to sleep.

CHAPTER 53

Jeff and I left early the following morning and headed across the vast and empty English Moors, land of legends and mystery novels. Since I had a flight out of Gatwick to Los Angeles the next afternoon, we had to move quickly – really quickly – in order to cover so much territory in a single day. We had lunch in the small fishing village of St. Ives. We found, and I photographed, two charming stone sites. The first was The Merry Maidens, where the energy seemed to be almost lyrical. The second was Men-an-Toll, which was clearly a fertility site. However, I knew neither of them was a major activation site for me.

Unlike our other times together, we did not talk much, and what conversation we did have consisted of small talk. I think Jeff was uncertain how to broach what had happened at Stonehenge and what we had later seen on television that night. Obviously, he didn't want to push, which was fine with me, because I didn't know where to begin or how much I was comfortable saying.

Photography was a safe topic, and one time, while Jeff was helping me pack up my camera gear, he asked a safe question.

"I've been meaning to ask you, what exactly is all this stuff you carry around anyway?" Relieved that he was not approaching the real subject, I was more than willing to be very chatty about my photography. "Well, even though I have two digital cameras, which I use for most of my professional work, I prefer to use film. It's so tangible. As for my stuff, it's all used for different things. I always carry two camera bodies because I like to keep color film in one and black and white in the other. What else? Oh yes, I usually have four lenses. Two are wide angle, one is for close-ups and one is a zoom lens. I interchange the lenses between the two camera bodies.

"The filters have different purposes, too. One is a polarizing filter. It bumps up the contrast and takes out the glare. Some filters warm the color up in varying degrees while others cool the color down. And some like these," I said, holding up some of my color graduated filters, "alter the color dramatically. They intensify the color in one area of the image and fade it down to almost nothing in another part. You can manipulate the color in all kinds of different ways using filters."

"Hmm, it looks like you're working on some sort of big project."

This is a lead in for me to talk about more than photography...but I just can't go there right now. "I guess it does, but the truth is I'm not at all sure I know where it's going to end up. It seems to be evolving into two different series of photographs. I've already blown up some of my black and white images and hand-painted them but that's a whole other story."

"And it's more than I can understand," Jeff said. "I think I'll stay with my little digital point-and-shoot that does everything on its own. What you're doing sounds way too complicated for me."

"Sometimes it is for me, too," I laughed. "Let's get going while we still have good light. I just might be ready for a little more punishment."

We drove to Lands End, Cornwall's most southerly tip, and looked out across the water to a small island, St. Michael's Mount. At one point the Mount had been home to an old monastery, but legend told of an even earlier time when it was the location of a stone circle.

I had a sense this was a major activation site for me, but I didn't know why.

I closed my eyes, slowed my breathing and waited for something – anything – to take place, but nothing did. Frustrated and perplexed, we were about to leave when I felt several flashes of lightening, one after the other. Everything around me became very sharp and luminous.

I looked back at St. Michael's Mount and saw a sudden spark of light. The spark turned into a line of light that skimmed across the water and raced past me. I quickly turned, my eyes following the light. It continued for miles and miles. *Oh my god! It's a major line of energy!* I could actually see that the line started at St. Michael's Mount and ran all the way up through the major sacred sites and churches, including Glastonbury Tor, Avebury and finally, St. Edmonds' Abbey. For a long minute, the ley line was as clear to me as the reflective lights that illuminate a highway at night – then it disappeared.

So that's why I'm here! It's not about a particular site. It's the entire ley line I am meant to experience...and influence. Mary had said my sensitivity to energy would grow, and it had. I could never have experienced something like that even a few days ago. Now I was seeing, in real life, what I had read about in the diary. I wonder if Jeff saw anything? I looked at him and, although his body was unusually rigid, he was staring straight across at the Mount.

I followed his gaze, but couldn't see anything. Leaning down to pick up my camera case, I asked, "Are you ready to go?"

"Did you know that at one time that island was connected to the mainland and that the remains of an ancient forest still lie beneath the water that separates them?" asked Jeff, his body still rigid.

"No! How did you find that out?"

"I don't...." he started to answer, slowly shaking his head, "I...I just know." His body relaxed, and he looked at me with a crooked grin. "It must be the company I've been keeping."

"Jeff," I blurted out, unable to bear my secrecy any longer. "I'm so sorry I haven't talked about what happened at Stonehenge. It's just a long story, and I don't fully understand it myself, so it's really hard for me to talk about."

"I'm sure it is. I could see that whatever it was, it was big. Look, it's getting late. Why don't we get going, and you can tell me as much as you're comfortable with."

We gathered my gear and walked to the car. Jeff headed east, back to the Bed and Breakfast. Once we were comfortably on our way, I turned toward him. "Well," I began, "it all started with a trip to Egypt. No...that's not quite right. It actually began long before that, when I was a child."

I told him about my childhood powers and about the beautiful lady who visited me at night. I described how my parents had punished me and that I had to bury my special abilities. I mentioned Mary, but I didn't tell him anything about what I'd learned from her about my mission in life. And I definitely didn't tell him about the diary – or David.

We talked for the rest of the ride. I explained what I felt I could, and Jeff was incredibly patient with me. He let me go at my own pace, never pushing, never questioning. Curiously enough, it ended with him reassuring me – reassuring me that he knew I wasn't crazy, that he understood, that he would do his part for the planet – and that, no matter what, he would be my friend for life.

It was dark long before we finally arrived back at the Moseley's. Jeff helped me switch my equipment into the trunk of my car before we tiptoed up the steps and into the inn. He led me to the sitting room, where dying embers glowed in the fireplace. Handing me his card, he whispered, "Put this in your breast pocket, close to the thing-a-ma-jig you're wearing around your neck. Yes, I know you have something important there. It's been giving off some kind of signal since the moment we met. I want you to promise that if I can ever be of any kind of help, and I mean any kind, that you will call me. My card has every phone number on it you could possibly reach me at. Do you promise...even if you're just feeling lonely or...or...anything?"

"I promise." He gave me a great big bear hug, and I sank into the comfort of his arms. "I can't tell you how important it is that we met," I whispered.

"There are no accidents, my dear Cassie." I hugged him again, and even though we would each go our separate ways, I knew we were companions for life – on a sacred journey.

Tired as I was, when I got back to my room, I pulled out the talisman. The mirror face was blank. Jeff was right – it was vibrating. *How could I not have felt it?* I closed my eyes and focused as I had when I was a child, then opened them and looked back at the talisman. Sure enough, there was a close-up of John talking to another man. *That's strange…I'm supposed to command it, not the other way around. Mary never mentioned anything like this. I wonder what it means?*

I couldn't think of what I needed to ask, so I commanded, "Further!" The picture widened but all I could see was a jungle-like landscape in the background. I went deep inside but I still had no idea why it had called me. After a time I commanded "Off!" and it shut down.

One glance at the clock told me it was late, and I had another very early morning. I put the talisman on the nightstand, brushed my teeth, got into bed and switched off the lamp. But tired as I was, whatever position I settled into was soon uncomfortable. Sleep was as elusive as a mirage. My thoughts rummaged over the many things I had discovered in England and Scotland. I had come to learn about Atlantis, but ended up finding out a lot about myself – and so much more.

Never could I have imagined that mild-mannered John from Egypt, who had helped me so much when I was sick, would turn out to be the personification of Evil. And who would have ever thought that defeating him would become my primary objective in life? There was still so much I needed to learn. *Well, from what Mary said, I guess I'll be learning it soon.*

CHAPTER 54

The plane thundered through blue skies and billowing clouds. *Ahh! Right on time! That's a good start…for a fifteen-hour flight.* I had settled in for my direct flight, when I remembered that I had never marked my film from the day before. I pulled out my camera case and reached for the film and the small notebook in which I kept track of my film rolls.

As I was thumbing through the notebook, I ran across the doodles I had

drawn in various dribs and drabs over my travels. I had been so busy, I'd forgotten about them. It was a surprise to discover there were nine different symbols going all the way back to ones I had seen on the bus ride in Egypt.

The symbols were fascinating – and beautiful. In fact, they were works of
art! It was like stumbling upon an old treasure chest full of things I had created
– except that it felt like I had nothing to do with creating them. It was more like
they had simply come through me.

The images seemed to share a commonality, to be related to one another.
The more I stared at them, the more mesmerized I became. *They're so magical!*
I was intrigued. So now, with nothing but time, I crossed my legs yogi style, sat
back in my seat, slowed my breathing way down and allowed myself to drift
into a meditative state.

I focused on the images one at a time, quietly hanging out with each one
of them. After a time, I noticed that the lines seemed to shift and change. Some
moved closer and others further away. The lines would shift again and again
until the entire image pulsated. The same thing happened with each drawing.
I easily spent long periods focusing on individual symbols, closing my eyes and
resting after each session.

My body was operating in the strangest "no-time" time. Everything appeared
to have slowed down, yet at the same time, my brain seemed to be accelerating.
I was startled when three new symbols appeared to my inner vision, and even
though I was in a meditative mode, I was able to draw them in great detail in my
notebook. And exactly as with the original nine, they also had the ability to shift
and change.

Continuing to experiment, I soon discovered something else. If I softened
my eyes while focusing on one of my images, I slipped into an altered state
where time seemed to stand still. *It feels like I've come across a whole new
language…only it is a language of images. It also seems like I am "learning"
from the symbols, though I have absolutely no idea what that learning might
be.* I was very excited.

At some point, I dozed off. In my dreams, the symbols were dancing before
my eyes. They carried me back to many of the sacred sites I had visited. I saw

myself at the sites in Peru, at Tiahuanaco in Bolivia, Callanish as well as Stonehenge, Glastonbury, Avebury and St. Michael's Mount. I experienced a lightening flash at every site – even at places where I had not felt one when I was actually there – and with each flash came a new rush of symbols.

As I woke up, the words, *"Glyphs…we are glyphs…call us glyphs…"* were ringing in my ears. I came fully awake with a start. *Glyphs! Where did that come from?* I rubbed my eyes. Glyphs! The name seemed strange but at the same time, it was so right. *My little drawings, my doodles, are not random symbols. They have a name…Glyphs.*

Darn! I wish I had my computer! I remembered reading somewhere about glyphs, but I hadn't paid attention to it. Let me think…. I knew the ancient Maya had used glyphs, and the Hebrew language was composed of glyphs. I remembered that much. And, of course, there were the Egyptian hieroglyphs. In all of those languages, each image had both a name and a meaning of its own. *I wonder if my glyphs have names…and meanings.*

I looked at my notebook, and at the glyphs I had drawn. The artist in me longed for some watercolor paints or dyes, like I had used on my black and white photographs. I thought the images would look great filled in with pastel colors, but the second I had that idea, I changed my mind. I realized that color would work against the glyphs natural sense of movement. It would fix the painted areas into single shapes. I didn't want that. Movement was what made them so intriguing, so powerful.

Whew! I need to give myself a break. Reluctantly, I put the notebook in my camera case and pulled out a book that had caught my attention in the airport bookstore, entitled *Sacred Sites of the Americas.* The irony of my find didn't pass unnoticed. I had been chasing sacred sites across the globe, then I had found a book about sites in the Americas in an airport bookstore in England. Go figure! *If it's true that I'm being guided, the answer to where I am supposed to go next might be in this book.* I read a bit but found I couldn't concentrate. I had a strong desire to see the glyphs again. I couldn't seem to get enough of them.

Giving up the struggle, I put the book away and pulled out my notebook. I turned to the first glyph I had drawn, got comfortable and focused on it. After a while, the symbol began to move and shimmer, then fade away. In its place, three letters appeared, E-K-R. I had no idea what they meant, but I copied them into my notebook right above the drawing. I spent time with the second glyph and, once again, "saw" three different letters, S-K-N. This happened with all of the twelve symbols I had drawn, each one showing its own arrangement of three letters. I carefully wrote the letters that appeared for each glyph. *This is getting interesting! I don't understand it…but it's certainly interesting!*

I flipped back through the glyphs and randomly picked one to focus on. I saw the same three letters I had seen the first time. I randomly picked another glyph and saw the same three letters associated with it. This happened time and time again, always with the same results. Finally, it dawned on me that the funny, unpronounceable three letters were actually words, and in fact were the names of the various glyphs. Moreover, these three-lettered words seemed to be part of a language – a very strange language that was somehow familiar. That had to be the answer to my earlier question, the one about meaning and names. It was as if I were on an archeological dig and had just hit pay dirt.

A peek at my watch revealed that five hours had passed. I was shocked, but instead of being tired, I felt highly energized. I went back to the first glyph and started to work with it again. Immediately, the unpronounceable words became pronounceable. I had no idea how it was happening. *It's like I've known these words before, but have forgotten them. And now, somehow, my memory is returning.* The same thing happened with the other eleven – the words became pronounceable. It was a unique and exquisite experience, like nothing I had ever done before. *I'm remembering something I had no idea I had forgotten.*

As I continued to operate in this no-time time, I saw four new glyphs, each with its three letter name that became pronounceable. I quickly added these to my growing collection.

Everything around me seemed to be moving in slow motion, and I could see and feel the beats between beats. At the same time, I felt like my brain had been plugged into an accelerated learning program. *I think the glyphs are teaching my brain things that will take the rest of me a while to understand.*

At that point, all I knew was that each glyph had its own meaning – and something special to teach me. Together, they formed a unique language and a world of knowledge they had yet to reveal. *That's why it seems like I'm learning…because I am! Not only with my mind, with my entire being. I'm so riveted because, as I focus on each of you, one at a time, I am absorbing your very vibration into me.*

I looked back at the first glyph with the name EKR and understood its meaning to be *The Celestial Messenger.* As soon as I had written the name, a tumble of words came pouring out of me like a veritable rush of water – through my hand, out my pen and down onto the page. It was the same with all sixteen of the glyphs. My hand was numb by the time I was finished. Hardly conscious of what I was doing, I dropped the notebook and pen into my bag, and promptly fell deeply asleep.

> A man, dressed in some kind of dark uniform, is standing in the shadow of a tall building. His eyes search the street in front of him. He seems impatient – almost agitated – at not finding who or what he is looking for. A smile crosses his face. He cups his hand over the ear piece of the headset he is wearing and hisses, "He's here…I can see him right in front of me…going in."

> Two other men, also dressed in dark uniforms, run out into the street. The man with the headset rushes out as well. One of the men is Middle Eastern and another Caucasian, but the third, the one who was doing the talking, has features that are somewhat amorphous and totally unfamiliar. They circle in toward a single figure on the street. As they draw closer, I can see the lone figure. It is David.

I awoke abruptly in a cold sweat when the plane hit a patch of turbulence. My head was pounding and my heart racing. *What's going on? Is David in some kind of trouble or was that just a crazy dream?*

The plane pitched sharply as the voice of the attendant broke through my thoughts. "Ladies and gentleman, we are experiencing turbulence, and the captain has switched on the fasten seat belt sign. Please return to your seats immediately, put up your tray tables, pull your seat backs into an upright position and make sure your seat belts are fastened. Stow all your belongings under the seat in front of you. We are going through a storm front, and our pilot is assessing the situation. We may need to fly a bit higher or alter our flight path to go around the storm. There's no reason for panic. Just hold tight, and make sure your seats are in the upright position and seat belts fastened."

A murmur went through the crowd. A few moments of static was followed by an unintelligible voice that briefly blasted over the loudspeaker. The plane lurched sharply to the left. Purses and peanuts went flying. Coffee and coke splashed everywhere. The plane steadied itself before veering brutally to the right. There were yelps as a woman hurrying back to her seat fell headfirst into the lap of an elderly man. A woman in the back of the plane screamed as luggage from an overhead compartment slammed down into the aisle and slid forward.

Noise seemed to come from everywhere and the air was filled with so much tension that my mind went blank. I couldn't worry about my dream. *My god, is this it…am I going to die right here and now?*

Static, followed by a piercing squeal, echoed through the cabin. One man yelled, "Is the plane safe?" Finally the words, "Ladies and gentlemen, this is your flight attendant. Please stay calm," buzzed through the plane. We bounced several more times before the plane righted itself. There was a collective exhale.

The sound of relief was not only audible – it was palpable. The loudspeaker whirred and squealed again. "Ladies and gentlemen, please stay calm. The captain is in complete control of the situation. We are currently flying over Quebec, Canada. A sudden storm has come up from the west. It seems to have come out of nowhere, so instead of heading southwest toward Bismarck, Wyoming, the pilot is altering our flight plan. We will continue to head south until the storm is behind us, then we will pick up an alternate route heading west that will take us directly into Los Angeles.

"As a precaution, please remain in you seats with your seat belts buckled for as long as you see the fasten seat belt sign. There is no reason for concern.

The aircraft is functioning perfectly, and we apologize for any inconvenience." There was a brief pause. "Oh, one more thing. As soon as we are out of the turbulence, the captain has offered to buy everyone drinks...that is, everyone who is eighteen or over." There was a round of nervous laughter as people began to talk amongst themselves. I held my feet firmly on either side of my camera case, not trusting it to stay put under the seat in front of me.

The plane continued bouncing. After a few agonizing minutes, the audio came back on. "Ladies and Gentlemen, this is your captain, Mark Stuart. As your flight attendant Penny has assured you, we are in good shape. At this time we are continuing in a southerly direction and will soon be flying over Albany, New York. This is a particularly stubborn storm front, so we will continue south until we have cleared its path and can head west. You can follow our revised flight-path on the video monitors located throughout the main cabin. We are picking up a tailwind, which will help offset the time delay created by our diversion. As a precaution, please remain in your seats and keep your seatbelts fastened. On behalf of myself, my co-pilot Frank, and your flight attendants, I want to thank you for your patience."

Everyone settled down and tried to relax. The ride was bumpy but not terrible. I kept an eye on the monitor as we continued to head south. Penny came by with our free drinks and some snacks, and was welcomed by a round of applause. There were still plenty of white knuckles, but except for the wailing of a baby, everyone seemed to be in good spirits. It was a bit of a party atmosphere as people released their tension and struck up conversations with their seatmates. I, however, was in no mood to party. My head was still pounding, my dream unresolved, and I felt drained.

There was a lull in the storm, and I managed a short nap before I was bounced awake again. Still not wanting to think about my dream, I picked up the book *Sacred Sites of the Americas* and opened to where I had left off. I read about the mysteriously abandoned pre-Hopi site in New Mexico, Chaco Canyon, various sites in Mexico proper, as well as the Mayan sites in Mexico's Yucatan Peninsula. This last area really held my attention. *Hmm...! That's probably where I need to go next,* I thought, as I pushed my seat back as far as it would go and dozed off.

I opened my eyes for a minute and glanced at the monitor. We had just passed over Charlotte, North Carolina and were already heading slightly westward. *Good! That means we should be back in Los Angeles in about four hours.* Feeling comforted, I drifted off again but woke up when the airplane abruptly dropped what seemed like several hundred feet.

The lights in the cabin flashed off and on, then off again. The pilot was trying to talk to us, but his voice crackled and broke up like a bad cell phone connection. The plane eventually stabilized, and although there was still static on the sound system, we were able to hear more clearly.

"Ladies and gentlemen, this is your pilot Mark again. I guess it's been pretty bouncy back there, but the good news is that you're in a great airplane, and all of us up here have been through this before. You can rest assured that we are not in any danger. However, the storm seems to be chasing us, and now we're locked in by another storm front that has made a quick change of direction and is heading northward up the Atlantic Coast. That's the cause of the current turbulence.

"In order to get around the storms, we have had to change our route and are presently heading out over the Gulf of Mexico towards Mexico's Yucatan Peninsula. We are waiting for confirmation to land at the airport in Mérida." There was a moment of silence before the captain cleared his throat, and trying to sound cheerful, said, "Well, it looks like you folks will be getting a free vacation on us. We've gotten the go ahead, and will be landing in Mérida shortly. Our ground staff is making hotel reservations, and preparing food and transportation vouchers for all of you. Penny and the other flight attendants will be coming around to handle any special problems. We are sorry for any inconvenience this causes, and we will do everything we can to get you back to Los Angeles as soon as possible."

Unreal! I can't believe what I'm hearing! Two hours ago I was thinking about going to the Yucatan Peninsula and now the entire plane is flying there!

CHAPTER 55

The weather was calm over the Yucatan Peninsula, and our plane landed uneventfully. There was, however, a flurry of activity in the small airport terminal – and we were at the center of it. Apparently the storms were stronger than our pilot had indicated, and everyone was relieved when we arrived safely.

We were led into a large room where custom agents swiftly checked and stamped our passports. Hotel representatives handed us room, food and transportation vouchers, and we were told that the airline would cover any international calls we needed to make. Much to our relief, we were assured that the new disease breaking out all over the globe, now nicknamed "Mad Man" disease after the debacle of "Mad Cow" disease, had not made its appearance in this part of Mexico. There had been a number of deaths in Mazatlán, but that area was now quarantined, and no planes had been allowed in or out. I couldn't help but wonder if this newest bit of nastiness in the world was one of John's creations.

Everything was managed in an organized fashion. We were divided into groups according to our hotel assignments, and each group was given a dedicated multi-lingual agent. We were handed our agent's phone number for any additional problems that might come up, as well as a number to call in the morning for weather and travel updates. Everyone was very considerate, and we were encouraged to relax and enjoy ourselves. However, they couldn't help us with the questions that were foremost in everyone's mind – when would the storm break and how soon could we get back to Los Angeles? The continuing onslaught of unseasonably strong high altitude storms made that prediction impossible.

When we left the terminal to board the minivans which would take us to our various hotels, the hot, humid tropical weather hit us with surprising force. Many of my fellow travelers were in various states of panic, exhaustion and confusion caused by the day's events. I, on the other hand, was calm, collected and excited. And I couldn't get over the fact that I was in Mérida, the capital of the state of Yucatan!

I settled into my hotel room and opened the shutters to take in the early evening air. My room looked out on the bustling colonial city with its wide avenues and white buildings. I spotted an inviting-looking outdoor cafe nearby, replete with stripped umbrellas and hanging flower pots, which called out to me. After inhaling the fresh air – and the beautiful view – I decided I was more than ready for dinner.

Stopping briefly in the hotel's lobby, I picked up a couple of brochures on the Yucatan pyramids and ventured out into the tropical evening. It had been a hard day, and I had slept only fitfully on the plane. I should have been exhausted, but I guessed working with the glyphs had had a positive effect on me.

I got hot just walking the couple of blocks to the restaurant, and the thought hit me: *I have nothing to wear tomorrow.* I burst out laughing. For once, that was, literally, an absolutely true statement. Heavy parkas and sweatshirts definitely wouldn't work here! Fortunately, it seemed that the shops were open late in that part of the world. I darted into one little shop, and bought a couple of tank tops and a pair of shorts.

Sitting in the restaurant, enjoying my meal of fresh cooked tiny tortillas, known as *salbutes and panuchos,* I began to study the brochures. I was excited to learn that Uxmal was fairly close by, and Chichen Itza, though further, was not terribly far away. I wondered if the hotel had any day trips there? *Even if our plane is able to leave tomorrow, I could stay on for a couple of days. I already know I need to visit these places...especially Uxmal.*

I was ecstatic when the desk clerk told me there was a tour going to both sites three days a week and that the following day was one of the days. "But," he said, "it leaves very early in the morning, and we only have one seat left in the bus."

What if the weather clears tonight? *Well...what if it does! I can't wait to find out.* I would have to chance it and make other travel arrangements if I needed to. There was one seat left, and it was meant for me! And I didn't mind how early it started.

Hurrying up to my room, I gazed out the window at the lights of the city.

It's so beautiful here! The warm air...the tropical breeze.... It's a shame to close the windows but tomorrow is almost here. I paused for a long, lingering look and quietly closed the shutters.

My *Sacred Sites of the Americas* in hand, I crawled into bed to read about the two sites I would be visiting the next day. *Everything is happening so easily. I find the book, read about the Yucatan, think I want to go...and here I am!*

However, my delight quickly vanished, as I suddenly felt engulfed in a giant wave of fear and dread. It was so strong and came on so fast, I couldn't move. My stomach had tied itself into a knot, and the book fell from my hands.

Whatever this is about, I will not let fear control me! I may not be in charge of my body, but I can be in charge of my mind. I lay still for quite some time, holding my belly, and reminding myself who I was and what I was destined to do before eventually falling into a fitful sleep.

* * * * * * * * * * *

I was jangled awake very early the next morning by a call from the front desk letting me know the tour bus would arrive in a few minutes.

"Oh, no! Can they wait? I'm not dressed yet," I pleaded. *Damn! I must have fallen asleep before asking for a wake-up call.* For a moment I lost my bearings. My mind was gummy and unfocused, but I recovered enough to say, "Please have them wait just a few minutes. I'll be fast."

I dressed hurriedly, grabbed my camera bag and raced downstairs. There were several people gathered in the lobby. *I hope there're from my tour.* I ran to the front desk.

"The tour to Uxmal....?"

"Sorry for your rush. The bus not here yet."

"Great! Thank you for the call. I...I...."

"*De nada, Señorita.* We know you from the airplane. Thanks god everything was all right. She was a very bad storm. They say nothing flying today. Maybe not even tomorrow! Quien sabe? You want coffee?" she asked, pointing to the dining room. "I tell driver to wait for you."

Well, that answers the airplane question, I thought, as I walked to the dining room. *I'm sure glad I decided to take this tour.* I got a coffee to go and picked a few things off of the buffet table, wrapped them in some napkins and signed my room number on the check. By the time I returned, the bus had arrived and people were beginning to board.

I settled down onto a seat in the back of the bus, still feeling dazed and not fully awake. My head was full of jagged dream images – images of John, of David, of glyphs, and even of the camel named California. Without thinking, I reached for the talisman, but it was not there. *Damn! I must have left it on the nightstand this morning. God, I hope the maid doesn't take it.* It was the first time I had been without it since Mary's. *This is not a good sign!*

In the hour it took us to get to Uxmal, I managed to pull myself together – more or less. However, I still had no idea what hit me last night, and why I was still so nervous and jittery. I was one of the last people out of the bus and followed the group as they filed into the archeological park. The park had just opened, so there were very few people around.

The first place that our tour leader, Gustavo, took us was to the pyramid called The Temple of The Magician. He explained, in both English and Spanish, that while it seemed to be one pyramid, it was actually five different temples. They were built, one over the other, during the history of the ancient city, but parts of each of the temples were still accessible.

The hardiest of the group followed Gustavo up the various staircases to identify the different temples. I was still out of sync with myself – and the site. Whatever I was supposed to feel here wasn't likely to happen with so many people around. I wandered to some of the other structures, taking a few pictures here and there but not noticing anything in particular.

Finally, the group moved on to another area, and it was my turn to explore the pyramid. It was an amazing structure with an elliptical base, and each of its four sides, or "faces," was different. Every face not only had its own staircase, but its own unique pattern of carvings. I randomly picked one staircase and started to climb. It was quite a haul. At the second level, I came across a giant mask of *Chac,* the rain god. I noticed an opening in the mouth of the mask that led to an inner chamber. Leaning in, I saw that it was dark and musty inside, but suddenly I wanted – *needed* – to be inside that chamber.

I climbed over the lower lip of the mask and dropped into the cavity. A slight shaft of light illuminated the chamber and was just enough to keep the interior from feeling ominous. As my eyes adjusted to the darkness, I spotted a small, round stone disk on the chamber floor. The disk had been carefully carved so that the profile of a Mayan face stood out in bas-relief from the rest of the stone. Over the profile of the face, the head of a snake and a feathered plume arose. The snake's body, composed of some type of hieroglyphs, undulated around the edge of the disk. The entire thing was no bigger than my hand. I could understand the Mayan face, but I wondered what the image of a snake with feathers meant.

The disk did not seem to be a part of the temple and was not attached to anything. When I walked the few steps forward and kneeled down beside it, I realized I was in complete darkness. I looked toward the shaft of light, then back at the disk. It was not illuminated from the sunlight – it was glowing from within. Energy was radiating off its surface and my nervous system seemed to be absorbing that energy – that information.

I put my hand on the disk, and suddenly a great shudder ran through my body. I felt myself slip into a state of hyper-awareness and experienced a jolting flash of lightning. It was as though I were transported to another time and another place. I could feel the blood coursing through my veins – Mayan blood.

Still kneeling beside the stone, I closed my eyes and an entire vision opened before me. I saw the ancient Maya from a time long before the habitation of this site, and I understood immediately how deeply the Mayan Culture had been influenced by teachings from Atlantis. I saw how, just before the sinking of Atlantis, the high Atlantean priest Iltar had brought a migration party from Atlantis to the Yucatan Peninsula. They had built the first pyramid, the Temple of Iltar, which was now underwater off one of the peninsula's coasts.

I remembered that the Mayan culture had also benefited from the extraterrestrial knowledge of the Star Beings, the wisdom of the proud Lemurians and the Lost Tribe of Israel. Most importantly, I learned that the ancient Maya were the Masters of Time, planetary record keepers. Being aligned with true time – Cosmic Time – they had created and lived by a calendar that reflected that deeper understanding.

This calendar identified, from the ancient past into the future, the cycles of time for Planet Earth. The Maya were very sophisticated astronomically as well as mathematically. Their calendar demonstrated an understanding of earth's place in the cosmos. This calendar made it perfectly clear that one age of earth, a thirteen thousand year cycle, was now coming to an end, and another cycle was beginning.

In a flash of insight, I grasped the importance of the Mayan legacy in what the diary had referred to as the New Era of Light. This New Era was all about a different relationship to time. In their comprehension of time and mathematics, the ancient Maya had seen that a giant synchronization wave– a wave of information originating in the center of the galactic core – was tearing through space on its way toward earth.

I also recognized that we were already experiencing the wave's pull, and that the ancient Maya had predicted when it hit, it would change everything. It would be the end of time as we had known it –a shift in the way life had been lived on earth for millennia. I saw just as clearly that the Mayan Calendar was symbolic. No human on earth had figured out exactly what it meant, or precisely the year, date and hour when that information would actually penetrate the earth's atmosphere. Everyone was simply guessing, attempting to decode the ancient mystical enigma.

In that instant, it made sense that it was I who had to be there to receive that piece of the puzzle. I understood, because I carried those ancient encodings in my own DNA. *It's in my blood, my Mayan blood. And whenever the New Era comes, I have to be ready…humanity has to be ready…or we will miss our chance.*

If it had been at all vague before, I was now completely clear about what both Mary and the diary meant when they had said the Peoples of Earth needed to come together in Love. *We will cease to exist if we remain separated from ourselves, from one another and from the earth, the way we are now. Enough of us need to hold a single unified intention…the intention to live in harmony with the earth and with all life.*

We can't afford to think of ourselves as a part of this culture or that. We need to come together in one planetary consciousness. We must also learn to inhabit our bodies in a completely new way, a way that will allow us to rejoin the natural cycles of life…of time…of the cosmos. The evolution…no, the very continuation of the human race depends upon it.

Now the diary spoke to me in a very personal way. I understood that if enough of us could come together with a sense of cooperation, our combined intention would be so powerful, it would automatically raise the earth's magnetic field. David would then be able re-connect the grid and prepare the earth to receive the energy of the New Era. *And I…I have a part in all this.*

It may have been the confinement of the cave – or the power of the information – but I must have passed out. The next thing I was aware of was a gentle massage on my neck and shoulders. I slowly opened my eyes and I saw a young couple, one on either side of me. I tried to speak.

"Shhh," said a comforting voice. "Just take it easy, everything is alright." I looked around and realized I was lying on the floor of the cave.

The woman asked if I wanted some water. I nodded, and a canteen was brought to my lips. Some water dribbled down my neck and felt refreshing.

The young man spoke softly, "Are you hurt?" I stretched my body. Everything seemed fine.

"I think I'm alright," I whispered, my throat still parched.

"Do you want to sit up?"

"Yes…I think so." Two sets of strong arms helped me into a seated position and moved me so I could lean against the wall of the cave.

"What time is it?" I asked.

"A little after eleven," said the woman.

I signaled for more water and drank thirstily. "My god, I've been in here for so long. I hope my tour bus hasn't left. I have to get out of here and go look for it."

"Are you sure you're up to it?" asked the man.

"Yes, just give me a moment."

"Here, have some trail mix before you get up." He reached into his open daypack. "Or would you like an apple instead?"

"No, thank you. I'm alright now, and the tour guide has lunch for us. But I'll take another sip of water."

It wasn't until the young couple helped me up that I noticed a small but very bright flashlight illuminating the chamber. "I always carry this," the man quipped, "you never know who you're gonna find in a cave!"

"Well, I'm sure glad you do," I laughed. "I would have hated to wake up in the dark. By the way, may I use the flashlight for a second?" He handed it to me, and I aimed it on the ground, looking for the stone disk. I searched from one end of the cave to the other, but I couldn't find it. It had vanished. *I guess it was meant for only me...and I've already seen it.*

Feeling deeply grateful, I thanked the couple and started for the mouth of the cave. "Oh no you don't," said the man. "We didn't rescue you to have you fall going down those steps." He slung my camera case over his shoulder, and the two of them helped me out of the mouth of the chamber and down the steep steps of the pyramid.

At first, the sun was so glaringly bright it blinded me, but my eyes slowly adjusted. We gingerly made our way down the pyramid, using the chain rope that was there for that purpose.

I was relieved that the bus had not left, but embarrassed when I saw Gustavo's look of disapproval. I thanked the couple again and turned sheepishly to face him.

"I was worried about you! We're ready to leave, and I had no idea where to look for you. From now on, you have to keep better track of time."

After profuse apologies, I slinked to my seat in the back of the bus. Gustavo had already handed everybody a box lunch and made a special trip to deliver mine. After a stern warning to the group, "Make sure you drink plenty of water. Is very hot here in the tropics," we were off to our next stop. I leaned back in my seat and tried to integrate everything that had just happened inside the cavern of the ancient temple.

CHAPTER 56

I t took almost three hours to get to Chichen Itza. I had plenty of time to think – and to feel. Although the diary now spoke to me in an increasingly real way, I was more worried than ever. *Will people...enough people...be willing to change?* I spent some time pondering that thought before I realized there was no point to the question, no way to get an answer. The only thing I could do was my part – whatever that turned out to be.

The wild card was John and his people. *What were they up to and what was I going to have to do to stop them?* But again, the only answer was to wait and watch. Mary had said I had the power, that it was my destiny. *I guess I need to let go of all the thinking, allow the mystery to unfold and trust I'll know what to do when it does.*

"Mystery" was certainly the right word. What had happened to the glowing disk I had seen in the chamber? I knew it was there, because I remembered walking over, kneeling down beside it and touching it. And I was in the middle of the cavern when I had woken up. My "rescuers" certainly hadn't taken it. They were too busy – and too surprised – when they saw me. Besides, the young man had opened his backpack right in front of me. I had to laugh. *Why am I still so surprised when things happen that I don't understand?*

Our bus traveled over the countryside and through a changing landscape. Uxmal had been dry and desert-like, but now, approaching Chichen Itza, we were in the midst of a jungle. I looked at the site map Gustavo held out for us and could see that the ruins of Chichen Itza were much larger and more complex than those of Uxmal had been. Chichen Itza had many different temple structures – an observatory, a ball court, an enormous pyramid and a large cenote, or sacred "sink hole," that had possibly been used for human sacrifices.

The first place we visited was the Kukulcàn Pyramid, which was located roughly in the center of the site. Although it was not as large as the Great Pyramid of Egypt, its presence dominated everything around it. I could see I wasn't the only one who felt dwarfed as we gathered in the shadow of the ancient man-made structure. Gustavo told us the pyramid was named after the god Kukulcàn and explained that "the Mayan symbol for Kukulcàn is a plumed or feathered serpent...in other words, a snake with wings."

My breath caught in my throat. That was the image I had just seen on the glowing disk at Uxmal – a snake with feathers rising over a Mayan head and the snake's body coiled around the rim. I was excited, but a bit apprehensive, as I asked Gustavo why Kukulcàn and the snake symbol were tied together.

"Good question! Kukulcàn is the most important god of the Mayan pantheon. He is connected with the heavens in general, and Venus in particular. The symbol of the serpent, or snake with wings, represents 'the one who connects Heaven to Earth.' It is said that Kukulcàn brought to the Maya the skills of agriculture, medicine and how to run a civilization. You can see this image in many, many places, but here...here the temple is dedicated to him."

Gustavo also told us about a structure on the site that had a painting of the god Kukulcàn in the shape of a man – a tall white man with silvery hair and blue eyes. *A white man with silvery hair and blue eyes! That's how Zev Moab and The Twelve Beings were described. It sounds like the Mayan god Kukulcán was a Pleiadean! Could it be that the gods of other ancient civilizations around the world were Star Beings as well?*

"This pyramid," Gustavo continued, "like the pyramid at Uxmal, was also built atop another pyramid. But the important difference is that the Kukulcàn Pyramid was constructed with amazingly advanced astronomical knowledge. The ancient peoples who built this structure also built an observatory to study the alignment of the sun, the moon and the planets. They developed the ability to analyze – and to predict – where and how the sun would shine at any particular time.

"The Mayan people positioned the Kukulcàn Pyramid so precisely that every year, on the afternoons of the spring and fall equinoxes, the sun hits the northern staircase in a way that forms a distinctive shadow. The shadow imitates the body of a great diamond-back snake and, as the afternoon progresses and the sun moves across the sky, the snake appears to be creeping down the staircase until it joins with a huge stone serpent's head at the bottom. To this day," remarked Gustavo, removing his hat, wiping his brow and looking up at the pyramid with awe, "people...many, many people... come every year to view the Great Serpent and to marvel at the wisdom of the ancient Maya."

The group moved on to the next structure and the next. I followed them for a while, snapping a few pictures here and there, but by the time we reached the observatory I knew I needed to explore the rest of the site on my own. *Something here is calling me, but I don't know what it is.*

This time I checked in with Gustavo, and promised him I would be back and in the bus by six o'clock. He warned me sternly, "Do not be late...we have the dinner arranged, and it will already be late when we get back to Mérida."

"I won't," I replied, as I turned and wondered off to explore. The sun was blazing. *Good thing I brought an extra bottle of water.* I had walked some distance and snapped a few uninspired pictures before I realized that I wasn't sensing anything special here. I sat down under a shady tree to change film and make sure all my rolls from the morning were marked down in my little notebook.

I was focused on what I was doing when I felt the presence of someone standing near me. Before I could turn around, I heard the words, "Well, if it isn't one of my favorite people on the entire planet...Cassandra Wolfe. I've missed seeing you!"

John! I recognized the voice and instantly understood where the fear and dread of the night before had come from – and what the talisman had been trying to warn me about – even before I left England. I grabbed hold of my camera case, took a deep breath and forced my voice to remain calm. "Hello, John," I answered, without looking up. "Imagine meeting you here."

"Really Cassandra, it's so good to see you again," he said, carefully kneeling on one knee beside me. "How is the little traveling earth priestess?"

My mouth twitched. "What do you want, John?" I asked, each word flat and measured.

"Well, that's cutting to the chase. I thought we could have a nice chat. It's been such a long time since we did that."

I took another deep breath and stood up. He stood up too and, as usual, he towered above me. I tried my best to ignore that fact. "I have pictures to take," I said, as I picked up my camera case and turned to leave.

"Please Cassandra, don't go...we need to talk. I think you're still angry about Peru. I'm sorry about that. I know it was a mess, but it just wasn't the proper circumstance for you and David to meet. Right now, we have more important things to discuss, things you need to understand in order to see the bigger picture. Please, for your own good, you need to hear me out. We have more in common then you might imagine. For starters, we both want the same thing...we want planet earth to survive."

I stared at him in disbelief. *He wants planet earth to survive! Under what condition, total mayhem! How in the world can he possibly think we both want the same thing?*

"Okay, that's better. I can see you're willing to listen to me, at least for now, and I so appreciate that. By the way, I thought you might be interested in knowing that it was me who created the storm fronts and shifted the winds to bring your airplane here."

I was so caught by surprise that my jaw dropped, and before I realized what I was doing, I had locked eyes with him. "You did what? You idiot! You could have killed us!"

"Now don't get upset. I had complete control of the situation. Truly, it was for your own good...our mutual good. I wanted you to get a sense of how powerful I am. Just give me time and I'll explain why I had to do it, then we'll get on to the other things you need to be aware of. Once you've heard me out, you'll see that I'm on your side, and we both are here to help one another. Cassandra please, please sit down."

"No! No sitting! And you've got exactly two minutes."

"Two minutes? Well...alright.... So, where to start ...." He mumbled as he patted his forehead. "I know! Why don't we begin with Stonehenge! I want to make sure you grasp exactly what took place there. You shot out that amazing energy across the grid and managed to turn lights on all the way over in Africa. It was great! You did a wonderful job. It shows how talented you are.

"Unfortunately, I had to shut them off. It's a long story, but it simply wasn't the right time. Progress will happen there eventually, just not now. In the meantime, it was great for people to have that experience. It let them believe that 'miracles' can happen. That's good for the psyche. It gets people prepared for things to come."

I stared blankly at him. Full comprehension of what had taken place at Stonehenge – and what I had later seen on the television at the Moseley's – slowly percolated through my consciousness. *It was true, the unfinished electrical plant had started operating and then had stopped, but John...?*

"Hmm! I see you didn't quite understand the situation. Perhaps, my dear Cassandra, your sweet little Mary neglected to tell you the truth about how much power I have."

I knew he was looking for a reaction from me – and he got it. He had said the "Mary" word, and immediately both my defenses and my curiosity soared. In spite of myself, I reluctantly sat back down, but I held on to my camera case, ready to bolt at any moment – and I didn't look at him.

"I'm so relieved," John said, patting his forehead again with his handkerchief. "Do you mind if I sit down next to you? It's so damn hot here."

God, no! I don't want...I can't...answer him....

"Well then, I'll take that to mean you don't mind," he said, sitting near me under the tree. "Okay, I brought you here because I knew you had work to do. There were some things you needed to find out at Uxmal this morning. And I was right, wasn't I?"

How does he know these things about me? How much does he know?

"That's fine, you don't need to answer. And don't worry, I'm not a 'peeping Tom.' Whatever you found out is entirely your business. But since you needed to be here...and we needed talk, I seized the moment, so to speak, and created a convenient little storm. Now, I'm going to be perfectly candid with you, because that's the only way for you to understand why we need to work together. It's important for you to realize, to fully grasp, who I really am, what I can do in general...and for *you* specifically."

I turned away from him.

"I know, I know! You find it impossible to believe that we have anything in common, but that's not true. For example, we both agree that the human race needs some help, right?"

My head made a small, almost involuntary nod.

"Good! See, we agree already. Now, there's something else Mary neglected to tell you. Your job, the thing she called your 'destiny,' well, it's doomed to failure."

"You think you're going to scare me with that...."

"I'm not trying to scare you," John interrupted. "The reason it's doomed is because you're going up against how humans operate. I understand them perfectly. You, my little innocent, haven't got a clue. You give them way too much credit."

"I don't believe you!"

"That doesn't matter," John said calmly. "It doesn't change the truth. Here's the thing, humans are not very good at life. They need someone to lead them, to give them a direction...a purpose in life. Humans feel so much better when they have a sense of purpose, when their life has meaning. Now, I know you agree with that, don't you?"

"About that, yes, but...."

"There's more! Here's the scoop, the big news, the real insight! It doesn't make any difference what that purpose is, just so long as humans think they have a job to do. They need to believe they matter. And that's exactly what I do. I give them a purpose."

"And just how, pray tell, do you do that?"

"Now, here's where it gets really good. You see, humans also have a deep-seated need to feel valued...and special. Oh, and they also like to be 'right.' That's really important. It's a great combination...feeling special and being 'right.' And I'm a conduit to give them exactly what they want." John snickered as he wiped his sweaty brow.

The slimy bastard! He's setting me up for something. I don't trust him for one second, but it might be important to hear what he has to say.

"The truth is, the way humans operate makes my job not only fun, but really easy. All I have to do is covertly show one group of people how they are smarter, better, or more deserving than another. Then I do the same thing with another group, and on and on, all over the world. Humans really get into that shit, and then they're off and running. They formulate opinions and whole belief systems based on their importance. That leads to borders, alliances and treaties.

"Before long, they divide into factions and start squabbling amongst themselves about which way of thinking is right and who should have the power to lead their particular group, so they can show the other groups how 'right' and powerful they are. Then, of course, they live in constant fear that another group with a different opinion will threaten their way of life, so they get angry and go to war with each other.

"Yes, indeed, the ultimate experience for humans is when they think they're better than everyone else. It's amazing! They get such a rush out of it. I love to puff up their egos and watch them walk around like proud peacocks defending their point of view," he chuckled. "Even *you* have to admit it's what is happening all over the world. Look at the dictatorships, Rwanda…Darfur…North Korea…China…. Everywhere you look. You see it in the news every day, now don't you? You can't deny it."

I felt my face flush – but not from the heat.

"Good! Very good! I can see you agree. You can't help it. It's a simple fact. And I'm sure you will agree with another thing I have to say. It's one of my favorite topics, greed! You see, humans relish their toys. In fact, they value them so much, they will do anything to have them. Humans! They believe that things will make them happy and successful in life, so no matter how much they have, they always want more.

"It goes back to the first thing we agreed on, humans are not very good at life. In fact, they've created, or *think* they've created, an entire industry to convince one other that what they *want* is actually what they *need*. They will buy what they don't need and can't afford, just to keep up an image of who they think they need to be. It's not my fault! Somehow they just can't seem to sort out the difference. Ah yes, advertising! A multi-trillion dollar business worldwide. Another one of my brilliant ideas.

"By the way, who do you think really causes inflation and deflation in housing, bonds, stocks…everything? You think it's the government, banks and big financial conglomerates? Well, in a sense, they do, but they're all working for me. We control everything on this planet! You see, my sweet, as one of your leaders who works for me once said, 'If you control the monetary system, you control the world. The *entire* world," emphasized John, now almost snorting in glee. "I hate to admit it, but if humans weren't so easy to manipulate, I'd be out of a job.

"You're probably wondering what this has to do with you and me. Am I right?" John paused, waiting for the response that did not come. "Okay then, we'll get back to that one. Here's another question. How do you suppose humans have gotten themselves into such a mess? Now, that's a good question, isn't it?"

My head was spinning. It was a very good question. John seemed to be making some kind of sense, but there was an undertone that felt really, really bad.

"It's very simple. We're behind the scenes pulling the strings. We play on human nature. Humans want their toys, so we create a strong economy by producing goods with planned obsolescence. They buy it, then they have to buy it again…and again…and again!"

John turned his handkerchief and mopped his now-dripping brow. "Humans want power. Well, we've already talked about that. They also want to have meaning in their little lives. Ok, we give them meaning. We give them something to fight for…or fight against. We can work with almost anything. We use religion, skin color, personal preferences, country of origin. Hell, we can use what they eat for breakfast!

"But wait I've left out the main draw…fear itself! Your average human joins us out of just plain fear. We create bad things, people panic…and then they come to us in droves. They're eager to give up their puny little lives and whatever power they actually do have in exchange for our promise to keep them safe. In other words, I have power because humans give it to me!" John bellowed, evidentially pleased with the point he was making. "Even so-called world leaders can't function without us." Still laughing he added, "And if you are wondering just who the 'us' is, you're in for a real treat! But that comes later in my story.

"Now where was I? Ah, yes! Some of our methods might be a little, well, different than you would expect. But when you hear the logic of it, I'm sure you'll agree I'm on the right track. Take any period in history, and you can see what we've been able to accomplish. It's truly impressive.

"Let me give you a little example from modern times. Ever hear of World War II? I realize it was before your time, but I'm sure you've heard about it… and the atomic bomb. That whole scene was ours. It's gotten a bad rap, but the good news is everyone involved felt they were fighting for a purpose, for something important. And it really didn't matter which side they were on. They had a job to do, a reason to get up in the morning.

"And then of course, we have the war economy to consider. Think of equipping all those soldiers. There's the airplanes, boats, tanks…the ammunition. Why, World War II rescued America from the Great Depression. Everyone was working. Even women! Factories were operating night and day. One day people were jumping out of windows and then, in the blink an eye, new millionaires were being hatched. After all, someone had to house, educate and entertain all those returning soldiers.

"Things may have looked a little different on the surface with the Korean War and Viet Nam, but underneath the same thing was going on. Now Viet Nam, That was a real piece of work! Honestly, I didn't think it would fly. Humans…. One thing they never seem to catch on to is that wars never prove anything and nobody really wins. The same people make money and, well, the same people don't. And I'll give you one guess who was behind all of that. Me! It just goes to show you that even I, with my deep understanding of human nature, have been known to overestimate the human race.

"It might take a bit of mind adjustment, but you can see that from this bigger perspective wars are a good thing. I mean, people get killed and that might appear tragic, but in the end, it helps keep the population down, and that's a good thing. It's too bad! Really too bad, but that's the way it has to be. You see, it's all for the greater good of humankind. The main thing is that wars are good for business, and I'm in the business of business. And you can be, too."

I was shocked, confused and angry, but my body was steady as a rock. I turned to face John, and in a voice as cold as steel, asked a burning question, "John, what exactly is it you're trying to say?"

"I'm saying that once you understand the reasoning behind things, you'll see why we need each other, and why it would be silly not to work together. It's time for you to be on the winning side. You've spent your whole life feeling like an outcast, and you've been struggling financially ever since you left home. I'm offering you an opportunity to finally put that to rest and be a winner. You would not only fit in, you'd be appreciated for who you are...and make money, too!

"You might as well listen to me Cassandra, because honestly, most people are so numb they hardly notice the bad parts of their lives. Besides, people need tragedy. That's why I created Earth's newest plague. I love what you humans are calling it, Mad Man disease. That pretty much says it." John slapped his knee with enthusiasm. "A little pain is a good thing. It keeps them invigorated."

"John, you're crazy!"

"Ah, Cassandra, you're only making things more difficult for yourself, and it won't change anything. All the truly smart humans recognize this dynamic and have learned how to work the system. They use it not only to benefit their own groups, but also to gain personal power. They know what I know...how easy it is to manipulate people, to get them to believe they need you.

"In fact, there are only a handful of people running the entire planet. Some of them realize they're working for me and some don't. But those who do know, my little innocent, don't care. Just threaten to take away their money or their power, and they can be led around like ants to a picnic. Do you get my drift? Can you see how I am giving people exactly what they want? It's a fair trade. They get what they want, and everything our side wants is ours for the taking." John snorted, his eyes beady and snake-like.

That's enough. I've got to get away from him!

I started to get up when John leaned toward me and sleazed, "I guess you don't quite realize that every time you connect the energy, like you did at Stone-henge, you're putting more clout in my hands, too. Yes, *indeedie!* You reactivated those sites, and I have access to their power, as well. So you see, we're already working together, after all. It's really quite ironic. But since we both want what's best for the human race, we're actually helping each other."

My stomach was churning, and I thought I might be sick. "Why do you do it...what's in it for you, John?"

"Ah! Finally you've asked the 'ultimate' question. Why do I do it? You mean aside from getting to be the most powerful person on the entire planet? Because I get immortality! Is that good enough for starters?" John's roar of laughter thundered in my ears.

"Immortality?"

"Well, let's call it an 'energy exchange.' I have a special relationship with some folks of the extraterrestrial persuasion. You may have heard them called the Forces of Darkness, but what's in a name? Anyway, since the time of Atlantis, which unfortunately turned into a bit of a fiasco, I've had this little deal going. It's a simple process, and I'm sure I could get them to agree to give you the same thing. I keep a certain level of chaos, confusion and fear happening on the planet. The extraterrestrials feed on this energy. It keeps them alive. Who am I to judge? In return, they give me eternal life. When I've worn out one body I just walk into another one.

"Now, I am very conscientious about this, and I never take a body without permission, but you would be amazed at how many humans there are on the planet who don't really want to be here. I wait for a time when they are feeling low. They could have lost their job, gone through a divorce, or maybe someone they loved just died. I calmly ask them if they would like to leave. They are thrilled at my offer and...*viola!* I have a new body. Everyone is happy."

John laughed until he nearly choked. Then, having completed his moment of knocking his own socks off, he pulled himself together and resumed his normal cloying tone of voice.

"Sorry, but humans crack me up!" He mopped his forehead again with the drenched handkerchief. "How can you stand spending so much time outdoors?

It's so…well… *outdoorsy.*

"Okay, back to business. So, here's the deal. You can have the same arrangement I have. And the same benefits! The truth is, I'd be Joe Nobody without those extraterrestrial Forces of Darkness. Well, I'd still be a lot smarter than the rest, but I'd lose my 'special powers.' Fortunately, they're right there with me. So now you know who the *we* is…and how much power I have at my back," John bragged, beginning to chortle again.

I sat unable to move, staring at him as the true horror of what he had been saying began to sink in.

"Now really, Cassandra, do you think you can go up against that kind of power? Do you honestly believe that you're strong enough for that? I mean, I think you're great, but there's great and then there's *great!* And frankly, while I respect your gumption and pluckiness, I don't think you have the kind of power or talent or just plain inner strength that can match us. After all, what do you have to offer people that can begin to compete with what we've got going on here?

"Besides, it's not just me you'd be working with. We've got people in high places all over the world, and our legions are growing daily. We have plenty of new recruits. 'Human nature,' you know. Fear, power and greed can lure the noblest of men. We dangle any material possession they could wish for, and trust me, we have them all. And gorgeous women, gorgeous men…! Whatever they've got an appetite for, we've got it.

"You really need to think about it, Cassandra. You're young, you're beautiful, and even though you may not be brilliant, you're a smart cookie. The sky's the limit for you in our world. You can have anything your little heart desires…except peace, that is. And face it, peace is boring when you come right down to it.

"Why not just call it a day and come over to our side? We could use your skills and you could have more money and power than you've ever dreamed of. You have to admit you need money, Cassandra. It's a constant struggle for you. All that can end. *Poof…*gone in a flash! Think of the fun you could have. After all, everyone knows that the real purpose in life is to have fun! It might be a bit difficult at first, conscience and all. But, you'll be surprised how quickly you get over it. I did, all the way back in Atlantis."

I felt a clutching sensation around my heart. Fear and insecurity, the constant companions of my childhood, came folding in on me. *Maybe he's right. Maybe I'm not strong enough to go up against him...and human nature! Maybe everything he said is true. What have I gotten myself into?*

"Now, now, my pretty," John cloyed, his voice offering the comfort he thought I needed. "It's not going to be that bad. You'll find...."

A great fury welled up within me. *He's playing with me, and I won't fall for it! I know he's powerful, but so am I. He may have shut off the electrical plant, but I'm the one who turned it on.* In a blaze of recognition, I knew that if I gave into anger in any form, I, too, would be giving him power over me. The fear that had turned to rage now became a sea of calm.

I rose to my feet and turned to face the monster. "John, in your contempt for the human race, you seem to have forgotten one important thing. Regardless of your little 'arrangement,' you're only human yourself. No matter whom you think you've got on your side, in the end, with all you've done to separate yourself from everyone and everything. You're all alone."

One of his eyes twitched, and I knew that no matter how minutely, I had hit a nerve. He quickly recovered and opened his mouth to speak, but before he could get a word out, I turned and left.

"See ya around, John," I shouted over my shoulder. My body was shaking and I could barely feel my feet as they quickly moved across the ground, but I had gained one vital piece of information. *He needs me, so he won't kill me... for now. But how far will he go to get me over to his side...that's the question!*

"You'll be back, Cassandra. Once you've put that itty-bitty little brain of yours to work, you'll be back. You'll beg me for another chance. Soon we'll have our own satellite in space. We'll be able to do anything we want, even take out whole cities in a wink! Before you know it we'll have everything. The planet will basically belong to us. You'll see there's no way to fight us. You'll have to join us. There's really no alternative."

His voice faded as I rushed to find my group. I was almost there when I felt a slight vibration coming from my camera case. *That's weird!* I took a few more steps but the vibration was even stronger. I hastily opened it, unable to imagine what it could be. Nestled in amongst my cameras and lenses, I saw the talisman. *Oh my god! I didn't leave it behind! I must have put it in here last night before I went to bed.*

I looked around to make sure no one was close by. I reached for the talisman and quickly commanded, "On!" John's face and upper torso appeared. He was holding something that looked like a metallic domino but without the spots. He held it up to his ear and nodded his head. "Further," I commanded.

The scene opened. John was still under the tree where I had just left him. A ringing sound came through the talisman. I heard his voice as he talked into the object, "I didn't get her this time but don't worry, she'll cave. She's still clueless that the only way to defeat you is to put you out of commission. And to do that, she'd have to convince a whole lot more people to take responsibility for their lives. And trust me, she'll never pull that off. I've got the human race and their little egos by the short and curlies. Hell, the majority of them don't even know they have a choice in things!" There was a short silence, then, "Okay, partner, I'll talk to you later."

I watched as John put the tiny cell phone in his pocket, then turned and walked away. It was a few moments before I could command the talisman "Off!" and rejoin my group.

CHAPTER 57

Not since Egypt had I felt so alone in the midst of a group. Everyone was in awe of the sophisticated Mayan culture, and their animated conversation made the long bus ride back to Mérida fly quickly – for them. For me, it had been a completely different story. I was in silent turmoil, in the midst of a great tug-of-war within myself.

Mary had said I could defeat John and his people, that I had the power within me to do it. And certainly what I had been doing at the sites seemed right. But now, to discover that I might be helping John broke my heart. The entire inside of my body quivered and shook. *John is insane and…I have charged up some of the most sacred and powerful energy points on the planet to accelerate his evil plans!*

A deep sense of betrayal washed over me when I considered that my actions might be making the world more miserable. It was a real conundrum. *Knowing what I know, how can I go on? Should I even bother? What if I really don't have that kind of power, anyway? I might have just been kidding myself. And damn it, John's not far off about human nature.*

I was very close to giving up, which led me to thinking about Mary. Could she have underestimated John and the Forces of Darkness? I took a few deep, conscious breaths. *That's exactly what John would want me to do, doubt myself and doubt Mary. That would give a little more food to his extraterrestrial partners.*

I closed my eyes and leaned back in my seat. I went over my discussions with Mary, looking for something I had missed. She had said it was my destiny to defeat John and bring the Light, what I was born to do. I found myself re-membering life as a little girl. How excited I had been when the beautiful lady came to visit. She understood me, knew who I was.

As my mind tripped longingly over the years, I played back the tapes of those magical moments. They were moments before I had experienced doubt or fear – before I learned the words "can't" or "won't" or "shouldn't." One particular image jumped out from the rest. It was the first time I had levitated an object. The beautiful lady had placed a sparkling golden coin on the floor and said that if I could pick it up using only my mind, I could keep it. I hadn't hesitated. Instinctively, I focused my mind on the coin, and it lifted up as if borne on fairy wings. The beautiful lady smiled, then laughed, and her laughter was like the tinkling of little glass bells. In that moment, I knew the truth – I could do anything I set my mind to!

Everything became clear. *That's right! I can do anything I set my mind to. Choice really does exist. And if it exists for me, then it has to exist for the rest of mankind.* The darkness that had enshrouded me immediately lifted, and it was as though I had bathed in a cool spring of pristine water. I felt a rush of trust in myself, and with it came the certainty that the power did lay inside of me – had always lain inside of me. I must keep my mind…and my heart… focused on that power, move slowly and listen deep inside.

Suddenly, I was positive that if I kept my focus, the path to defeating John would show up in the moment it was needed. I did not need to know the "how" yet. Mary had said I would know what I needed to know when I needed to know it. Defeating John and bringing the Light, so the human race could choose to evolve was exactly what I had already chosen to do. And if I had chosen it, then I could do it.

It was dark when we arrived back in Mérida. Nothing had changed – but everything had changed. I was no longer afraid of John. Well, not exactly. I was still anxious about him, but having everything out in the open made all the difference. Although it had been a rollercoaster of a day, I felt oddly peaceful.

The storm front weakened sometime during the night, and our plane was scheduled to take off shortly before noon. *I guess John doesn't need me here anymore.* A dark shutter raced through my body just thinking about his claim of creating all those "convenient" little storms to force us to land in Mérida.

Our departure from Mérida was handled with efficiency. Of course, we had the same flight crew, and once we were airborne, our pilot asked, "So how did you like the little side trip I arranged for you?" Cheers and moans, in almost equal amounts, rang throughout the cabin. Someone called out, "You should've made the storms last longer!" More cheers and whistles and clapping.

If they only knew….

Other than the *What did you do?* and *Where did you eat?* chatter among the passengers, the general topic of conversation was the Mad Man disease. We had all seen reports on the television, and the subject was obvious even in a foreign language. Everyone was concerned – but I was furious. *John…you bastard! I can't believe how a person can be so evil. But you're not a person, you are "evil" incarnate. And I'm the one who can stop you!*

Tina was supposed to pick me up from the airport before our two-day "delay." Knowing she would be worried, I had phoned her as soon as possible after we landed in Mérida. She was relieved to hear from me but managed to quip, "I'm certainly glad I wasn't with you on that little adventure." She made me promise to tell her my new arrival time. "I'll be there. I want to make sure you're all in one piece." And, of course, she was right there waiting for me when I finally reached the baggage claim.

"I still can't believe what you've been through. Weren't you scared?"

"Well, we did toss around a bit," I said, trying to make light of it. I hurriedly put my suitcase and camera bag in the trunk, slammed it shut and sank onto the soft leather seat of her semi-luxury car. The seat was moved all the way back. "Ah, leg room! This is what flying first class must be like."

"You deserve it," Tina laughed. "But seriously, I would have been totally freaked out if it had been me," she exclaimed, starting the engine and pulling away from the bustling airport. I looked at the jumble of cars vying for their place in the mess that is LAX.

"Hmm…. Look at this! I'm risking my life just getting out of the airport in this rush hour traffic."

"Come on now, honestly, weren't you scared knowing there were storms on both sides of you? I mean how did you feel when the pilot said you were forced to head out over the Gulf of Mexico?"

"It gave me pause to think, that's for sure. But what's funny is that in those kinds of situations, when things are just laid out in front of you like that, you just go with the flow. What else can you do?" *I love Tina, but I can't stand all the questions right now.*

"I don't think I could have ever been as calm as you. And look at you now! No one would ever guess what you just went through."

She has no idea how right she is on that one.

Tina chatted on, telling me how sick she had been on the train down to her parents and how her mother literally "fed" her back to health. "Chicken soup, meat pies, fish and chips…. I had to get well, or I'd have died from 'stuffication.' It was a great visit, but I was so happy to get home."

"I'm so glad. I was really worried about you. By the way, did you have a chance to check on the photos I took to the lab before we left for England?

Those labs always need prodding or your work gets put behind all the more urgent jobs, and I'm anxious to get them framed."

"Uh…yes I did. I know you asked me to call them, but I was in the area, and so I stopped by. They had one ready, the one of Machu Picchu. Cassie, they blew it up really big, and it's absolutely beautiful. Everybody was commenting on it. I'm so proud of you."

Tina was full of conversation as we zigzagged our way through the slow Friday evening traffic, but after awhile she grew strangely silent. *She would never get quiet over traffic. I wonder what's going on?* Finally, I couldn't help but ask if everything was alright.

"Yes," she answered, somewhat distractedly, "everything's okay." But the silence continued. *This is so not like Tina.*

"Are you sure? Is it something about you and Martin? Have you broken up?"

"No! No, it's nothing like that. Okay, Cassie, I need to tell you something, and I don't want you to be upset because everything's turned out perfectly."

Her solemn tone of voice got my immediate attention. "So tell me!"

"It has to do with your beloved roommate, Gail. You know how you're always saying how messy she is and how she screws things up, because she's so forgetful? Well… she really did it this time. She turned on the water for a bath and…."

"Don't tell me! Let me guess. She flooded the bathroom."

"It's worse than that but don't worry, all of your things are okay. I mean it only got to the bottom of a few crates of books and some clothes you left folded on the floor of your bedroom. But all the portfolios and art you had stacked on top of the crates are fine. So is everything on your desk…your computer and box of flash drives weren't touched. And of course, the digital cameras and CDs on your shelves are safe."

"Thank god! So all my negatives and prints are okay?"

"Yeah, the water only got to what you had in dead storage on the floor."

"Great! What did Gail say…how did it all happen?"

"Well," Tina said grinning, "You're gonna love this. She said she got a long distance call from a girlfriend she hadn't talked to in ages. Her friend was calling from an unlimited access phone and…."

"She forgot all about the bathtub. Damn! I'm always reminding her about that. I told her it would happen someday. How bad is it?"

"Pretty bad, but at least now it's easy to tell that the floor of your apartment slopes toward the living room and kitchen," Tina said, trying hard not to laugh, but failing.

"No way! All the way down there? I can't believe it!"

"Wait…there's more. She must have dozed off after the call, because the water was running for a long time. Eventually it started dripping into the apartment below, and I know how much you love the two guys who live down there. By the time they got home from work, they had a swimming pool in their place."

"Oh, my god! Alright, go on."

"They were livid and called the manager. He called Gail on his cell, raced up the stairs and started banging on your door. By that time, the water had started to come into her room. She got up from her boat of a bed and stepped into a rushing river. Can you imagine? Then she had to face the manager while he's screaming at her on the cell…*and* in person.

"Now here's good news. Number one, you have no liability in this. Remember, you sub-leased from her. So she's the one on the lease. You're not involved.

"Number two, we've finally finished the repairs on Martin's new house and we've moved in. You've seen it. It's big and beautiful…and very private. We have two extra bedrooms and that bonus room. I've already moved you in. There's plenty of space, and you can stay as long as you want. It's certainly not like having your own place, but it's much nicer than Gail's, and both Martin and I are thrilled to have you."

"I…I don't know what to say. I've always hated Gail's stuffy little apartment but I can't just…."

"Yes you can, and it'll be great. Just wait, you'll see. Besides, you're already in, installed, done! It doesn't have to be forever. We're gone all day anyway and you remember how much Martin travels. And I'm not thrilled about being alone in that big a house."

"You've done so much and I appreciate it, you know that. I'm…I'm just shocked." *I can't live with them! I'm already living with frigging John and the diary and David and Mary. It's too crowded! I need my own space. Damn!* There I was trying to figure out how to stop John from ruining the world, and I got flooded out of my apartment. And John, who couldn't care less about anyone but himself, was living like a king!

"…Cassie…Cassie," Tina said quietly, "we're almost home."

There was a dead spot in the pit of my stomach where gratitude should have been. Tina pulled into the driveway, and Martin came out to meet us. A jolt of crisp night air hit me, and I managed a cheerful greeting for Martin as we unloaded the car and walked into the welcoming light of their new home.

The house was a two-story Mediterranean, and their remodel had opened it so you could see right into the garden from the front door. Even in my agitated state, I could appreciate how warm and inviting the house was. *Just like Tina and Martin.* I had barely peeked into the living room before Tina took my arm and whispered, "Cassie, we'll show you around later. Right now we have a surprise for you."

Martin had taken my luggage through the living room and was waiting for us out on the flagstone patio. "Welcome to your new home," he said, as he turned and led us down a stone path that meandered around the swimming pool toward a guesthouse at the rear of the yard. "It's funny how things work out! We weren't going to fix up the guesthouse just yet, but when we took a closer look, it wasn't as bad as we had thought. All the old features were basically in good shape, and it only needed some sprucing up. Since our workers were already here, it turned out to be less expensive to have them do it now. So here you are…our new neighbor."

Tina opened the door and I entered a small but charmingly furnished living room. It felt light and airy because of its peaked ceiling and large windows that looked out to the garden. To the left was a dining area and beyond that, a very well laid out little kitchen with lots of storage and countertop. Martin told me the cottage was built in the late thirties and was the first structure on the property. It still had the original oak floors and moldings. The main house wasn't built until the mid-forties.

"This way to your boudoir," he said, leading me into the comfortably sized bedroom. It was furnished with a double bed piled high with pillows and a beautiful little rosewood desk that Tina had purchased at an estate sale years before. My rescued clothes were neatly arranged in the closet and a little old-fashioned cabinet in the bathroom held all of my personal items. "You two are amazing! My things look right at home."

"This was Tina's mission, but I've saved the best part for last." With obvious pride, he walked over to a pair of French doors that opened into yet another room. He flipped on the light, revealing an art studio fit for Picasso. "This was a covered patio that allowed the guest house complete outside privacy apart from the main house. I didn't think that was necessary so I enclosed the patio with windows to make a sunroom. You can't tell now, but during the daytime it gets incredible light. I think it will be the perfect studio for you."

"Martin, it's just beautiful. How can I ever thank you?"

"You don't have to because I'm going to be thanking you in a minute!"

"The minute is now," called Tina, busily clinking something in the living room. "Cassie, come back out here so Martin can tell you the really wild and wonderful part."

"This place is pretty wild and wonderful on its own," I called back. "I can't imagine what else you two could've cooked up."

Tina had lit candles, and the coffee table was laden with champagne on ice and veggies, along with cheese and crackers. *Oh god! I'm happy but I don't want a party!*

"Come, sit next to me," Tina said, patting the sofa, "we have another surprise. And have a bite of something to eat. You must be starving." *What now,* I wondered as I sat down and reached for a carrot. When I looked up, I noticed that a large sheet was covering the wall opposite the sofa. Chomping on a cracker, Martin walked over to one end of the sheet. Tina jumped up and went over to the other end.

"Ready?" he asked.

"Ready!"

They removed the sheet, revealing two of the large multi-image color photographs from my trip to Peru and Bolivia that I had left in the lab for Tina to check on. "The third one is right here," Martin said, removing a sheet from an adjacent wall. The two images of Machu Picchu and one of Tiahuanaco were all beautifully mounted between two pieces of quarter-inch Plexiglas that were then sealed together and the edges polished. The pieces looked gorgeous – and huge. The result was truly dramatic. The vision of ancient stone sites combined with modern technology was unexpected – and strangely compelling. I was speechless.

"What do you think?" asked Tina. "It was Martin's idea."

"I love your work, Cassie. And I hope you like the framing. I was with Tina when she stopped by the lab. The lab owner knew you wanted to keep the sprocket and edge numbers visible, and he showed me this new type of framing he thought was perfect for your work. Putting them between two pieces of Plexiglas forms an unframed-frame and the picture just sort of floats there. It's an amazing look, and I just couldn't resist. I hope you don't mind."

"Mind? They're incredible…really beautiful! Thank you both." I stood up to get a closer look. The framing was perfect. "I…I can't believe it. How in the world did you get it done so fast?"

"I sort of finagled my way," Martin replied with a grin.

"You know Martin," laughed Tina, as we settled back onto the sofa. "He always has his ways! Besides, he had a personal agenda this time."

"She's absolutely right," Martin said, as he poured the champagne, and we had a quick toast to our new homes.

"Cassie," he began, "the only reason I went to the lab with Tina was because we had a lunch date and the lab was on the way. But once I saw your work, something happened. Now, I'm the biggest critic you could ever find, but I couldn't take my eyes off of your photographs. They were absolutely riveting. I don't know what it is, but there's something…I can't explain it, but I feel some… some kind of aliveness when I look at your images. It's an aliveness I've never felt before. In fact, I made Tina go back with me after lunch for another look. That's when the technician showed us the framing, and I decided, right on the spot, to do it. It was so perfect for your work. Then, when we saw the finished pieces, they were.... I can't describe it exactly. I'm at a loss for words."

"And Cassie, trust me, Martin is never at a loss for words."

He cleared his throat, and in his "business voice" said, "So, for starters I want to buy those three pieces from you and...."

I cut him off. "No way! You can't buy those pieces, Martin. They're yours. With all you two have done for me, I'm thrilled to have something I can give back. And I'm thrilled to hear your response to them, because the places in the photos are energy vortexes. They're very magical, and somehow I've been lucky enough to capture their essence on film. I've had some mind-boggling experiences myself, both with the film and at the sites."

"We want to hear all about your trip, and your added excursion, but right now I want to continue my little saga about your photographs. I hope you don't mind, but I have a friend who owns a gallery, and I had her stop by yesterday to see your work. I showed her these three, as well as the two large hand-painted Egyptian pieces you did just before you left. She is planning an exhibit of ethnic sculpture from around the world and has been looking for an artist whose work would complement it. She loves what she saw and wants you to be in the exhibit."

My sense of time warped. *This cannot possibly be happening. Was it only yesterday that I was at Chichen Itza listening to John's tirade about destroying the world? Then I get flooded out of my apartment and moved into this amazing guesthouse. I ask Tina to check on my photographs and presto, they're framed. I start to think of myself as an artist, and I come home to being in an art show.*

"I think we've overwhelmed the poor girl," Martin said. "We didn't mean to drop all of this on you at once, but we were just so excited."

"We were...we are," Tina gushed. "And Cassie, it's such a fantastic opportunity for you. I know how much you love doing the hand-painting, and your photographs have always been incredible, anyway. This show will give you so much exposure. It could be the beginning of a whole new career! The gallery is beautiful and Marguerite, the owner, is very sharp. She loves discovering new artists, and when she finds one whose work she really likes, she becomes their advocate. She knows you're just a 'babe in the woods' at this, but she thinks your work is terrific so you don't have to be nervous about anything. What do you think? Isn't it great?"

Tina's eyes widened with anticipation as I searched for my voice. It was there, but I couldn't seem to find it. The dead spot that had filled the pit of my stomach had turned into a quiver of nervous excitement. Finally, I managed, "Unbelievable! It's just unbelievable. An art show…. I feel like I'm in some sort of a dream where a magic wand has been waved, and I have been turned from a frog into a princess."

Martin laughed as he leaned over, put his arms around me and said, "You're Tina's best friend. We can't have Tina being a princess without you being one, too."

He stood up and gazing at my photographs, said, "They grab me every time. I can't wait to see what you're going to come up with next. But don't think about it now. You've had more than enough for one day. Get some sleep and take care of yourself. You've just been through a bit of an ordeal. I'll make an appointment with Marguerite so you two can get acquainted."

We talked a bit more, then Tina showed me the refrigerator they had stocked with food and where the kitchen things were. "And you have one final surprise," Tina said, as she unwrapped a brown paper bag. "Ta da…your favorite coffee!"

That bit of thoughtfulness, and so much more, brought tears to my eyes. After another round of hugs, Martin said, "Honey, I think we should go. And Cassie, I'm really glad you're here. Sleep well."

"Call me when you wake up," Tina whispered as she gave me one last hug.

"Thank you! Thank you both so very much."

"Just don't forget us when you're rich and famous," laughed Martin, as he bent to place a tender kiss on my forehead.

"I promise," I replied, as I watched Tina and Martin, and their magic wand float out the door and down the path to their new home.

CHAPTER 58

I awoke shortly before nine the next morning, "knowing" that my glyphs – the symbols that had appeared to my inner vision – needed to be in the art show. I tried to dismiss the idea. *It's crazy…they're important to me, but they're not really art!* However, the idea would not go away. I reached for my photo notebook and examined the glyphs from an artistic point of view, remembering the feelings I'd had each time a new one appeared.

As I continued to look at the glyphs, I become certain they were somehow connected with the sacred sites I had visited and should be seen alongside them. *Well, I love you exactly as you are, but I think I'll have to spruce you up a bit before your "public appearance."* I spent a large part of the day copying each glyph with a black design pen on graph paper to make their shapes more exact and the lines cleaner. I wrote the three letter name for each glyph above the image and its meaning below.

A quick call to Martin proved that, true to his word, he had scheduled a meeting with Marguerite, the gallery owner, for lunch the next day. My fashion portfolio was always ready to go, but preparing an art portfolio required some thought. I gathered a few small black and white sacred site images, two of my small hand-painted pieces, and proof sheets showing the amazing, multi-image, color-manipulated strips of film, the unexpected gift from my dented camera scenario in Peru. And, of course, I took the glyphs. It was a pretty skimpy collection, but she had already seen the big pieces.

I glanced over at the rattan end table and noticed a pile of mail that Tina must have stacked up for me. I knew what was in it – bills, bills and more bills, at least one of which was going to collection. My rent might have been covered, but the rest of my life wasn't. *I need this show to happen and I need to sell a lot of work. I've got to have the funds to do whatever it takes to defeat John…and find David.*

Martin had made reservations at an upscale restaurant in Beverly Hills and joined us for lunch. I was nervous but Marguerite and I took an instant liking to one another – kindred spirits under two very different skins.

"I'm always on the lookout for new artists, and when Martin showed me your work, I was impressed. It has an interesting quality to it. There is a certain, I don't know, energy…a vibrancy to your images that's unusual. It's like you've brought these ancient places back to life." Martin looked at me with a smug grin.

I was thrilled by Marguerite's words and eagerly showed her the rest of my work. Then, though I was a bit apprehensive, I showed her the glyphs. She loved all of the photographs, especially the hand-painted pieces, but wasn't at all certain about the glyphs.

"What do the three letters on top mean?"

"They're the names of the glyphs. Each glyph has its own name and meaning. For instance, this one, AGN, means *spiritual evolution*. I know the drawings seem simplistic, but they're very interactive. When you hang out with them, give them your undivided attention, they pull you right in. Trust me," I said hurriedly, "they'll look very different when I have them scanned into the computer and printed on watercolor paper as Gliceé prints. Then, with the framing, if we keep it very simple, the images will just pop out at you. They're a good compliment to the sacred sites photos. They really are." *I hope this works! The glyphs absolutely have to be in the show.*

I promised I would have a few ready for her to see by the end of the week. But for sure, we would show the large, single and multi-image, color-manipulated photographs, and, of course, the hand-painted ones. We discussed how many pieces and of what size it would take to fill the gallery. Framing the photos would not be a problem, but I needed to have more of the hand-painted ones and that would be time consuming. We parted ways, Martin, Marguerite and I, in high spirits and with great enthusiasm for the project.

George, my printer opened at 7:00 a.m., and I had the first appointment. I took four of the sixteen glyphs and left them to be turned into computer images, enlarged and printed on fine English watercolor paper. Then I took my color film, as well as the black and white film from England, Scotland and the Yucatan to the various labs to be developed.

Next, I began the monumental task of going through at least one hundred slides and filmstrips from the color-manipulated series. I picked out my favorites to have blown up as large colored prints. No decisions would be needed on the framing! I wanted them done exactly the way that Martin had "non-framed" them in the Plexiglas mounts. And I decided to keep the distinctive style of showing the sprockets and edge numbers, whether they were single or multi-images, for the entire series. I wanted the viewer to have the same sense of immediacy I had felt when I first viewed the raw film at the lab.

Then I began to assess the black and white images. *How big should they be and how long will it take me to paint them?* Marguerite had made it clear she was anxious to make plans for the show and get the publicity out. Her gallery was new, and while the schedule was still open, it would fill up quickly. *Now is when she has room for me, so I just have to go for it. I'll paint night and day if I need to!*

Several things were pushing me toward an early date for the show. The first was that the show felt very important – like it would give me a necessary piece of the puzzle. The next thing was John. He had put all of his cards on the table at Chichen Itza. And, with everything I had learned from both the diary and Mary, especially with the fast growth of the Mad Man disease, I knew that time was of the essence.

And, of course, there was David – dear David! He was never far from my mind – or my heart. In fact, he had become the background music to the movie that was my life. Considering all of those things, it was important to have the show soon.

Marguerite, Martin and I met again on Friday. I held my breath as I showed her the glyphs done as Gliceé prints. She looked at them intently.

"I don't understand what it is about them that makes them special, but they clearly are. All right, you've convinced me. We will include your glyphs in the exhibit." We decided on a 16" by 20" size for them with my idea of very simple white frames and mats to make the graphic design quality jump out.

I told her about the color-manipulated pieces I had already put in the lab to be blown up very large. "I will pick up all of the film from England, Scotland

and the Yucatan this afternoon and start making my selections." The big question was time. *Will I have enough time to do the hand-painted pieces?* I already had the two large ones from Egypt. "I think I can manage at least two more large painted pieces, possible three, and probably a few smaller ones, but the framing…"

"Don't worry about the framing. I'll take care of everything. You just take care of the painting!" Marguerite gave me a date and then watched as my face must have registered my panic. Oh god! Can I pull this off? Both Martin and Marguerite burst out laughing before quickly reassuring me, "You can do it! We'll do everything to help you…we'll even feed you. All you have to do is paint!" I would have the major room and the ethnic sculptor the smaller one adjoining it. We shook on it, and I scurried out to make my pick-ups at the labs.

It was a very hectic period. I went into a kind of time warp, painting for hours at a stretch, day after day, just as I had with the two pieces from Egypt. And the little cottage was perfect. *It's so quiet and the light is incredible. Everything is turning out even better than I could have imagined…I hope!*

CHAPTER 59

On opening night, I was very excited – and very nervous. All of my friends were there to lend moral support. A wonderful crowd of art lovers turned out as well. Martin, Marguerite and I had decided that the exhibition should be a benefit for an environmental organization. I was delighted, because it focused attention on the current plight of the planet and what was needed to turn things around. Even more exciting was that my art inspired a number of probing discussions about the length of time humankind had existed on earth and debates about the sophistication of our early development.

But what I was most curious about was how other people would react to the glyphs. The glyphs felt like a part of me. *For god's sake…they "spoke" to me…but I wonder if anyone else will be able to feel their energy the way I do?* I wanted to watch the people, but it was my show and someone was always asking me a question. The ones most frequently asked were, "Where did the glyphs come from?" and "What do they mean?" I scrutinized their faces as I offered the simple answer, "They came to me in meditation." *This isn't the place to get into the meaning and messages of the glyphs unless someone experiences….*

Several times throughout the evening, various people suggested I put the glyphs together in book form. Tina was standing next to me at one of those times. She squeezed my hand and said, "That's my Cassie," sounding much like a proud parent.

The crowd thinned as viewers migrated to the second room of the gallery. With the main room less congested, people were able to get a better view of the art. That was when the glyphs really became a focal point. Many people walked up close to the glyphs and were studying them intently. The large room was completely a-buzz with energy.

I could literally see energy coming off of the walls. I watched it move from the glyphs to the people who were looking at them. The energy also radiated from one sacred site photograph to the next, connecting them. Finally, it moved from one person to another. In fact, I was looking at one large energy soup.

Is anyone else seeing what I'm seeing? I was so absorbed and fascinated by what was happening that I did not notice the tall slender man, dressed in black slacks and a black silk shirt, standing at my side.

"Quite remarkable," he said.

I turned to him and smiled. Then the weirdest thing happened. I wanted to speak, but when I opened my mouth no sound came out. I stood frozen, mouth slightly ajar, literally unable to say a word. It was his eyes. There was something about them that was both strange – and familiar.

"My name is Professor Daath," he said, shaking my hand. "I want to tell you how much I am enjoying your show." My eyes were still fixed on his, but I managed to notice his voice. He spoke with an accent that I could not identify.

"I'm sorry," I said, clearing my throat and shaking my head a bit to clear my vision. "I didn't mean to stare. Do I know you?"

"I don't believe so. I'm not from around here. This is the first time I've been to Los Angeles."

There was that strange accent again. It was not British, not Australian, not South African, either.

"I have been waiting for a chance to speak to you about your art. How did you discover the Pleiadean glyphs? You see not many...."

"The what?"

"The Pleiadean glyphs. I'm a Professor and have a doctorate in archeology and...."

"I'm sorry, the what?"

"Hmm, sounds rather like you don't quite realize what you have here. Is there someplace where we can talk privately for a few moments?"

"Um, well, yes. The gallery has a viewing room. I'm sure Marguerite wouldn't mind." I led him down a small corridor, through a glass door and into a dark room. I fumbled around for the light switch and an indirect light softly flooded the space. The entire office was tastefully designed around a slightly Asian theme. I motioned him to sit in one of the chairs by the koi pond. The sound of its gently running water felt reassuring.

I was still intrigued by his large eyes. We sat quietly for a moment before he broke the silence. "You seemed surprised when I referred to your drawings as Pleiadean glyphs," he said matter-of-factly, but with a slight smile. "Many of the line drawings you are exhibiting have been found etched on small rocks at certain sacred stone sites around the world, even at some of the sites you have photographed. The idea that they are Pleiadean glyphs is simply a theory at this point. I am one of only three archeologists in the world who have committed themselves to solving this mystery."

"What mystery? My drawings? But Professor...."

"Please, call me Kevin."

I felt a surge of nervous excitement. *This is so bizarre. What is he talking about? These are simply my drawings.* I forced my voice to remain calm. "What mystery? Why are my drawings called the Pleiadean glyphs? Where can I see some of these rocks?"

"What a flood of questions," he said with a smile. "Alright then, I believe

I can answer your first and third questions together. I'm not sure that you can see any of the rocks, however I can show you photographs." He reached down to retrieve a black leather briefcase I had not noticed before. He snapped it open, pulled out a stack of black and white photographs and handed them to me. I was in shock as I quickly thumbed through them. I could not believe what I was seeing. They were pictures of my glyphs. I silently handed them back to him, searching for some kind of answer in his large eyes.

"The odd thing," he continued, "is that a few stones were removed from their original sites for protective purposes. All of those have vanished. At other sites, our people photographed the stones but left them exactly where we found them. Now, I realize this might sounds a bit strange, but they seem to have vanished as well. To date, the largest collection of stones found at a single site was on Easter Island. One of my collogues visited there just last week. We don't know how or why, but he reported that those stones had also vanished." He cleared his throat. "It's quite embarrassing, actually. My colleague seems to believe that the stones are still on the island, but that for some reason the natives don't want 'experts' sticking their noses into the island's business or…. The truth is, it's a bit of a mystery. We don't really know what to think."

"And my other question?"

"Why are they called the Pleiadean glyphs? I'm afraid that my answer is going to be a bit vague here, as well. There is a whole new field opening up in archeology known as *astro-archeology.* This discipline attempts to correlate ancient stone sites with events that take place in the heavens." He paused, assessing my interest.

"Yes?" I prodded.

"Ah, well, we have discovered that many of the ancient civilizations were sophisticated astronomers. For instance, we have discovered that at sites such as Stonehenge, the stones are aligned in such a way as to mark off the equinoxes, the solstices and even predict lunar eclipses. In fact, Stonehenge is often referred to as an 'astronomical computer.' And I can see you have been to Chichen Itza. Can you imagine…in 600 B.C., they built a pyramid that still shows the shadow of the serpent as it appears on the equinoxes?

"My colleagues and I also look at the myths and legends surrounding some of the most enigmatic sites. These stories abound with references to events that have either already taken place or are currently taking place in the heavens. We search for clues that might help us date the site's construction and possibly, its purpose.

"Now, to try to answer the question as to why your drawings are called the Pleiadean glyphs. Many ancient civilizations have some kind of reference to the star system known as the Pleiades. And these particular places just happen to be where we have found the stones bearing your glyph drawings. For instance, Callanish, on the Isle of Lewis, which you have photographed so beautifully, is known to mark off an alignment to the rising of the Pleiades. This star system is also known as The Seven Sisters. The Pleiades...."

"But how could I...?"

"Let me continue. The Pleiades makes this alignment on...."

My mind raced. *How could my glyphs have been found all over the world?* I stared into the koi pond, only partially listening to his words. *There it is again, Callanish and the Pleiades! The people at Mary's made that connection too.* And I knew the Pleiades played a very important role in the diary. It's where Zev Moab and other of the Galactic Visitors were from. But if what he was saying about the glyphs was true, why in the world had they come to me? Every muscle in my body snapped to attention, as question after question went wildly tripping through my mind. I closed my eyes for a long moment trying to get my bearings. I opened them and looked up, but the professor was gone.

I jumped out of my seat and quickly looked around the room, but he wasn't there. *What in the world just happened? Where did he go?* I ran back out into the gallery, but I couldn't see him anywhere. I raced out the front door and looked up and down the street. Nothing! I hurried over to Tina and breathlessly asked, "Did you notice that tall man I was talking to earlier?"

"What! You've got a crush already?" she said, jokingly squeezing my arm.

"No, Tina...this is important! Did you see the tall, unusual-looking man I was talking with a little while ago? He was wearing black slacks and a black silk shirt."

"Um…no, I didn't. There were so many people, and most of them were wearing black."

"Think! This is really important. It was just after the discussion about how the glyphs would make a good book. Remember?"

"Yes…vaguely."

"Then…?"

"Honestly, I just don't remember. There's been so much going on here tonight, and your show's been such a great success. What is it? You look really upset."

"Never mind," I said, still looking around in disbelief. "There was this man that I was talking to and he kind of vanished. It's a long story. I'm going to walk around and see if I can find him."

I walked the length and breadth of the gallery several times – searching, searching. I questioned a few people, but their response was similar to Tina's, "…there were so many people." Finally, after frantically looking for about fifteen minutes, even having someone check the men's bathroom, I had to face the fact that he simply was not there. The rest of the evening was a blur. I received more congratulations and thanked everyone for coming, but I could not wait to get home.

Later that night, in the quiet of my little cottage, I ran through the entire scenario again. I knew I wasn't crazy. There really had been a man I was talking to in Marguerite's office – and he really did vanish. *There was something about him…!*

I went into the bedroom and sat cross-legged on my bed. I closed my eyes, leaned against the wall and began to breathe. After a few, long even breaths, time began to slow down, and I could feel myself go deep inside. Images of the glyphs passed before me, one by one, much like a slide show. Then I saw myself in a desert. A group of men dressed in long robes were deep in conversation. One of them turned toward me. Our eyes met for a brief moment –but that was enough. I easily recognized him as the unusual looking man, Dr. Daath, from the art gallery. It was his eyes that gave him away.

The vision faded, and in its place I saw a picture right out of a book I had browsed through at my chiropractor's office. There was a line of stone statues. In a flash the dots began to connect. My eyes flew open. *Easter Island! That's where most of the glyph stones were found...and they're probably still there. Clearly, I need to go to Easter Island.*

Lying down on the bed, I closed my eyes again and could see myself in the picture of Easter Island, walking amongst the tall statues, cameras in tow. Within a short period of time, and with my lips curled into a gentle smile, I was deeply asleep.

CHAPTER 60

The telephone jarred me awake far too early the next morning. I fumbled with the phone and heard Marguerite's excited voice even before it reached my ear.

"I'm sorry if I woke you sweetie, but I couldn't wait to tell you. You're a genius! The show was wildly successful! We sold three of the large hand-painted pieces last night, and I have holds on the rest. And your multi-image photographs, I've never seen anything like it!

"The photographs are spectacular, but I think the framing is what did it. People kept commenting that it was like looking at a raw strip of film. They loved the idea of floating the image within Lucite. I tell you, the framing itself is art. I couldn't write orders fast enough. We've sold them all, and I've taken orders for more. People are going to hang them in a series. And your glyphs, they've sold, too. I don't know what it is about your work, but I've never had this much response to a show in any of my galleries before."

"Wow, that's great! Really great. I can hardly believe it."

"Well, it's all true, honey, but there's more. A man showed up at the gallery right after you left, in fact, just as I was closing, and ordered your entire set of glyphs. He also wants to publish them as a book, and sent over a proposal and a contract first thing this morning. It's a great publisher. They've made a nice niche for themselves in the international art book market.

I think you should seriously consider it. Can you come in this afternoon about two so we can talk?"

"Absolutely! I'm so high I might just fly over."

Marguerite laughed. "I'm really happy for you…for us. See you at two."

I hung up the phone, grabbed my pillow and hugged it tightly. I was numb and excited at the same time. *My show's a success and someone wants to do a book of my glyphs!* Now I understood why I had felt so strongly that the glyphs needed to be a part of the show. And after seeing the energy interaction between the glyphs and the people at the gallery, I realized that the glyphs hadn't been just for me – they were important for everyone. *I don't quite "get it" yet, but I know they need to be out in the world.* And who would have thought my camera's "accident" in Peru would create such magical images that they would pay for my trip to Easter Island – and more.

Easter Island? Easter Island? Had the diary said anything about Easter Island? I couldn't remember. *I guess I'll have to go get it out of the vault and take a peek.* I hated to do it, but I hadn't seen John or his men since returning from Mérida. I looked at the clock. *If I go right now, I'll just have time to bring it home, scan through it and take it back on my way to the gallery.* I threw on some clothes, jumped into the car and headed to the bank.

I had barely settled in on the sofa when the phone rang. "Sweetie, its Marguerite. Listen, I just got a call from my morning appointment. She has a conflict and wants to move our meeting to two o'clock. I hate to mess up your day, but could you possibly come in now?"

"Okay, sure. No problem. I'll be right over." I put the diary in a paper bag and tucked it into the middle of the dirty clothes hamper. *This is probably overkill but just in case….*

There were several people in the gallery when I arrived, and Marguerite proudly introduced me as her latest '"find." I was welcomed with congratulations and questions. One woman said, "I know a little bit about using film, but I don't really understand how you got the multi-image photographs. And how did you get them to be so specific?"

"I didn't actually *do* anything. The images were a 'gift' from the site."

Their questions continued. They wanted this and that piece of technical information about both the hand-painted pieces and the glyphs. I told them the details weren't important. "What's important is to experience them."

Tactfully, Marguerite said, "Why don't you do just that…experience them. I have something in the office I need to go over with Cassandra. If you have any more questions, we'll be back in a few minutes."

"Don't worry about us," one of the women chimed in, "you always have such thought-provoking shows at your galleries. We might just want to spend the day here."

Marguerite had placed three beautifully produced art books on the table by the koi pond. "These are by the publishing company who wants to do your glyphs," she said, as I sat on the same chair I had occupied during my discussion with the disappearing Dr. Daath. "This company knows the business and does a beautiful job. I have to say that never, in my entire career, have I seen anyone put together a proposal with this much detail in such short a time. I'm sure they recognize your work is going to be big and want to grab you before anyone else does. That's why I'm so excited and want you to get on this right away."

"They really are beautiful! The paper quality, the color…."

"Here's their contract and proposal. I've already looked them over and faxed the contract to Martin. He made time to review it and thought it was an excellent deal. You have a good advance, a good percentage and an established company. The only thing he added was a statement stipulating that you retain the copyright to the glyphs themselves. Why don't you take a few minutes to look over the basic layout and design sheets and see what you think? I'm going to check on my clients, and then, if you have any questions, we can call the publisher."

The initial layout was wonderful. The book would be nine inches square and printed on heavy stock, semi-gloss paper. The cover would be a deep purple with a six inch gold square in the center. One of the glyphs would appear in black within the center of the gold square.

The book itself was also thoughtfully laid out. When opened, each glyph would appear on the right-hand page and the accompanying text on the left. The book package included individual "glyph cards," all sixteen glyphs printed on card stock just slightly smaller than the book. That made it easy for the images to be individually held or hung.

It was as though they had read my mind. It looked exactly like it would have if I had designed it myself. But there was the text to consider. I knew the glyphs had to be out in the world, but I had been given some pretty heady information for describing them. *What did I want to say about them – what should I say?* I didn't have the answer, but it was clear to me that I needed to have final say on whatever text would to be in the book.

Marguerite burst back into the office, anxious to hear my response.

"It's really beautiful! It is exactly how I would have designed it myself, and I'm good with the contract, since Martin gave the okay, but I have a few concerns." We discussed them and agreed that my concerns needed to be addressed in the contract.

Marguerite phoned the publisher who came out of a meeting to take her call. "The artist is really happy with the conceptual layout. She thinks you did a beautiful job. As for the contract, we've already had our attorney look it over. Basically, it's fine, but we've added two amendments. The first is that the artist will provide the text and has final approval over all text and images that are used. The second is that she retain the copyright to the glyphs themselves."

I hope this doesn't kill the deal. I watched as Marguerite listened intently to what was being said on the other end of the line. "Um…um hmm…I understand. Just a minute, I'll ask her."

She covered the mouthpiece with her hand and whispered, "They're okay with the changes, but they also want to buy the right to produce fine art posters."

"They do? I…I have to think about that one."

"The artist wants to wait on that," Marguerite told them, "but we're ready to sign the contract." There was a pause in the conversation before she said, "All right then, we'll FedEx the contract right over."

She hung up the phone, and we erupted in blur of laughter, kisses and hugs. "You're definitely on your way, my girl!"

"Amazing…!"

"Now get out there to your adoring public. I've got to call FedEx. The publishers want it ready for the next book fair and need to get started right away."

I spent a few more minutes with "my public" before hurrying home. *I need to look through the diary really quickly and get it back into the vault.*

My mind was spinning as I opened the door to the cottage but froze at the sight that awaited me. It was a disaster! Things were strewn everywhere – the living room, kitchen, bedroom and into the studio. *What the f…!* Suddenly it dawned on me – the diary! I raced to the dirty clothes hamper. It was tipped over, clothes clumped all around. *They took the diary!* I franticly searched through the clothes anyway. Clearly, the diary was not there.

I tore through the house like a madwoman, turning over everything lying about. Nothing else seemed to be missing. My legs gave out, and I slumped down on the floor. *Damn that John! Son of a bitch!* I ran my fingers through my hair, thinking, *He must have had his men watching me…constantly.* Then an even more horrific thought entered my mind. *The glyphs! It has to be him! If he doesn't own the publishing house, he owns the publisher. He doesn't want those glyphs to get out into the world…I know it!*

My hand was shaking so hard I could barely grab hold of the phone and dial Marguerite's number. The phone rang once. It rang a second time, then a third. *Pick it up! Pick it up!*

Finally she answered. "Marguerite, you have to stop the deal."

"What? FedEx just left…."

"I'll explain later, just stop the guy! You have to get that contract!"

"I can't…."

"You have to! Where does he stop next? Get in the car and find him. Just do it! Call me when you have it back." While I was waiting for Marguerite's call, I ran to the main house and looked in through the windows. Nothing was disturbed. *I knew it!*"

I counted the seconds waiting for her call. *What if she doesn't catch him?*

And if she does, how in the hell am I going to explain this to her? A moment later the phone rang. Marguerite was completely out of breath. "Alright, I have it," she said, sounding a bit harsh. "Now, what's this all about?"

"This will sound crazy, but I…um…I…."

"Cassie!"

"Okay, okay! It's a long story, but believe me…the person who wants the book doesn't intend to ever publish it. His real reason for buying it is to tie up the rights and make sure that the glyphs never get out to the public."

"What…?"

"Check it out. Does the contract stipulate when the book will be published?"

There was a rustling sound. I could hear Marguerite tearing open the FedEx package and thumbing through the contract. "No, it doesn't, but they told me on the phone that they wanted it ready for the book fair. What if I called them and get them to put it in writing?"

I can't trust them…they'll say anything to get the glyphs. "Marguerite, there's a reason people were so excited about my work last night, and it isn't only because the images are beautiful or the framing is great. The work is energetic. It affects people on a visceral level, and the glyphs, especially, are transformative. They work on people's energy fields and strengthen their ability to connect with each other in a positive way. That's why it's so important that the glyphs really do get out into the world…and that's exactly why some people don't want them out."

Marguerite was quiet. "There was something magical here last night. I… I don't quite get it, but if you feel so strongly about this that you're willing to give up the advance and royalties, I…I guess I have to trust you. Do you want me to shred the contract?"

"Yes, please, and thank you for your understanding. It means a lot to me. Just wait, you'll be amazed at how many people buy one or more of the glyphs. And Marguerite, I'm sorry I can't explain more now…but I just can't."

Thank god she caught FedEx in time, I thought with a brief sense of relief. *Now I have to to get myself together and clean up this mess.* The last thing I wanted was for Tina or Martin to see what had happened.

Beginning in the living room and kitchen, I slowly made my way into my bedroom. My sense of violation competed with my worry about the diary. *What could David have written that John wants so badly? And what happens to David if I can't give it back to him?*

I was almost finished when I picked up a little pouch. *Wow! I forgot about this.* I opened the pouch and poured its contents out on the bed. There was a beautiful piece of malachite, a small handful of seed crystals and a scribbled note that read, "For you from Egypt." I flashed back to the day in the Old City of Jerusalem when I had become separated from my friends. I had met an Arab boy who had insisted I follow him. He had led me up a steep stairway so I could get a better view and had given me the pouch. He had pointed to the crowd below and I thought I saw David. But then both David and the boy had vanished.

Knelling beside the bed, I ran my fingers over the seed crystals. I picked up the piece of malachite and held it in the palm of my hand. It felt unusually warm. *Oh, my god! Could these have come from David?* I put the malachite and seed crystals back into the pouch and held it within the protection of my hands. *Why do I feel I have to take this with me to Easter Island? It's like I'm supposed to do something with it when I get there.*

I put the little pouch on top of my nightstand where I couldn't miss seeing it and reached for the phone to call Marguerite. I told her I wanted to add to my sacred site series by photographing the statues on Easter Island and asked her if she could cut me a check for at least some of the sales.

"Honey, you're my Golden Girl. You can have a check for as much as you want." Then she laughed her deep throaty laugh. "Within reason, that is."

Once again, as with all of my other journeys, events in my life had created a clear and easy pathway for me to travel to some distant place. There was a lot to figure out, but one thing was for certain, I was headed for Easter Island – and I needed to get there as soon as possible. I had to find out more about my glyphs – the Pleiadean glyphs – and why John was so afraid of them getting out into the world.

CHAPTER 61

Once I was over my rage at John, the days I had left in Los Angeles flew by in fury of activity. I had returned from one trip, painted like a fiend to prepare for the art show and was now about to head off on another adventure. There were orders to fill for the gallery, an interview for a photo magazine and the "stuff" of life to catch up with.

Before I had time to catch my breath, I was on an airplane headed for Papeete, Tahiti, and then on to Easter Island. I knew each leg of the journey was going to be long and felt impatient beyond belief. *I need to be transported over, not spend fifteen hours cooped up on an airplane!*

Fortunately, the time sped by because I seemed to enter some kind of altered state. There were extended stretches of time when I was not quite awake but not really asleep, either. During these periods, I found myself downloading tidbits of information. It was as though, by my very intention of going to Easter Island, I had tapped into a channel of universal knowledge – knowledge that came to me in the form of an inner voice that seemed to "speak" to me.

First, the voice gave me a brief description of the Island. "It is triangular in shape, with an extinct volcano on each of its three points. Long ago, when the volcanoes were active, their very presence made Easter Island a place rife with 'geophysical and paranormal' activity."

The voice went on to say, "In a very ancient time, the entire island was a ceremonial center and a communications device. And because it is the most isolated land mass in the world, the island was a perfect landing site for...." A blast of static interrupted the voice, as if its signal had become jammed. *Damn!*

I drifted through the hours, hearing words here and there, all of them telling me I was going to a very special and important place. I was excited about that but couldn't get past trying to figure out what I had missed when the voice had turned to static.

The second leg of the journey was on a small plane, so there was always a fair amount of turbulence, but I was now a veteran when it came to bumping and shaking. The voice was silent for most of the trip, but I had a series of distorted dreams with one common thread – David. He was always in some kind of trouble or struggle, but each time, just as I was about to discover what was going on, we hit a bump and I was jostled awake.

Are these dreams trying to tell me something? Is he in some kind of trouble? When I wasn't dreaming about David, I was thinking about him. But now it was more like a longing. My mind – my heart – kept returning to him again and again and again.

Shortly before landing, I heard the voice once more. This time it seemed to call out directly to me. "There are things you need to learn on Easter Island. Look and listen closely and carefully, with your feelings as well as your eyes and ears."

I was stunned. *Is the voice talking about the glyph stones or…?* Then, as if to reassure me, the voice said, "You will receive additional information during your stay."

CHAPTER 62

I arrived on Easter Island in the middle of a rainstorm. The air was so muggy and damp, I felt my clothes begin to mildew the moment I stepped off the airplane. I made my way to the "hotel," more like a Bed and Breakfast, unpacked and began to get myself oriented.

Easter Island is an odd place. It is very small, about one hundred and fifty square kilometers, and most of the island is uninhabited. The country of Chile annexed the island in the late eighteen hundreds and, with the exception of Hanga Roa, the little town at one end of the island, declared the island an open-air museum. Hanga Roa is the only place where the island's residents are allowed to live and where all telephone and electrical lines are located. Up until recently, there were no paved roads, and even agricultural pursuits were, and still are, tightly regulated. My hotel was located on El Correo Central, the main road, which led to the center of town.

The only contact I had on the island was one I'd made through my friend, Jesse, who had visited there a few years earlier. His fluent Spanish had made it easy to converse with the natives. One of the people he met was Mateo, a remarkable man who had made it his life's mission to restore the island's lost heritage. Jesse was very taken with Mateo's work and had stayed in contact with him. He informed his new friend that I was coming to visit and asked him to take good care of me. And fortunately, Jesse had said Mateo spoke decent, if somewhat broken, English.

Anxious to meet Mateo, I dropped off my luggage and went to ask the innkeeper for directions. He was sitting in the doorway fanning himself with his hat. "Is very humid, but lucky for you, you came during the rainy season. Not so many tourists. Now, to Mateo's house…is easy, but you have to know which one is it. The houses have no numbers, because here everybody knows everybody else."

I jotted down his directions and set out for Mateo's, questions about the glyph stones ready to burst out of my mouth. But I knew I had to be smart. After the craziness of John stealing the diary, his attempt to keep the glyphs from getting out into the world and Dr. Daath's belief that the glyph stones on the island might have been hidden by the natives, it seemed wise to err on the side of caution. *I'll have to see how it goes. I'm sure I'll know when the time is right, but it had better be soon.*

It did not take long to find the house. Mateo greeted me warmly and we conversed fairly easily. I had brought along a sampling of my photographs so he could see that I was sincere about my interest in the ancient sites and not just a tourist. I asked him if he would like to keep one or two, and without a moment's hesitation, he reached for one of the photographs from Tiahuanaco. It was a multi-image piece of the Kalaysa Temple, showing the sunken courtyard with the faces of "all the races on earth and then some." He declined my offer of a second photograph, but thanked me profusely for the one he had selected.

Hmm! Fascinating…. I wonder why he chose that one…and so fast? He was clearly moved by my work, or by the image he had selected, because he immediately offered to personally show me around his "special island" the following day. I was thrilled.

Mateo was working on an old jeep when I arrived at his house the next morning.

"I need a few more minutes to work on her, but come inside, I have something to show you," he said, ushering me into his simple but comfortable home. He opened a metal lockbox, and handed me two faded yellow manila envelopes, and a stack of old pictures and artist renderings of the island. "This will keep you busy while I finish." He indicated that I should read the contents of the envelopes before looking at the pictures. Then he motioned me to a comfortable-looking old chair and hurried back out the door.

Great! I hope there will be some pictures of the glyph stones. The artist in me hesitated only a millisecond before rifling through the pages of renderings. There were dozens of drawings of the famous Moai, the enormous stone statues for which the island is known. Some depicted Moai standing alone, others showed them in various groupings, from five to fifteen, perched atop low stone platforms. Still others showed Moai either partially buried in the ground or lying broken, parts scattered about. They were amazing, but there was nothing that even remotely resembled my glyphs.

I carefully – and quickly – looked through the remaining drawings. They seemed a bit older. The last one jumped out at me. Even though it was not a glyph stone, it stood apart from the rest and was by far the most unusual. It was not exactly a rendering, but more like some kind of mechanical drawing on an unusual type of paper, one I had never seen before. It showed the island as it must have looked from the air, perhaps from a helicopter. The entire perimeter of the triangular island was ringed with Moai standing on individual platforms as if guarding the island. However, instead of facing outward toward the ocean, as one might expect, they were faced inward toward land.

Where could this drawing have come from and how was it made? It almost looks like it was computer generated. I glanced back at the first drawings, looking for some indication of when they were created. I was able to find both signatures and dates. The dates were easy to discern and ranged from the early seventeen through the mid-eighteen hundreds. I looked again at the "computer" drawing, back and front, but couldn't find a signature or date anywhere. *Hmm, every drawing is dated except this one. Why…? And there were no helicopters back then. How could they have known the island looked like this?*

I glanced again at a couple of the dated drawings, searching for my glyphs. *I suppose it's possible that the glyph stones came later. Maybe I'll find some answers here,* I thought, as I reached into the first manila envelope. The moment I felt the papers inside, I could tell they, too, were old. I pulled them out very carefully and was rewarded with a treasure-trove of handwritten information, except that none of it was in English, so I couldn't read a word of it.

I was becoming impatient. I really needed to learn more about the glyphs – find out why they were so important that John wanted to stop people from seeing them. *The glyph stones are the reason I came here. Well, that and whatever it is I'm supposed to be looking and listening for.* I reached into the second envelope and inched the papers out. They were slightly larger than the others, and appeared to be written more recently by archeologists and scholars visiting and studying Easter Island. And they were all in English. Apparently, whoever had written them had been able to translate some of the original material written by the earlier visitors.

One paper claimed that the first modern day inhabitants of the island were Polynesians who, led by their king Hotu Matua, had come to the remote island about fifteen hundred years ago. I also learned that all of the Moai were carved from the soft stone found in only one place on the island, the ancient and extinct volcano of Rano Raraku. The volcano was located at the far end of one of the triangular island's tips. *But again, no mention of glyph stones!*

Peeking out, I saw that Mateo was still busy tinkering with his jeep. *Is it possible he took out all pictures, even written references to the glyphs, before giving me this information?* If that was the case, the subject might be even more delicate than I had imagined! Hmm! *Can't worry about that now. There are still a few more pages to go. Something might turn up yet.*

Whoever had written the next account reported that, "…over one thousand

Moai have been carved. The platforms the Moai stand on are called ahu, and the natives consider them to be ceremonial in nature. The Moai themselves average fourteen feet in length and weigh about fifteen tons. However, some Moai are over thirty feet tall and weigh up to eighty tons." It also said that at one time there were two hundred and fifty Moai, placed about one half mile apart, forming an almost unbroken line along the perimeter of the island, and just as the strange "aerial" image had so strikingly shown, all of them, save one, faced landward. I looked back at the "computer generated" image, wondering again how it had been made.

Mateo poked his head in the door to check on me and said he'd be ready in a few minutes. I scanned the last several pages of information, focusing on anything glyph-like, but there wasn't a thing. Then I looked once more at the drawings. There was definitely nothing related to the glyphs there, either.

CHAPTER 63

Mateo was whistling when he came through the door. Obviously the jeep repair had gone well. He went in to wash up and came back wearing a fresh shirt and a broad smile. He indicated it was time to go by carefully gathering up the papers and drawings, and putting them back in their lockbox. Then he took me by the hand, and we were off.

We drove over what seemed like miles of empty land to our first stop, a site called Ahu Vinapu. There, not far from the airstrip where I had landed the day before yet out in the middle of nowhere, was a wall about eight feet long made of large stone blocks. One end of the wall was crumbling, turning into rubble. It didn't look important, and I wondered why Mateo had stopped there, but once we got out for a closer look, I was glad he had.

The wall looked exactly like those I had seen in Peru – the blocks were fitted together with the precision of a jigsaw puzzle. There was nothing else around except the very weatherworn head of a Moai buried up to its chin. *How odd!* I looked back at the wall. *This is such a small, isolated island...where could these people have gotten the sophisticated technology to build such a wall?* I thought of the pictures I had seen of Easter Island before I arrived and of the renderings Mateo had provided me. This wall was not like any of them. It felt completely out of place.

I told Mateo I had seen similar stonework in Peru. "In fact, this wall looks a bit like the courtyard wall at Tiahuanaco, the photograph you liked so well. Is it common on Easter Island?"

"Well…" he said, his brows pinched in concentration, "No…only here."

I asked him to tell me more about the wall. His eyes probed mine, as if he was considering whether or not to answer my question, then he shrugged his shoulders and said, "It's an old wall…that's all." *That can't be true. He wouldn't have brought me all the way here to see it if there was nothing to say about it!*

I wandered around, studying the wall from different angles and taking a number of photographs, but soon, on the pretense of examining the site more closely, I searched the area for glyph stones. I even poked around in the rubble but couldn't find a single stone with glyph markings. I looked back at Mateo. He was leaning against his jeep, smoking a cigarette, a slight Buddha smile curling the corners of his lips. *There's something he's purposely not telling me, I'm sure of it!*

Our next stop was somewhere in the interior of the island, a site called Ahu Akivi. There, again in the middle of nowhere, stood a row of seven towering Moai standing side by side on a long platform. "I recognize them from the renderings, but it's amazing to see them just standing there." Mateo smiled warmly.

The combination of a row of seven Moai and their sheer size made for some pretty spectacular photographs. I took shots from all angles, using a particular filtration pack that brought out colors not visible to the naked eye. The filters enhanced the colors of the billowing clouds floating through the tropical sky and increased the warmth of the statues, turning them almost copper–colored as they reflected the hidden hues of cloud and sky.

I glanced at Mateo now and again, but he seemed fine with the time I was taking. Then, as at the earlier site, I moved in closer pretending to study the carving technique used on both the statues and the ahu. In reality of course, I was inspecting the area for glyph stones, but again there were none to be seen. *If any of the stones were at this location before, they're certainly not here now.*

I wiped the perspiration from my face and stood back a bit, this time focusing my eyes, not my camera, softly on the row of Moai. I tried to "feel" the energy of the place – see if there was anything unusual – anything the voice on the airplane might have been alluding to. *Nothing! Absolutely nothing!* Reluctantly, I turned and walked back to the jeep.

"You get some good shots?" asked Mateo.

"Definitely," I replied, hiding my disappointment at what I hadn't found – and what I couldn't ask.

He laughed with pleasure as he handed me a bottle of cold water. "Wait till you see what's next."

Mateo turned the jeep around, and we headed off in another direction. Soon, just as I had seen in the drawings, we were passing Moai lying broken on the ground as well as partially buried. After having just seen the full-bodied statues, it was eerie to drive past Moai buried up to their shoulders, even to their necks. I wanted to stop, but Mateo said, "There's plenty more. I'm taking you to the place where they were born."

"The volcano? I can't wait!"

It wasn't long before Mateo pointed and said, "There she is, Rano Rarako."

The closer we got to the volcano, the more Moai we saw. The information Mateo had given me had been helpful, but none of it prepared me for the experience of seeing Rano Rarako for the first time. We left the car in a designated area and began hiking up a meandering path, wandering up and over grass-covered mounds that formed much of the base of the volcanic cone. We were literally walking amongst the Moai. It was eerie – and amazing. Giant heads were sticking out from the grass. We passed heads that seemed to be looking at us as well as full Moai lying on their backs, like they were taking a nap.

Mateo explained that all the Moai heads had full bodies exactly like those we had seen at Ahu Akivi, but over the years, erosion from the volcanic mountain had caused them to become buried in this way. He also said these completed Moai had been positioned here, waiting to be transported to the various ahu located around the island. Then he got a strange far-away look. I felt like Mateo had just vanished on me. I pushed those thoughts aside and focused on the figures that surrounded us.

Soon the grass gave way to the gently sloping, barren creator wall itself. As far as I could see, Moai were lying in all directions, vertically, horizontally and diagonally. They had been carved from the outer walls of the volcano itself and were in various stages of completion. Some were barely carved, others completely carved, and many were still attached to the volcanic wall by the thinnest of stone strips – almost like an umbilical cord. The site took my breath away.

I gazed at the obviously abandoned Moai in wonderment. "How did they carve them?" Mateo told me the carvers were master craftsmen. They would examine a section of the volcanic wall to determine the best placement for their work and then draw the outline of the Moai directly on the wall itself. The craftsmen had only primitive stone tools to work with, but they managed to chip away until the form of the Moai "appeared."

"It looks like one day the carvers just put down their tools and stopped working."

Mateo smiled his enigmatic smile and said, "Nobody knows. People think many different things, but nobody really knows."

I asked Mateo what he thought had happened, but he got that faraway look again and said, "I'm going to sit down for a while, but don't worry about me. You traveled so far to get here. Take your pictures…and take your time."

I watched as he walked to the only shade available – the shadow of one of the Moai. *That's very weird! It seems like he's avoiding most of the questions I ask. I wonder why?*

I turned back to the task at hand, but I hardly knew where to begin. I stood motionless, feeling the majesty of the place and tying to take it all in. But soon, without really thinking, I began taking pictures like a crazy woman. I took close-ups, panoramas, and everything in-between. I became so caught up in what I was doing that I completely tuned out the intense heat and humidity, and captured some of my most incredible images yet.

Finally, I reached a point where I could pause and look out at the "bigger picture." Still totally entranced, I walked up and around to the east side of the crater wall, and found myself looking down the slope into a kind of rubbish pit far below. I spotted a figure that was totally different from any of the Moai. I changed lenses to get a better look.

The close-up lens made all the difference, but it did not make my find any more understandable. Lying amongst discarded rock and broken pieces of Moai was a bearded figure whose face looked exactly like the stone figures I had seen in the sunken courtyard at Tiahuanaco. The figure had been carved into a sitting position, but at some point it had toppled and was now resting on its side. *What is this doing here? It's another "out of place artifact," except this one was out of place even at Tiahuanaco!*

My discovery reminded me once again of the real reason I had come to Easter Island – to find out about the glyph stones. And the voice I'd heard on the airplane had said to be on the lookout for anything unusual – whatever that meant. *Okay…the wall I saw earlier was unusual, Mateo's response to my question about it was unusual, and now this statue. What's next?* I looked around, but nothing caught my attention.

Not knowing what else to do, I took a breath and closed my eyes. This time I felt a jolt of energy – big time energy! It was in a distinct line running straight out from the volcano, but it was a different sort of energy then any I had felt before – anywhere. It seemed fragmented, spotty and disconnected. *I don't understand.* I walked to another section of the volcano and tried again. The result was pretty much the same. *What's wrong? There is definitely something weird about this energy.* I looked over at Mateo to see if he had noticed anything, but he was still leaning against an angled Moai, eyes closed.

Even though he appeared to be resting, I did my little ritual of pretending to take more pictures, while my eyes grazed the ground on the lookout for glyph stones. I not only looked as I walked around, I also used my close-up lenses to scan as far as I could. But I didn't see anything that remotely resembled what I was searching for.

Eventually, the heat got to me, and I went back to Mateo, exhilarated by the picture-taking, confused by the strange energy, and disappointed at not finding any glyph stones. *I just can't let this go on. I'll ask him about the glyph stones tomorrow.*

"Ready to climb to the top?" he asked, his face creased into a teasing smile.

"Mmmm," I groaned, looking up at the volcano and wiping sweat from my brow.

"No, really! You have to see the lake."

And so we left the Moai behind and followed the meandering path up the volcanic wall. The path was gradual – until it wasn't. We climbed up and over rocks and boulders until we reached the rim of the crater. Then, standing on the wide ledge that had been flattened by the centuries, we gazed into a lake that had been formed in the empty crater that was once the volcano's core.

Without warning, I felt a force – no, I became engulfed by a force – of energy that was so powerfully alive, it was almost tangible. *Okay, this has definitely gotten my attention! Now what?* But before I could ponder my own question, the ground beneath my feet began to vibrate. *My god! It's an earthquake!* I grabbed Mateo's arm. "Did…did you feel that?"

"Feel what?"

"That vibration…you didn't feel it?"

"No" he said, pausing for a moment, "but it's really quite a sight, isn't it. I'll leave you alone with it for a few minutes."

The vibration had ended, but the strange energy was still there. *That was bizarre. How could he not feel anything? Or did he…?* Maybe that was why he jumped subjects on me. The crater lake was visually captivating, but to say I had to be alone had nothing to do with anything. *I wonder what's really going on here, and what he knows about this place?*

Mateo had walked some distance away and began talking to a group of tourists. No one appeared to notice the strange vibration that had seemed so intensely powerful to me. But I continued to feel the energy – and it still felt very strange. It was not as disjointed as it had been earlier, but something – I couldn't tell what – was very wrong. *I wonder if this is what the voice on the airplane was talking about? Everything I've experienced at this crater so far is so extreme it has to be important! Could it be of such great magnitude that it holds the very key to why I am here?*

I closed my eyes and focused on my feelings. I knew that everything that had happened since the moment I first met Mateo was of great consequence. It was a riddle that, one way or another, I had to sift through and solve.

Forcing my emotions aside, I spent the next few minutes photographing the crater, but I could not get over the strangeness I was beginning to feel about the entire island. It wasn't long before I walked over to Mateo and said, "Ready?"

"Ready when you are," he answered, "but it's trickier going down. Let me hold your camera case."

I must have involuntarily flinched, because he looked embarrassed and turned away. I ran my fingers nervously through my hair, and then, remembering his importance on the island, I touched his arm and said, "I'm sorry! They're my babies, but here, you're right. It would be better if you held on to them." And it was. It was not as easy to keep my balance going down as it had been coming up.

When we reached the more gentle mounds and were once again walking among the Moai, I asked Mateo if he knew why the natives would carve such statues and continue carving them when they already had so many. He said that nobody had the answer. "There is a tradition of statue carving in Polynesia, but nothing like these on Easter Island."

"But the Moai are so huge, I can't even imagine how many tons. How could such giant statues have possibly been moved to their positions on the ahu without being damaged?"

He replied that over the years many scholars had come to the island to try to answer that very question. Some believed the Moai were rolled on a bed of logs and had even done experiments to prove it, but the results only brought up other questions and created even more of a mystery.

"What kind of other questions and mystery?"

"That's just it," Mateo said with a laugh. "All of it is a mystery. Everything about why the Moai were carved in the first place, and how and why they were moved is mysterious."

I looked at Mateo in surprise. *Was he hinting about something else that might be mysterious?* "Speaking of mysteries, Easter Island is so isolated…are there other mysteries here?" *Like the glyph stones?*

His expression did not change as he replied, "All places have their mysteries, don't they?" It was clear this part of the conversation was over. Finally, we reached the jeep and climbed into what, literally, felt like a sauna, and began our drive back. We talked about the many other places on the island that I should see. I listened to every word, hoping to hear some small piece of information that in some way might end up relating to the glyph stones, the strange energy I had experienced, or anything else of importance.

Although Mateo was warm and open, the nagging feeling that he was leaving something out would not go away. *He's the expert on the island, the one trying to keep the culture alive. But there's something…or somethings…he's purposely not telling me. Why?*

Mateo said he was busy the next day but offered to continue our tour the following day. He dropped me off at my hotel, and I thanked him with genuine appreciation, and I was completely sincere. Despite the heat, the mysteries, and no clue about the glyph stones, I had loved every minute of the day. There was still plenty of time for me to ask him directly about the glyph stones – and everything else.

CHAPTER 64

The next morning was hotter, and if possible, even more humid than the day before. The air felt thick as I pulled myself out of bed and moved into the coolness of a shower. Mateo had suggested I go to the museum, which was in walking distance of where I was staying, so after a light breakfast and a lot of water, I got directions from my host.

It's possible somebody there might know something about the glyph stones. After all, I reasoned on my walk, that's what museums are for – sharing information.

And sharing information is exactly what the museum curator did. She told me the original name for Easter Island was Rapa Nui and rattled off all the "must see" spots on the island, many of which were away from the usual tourist stops. Even though Mateo had promised to take me around, I took copious notes. Then I casually asked her about the glyph stones – or about any type of glyphs that had been found on the island. Her face brightened immediately, and she said, "Let me show you the Rongo Rongo boards."

My heart leapt in anticipation – then fell in disappointment. She led me to some tablets that were made either of stone or petrified wood. There were markings on them that might possibly be classified as glyphs, but not anything like my glyphs.

"The 'old ones' here had a written language," the curator explained, "the only written language in all of Polynesia. Unfortunately, we don't know what the boards are saying. Nobody has been able to translate them, and you're the first person who's asked about them in years."

"Thank you for your time and the other information, but this is not at all what I'm looking for." I was starting to leave when she called after me.

"Oh, how forgetful of me. There is a scattering of *petroglyphs* – rock engravings – around the island. The most concentrated group of them is in the caves below Orongo."

I spun around. "Really?"

"Oh, yes! They're very unusual. But it's a bit treacherous. You'll need a guide."

"I've already arranged for one tomorrow, but thank you so much for the information. You've been a great help."

Energized and excited, I headed off for the one "must see" spot I could reach on foot. Ahu Tahai consisted of a grouping of five Moai standing on one platform, but for some reason the carvers had deliberately made the statues look different from each other in both size and shape. I asked a nearby tour leader what the differences were meant to represent. As usual, there were all kind of theories, but nobody could give me a definitive answer. There seemed to be so little that was really known about this place. There was lots of speculation, but not much agreement.

My eyes were constantly and automatically searching for the glyph stones, and I asked everyone I met if they had heard about them. However, no one could – or would – help me. *I don't get it. How can something have been "mysteriously" found if no one has even heard of it?*

I was still getting used to the humidity and wanted to be fresh for the next day, so after dinner and a shower I went directly to bed. My room had no cross ventilation, and the air was heavy and hot. I could not stop thinking about Mateo's strange behavior, the powerful energy I had felt on the side of the volcano, the vibration that had almost knocked me over on the rim of the crater and the petroglyphs the curator had told me about. *Is it possible these are my glyphs? I've been basing everything on what the disappearing Dr. Daath had said. All my diplomacy…waiting to ask Mateo about the glyphs… might have been unnecessary.* I fell asleep with my head spinning.

Mateo wasn't at his house when I arrived there the next morning. I talked, or tried to talk, to an elderly lady who answered the door. By the use of hand signals and my pigeon Spanish, I finally understood her to say that Mateo probably wouldn't be back for three days. *Great! Why didn't he tell me! What am I going to do now?* I was shocked and agitated as I turned and walked away. I hadn't gone far when I heard the old woman calling me, "Senorita, senorita." I turned and saw her scurrying after me waving a folded piece of paper. "Para tu," she said, handing it to me. Then she turned and trotted back toward the house.

I unfolded the paper and read Mateo's hurriedly written note. "Sorry. Was called away on emergency. Hope to be back in a couple of days. Mateo."

So what now? Mateo was the one who knew the most about the mysteries and legends of the island. I felt completely lost, but I quickly recovered and knew exactly what to do. I walked back to the museum and asked the curator to recommend her best guide. She was glad to help, and luckily the guide happened to be available, but not until the afternoon.

CHAPTER 65

The first thing Roberto, the guide, asked me when he picked me up was what I was most interested in seeing. The word *petroglyph* flew out of my mouth. "The curator at the museum told me there were some at a place called Orongo."

He laughed and said, "Then Orongo and petroglyphs it shall be." Roberto was a middle-aged man, born on the island but schooled in Chile. He had learned English at university and spoke very well. As tourism on the island had increased Roberto returned, "…to help people understand and love my island."

What luck! Hopefully, he'll be able…and willing, to answer my questions.

On the way, Roberto took me to Rano Kau, the biggest crater on the island. Unlike the places I had visited with Mateo and on my own, this site had neither Moai nor ruins. However, it did have one of the most dramatic views I have ever seen. Once Roberto and I had climbed to top of the trail, it was as if we had landed on another planet. We gazed down into a giant crater whose sides seemed to have been painted in streaks of blue green, yellow and brown. Its huge caldera was glistening with lakes and marshes. Words cannot possibly describe the spectacular, unearthly appearance that lay before us.

"The reason I brought you up here, other than the fact that it's breathtaking, is because the carving of the *petroglyphs* you want to see was part of a ritual that began over there at the village of Orongo," Roberto said, pointing to a stone village built alongside the rim of the crater. "Orongo was a ceremonial center, one of the last sites developed by the Rapa Nui culture, but a very important one.

"The main ritual took place there every July. It was coming-of-age ceremony for the young men of the island. Legend has a remarkable story about why the ritual took place in that particular month. Some say it was set to coincide with the rising of the constellation called The Seven Sisters, or the Pleiades."

The Pleiades! I perked right up on that one. *He might know about the stones!*

"Anyway," he continued, "there would be some kind of ceremony at Orongo after which the young men would climb down the steep, rocky slope that drops directly from Orongo to the ocean over a thousand feet below. The shoreline is full of caves, and that's where they would carve the petroglyphs. It's really steep, Do you still want to go down?"

"Definitely! Let's go."

"You are a hearty soul, and I can see you're wearing sensible shoes. There's a second path a bit away from the village that's not quite so steep. We can drive the jeep over there and give it a try."

It took time – and a little help from Roberto – but we made it down. "Look, see there," he said, pointing to *petroglyphs* on one spot, and then another and another.

"What are they?"

"They are creatures that are half-bird and half-man. They're called *birdmen.*"

The large images were well weathered by wind and water, and probably not etched all that deeply into the rock to begin with, but once you noticed them and recognized their shapes, the *petroglyphs* were everywhere. I looked around, hoping my glyphs were a part of the drawings, but I didn't see anything even close.

"Are there any other ones, maybe some that are carved onto small stones?"

"No, they're all big like this, and all carved into the walls of the caves."

"Well, are there any other images?"

Roberto scratched his head thoughtfully. "There are some of turtles in one of the caves. Does that interest you?"

"No, not really, but I've heard stories about some Pleiadean glyph stones that were here at one time. Have you heard of them?" I held my breath waiting for his answer.

"No, but it sounds fascinating. I wish there were some. I'd love to have seen them."

I watched him carefully as he spoke. Everything in his body language said he was telling the truth. *But...is he?* My glyphs are such simple designs and he said the ritual took place at the time of the rising of the Pleiades. *It's possible my glyphs are here somewhere hidden amongst the birdman petroglyphs, and no one noticed them because there're so small.* "As long as we've made it down here, can we look around for a while?"

Roberto was happy to oblige, and we spent the next hour climbing over the rocks and exploring many of the caves carved into the land by the relentless ocean. The large birdman *petroglyphs* may have been impressive to others, but they were not the glyphs I was looking for – they weren't my glyphs. *Damn!* My eyes were constantly darting around, searching between the rocks, on the walls and ground of each cave. I was incessantly pushing on when Roberto yelled above the pounding surf, "Cassandra, all the drawings are the same. This is all they drew, birdmen. Besides, it's getting too windy. It's not safe. We have to get going."

As Roberto helped me back up the steep path, he jokingly asked, "This is great exercise! Do you want to go back down tomorrow?"

"Thanks, but no thanks. I've seen enough birdmen to last a lifetime."

By the time we reached the top I was definitely done for the day. And I was more than disappointed that my glyphs weren't there. *I guess I'll have to wait for Mateo after all.*

On the drive back Roberto explained why it was that birdman petroglyphs were created in the first place. I was only half-listening, until he added off-hand-edly, "At least that's the commonly known version. There is a more mythical, less well-known story. Some say the birdman cult may be a recollection of ex-traterrestrial activity...a memory of visitors from the sky. It's an intriguing idea, like your stones. I wish I knew more about it."

Roberto interrupted himself by pointing out two groups of people on horseback. "Ah! That makes me so nostalgic." He explained that horses were once the only means of transportation on the island and complained that civilization had taken its toll. "Now people mostly prefer to explore the island by motorbike, jeep or in groups on the tour buses."

"Not me!" I blurted. "I mean, jeeps are great, and I'm glad I'm in one, especially after that climb, but I definitely want to do some exploring on horseback."

Roberto smiled appreciatively, and we talked about how we might manage it. He was booked for the following morning but was free that afternoon and could pick me up by one o'clock. "But it will probably be too late in the day to set out on horseback."

I was disappointed but not about to change guides – and Roberto was delighted. As he dropped me off at my hotel, he said, "You're not like the average tourist. You're a true adventurer. I can tell how much you want to understand our island."

Adventurer! That's an interesting name for what I'm doing, I thought, as I went up to my room, grabbed fresh clothes and headed for the shower. The cool water refreshed me – as long as I stayed in the shower. I tried not to think, but my mind would not be still.

I went over and over the various energies I had experienced in the past two days. The first day, I had felt a powerful vibrational energy underfoot while standing on the slope of Rano Raraku. Then I had experienced the same odd, disjointed energy while on the rim of Rano Kau looking into the caldera. I even felt something at the village, but very little anywhere close to the birdman Petra glyphs.

The voice on the airplane had talked about geophysical and paranormal activity. It seemed to have been referring to the island's past, but what I encountered the day before and again that day could certainly be classified as "geophysical." *And, this is definitely the present. Then Roberto connected the ritual to the Pleiades. What does it all mean?*

I tossed and turned all night, the refreshing sleep I needed totally eluding me. It felt like I was being torn apart. That must have been a harbinger of things to come, because the following morning I woke up feeling strange. In truth, it was more than strange. It was as if I were living in two worlds at the same time – but I had no idea where the "other" world was. In one moment my energy was boundless, my thinking and sensing so clear, it seemed as though a veil between the physical world and an invisible one had been lifted. I could almost see things before they actually happened. But, in another moment, I was exhausted and massively indecisive.

I made myself stay in bed for a while, then showered and slowly dressed, trying to bring the other half of me present. I hated to waste the entire morning but wasn't sure what to do with myself. Aside from the town, which really did not interest me, the only place within walking distance was Ahu Tahai. I had already been there and had not seen or felt anything special. However, while at breakfast, I experienced a distinct pull to go back there. I tried to ignore it, but the feeling wouldn't go away. *Alright, I was warned to listen and look both externally and internally. Guess I'd better pay attention to myself.*

Walking through the sweltering, muggy air, I could not help but question what I was doing. *I'm wearing myself out for nothing!* When I arrived at the site, I noticed a group of people were standing in a cluster. I went over to see what was going on and saw an elderly woman lying on the ground. Everyone seemed afraid to touch her. I heard someone whisper, "Mad Man disease," and understood why no one was helping her.

I wedged myself in closer and saw that the failing woman's lips were moving. A knowing that I would be safe sprang into my being with a force that surprised me. I pushed forward and kneeled down beside her. I put my ear close to her mouth. I could barely make out the words, "My heart! My heart! In my handbag...."

"Don't be afraid," I shouted to the group, "It's not the disease, it's her heart." I pointed to her, to my heart and then to hers. "Where's her purse? Someone find her purse!" I looked around, spotted it and motioned someone to hand it to me. I fumbled around until I felt the small bottle of nitroglycerin. My hands were shaking as I unscrewed the top, took out a small tablet and placed it under the woman's tongue. I watched closely as she began to recover. Her breathing eased and color came back into her face. I lifted her head and put her handbag under it.

Within moments, a doctor appeared. I waited until everything was under control, then turned and left. I was furious! *That woman could have died... for nothing! Damn that John and his stupid disease! He has people afraid to touch one another.* Not only was the disease gaining ground, but fear of it was becoming pandemic.

I marched toward my hotel, vowing to get my answers and hell–bent on destroying John – whatever it took. But soon, other thoughts began to wiggle their way into my brain. *That woman would have died if I hadn't been there? How did I know to go there? How did I know I would be safe?* I stopped at an empty little café for coffee and some quiet thinking. *This is a whole new dimension to my abilities. I can't even imagine....*

The sound of voices and scraping chairs told me it was lunchtime. *Roberto! I need to pull myself together!* I grabbed a sandwich to go and went back to the hotel to get ready for my afternoon adventure.

CHAPTER 66

Roberto arrived just after 1:00 p.m. and took me to Ahu Naunau, a site on Anakena Beach where a line of Moai were standing with their backs to the ocean. It was a great spot, but the sun was all wrong. I would have to come back in the morning to photograph this place properly.

After a few shots I focused on the Moai, which were somewhat different than the others I had seen. They had the same body and head shape, but the carving itself was very meticulous and refined. These Moai had sharper, more detailed ears, and their noses had pronounced nostrils. But the biggest difference was that each of them had some sort of red "hat" on the top of its head.

Roberto told me that the islander name for the hat-like objects was *pukao*, and that they were carved from a different quarry than the Moai, one that had red, lava rock walls. "This site has been reconstructed, but we think that all of the Moai on the island had pukao when they were originally placed on their ahu. If you look carefully, you can see their red rock remains scattered around the island."

"That's interesting, but what's the purpose of the pukao, and why are they red?"

Roberto paused, as if he were listening to something I couldn't hear. Then, with a slight hesitance and a lowered voice, he answered. "Well, that's a long story, and nobody knows if it's true, but legend tells of an ancient race of light-skinned, red-haired people who once lived on the island. In fact, they may have already been here before the Rapa Nui arrived. And they had quite a story prior to that."

"Really! Do you know their story…where they came from?" I tried to keep my voice calm, but my heart was thumping. *Light-skinned, red-haired people! I heard about them in Tiahuanaco.*

"Well," he continued, a bit conspiratorially, "I haven't heard any stories about where the red-haired people originated, but they are said to have come to the Andes Mountains in South America, specifically to Tiahuanaco. There is some evidence that they either established, or at least participated in, a culture that spread all the way to the Moche people of Peru.

"In fact, there is a group of rogue archeologists, a small group, but still, who believe this empire once encompassed all of Peru and Bolivia, and that it was the most ancient culture in South America. They also believe that ancient empire was responsible for all of the remarkable stonework found there.

"It could be the redheads got wanderlust, or who knows what, but legend tells us that some of them eventually took to the sea, headed west to Easter Island and established a culture here as well."

"Wow! They sure got around, didn't they? I guess Easter Island was the next chapter in the saga of these people. I heard about them when I was in Tiahuanaco. They were an oddity there, and they're even more of an oddity here. So the red hats, what are they called, *pokos*?"

"That's pretty close. Pukao means "topknots," and it's possible they may have been symbols of the red hair. When the famous Norwegian explorer, Thor Heyerdahl, came here in the early 1950s, he photographed a young boy who was a direct descendant of those early people and had inherited the fair skin and red hair. You see, there is more to the history of our island then just legends."

"You mean the kinds of things the rogue archeologists talk about?"

"Exactly!" He paused again before continuing even more quietly. "They believe Easter Island has had a long and varied history, beginning far earlier then the arrival of the Rapa Nui people. The rogue archeologists also believe mainstream archeologists have completely missed the point, because they have insisted that the history of Easter Island is related to the rest of Polynesia. Of course, to a certain extent it is, but this," he said, pointing to the pukao, "and the stonework...I'm not so sure."

"The stonework?"

"Yes! All of the archeologists agree that this site was one of the first established by the Rapa Nui, and they excavated it extensively before restoring it. They were able to unearth the remains of several other ahu that were beneath it and much older than the current one. But, although they verified that this site had been occupied for a very long time, they ended up with a whole new set of questions.

"You see, the stonework on the more ancient ahu was created with far greater...and very unusual...precision. The individual stones fit together in a much more exacting fashion than those on the later ahu. In fact, the older ahu were built exactly like the wall at Ahu Vinapu, which of course, is odd. You would expect that the expertise of the builders would have improved as they reached more modern times. But it's quite the reverse. The older ahu were much more sophisticated."

So, I was right! There were things Mateo wasn't telling me. "Ahu Vinapu was the first place Mateo took me. I had seen that kind of carving in Peru, but I couldn't understand how the natives here could do work like that."

Roberto shrugged and shook his head. "That is the big question. It really messes up the Polynesian 'origin theory,' but here it is, and someone built it."

"This is fascinating. Do you know, or have you heard, anything else that's unusual like this?"

"Not much. Most of my clients are just your average tourist, but occasionally...." His voice trailed off, deep in thought. He hesitated before saying, "Well, there was one time, soon after I had moved back to the island. Mateo had been showing an elderly gentleman around the island but was having communication problems, so he swung by my place and asked if I would come along and act as a sort of translator.

"The man was a Maori Elder, born and raised in New Zealand. Now, don't be confused by the similarity between the word 'Maori' and our 'Moai' statues. The Maori are the aboriginal peoples of New Zealand.

"Anyway, we took him to the usual spots. The man understood everything I was saying, nodded and smiled appreciatively but never said a word. The last place we went was Rano Kau, the crater we saw yesterday. Of course, it has an amazing view, but the moment the elderly gentleman looked over the rim and into the caldera, with its painted walls and glistening lakes, his eyes welled up with tears.

"I'll never forget him. He was silent for some time, just staring into the caldera and patting his eyes, before he finally broke his silence. He said, 'No Maori is known to have ever visited Easter Island, yet our ancient migration chants describe Rano Kau perfectly. I've heard these chants…this description… all my life, but I never believed it was a real place. To me it was…a fairy tale.'

"Once the man composed himself, he explained that their migration chants, which in all cultures are the transmission of ancient sacred knowledge from one generation to the next, tell the story of their ancestors who started out from Egypt, traveled across the Indian Ocean to Central America, and settled in the area now known as Peru and Bolivia. After many generations, a group of them traveled on to Easter Island, then to Hawaii, and eventually settled on Aotearoa, the island known today as New Zealand. It was an amazing story, and I've never quite gotten over the look on the old man's face."

My eyes were wide open, and my mouth too dry to speak. My heart started racing. He was saying there was a connection between Easter Island and Egypt. I was stunned. The diary had specifically said that a great majority of Atlanteans had red hair. *I'm sure those ancient red-headed people were Atlanteans. Not only is there a connection between Easter Island and South America, but they both connect back to Egypt!*

"Well, I can see my little story has left you speechless. You look like you have just heard about your long-lost relatives," laughed Roberto, handing me a bottle of water.

I tried to keep my voice calm. "This is so amazing! It's hard to understand...and believe, but that would explain the similarity in the precision stonework. It would even explain the red-haired people. Do you have any other little stories in your back pocket?" I held my breath, still hoping, in some roundabout fashion, to hear something – anything – about my glyphs. But after the information he had just given me, it almost didn't matter.

"I can't think of anything right now, but I'll keep the wheels spinning," he said, pointing to his head. He started to take me to a different site but noticed something didn't sound right in the jeep's engine, so we headed back. "I want to check on this before dark. I can probably fix it, but Mateo's been gone three days so he should be back by tonight anyway. You'll be fine."

But as I lay in bed that night, I wasn't feeling fine – I was feeling perplexed. Why had Roberto been so open with me while Mateo was so secretive? And the theories of the rogue archeologists.... *My god! That takes us all the way back to Atlantis. It's the only way it makes sense.* The statues in the courtyard at Tiahuanaco, the red topknots and the precision stonework could not be explained in any other way. And Roberto had said that there might have been a relationship between the timing of the coming of age ceremony at Orongo and the rising of the Pleiades.

Pleiades! Atlantis! I suddenly understood what the voice on the airplane had been trying to tell me before the signal got jangled. Easter Island was once used as a landing site as well as a communications device for those from the Pleiades.

Mateo had to have known about all of that, too! Well, maybe not about Atlantis or the Pleiades, but certainly about the connection to South America and the precision stonework. That must have been why, without a moment's hesitation, he chose the photograph of the courtyard in Tiahuanaco. *Could it be that these ancient red-haired people are a part of his ancestral heritage as well?* I fell asleep confident and comforted. Things were beginning to make sense.

I woke up in the middle of the night – in the middle of a dream. The dream was a jumble of images and feelings about the spotty, jumpy, bumpy energy at Rano Raraku, the read-haired people, and the old man from New Zealand. Intuitively, I knew the real reason I had come to Easter Island. And it wasn't about finding glyph stones. They might not even exist.

I had come here to do something special – a kind of healing to connect Easter Island back to Egypt. That was the reason I had felt the need to bring along the seed crystals and malachite given to me by the Arab boy in the Old City of Jerusalem – stones that came from David – from Egypt. They were the physical tools, along with my intention, to create the link. *But, how could David have known all of this back then? David…dear David! Will I ever meet you in this life?*

CHAPTER 67

Later that night, I dreamed that the sky above me began to weep. Then, just before I awoke in the morning, I saw a strange image – a perfectly round stone that appeared to glow from within. I woke up happy. Something inside of me felt settled. However, as the day moved on, I had two disappointments. Mateo had not returned, and Roberto was still working on his car. *I don't want to waste today, and tomorrow is my last day. Mateo might not be back, and now I can't rely on Robert, so I'd better set something up myself.*

However, time moves at a different pace in the tropics, and plans never seem to go forward as one imagines. The intense humidity made everything feel not only damp, but also strangely alive. The very essence of the place discouraged logical thinking and planning ahead, making follow-through almost impossible. And, in the back of my mind, I was still waiting for Mateo, and so the day passed.

Although I had managed to see and photograph most of the sites, and met many of the locals, I now had a new concern. I had to find a place to do whatever it was I needed to do to heal the energy on Easter Island – to connect it back to Egypt. I thought about all of the places I had seen on the island. Rano Raraku had definitely been the most energetically powerful. It was also the most distorted, so I guessed that was where I needed to go next. I was not at all sure what I would do when I got there – but at least I knew where I was going.

I decided to spend my last day touring Easter Island on horseback. My goal was to go back to Anakena Beach in the early morning when the light would be perfect to photograph the seven red-hatted Moai that Roberto had shown me. Then I would go to Rano Raraku and do "whatever." I would top it all off with a swim in the crater-lake created by the volcano – a kind of mystical baptism. The depth of the lake had never been charted, and it was rumored to have healing powers.

Everything seemed settled except the meaning of the glowing round stone from my dream the night before. At dinner that evening, I asked my host if he had ever heard anything about a round stone that might be somewhere on the island. After some consideration, he recalled that his grandmother had told him of a special stone talked about by "the old people." He couldn't tell me much about it and had only a general idea of where it might be, but after my dream I was positive I needed to see it. Just thinking about it charged me up.

My host and his family warned me that I had planned too much for one day, but if I insisted upon doing it all, I should rent a jeep. However, even though I hadn't ridden in years, I had a romantic vision of myself riding on horseback around the magical little island, hair blowing in the wind, experiencing my kinship with the Nature Spirits. When logic failed to change my mind, their nephew Leu volunteered to accompany me as my guide.

It took Leu longer than expected to arrive with the horses so we left much later than planned. He was moving us on at a rapid clip for fear that we would never cover my proposed itinerary before dark. He kept checking with me to make sure we weren't going too fast, but I loved it. Just like riding a bicycle, once I mounted the horse it all came back to me. "Let's go faster," I called out, and Leu took off cantering ahead. The power of the horse beneath me, the rush of air against my face, and the sensation we were flying was exhilarating – everything I had wanted.

This is great! It makes up for all the heat and humidity. Then, out of nowhere, two riders came up behind us, spooking my horse so badly I nearly fell. My horse reared and turned. As I struggled to stay astride, I saw two men dressed in dark clothing galloping away. *What the...! Why are they here? John already has the diary.* I knew he had tried to stop "my glyphs" from getting out to the world. Maybe he was the one who took the glyph stones. It didn't really matter – I was going forward with my plan, and that was that.

However, within an hour of my communing-with-nature adventure on horseback, my upper back muscles went into a severe spasm, and we slowed our horses to a walk. By the time we reached our first destination, Anakena Beach, it was high noon, and the sun was merciless. *So much for my perfect morning shots of the seven Moai! Damn that John!*

I was in pain and lay down on top of a wooden picnic table in an attempt to release my back. Leu began to unpack the sandwiches and drinks his aunt had prepared. Obviously I was not going to make it to Rano Raraku either. It was far too long a ride. What was I going to do about my "assignment?" The voice I'd heard on the airplane said I would get more guidance once I was there. *I think now would be about the perfect time!* I took a deep breath. I knew this was the exact moment when I needed to slow down my thoughts and trust, so I did – sort of!

I suppose it's possible to do my thing right here at Anakena Beach, but it just doesn't feel right. I listened as Leu talked about what we could realistically do in what was left of the day, considering the state of my back and the distance to the various sites. Every place seemed too far except, possibly, the round stone his uncle had told us about. *Well, I did dream about the stone!*

"From what my uncle said, I think I can find the stone. It should be very close to where we are right now. Can you still ride, or do you want to go back?"

Leu's question bore much more significance than whether or not I could continue to ride. I thought about Manco, Jeff, Mary and so many others, and realized that Life had chosen strange packaging in which to clothe my teachers and guides. I searched down deep inside of myself for an answer. *Even if it's not "the place," something tells me I have to see that stone.*

I stretched my back as best I could, but it felt only minimally better. But, one way or another, I had to get back on that horse! "Okay, let's go," I said, as I climbed up the mountain of a horse and eased into the saddle. Then groaning and gritting my teeth I chanted, *I can do this…I can do this.*

Moving slowly, we began to head in the direction Leu's uncle had described. We spent what seemed like hours in the blazing sun, combing back and forth over the rocky terrain, one small section at a time. To be honest, I was ready to call it quits, but Leu encouraged me to go on.

"It's your last day," he said, emphasizing his words with impassioned Spanish. "If you don't see your stone today, you will never have another chance."

By the time we finally stumbled upon the stone, I was exhausted and in a lot of pain. I could have sworn we had ridden over that exact spot many times before but somehow had never seen it. Yet, as soon as he had called it out, there it was in plain sight.

The stone was about sixteen inches in diameter and lay close to the broken remains of what Leu explained was the largest of the Moai ever moved from the crater. At first, the stone appeared to be a perfectly round, but I quickly realized the top and bottom were slightly flattened. It was completely unlike anything else I had seen on the island.

The place was peaceful – and strangely quiet. I got down from my horse and stretched my back again. Something snapped into place and, to my amazement, the pain lessened immediately. I stretched to the left, then to the right, just to make sure. The pain was almost completely gone and I could move somewhat freely. I carefully kneeled on the ground next to the stone and lightly brushed its surface with the palm of my hand. It was surprisingly cool.

Instinctively, I leaned forward and gently rested my forehead on the cooling stone. The moment my head touched the stone, I was enveloped in a rich, velvety blackness. Vibrant colors began to swirl against the dark background. As the colors receded, a long tunnel opened and fanned out before me. It was a huge tunnel – long and high and wide. Some distance from me, somewhere around the middle of the tunnel, a large object suddenly appeared on the ground. I was about to pull back when I realized that the "large object" was the very stone upon which I now rested my head – but in my vision, it was at least five times bigger.

The rich, vibrant colors enveloped me again. When they faded, the stone was surrounded by twelve beings whose tall foreheads bore an uncanny similarity to the Moai scattered about the island. The twelve beings sat in a circle, their great eyes focused on the now glowing stone. All at once they made a humming sound, like a swarm of angry bees. The air around them filled with shimmering geometric forms.

I was somehow able to see beyond the beings and clearly through to the other end of the tunnel. It opened onto a vista where I saw the huge Moai, freshly carved from the crater at Rano Raraku. As the beings focused their eyes on the stone and continued to hum, I watched the Moai begin to glide, in solemn procession, to various locations around the tiny island.

When the Moai reached their preordained spots, they positioned themselves atop the stone platforms prepared for them and became inanimate stone again. Here they remained like silent sentinels, great guardians of this sacred place, until generations later they were toppled by an angry people who had lost the ability to access the statues' ancient magic.

Then abruptly, whatever I was attuned to came to an end. The vision disappeared, and I returned to myself. However, what I had seen was so detailed that I was shocked to find that only a few moments of actual time had passed.

Leu looked at me rather oddly. He sensed that something had taken place, but there was no way he could have imagined what it might be. "Do you wish you could build a house here so you could wake up every day close to your stone?" he asked.

I had no words. My experience was so profound that even if I could have explained it to him, I probably wouldn't have. It felt private. *I feel like I'm a part of this place. The stone has given me the gift of "seeing" into the island's secret. It is a privilege, an honor.*

The whole thing was amazing. Although Leu had lived on the island all of his twenty-six years, he was not aware that the stone even existed before I had spoken to his uncle about it. And of course, neither he nor his uncle had any idea how the stone might have been used in the island's ancient past. Because the oral tradition relating to the sites had long since vanished, probably most of the islanders had no awareness, either. Except for Mateo! He had to know about this.

Leu helped me up, but I was a bit dizzy. He handed me a cup of water and stayed close. It took a few minutes before I felt steady on my feet. *I'm positive that what I've seen is real. Something definitely happened, but I have no idea what it has to do with me?*

"Now, you must be happy we kept on looking until we found your stone."

"You're right, I am, and thank you so much for helping me. I'll be fine… I just need to be quiet for a few minutes." He understood and walked over to tend to the horses.

I had barely closed my eyes when the realization swept over me. *This island, this section of the planet's energetic grid, has come apart. It's broken…shattered!* That was what the strange fragmented energy I had felt at Rano Raraku and Rano Kau was all about. *I need to bring it back…to reconnect it. That's what I have come here to do, but how?*

Without realizing it, I had already pulled the sack of crystals out of my camera bag. The bag began pulsating. *No, it's the stones inside that are pulsating!* As I held the bag tightly between my hands, my heart began pounding to the rhythm inside. I closed my eyes and stood very still, allowing the place to speak to me.

I opened my eyes and looked down at the round stone lying only a few feet away. I experienced the familiar flash of lightening from the inside out and saw a rush of energy – of luminescent geometric forms – rise from the center of the stone. The forms rose high into the air and swirled about before plunging deeply onto the ground, transforming themselves into lines that radiated out in all directions from the stone.

Something guided me forward. I walked a few steps, then a few more. I followed my feet as they moved around to the side of the stone that faced the ocean. I stopped for a moment and then walked a few more paces, tracking the shimmering path of light. I lifted my foot to take the next step, but put it back down. My feet did not want to move. *This is it!*

Kneeling down, I picked up some small flat stones and used their edge to dig a little hole. After a few deep settling breaths, I closed my eyes and pictured Egypt, the Pyramids and the Sphinx. *Dear Mother Earth, I bring you malachite and seed crystals from Egypt. Help me to repair and reconstruct this part of the planet's energetic grid...to once more awaken and connect the powerful dormant energy of Easter Island, and all of the information it holds, back to the Motherland, Egypt.*

The sound of thunder that rumbled across the otherwise peaceful sky above did not interfere with my inner vision. I saw the face of Mateo, with his Buddha smile and gentle laugh, and heard his words. "My ancestors and I thank you for healing our island. Now you understand why I had to leave. You had to feel ... to uncover the problem and discover the solution. My presence would have made that difficult."

I was overcome with gratitude as waves of love and connection washed over me. Now, with a sense of purpose – and relief – I emptied the contents of my little sack. The malachite and seed crystals glittered in the late afternoon sun as I covered them with earth and rock. Hot as I was, a shiver ran down my spine confirming that the link had been set in place. The ritual was now complete, and I knew I had done exactly what I was meant to do. And I knew something else – I knew that I had to go back to Egypt.

Leu helped me up from the ground and onto my horse, and we began the long trek back to the other end of the island. Oddly enough, my back pain, which had been almost completely gone at the round stone, began to return. We had ridden about an hour into the coolness of the oncoming night when the pulling in my back made it clear I could go no further.

Easter Island was not exactly "civilization," where one could just go to a phone booth and call for help. However, using one's thumb still did the trick. So, with Leu's help, I hitched a ride from one of the few vehicles that appeared on the isolated road. A local family, in an old four-wheel drive truck with a covered cab, warmly welcomed me. I gratefully accepted the ride, leaving Leu with the horses, and managed to climb, backpack in tow, into the back of the already crowded truck's cab.

Only a trace of moonlight filtered in through cracks and holes in the walls of the cab. I looked around at the other people crammed into the cab. A young mother was holding a sleeping infant in her arms. She smiled silently. Two other children, young boys that looked to be about seven or eight, were sharing some food. They look up shyly before their eyes darted away. An elderly man gave me a toothless grin.

A man with blond hair and beard was sitting directly across from me. We smiled pleasantly at one another, as we bumped along in the darkness. I felt his eyes lock onto my camera case. *His face seems so familiar. I know I've seen him somewhere.*

"You look so…" I began, but he turned his head away, as if telling me not to continue. We were silent for a while, and I tried to remember where I had seen him. Then, it came to me. *He looks exactly like the man I saw at Mary's that day at Callanish.* He had been with the Mayan man, Carlos, and though we had made eye contact, he had never spoken. My mind was a jumble again.

His eyes returned to my backpack. "I have cameras inside," I said in Spanish. He nodded silently. "I was shooting pictures at a very special place," I continued. Although my Spanish is limited, I understand more than I can speak. However when I get nervous, I reach the outer edges of my vocabulary very quickly, which is when I generally smile a lot and use my hands. Something about this man was making me nervous, so I was smiling like crazy. He kept staring at my backpack, not saying a word. I was beginning to feel very uncomfortable.

"We had a hard time finding the place I was looking for, and I stayed on the horse much too long. Getting this ride back is a lifesaver," I babbled on.

There was complete silence, except for the bumping and squeaking of the ancient vehicle as it bounced on through the night. The man broke the silence with a harsh and abrupt whisper into the blackness, "Te Pito Kura!"

"What?" I said, startled.

"Te Pito Kura!" He paused before continuing slowly, still in Spanish. "You were at Te Pito Kura."

"I was at a round stone," I said in my best-accented Spanish.

"Yes, it is called Te Pito Kura, the Navel Stone." Swiftly glancing at the other people in the cab, he began to speak in English. "The ancient sacred name for this place, which you call Easter Island, is Te Pita O Te Henua, The Navel of The World."

"Really!"

He paused again before continuing, this time speaking very slowly, punching up each word and enunciating it with great care to make certain I understood.

"You were also at Rano Raraku, the volcano where the Moai were made."

"Yes, I was there earlier in the week."

"The ancient legends tell of a line of energy that runs directly from Te Pito Kura to Rano Raraku. That is how the statues were moved, you know... through the power of mind focused on Te Pito Kura. They were moved by mind...and by sound. Te Pito Kura was the 'control room.'" He paused, looking directly into my eyes. "The Moai were made to walk to their places on the ahu."

He let that sink in before mumbling what sounded like, "You know that." It was definitely a statement and not a question. He relaxed his posture and continued in a more conversational tone.

"I came here from Chile when I was still a boy. I wanted to uncover the mysteries of the island. I have never left."

"Never? Not even...." He turned away again.

There was so much I wanted to ask him, but the truck had come to a stop in front of my host's house. After many smiles all around and the driver's refusal to take any money from me, the blond man jumped out and helped me down from the truck. With a quick little bow, just as he had done at Callanish, he said, "Thank you," and climbed back into the truck. Feeling confused, disappointed and frustrated, I watched as the dilapidated little truck went jogging along into the night.

CHAPTER 68

My last night on Easter Island was a strange one. As I lay on my bed in my room, I felt a deep sense of satisfaction knowing that I had been able to help balance the earth's energetic grid. I also felt a sense of power because I hadn't let John's two creeps stop me in any way. There was so much to ponder. I knew the Chilean was the same man I had met at Callanish. Why had he not acknowledged me in the truck, yet said *thank you* after his bow? And I had no idea what John had hoped to gain by spooking my horse. It got him nothing. I still made it to where I needed to be, but that could have been why he did it. He had said that whatever I do to restore the grid helps him, too!

As for the twelve beings I'd seen surrounding the round stone in my vision, I could only surmise they were galactic visitors, Pleiadeans, like Zev Moab and the others who had been David's teachers. That explained the "computer-generated" drawings made seemingly from above. But I wondered if the statues were meant to represent the twelve beings, and if they were also meant to symbolize those visitors' protection of the small island?

While I had no idea what the answers to these questions might be, I still felt I had reached some sort of completion. I had experienced the most important aspects of the diary for myself – with the exception of seeing Atlantis or personally meeting any Pleiadeans. And as many learned scholars had put forth, I, too, had no doubt that Atlantis had not only existed but had left its mark on the world.

I had seen gigantic stones that could have only been moved across vast desert sands and over deep mountain valleys by a technology we do not have today. Now, on Easter Island, I had experienced that technology at work. And, just in case I should doubt what I had seen and felt, there was the blond Chilean to make sure I "got" it.

Thinking about the Chilean got me wondering again. *What was that funny little bow he made all about?* He had bowed when I had met him at Mary's too, and even then, I had thought it odd. I also pondered the concept of fate. If I had not insisted upon going to the sites by horse and had not strained my back, I would never have met the Chilean – or would I?

I let these thoughts and questions run like sand through the hourglass of my mind as it wound itself down into a deeply altered state – a meditative state, where I was neither asleep nor awake.

I am in the ancient Temple of Atlantis, watching as the young Priestess A-Lan entered her private chambers. She had just come from her final meeting with Prince-Priest A-Ta. She would not see him again until they met at the Pyramid in the time of the dark moon. Prince A-Ta would spend this period in preparation, and she would prepare herself as well.

Her heart beat wildly in her breast, and she felt flushed with excitement. She took herself down to the ritual baths, the great marble and travertine pools that were encrusted with gemstones. She chose the smallest pool, which was made entirely of quartz crystal. It was polished, but covered with a natural resin so its edges would not cut her flesh and its bottom would not be slippery to her feet. This is where the Elder Priestesses would have led her, now that she was fourteen and had begun to bleed. It was time for her coming of age ceremony. Her eyes welled up with tears, for there would be no ceremony – there were no Elders, no Priestesses of the Great Goddess, to guide her steps or show her the way.

Silently she unrobed, wiping away the tears from her aquamarine eyes. "Eyes of the Sea," the Great Mother had called them. Then she gently placed one perfect toe in the silent pool. The crescent moon was reflected in the still waters. The moon water rippled as she slid her lithe, now rounding body into the shimmering pool. The water was cooling as it gently caressed her. She thought of A-Ta, for she knew that he was in love with her, and she felt a warmth rise up between her thighs until it reached the nipples of her perfect teardrop breasts, making them hard. Oh yes, she knew about Prince A-Ta, for she was wise beyond her years.

All at once, she was overtaken by a sense of loss and deep grief. She grieved for her beautiful Atlantis, now all but destroyed. She grieved for her sister priestesses scattered about the planet, and she grieved for the Great Mother, who should be leading her through these final steps of Initiation but was not. In that moment, she felt very alone and very young.

Then, in a sudden rush of energy, she became herself again – only more mature. She entered into a deep meditative state and became aware of a great surge of power as the Codes of Light— the ancient memories that had lain dormant within the cells of her body until this very moment— surfaced. For the first time, she remembered her origin amongst the stars. She understood how life was made and experienced that self-same creativity within her own body. These were things that the Great Mother had intimated would come with puberty – and now they were here!

Intuitively, she led herself through the ancient Rites of Initiation, becoming at the same time both initiate and High Priestess. As she recited the primeval consecrated words, intoning them like a prayer, her past and future selves passed briefly before her eyes – and all became clear. When she stepped from the pool, her body glistening in the moonlight, she was a girl no longer. At that exact moment, she saw two dolphins leap together from the sea outside the temple walls, arching in silhouette against the low-rising slip of a moon.

The dolphins called out to her, and she answered in the primordial tongue known to both species from the time when they were one on another world. She quietly slipped into the plain linen robe she had brought with her, unclasping her heavy ebony tresses and allowing them to fall freely down the back of her damp robe. Softly, she shook her head with a remembering of her Self. Now she was ready for what she had to do – for she possessed the power and the knowledge of the generations of women before her. Now, she was the embodiment of the Goddess, herself.

And, now she could claim her rightful name – her childhood was behind her. Now she was the Priestess Diantha.

Diantha! I awoke with a start, the name blasting through my consciousness. The vision left me queasy and disorientated. For a moment or two, my mind was blank, then everything I had seen came back to me – in full force. I knew, beyond the shadow of a doubt, that the young woman in the dream was the Atlantean Priestess A-Lan, who I had read about in the diary. After her initiation, she was given her true name – Diantha.

Her name was Diantha…no…my name was Diantha! That was the reason I had chosen that strangely familiar name at the baptism ritual in the River Jordan. I thought back to the vision. My body remembered every moment of that long-ago day as if it were yesterday. I had seen the woman I would become – have become – today.

I was stupefied. I lay on the bed – needing to come back to the present, needing to feel firmly planted in the body I now occupied. *With everything that has happened, how could I not have guessed?* There had been so many clues – my unusual childhood, my picking the name Diantha at the River Jordan, David and I having the same dream, everything Mary had said, and so much more.

It was all there, right there, staring me in the face, yet I had never guessed.

My thoughts turned to David, the High Priest A-Ta. I closed my eyes and felt the same heat rise up within me. An overwhelming sadness flooded me as silent sobs shook my body and salty tears streamed down my face. It was all so familiar. I was in love with – him still.

David, I must see you! I will figure out a way. Was he still in Egypt? Was he alright? I had no idea what the dreams I'd had about him meant. I felt my lips move, forming a silent prayer. *God help me...I don't know how I'll do it David, but I will find you!*

A massive shudder raced through my body. It was as if something I had been holding onto my entire life had been shorn away – and I was free. Thoughts, memories and dreams merged, dancing before the singular eye of my consciousness. Things suddenly made sense. It was much like looking through the lens of a camera when it is out of focus. A simple turn of the focal ring makes everything that was blurry and difficult to see instantly sharp and distinct.

Now I know who you are, Mary...and who you were. You were the Great Mother, my devoted High Priestess in Atlantis, who so carefully guided my spiritual development in that long ago time – just as you have in this life. You were also the Beautiful Lady who visited me as a child. No wonder everything about her, from the first moment we met at Callanish, seemed so familiar. And, it was no surprise she was so easy to trust. *You were right Mary, I was never left to drift alone...I have always been led every step of the way!*

I thought of the disappearing Dr. Daath, the strange man I had met at my art show, who had told me about the glyphs and then vanished. He was also one of the ancient Galactic Visitors – like Zev Moab. That was why he looked so familiar, especially around the eyes. It was the modern clothing that threw me off.

One thing was certain, Dr. Daath had not come to inform me about stones appearing and disappearing around the world. His mission was to tell me what my glyphs were and where the ancient symbols originated. He also came to move me along on my journey. He was the reason I travelled to Easter Island, the place I needed to be in order to finally understand who I was and what I had come there to do.

My mind wandered back to the truck with the covered cab, and the blond Chilean with his odd little bow. *If I am Diantha, could he have known me back in the time of Atlantis as well?* He and Mary seemed to have a special understanding, but I had thought his bow to me was only a formality. Back then, there was no way I could have recognized how deeply he was acknowledging me – as Diantha.

And Mateo, with his Buddha smile and elusive answers, was one of the Great Brotherhood of Light – just like Tina's father. Of course, he couldn't give me answers, because I needed to experience everything I saw and felt on my own. *That's the only way I could have come to where I am now…exactly where I am supposed to be!*

Pieces of a giant puzzle began to flow gently into place, and with yet another new realization, I understood exactly what had been happening. At each of the sacred sites, I had been learning things – and accomplishing things – but I had also been becoming personally activated. *These activations have been my initiation process!* Somehow I had completely missed the importance of that, but now I knew.

The activations I'd been experiencing at each of the sites had brought back to life the ancient codes, the energetic imprints of power that had lain dormant in my DNA for so long. They were the very same codes that had been awakened in the "coming of age" ritual I had just witnessed in my lifetime as Diantha in Atlantis. Not only had those codes now come fully back to life – they had been upgraded. *I am now a vessel of Living Light, and David, with the complimentary codes activated in him, is waiting for me.*

I now understood what I needed to do and exactly why I had to find David. Once we found one another again, our energetic patterns would fit perfectly together, exactly like the ancient stonework I had seen around the world. With our combined power, we would be able to do what we had not been able to do on Atlantis – fully activate the Great Pyramid. Only this time, the activation would be for the entire planet – and it would take place in Egypt.

This would be the beacon of Light the world had been waiting for. It would energetically boost the human race right out of its history. People would be able to take a bold evolutionary leap and choose to live from Love – the full knowledge of their interconnection. The rest would be simple. David and I would enter the ancient vaults described in the diary and retrieve the keys to the Earth-Power System – the Planetary Grid. He would use those keys to clear the lines of energy, and together we would usher in the New Era of Light.

The Peoples of Earth are ready, and we are the Way-Showers.

I felt as though I had just awakened from a dream – a dream I had lived since my mother shut me down those many years ago. She had been afraid of her own powers and had buried them. She had taught me to be afraid of who and what I was, because she was afraid. But she didn't know that the end product of fear is more fear.

Now I understood how one's very soul could be raped by fear, and that the only way to break its hold was to recognize there was another option. That was the lesson I was ready to teach. I had lived in fear and denial, so I understood it well. If I could take back my ability to "choose," then so could everyone else.

That was exactly what John had been trying to stop from happening. He knew that if people realized they had a choice, he would lose his hold on them.

And he is right!

CHAPTER 69

I could hardly remember when, not too long ago, all I wanted was to return the diary to David and have him give me some answers. Now my need to find him had taken on a life or death urgency, and time was of the essence.

I can't go home! I need to go to Egypt immediately.

Between nervous excitement and formulating a plan of action, I barely slept. As soon as I heard movement in the house, I was in the dining room strategizing my itinerary with the help of my host. Thank god for computers! I had to smile. *No reliable telephones, but they have Internet. The Pleiadeans are probably having a good laugh at us for thinking our mega-gigabyte toys are so amazing.*

My travel plans shaped up quickly, because there wasn't much to decide. Fortunately, there was a complicated but acceptable solution – if you consider twenty-seven hours in an airplane acceptable. The shortest route I could find would start that evening with a flight to Santiago, Chile, where I would have a short layover before leaving for Egypt. The plane would make a stop in Paris before continuing on to Cairo.

Once my flight plans were finalized, I used my host's computer to make a reservation at the Mena House Hotel, the one near the pyramids where I had stayed with Gabriel and the group. I was in the midst of checking on transportation from the airport when the server went down. My host explained that the island had only one server and once it was down, they were so isolated it could be days before it was up and running again. *What a lucky break! I can't imagine….*

Now that the basics were handled, the next thing on my agenda was calling Tina. She was expecting to pick me up at the airport the following morning. *How am I going to explain all of this to her?*

My host told me about a service I could use to make an out of country call by credit card. As I dialed Tina's number, I tried to think of where to begin. *I guess at the beginning…more or less.* The phone rang several times. *What if she's not home? I can't leave this message on a machine, and I want to get it over with…now!* Still, as I was waiting for her to answer the phone, a bit of apprehension trickled into my resolve.

Finally, she picked up, but before she had the chance to be concerned, I reassured her. "Everything's fine, there's just been a little change of plans. I won't be coming home tomorrow. I'm going back to Egypt."

"To Egypt! Why?"

"Because…. It's kind of a long story, too long to explain on this phone call. I've wanted to tell you about it all for a while, but I didn't put all of the pieces together until last night. It started with a diary I found in Egypt."

"Found?"

"Well, that's not quite right. The diary turned up in my camera case the second morning I was there. I had hired a camel driver, and he must have put it there. I wanted to give it back, but the group moved around so much I couldn't connect with him again. The story the diary told was so fantastic I didn't think it could possibly be true, but now I know it is. For a long time, I was sure my having the diary was an accident, but I've come to realize that it was meant for me. It's what started me on all of the traveling I've been doing.

"Tina, there's just too much…it's too confusing to try to explain right now. There are things that go all the way back to my childhood. I'll write it all out for you today and tonight on the plane and mail it tomorrow morning. I have to change planes in Santiago, Chile. I'll talk to someone in the airport and make sure it gets out."

"But can't you send me an email and…"

"I can't, the server is down, Trust me! I'm not crazy and things will make sense once I tell you the whole story."

"You can't…! Never mind, where are you going to stay in Egypt?"

I gave her the information for the Mena House and did my best to reassure her, knowing it wasn't working at all. "This must seem very strange, and what I'm about to say will sound even stranger. But it is something I have to do. It's my destiny. I'll talk to you from Cairo."

Tina tried to protest and get me to say more, but it was pointless. She would only understand when she heard the whole story – maybe.

I was about to sit down and write the promised letter when a new and unexpected connection leapt into my awareness. My mother and I are of the same ancient bloodline. We both carry the same codes in our DNA. The lineage comes through her. It wasn't exactly new information, but I had been so wrapped up – and so secretive about everything I had been learning these last few months – I just hadn't thought of it.

My mother was afraid of her powers, but I wonder…? What was her experience? How much does she actually remember? She certainly had to know something, or she wouldn't have tried so hard to shut me down as a child. Had she been able to completely deny what was essentially the core of her being or had things occurred that had to be buried and reburied? *I wonder if she has some small piece of information…something she can tell me that will help me fulfill my destiny.* There was so much I wanted to ask her, but it wouldn't be easy to break her silence.

I used the same service to call my mother and hoped the line would be as clear as when I called Tina.

She answered the phone on the first ring. "Hello." Her voice was unusually soft.

"Hi Mom, it's me, Cassie."

"I know it's you," she whispered. "I knew you would call."

"Mom, why are you whispering? You sound strange."

"Your father and I are very worried about you. Don't go!" Her voice sounded stronger.

"What are you talking about?"

"Don't go!" Now she was speaking in her normal tone. "You're planning to go back to Egypt. Don't do it!"

How does she…? "Mom, please…."

"Cassie, just don't do it. Don't risk your life for this. It's not your place. The world can take care of itself. It didn't work before in Atlantis, and it won't work now. You'll just get yourself killed, and for what? For an idea!"

My god! She does know. What else…? "Mom," I said, interrupting her tirade, "please give me a second. The world is very different now and…."

"So now you think you know more about this than I do? You don't know anything! These people…they're ruthless! They'll never let you get away with it. You think I didn't have to learn these things? You think I don't understand what I'm talking about?"

"What do you mean? Have you had contact with them before?"

"Forget about before. They could do things now…things to your father and me and even your brother, if you're foolish enough not to care about yourself."

"Mother, has somebody threatened you?" A jolt of fear ran through my body.

"Don't you worry, they will! I know how they operate. I had to learn that lesson when I was young."

"But they won't...they won't do anything. They'd have nothing to gain. Hurting you or any of the family wouldn't buy them anything. I've talked to...."

"You talked, so what? You always were head-strong Cassie, and now you're going to go and get yourself killed for it...and maybe us, too."

"Mom, they won't hurt you. They haven't even threatened you. It's just an act anyway. They need people to be afraid. That's how they work, they frighten people. You can't give into it! And Mom, I realize this is difficult for you, but we can't deny that both of us carry the ancient bloodline. I really need an answer. Did anything else happen during your childhood, or later? Do you remember anything about the codes? Is there something you can tell me that might help me with what I have to do now?"

There was silence on the other end.

"Mom! Mom, are you there?"

I heard soft sobs.

"Please try not to be afraid. You have to trust me now. I'm not the Cassie you knew as a child. I've learned so much, seen so much. Mom! Mom!"

"Forget about the bloodline! It's not your job. Cassie, oh my Cassie...."

I wanted to shake her, to make her understand, but it was useless. My heart hurt for her worry – for her love for me. I wiped the tears from my eyes and did my best to keep my voice calm and reassuring.

"Mom, listen to me, no one is going to hurt you or dad. Please, trust me. Please! I know what I'm doing."

I waited for an answer, but none came. "Mom, I love you but I have to go now. I'll call tomorrow." My finger lingered on the disconnect button for some time before I was able to hang up the phone.

Is it possible...am I really putting them in some kind of danger?

I was frozen with indecision. *I can't go to Egypt if it puts my family at risk. I can't!* Thoughts raced through my mind, vying for attention. I clenched my jaw so tightly my neck went into spasm, but the pain broke my focus and brought me to my senses. *Wait! Wait just a minute! I have to think this through.* My mother had said that no one threatened her, yet obviously she knew something – was hooked into something – because she could tell I was going back to Egypt. But no one had contacted her, threatened her. It was just fear, and she had always been a frightened person. That had been clear since my childhood.

My mind went back and forth between doubt and certainty, until I relaxed into the truth. What I had to do was much too important for me to stop. *If I don't follow through, it could mean the end of human life on this planet! I can't be controlled by her fear…anymore.* My hand reached for the talisman hanging against my chest. It had come to me because I wasn't afraid to pick it up. *I know who I am, and I choose to do what I need to do.*

CHAPTER 70

The flight to Santiago de Chile seemed to take an eternity – and it was only the first leg of the journey. Upon arrival, we exited the airplane lemming-like and walked toward the baggage area. I had only a short layover and was carrying my luggage, so I went directly to the terminal for Air France, the airline that would take me to Egypt. Fortunately, the woman in the courtesy lounge was tri-lingual and spoke English. She agreed to include the letter I had written to Tina with other important documents to go out later in the day.

Great! Now I'm sure it will get there.

With Tina and the letter off my mind, nagging thoughts about my mother forced me to refocus on her. *She seemed so forlorn…so lost. I can't just leave it that way.* I found my way to a pay phone and placed the call. It took three attempts before the connection went through properly. This time my mother sounded even more anxious, more frightened. Her voice was somewhat strange, but she brushed it off as a slight headache.

It did not take long before the conversation shifted back to another version of what had gone on the day before. She pleaded and begged me not to go. I repeated, again and again, that she, of all people should recognize the necessity of my going. She grew silent the moment I tried to ask her a question, her quiet sobs the only sound on the other end of the line. Finally, I gave up and told her how much I loved her, but that I had to go. *She's just afraid…but how can she have all this knowledge inside her and choose to ignore it?*

So, I guessed, it was up to me – and David. I just had to go forward, and like Mary said, I needed to trust and I would know what I needed to know when I needed to know it. That was certainly the way things had been working so far.

CHAPTER 71

Not only was I now on a plane bound for Egypt, but I had also booked my old room at the Mena House Hotel. This trip would bring me full circle, and in some strange way, it felt like I was going home. Archeological facts, folklore, my experiences, the diary and my newfound memory had pulled themselves together into a completely new reality – and I was ready for the next step. I knew exactly what I needed to do. I would find Rashid and he would take me to David – or at least tell me how to find him.

I had brought a book to read, hoping it would make the long trip pass more quickly, but reading was a joke. My mind ricocheted from David to John, from Mateo to my mission. *I've learned so much! Hmm! I wonder if I can still move a pencil, like I did when I was a kid?* There was no pencil handy, but I was sure a pen would do. I put it on one end of my tray-table, focused on it and marveled as it slowly moved across. I tried it with my lipstick and had the same results. Then, holding my hand slightly above my lipstick, I felt it rise to touch my hand. I lifted the tray and levitated my handbag a few inches off of my lap, but stopped when I noticed a man across the aisle staring at me, mouth agape.

"Parlor trick," I quipped.

Moving into a subtler mode of experimentation, I scrambled the image on the little television monitors throughout the cabin. *I can't believe I'm doing this!* Each time, just as passengers were beginning to buzz the flight attendant, I would return the televisions to normal. There was no need to garner any special attention. Not only was I was having fun, I felt strong and powerful – ready to take on the task ahead.

Without any warning, my temples began to throb. I leaned my head back against the headrest, and a slideshow of images of David flashed before me. He was handcuffed to a chair in a small dark room. I could not hear any words, but it was clear he was being interrogated – and abused.

I squeezed my eyes shut to block out the vision, but it did not work. *How can this be happening? Who is doing this to him? Is it John?* The voice of the flight attendant rippled through the plane – and my thoughts. "Ladies and Gentlemen, we will be…."

My eyes flew open. A feeling of terror ripped my body in visceral response to what I had just seen. I clenched the armrests, and my heart pounded heavily in my chest. *What a nightmare…but I'm not asleep.* It was not the first time I had seen David in trouble. I'd had a dream on the plane that John hijacked to the Yucatan. In that dream, some men in dark uniforms converged on a figure that looked like David, but I had not been sure it was him, and it was clearly a dream. I had also seen something about David on the plane to Easter Island, and even once when I was there. Although David was always in some kind of danger, it had never been anything quite so graphic – and tangible.

This was different. It wasn't a dream – it was a vision – and it felt very real. *This thing with my mother must really be getting to me. It's probably just my imagination working overtime. Maybe I'm not as confident about all of this as I think I am.*

My hand reached up to touch the talisman. *I've got to see….* I turned my back to my seatmate and stared out the window. Do I dare? I removed the leather strap from around my neck. I clutched the talisman tightly in my hand before looking at it and whispering, "John!" As usual, his image appeared immediately. He was sitting on a lounge chair by a pool, a tall drink in his hand. I could hear his phone ring, and he began a casual conversation. Well, whatever he was doing, he wasn't with David.

The plane began its descent and finally bumped gently onto the ground. The breaks screeched and we slowed to a halt. I was still shaking as I stood up and prepared to exit. I felt tense and exhausted. *David is probably fine, but still….* I felt even more urgency to find him. What should have been a home-coming was now becoming a situation fraught with fear.

It took forever to pass through customs, but eventually I was back at the Mena House. I stood on the balcony and stared out at the pyramids. The night sky was brilliant with stars, but I felt fidgety and restless, hardly able to wait for morning. All I could think about was finding David.

* * * * * * * * * * * *

My day started early the next morning. After what I had seen on the plane, I began my search for David with a certain amount of trepidation. Nevertheless, I jetted to the sprawling village near the Sphinx, fully expecting to find Rashid who would then lead me directly to David. Seemed simple enough, but what was I thinking? *Nothing involving the diary has ever been simple.*

I probably asked ten people about Rashid and received at least twelve an-swers, all in broken English. "Yes there is a Rashid, but no…he is not here." "Rashid will be back tonight." "Rashid will be back tomorrow." "Rashid? He will be back next week!" "Who is Rashid?" And then, the most maddening reply of all, "…if he is one of the desert men, he will come back maybe never."

However, my presence did create quite a stir in the village. I was immedi-ately surrounded by a swarm of young men and boys who thought I was *inti-helowa,* meaning "beautiful woman," and although Rashid was not there, they would be very happy to take me on a camel ride. Noticing my disappointment at not finding Rashid, one of the boys grew quiet and looked deeply into my eyes. In a serious and charmingly mature voice, he said, "Do not worry. If it is the Will of Allah, you will find Rashid." *Well then, I sure hope it's the will of Allah that I find David too, and soon!*

Frustrated at not finding Rashid and at my inability to speak Arabic, I sought out the guide who spoke the best English. I asked him to talk to the oth-ers and find out which house belonged to Hadiga, Rashid's sister. He returned shortly, a broad smile on his face, proud that he had found the information for me. "She no longer live here." Apparently she had met with an accident and, along with her daughter Gameleh, had moved in with her sister's family in another village. "A far away village...no one know even the name of it."

The young man was disappointed that I was not happy with his message but quickly understood why. Then I asked about Hakim, the nephew of Rashid, who David had mentioned so often in the opening section of the diary. The guide went back to question the others and, after some discussion, headed back my way. I took one look at his face and my heart sank. He was obviously not pleased with his information – and I knew I wouldn't be, either.

"The news for Hakim is good. Some rich Americans make it so he can study English in America. He gone for...we don't know how long."

What am I going to do now? Hakim was my best hope of finding Rashid. Even if David was not in immediate danger, John was capable of anything, and things could change at any moment. Time was running out – I could feel it in my bones. I had to find David before it was too late. *But how?*

The young man stood watching over me, sensing my distress – and not asking for money. I pulled myself together, thanked him for his help and gave him a few American dollars. Then I gave him additional money and pointed to the young men who had tried to help me, indicating that he should share it with them.

I decided to roam around the village on my own, searching for someone – anyone – who could tell me something that might help. As I left the group of young men and boys to talk amongst themselves, I had the uncomfortable sensation I was being followed. The feeling persisted, but each time I turned around to check, no one was behind me. I spun around again, and this time spooked a teenage boy of about fifteen. He froze and then glanced behind himself, as if he were the one being followed. I watched as he narrowed the distance between us, looking back time and again.

When he grew closer, his words tumbled out, "You want Rashid? He not here, but I know where is another desert man. He in another village. I think he know Rashid." The boy turned and checked one more time, before boldly stating, "My name Abbas. For small amount of American dollars, Abbas will take you to desert man."

Oh my god! I never even thought to ask if there was anyone else who "came and went" mysteriously. I didn't know whether or not to believe him, but I didn't have a lot of other options, either. We settled on five dollars, and I trudged along the dusty road behind Abbas for what felt like forever.

However, when we reached the village, the desert man was nowhere to be found. Abbas spoke at length to a toothless old man. I couldn't make out any of their conversation, but they were talking far too intensely for it to be an ordinary exchange. At one point their interchange got very heated. It sounded like they were having an argument. When they finished, Abbas shrugged his shoulders and told me, "Desert man here yesterday but left in the night."

"What else were you talking about? It had to be more than that he's not here."

"No, no! Only that he was mad at me for bring a stranger to his place."

Hmmm! I don't think so. The old man was probably angry, because Abbas tried to bring me to one of the mysterious desert men. But it didn't really matter, it was just another dead end. *Damn! I can't afford any more of them. I know I'm supposed to find David…there has to be a way!*

I was hot, tired and frustrated. Abbas hailed a passing truck, and we rode in silence back to the Arab village by the Sphinx. He took the money I handed him and scooted away. *Okay, what's next?* Spotting an enterprising peddler who had set up shop with an umbrella, a couple of chairs and a cooler full of water and soda pop, I headed over to the "desert oasis."

It was hard to tell which felt better, drinking the refreshing water or rolling the cold bottle over my face, neck and arms. It would have been great if I could have made a list of what I know and don't know to help me figure things out. It had worked for me in the past, but right now, it would be absolutely pointless. The only thing I knew was that I didn't know anything.

I stared in the direction of the pyramids. I was too far away to see them clearly, but just the fact they were there – and real – gave me some solace. *Okay…what am I missing here? I thought of David and the danger he was in. David! That's it! I never asked directly about David. I'll ask the tour guides….* But I realized there was nothing – absolutely nothing – I could tell them about David. No one in the village had known his name or who he really was except for Rashid – and Rashid was definitely not around.

Well, sitting here is useless. Maybe a cold shower might spark a new idea. I was on my way to the Mena House when something clicked. *The porter's room!* I remembered how David had passed out in the porter's room of the Mena House when he had seen the Israeli professor on television. *It's possible someone there might remember something.*

With a new focus and a lot of determination, I trudged back up the long road to the Mena House. It was late afternoon by the time I finally arrived. Although I was gritty and parched and almost numbed with exhaustion, my shower would have to wait. I went directly down to the porter's room, the scene of David's collapse. The young men who apparently were on call were engrossed in a television news program that featured footage of the Mad Man disease spreading to yet a new part of the world.

Damn that John, I cursed under my breath.

When that segment was over, I got their attention and explained I was looking for a particular tour guide. To my relief, one of the guides understood some English and translated for me. I told him the man I was looking for had blue eyes, and had lived with Hakim's family and worked with him at the stables.

"The unusual thing is that one day, while he was here waiting for his customers, he had passed out. Do any of you remember him?" At first the translation was met with blank stares. The room was silent for some time before guides began to talk amongst themselves, shrugging and shaking their heads. "The television was on just like now," I continued, "and an Israeli professor was talking when the guide passed out. Everyone rushed to help. Doesn't anybody remember a guide with blue eyes?"

Suddenly one of the porters jumped up and called out. "Israeli! Blue eyes! Mr. David...you mean Mr. David? He come here often for meeting. He here now. I can find Mr. David for you. Come...come with me." My heart leapt in my chest as he took me up to the lobby in the slowest elevator ever invented.

The porter made a call on the house phone and then, pointing to couches and chairs in the lounge area, said, "Sit, please. The man, Mr. David, he will come soon. Excuse, please, I must go." I gave him some Egyptian money and thanked him.

Taking a seat facing the elevator door, I began my vigil. It was like waiting for water to boil – except with anxiety. *David! Israeli! Blue eyes! Comes in for meetings! Oh my god! It's got to be 'my' David! I can't believe it.* I waited – and waited – and waited. I looked at my watch. 4:37. I looked at it again. 4:38. I reached for a magazine and absentmindedly turned the pages. It was full of pictures of rare and priceless antiquities recovered from Egyptian tombs. I glanced at my watch. *Stop it!*

I read the descriptions of the artifacts, but two seconds later I couldn't remember a word I'd just read. Relax! Take a breath! He has to stop what he was doing and come from… somewhere. 4:46. I should have asked the porter how long it would be before David would arrive. I went back to the magazine. 4:51. My stomach was going crazy. I had to go to the bathroom, but I couldn't leave. I was about to go back to the porter's room when I felt a tap on the back of my shoulder. My body rushed with excitement, and I swung around expectantly.

"You wanted to speak to me? I'm Mr. David." He might have been Mr. David, and he might have had blue eyes and an Israeli accent, but he was at least seventy years old – and he definitely was not my David. He looked so eager and so sincere, that in spite of myself, I cracked a smile. Thanking him for his time, I explained there had been a misunderstanding. *What a joke! How ridiculous of me to expect them to remember David. It was just wishful thinking. Most of those guys probably weren't even here then…whenever 'then' was. I should have known it wouldn't be that simple.*

I wanted to scream. My brain was so fried I could not even think. But of course, I had to think. I had not come this far to give up now. I went up to my room, pulled off my clothes and took the most unsatisfactory shower of my life. *It's so hot in this god-forsaken place, you can't even get any cool water.*

Still damp from the shower, I reached for my notebook and flung myself on my bed, leaning against a stack of pillows. My fingers drummed on the notebook as random thoughts crashed against one another in my mind. *There's nothing else I can do here...unless...! Why didn't I think of that before?* My hand was shaking as I hastily scribbled a new idea.

CHAPTER 72

Early the next morning, I walked back to the Arab village ripe with a new plan – hopefully one that would work. But before I even got to the first stage of my plan, a voice interrupted my thoughts.

"Psst!" It sounded like a young voice. I looked around but couldn't see where it came from. "Psst!" I scanned again but didn't see anyone. "Psst! Over here!"

I searched once more and noticed a young Arab boy of about twelve almost hidden behind a mud brick house. He waved me over, and I took a few cautious steps toward him.

"You are looking for Rashid?"

I was surprised by the direct question but quickly nodded yes.

"He is looking for you!"

"Why are you whispering?"

He looked around furtively. "They are watching," he hissed at me.

"Who is watching?"

"You know who.... Them! Rashid wants me to bring you to him. He ask... do you know everything you need to know before you see David?"

That stopped me cold. *Who is this boy? Why would he ask me that? Did John send him?*

"Why do you want to know?"

"Rashid want to know, because David now ready to see you."

"Well then, I'll talk to Rashid about it."

"Okay, I am going. You count to ten, then follow me."

"Where...?"

"Don't ask! Don't look at me!" he hissed again, as he turned and walked out of the village.

I glanced around, but no one was looking my way and nothing out of the ordinary seemed to be happening. *How do I know he's not lying…that John is not using him to trick me for…whatever? Oh my god, I don't, but I'm desperate and maybe, just maybe, he really will take me to Rashid.*

Feeling very foolish but trying to look casual, I counted to ten and began to walk in the direction the young boy had taken. I cleared the village and spotted the boy squatting beside a wheelbarrow. I quickly reassessed him. He was probably only ten –or even eight. I began to breathe more easily. *He's much too young to be dangerous.* He stood up and beckoned me closer. Shining a big grin, he said, "My name Mahmud." Then, like a little man, he stuck out his hand, and I shook it.

"Are they…?"

"Not worry, they not here now but one of them was in village. Don't look back! Just follow me."

"How do you…?"

"Don't talk now…just follow me. Rashid will be explaining everything!"

For some reason I couldn't fathom, I did what he said. I followed him as he headed into Cairo. We dodged traffic, horns beeping at us and at each other. *This is crazy!* "Be careful," I yelled. "You'll get us killed."

"We're almost there," he called back. We wove this way and that through more traffic and down dark alleyways, the neighborhoods becoming poorer and dirtier as I became more and more tired and confused. Finally my legs buckled and my throat became so dry I could barely breathe.

"We need to stop…I have to rest," I said, clutching my chest.

"No, we will be there in a few minutes."

But I could not move. Soon a horde of angry men in dark uniforms seemed to emerge right out of the walls and dark alleyways, and quickly began to close in on me like a rush of angry wraiths.

I labored as I tried to breathe. *I have to get out of here! How…?* There was no realistic way to escape, but something deep inside of me knew what to do. *Focus your mind…David and the Atlanteans did it…I'm activated…my only chance!*

Forcing my mind to clear, I imagined myself inside my room at the Mena House. I thought of it detail by detail, picturing the king-sized bed and the beautiful Egyptian cotton bedding with the lace coverlet. I saw myself opening the large sliding glass door, walking out onto the balcony and looking at the Giant Pyramid silhouetted against the blue Egyptian sky. My concentration was so complete that I almost forgot to breathe.

Everything around me began to move in slow motion. I saw the men in dark uniforms converge on me – except that I wasn't there anymore. In fact, I was standing on the balcony of my hotel room at the Mena House Hotel. The Great Pyramid loomed before me, exactly where it had stood for eons.

My hand reached to touch the smooth iron handrail that surrounded the balcony, to reassure myself that I had escaped. As the reality of what just happened flowed through me, I began to shake uncontrollably.

A loud crash echoed through the room, and I awoke with a start. *What just happened? Is anybody here?* My eyes darted furtively around the room. I was alone. The early morning sunlight had begun to filter through the drapes. *What...what a nightmare!*

It had all been a dream – only a dream – but I remembered every detail. *It was so real... the young boy, weaving through traffic, the men in dark uniforms...and teleporting!* I had gotten myself out of there by focusing my mind. I had been able to save myself! *Was that just a really, really bad dream, or was it a vision preparing me for something I might need to do...soon?*

I got up and opened the drapes. The pyramids were right there, as was the glass door and the balcony with the iron handrail. I looked around the room again. Pillows were scattered all over and the bedside lamp was lying broken on the floor. The falling lamp was probably what woke me up. I must have flung my arm out and knocked it off the nightstand.

I straightened the pillows and bent down to pick up the broken lamp. My notepad had also found its way to the floor. I reached for it but hesitated a moment before looking at it. The last page was empty – I had not written a thing. I didn't have any great plan. In fact, I didn't have a plan at all. *That's the one part of the dream I wish was real.*

I curled up on the bed and stared at the blank page, willing a new idea to come. *There has to be something else…something I'm missing.* Minutes passed. Nothing, absolutely nothing came to mind. *Well, this isn't working.* I needed to look at things logically. *Okay, the best way to solve a problem is to look at the facts. No! First you have to have the facts. All right then, what do I know about David? Well…I know he was born in Israel and…. That's it! It's so insanely obvious…find his family.*

Closing my eyes, I tried to recall what else I knew about him – about his childhood. I scanned my memory banks, looking for pieces from that part of the diary and jotted down "the facts." He had been born outside of Jerusalem. He had fits when he was a young boy and would shout gibberish that no one could understand.

Cassandra…focus! Soon I was seeing David's scrawling script running across the pages of the diary. Then, as if I were holding the diary in the palm of my hands, I remembered. His parent's names were Benjamin and Sara, and his father was a professor in the Mathematics Department at the Hebrew University. *Damn! I can't remember if there was a last name!* David's fits were a serious problem, and his parents were terribly worried.

The father had inadvertently taped one of his son's rants and had played it while in his office. A friend of the father, a Professor in the Jewish language department, overheard the recording and recognized the gibberish as ancient Aramaic. Word for word, the boy had recited one of the speeches the biblical King David had made to his warriors.

David's fits stopped by the time he was four, but word leaked out about his "abilities." There was a rush of publicity, and the family, feeling they had to move, relocated to Tiberias.

Now, what…what was the other Professor's name? I could almost see it. It began with the letter H. I'd recognize it if I saw it. He was the man David had seen on the television in the porter's lounge the day he passed out. He would know how to find the family, for sure.

Dashing downstairs to the hotel's guest computer, I searched to find the name of the professor and see if he still taught there. Impatient but excited, I scrolled through the names of the professors in the language department. I was prepared to look through all the names, but the moment my eyes hit upon *Professor Abraham Hoffritz* in the Department of Hebrew and Jewish Languages, I recognized the name. *That's him! Yes!*

I tried to call, but only got his voice mail. *I can probably fly there faster than he'll return my call.* And given the delicate nature of everything, an in-person visit was probably the way to go. Besides, I was going to have to go to Tiberias to talk with David's parents anyway.

I jumped on the phone and booked a direct flight to Tel Aviv on El Al Airlines. The only one available would get me into Ben Gurion Airport just before nightfall.

CHAPTER 73

Since I only planned to be gone for a few days and did not want to deal with luggage, I had packed my necessities in my small tote. I had left my carry-on with the manager of the Mena House and my cameras in the vault. Although the Tel Aviv airport was bustling when I arrived in the early evening, the connecting bus ride didn't get me to Jerusalem until way after dark.

I had booked a room in the Hyatt Regency Hotel, which was close to the university. Brochures from the school, in both Hebrew and English, were prominently displayed at the front desk. I grabbed a few and changed dollars for shekels. Once in my room, I quickly looked through the brochures, hoping to find one that had a map of the campus.

There was no actual map, but one schematic showed an overview of the campus. *This will be handy,* I thought, as I opened the brochure on a table in the corner of the small room. I looked at the map to get the lay of the land, and even though I was tired, I burst out laughing. *I've definitely seen way too many sacred sites.* In overview, the campus looked like a long, giant serpent with kink in the center, causing both its head and tail to point in the same direction. The campus literally wrapped around itself, with a spacious green belt occupying the center area. It looked very open with walkways, seating areas and lots of greenery.

I awoke early and had coffee in the hotel lobby before taking a cab to the university. The campus was an unexpected sight. Perched high on a hill and adjacent to a national park, its modern sculptural stone buildings sat in profile against a clear blue sky. It was strikingly beautiful, however my focus was elsewhere – going over what I would say to Dr. Hoffritz. I became aware that the cab driver was talking to me, but I was in another world.

"Miss…."

"Sorry. What did you say?"

"We are here, Miss. The Faculty of The Humanities is right over there," he repeated, pointing to a building across the green belt of the "snake."

"I can't drive any further. It's just a short walk from here."

I hopped out of the cab and paid the driver. I was surrounded by an ongoing series of ultra-modern buildings constructed out of Jerusalem stone. The combination of stone and glass gave the complex a beautifully uniform ancient-modern look.

It took a moment to get my bearings, but I was in too much of a hurry to think clearly. *Okay, so I guess I just start…anywhere.* I walked into the first building, a building that could have been on any college campus except for the vast number of names engraved on the walls. It was evident that many people from various parts of the world had had a hand in the creation of the university. I walked down the long hallway looking for something that might resemble an office, but unfortunately all of the signs were in Hebrew. Eventually, I arrived at a spacious and sunlit indoor quad where a group of students were chatting between classes.

"Shalom," I said, using the universal Hebrew greeting. "Excuse me, do you speak English?"

"Yes, of course," said one of the students. "Most of us here do. Can I help you?"

"I hope so! I'm looking for the office of Professor Abraham Hoffritz. He teaches Jewish Languages."

"Oh, well, in that case he would probably be Atzmaut Hall," the student said, getting up and walking me over to a set of large glass doors. She pointed to a building across the open courtyard and said, "That's Atzmaut Hall. Somebody over there will be able to help you find his office."

I thanked her and raced to the other building. After a quick search, I tagged another student and asked the same question.

"Sorry, I don't know," he answered. "Never taken a class with him. You could try the Dean's office, or just go over to administration. It's closer."

"Where's that?" I asked, looking around a bit dazed.

He caught the searching look in my eyes. "Yeah, I can see why you might be confused. This place is kind of spread out." He led me to a different door and pointed to a building. "It's just beyond that one, but don't be afraid to ask someone else if you can't find it. People are always getting lost here."

I was excited and strangely nervous. *I'm about to personally meet one of the characters from the diary!* I had no trouble finding the right building, but the directory was in Hebrew, so I walked down the hall and into the first open office. A round-faced woman with curly red hair was sitting behind the desk.

"Shalom! I'm trying to find Professor Abraham Hoffritz."

"Hmm…what does he teach?"

"Hebrew and Jewish Languages."

"Just a minute," she said, rolling her chair over to a computer and typing in the Professor's name.

"Ah ha! Give me one more minute," she said, without looking up. "Our computers were down this morning, and they're still acting like a bunch of nutty kids." I felt time creep by.

"Come on Hymie," she said to the computer. She gave me an amused look as she said, "That's what I call him…Hymie. I find they work so much better when you treat them like real human beings." She laughed. "That's pretty funny, since they're not really human beings, but they think they are. Ah, here we go, Professor Abraham Hoffritz. Oops, he's on sabbatical until next March."

I was dumbfounded – totally unprepared for this turn-of-events.

"Is there anybody else who will do?"

What can I say…I'm looking for Ben somebody who is David's father, is married to Sara and taught mathematics here…sometime?

"No, thank you, there's nobody else."

I turned and walked zombie-like out of the office and down the hallway. A group of students, laughing and chatting and obviously having a great time, were right in front of me. I followed them out of the building. The sun seemed abnormally bright as it bounced off the grey-white stone buildings. I stood on the walkway beside the green belt, squinting in the harsh light and feeling completely blank. A few moments passed – and a few more – and a few more.

From some far-away place, I heard a voice and slowly turned. A middle-aged woman with short salt and pepper hair, beautiful skin and deep blue eyes with wire-rimmed glasses was trying to get my attention.

"Are you alright? I noticed you standing there. You seem lost. Can I help you?"

"Oh…no…I mean I'm all right, thank you," I said automatically.

"Why don't you come and sit down," she said, leading me toward a bench. I glanced around. I was still on campus, but nowhere near the administration building.

Once I was seated, I seemed to come back into my body. "Thank you… I…I didn't realize…. What time is it?"

"It's 3:30."

"You're kidding!"

"No," she said, grinning. "It's really 3: 30."

"I'm sorry," I said, smiling weakly. "I just got some rather bad news and…."
I…I must have walked around here for hours….

"You probably haven't eaten all day. I was just heading over to the Vitamin Meat Café. Why don't you come with me?"

I can't go eat! I've got to figure out what I'm going to do. "You're a lovely person. Thank you so much for caring, but that's not necessary. I have to…."

"Well, I think it is," she said, catching me as I stood up and almost fell. "I'm going to get you some water. Visitors aren't used to this kind of heat. Don't go anywhere. I'll be right back."

CHAPTER 74

Over a sandwich and iced tea, I learned that my rescuer was Rabbi Zahava Shalev, a professor at the university in the School of Jewish Studies. Her specialty was modern Jewish History and the Diaspora. When I expressed surprise over her being a woman, she explained, "I am what's known as a *reconstructionist* rabbi. Many of us are academics. Unlike orthodox and conservative rabbis, whose focus is on studying the Talmud and deciphering Jewish law, my real passion circles around what it means to be a Jew in the twenty-first century."

"Wow! I don't think I've spoken to a rabbi since I was a kid in Sunday school and, believe, me, they were nothing like you."

Just as I was beginning to feel my brain switch into forward gear, she broke the casual tone of our conversation. "So, what is a young American woman doing so far away from home and looking so intense?"

That stopped me cold. *How much can I tell her? Is there a way she can help?*

"Well," I said, taking a cautious approach, "I was trying to locate a man who used to teach here a number of years ago. He taught mathematics but had a close friend who still teaches in the Humanities Department. However, it turns out that his friend is on sabbatical until next March. So...I'm thinking it's a wash."

"Who is the man you are looking for?" she asked, in a very direct tone.

I considered again, this time taking full measure of her energy. *I can trust her...and she can help me.* "I don't know," I answered honestly. "As I said, he taught here some time ago but left abruptly. He had a son with some unusual, *umm*...talents. The papers got hold of the story, and the family became the center of a lot of unwanted attention. Apparently, it became so bad they felt they had to leave Jerusalem. He picked up and moved his wife and young child to Tiberias. The only information I have is that his name was Ben and his wife's name was Sara. Not much to go on."

"It's not, but you'd be surprised what a little information with a lot of intention behind it can get you," she said, cocking her head to one side and looking deeply into my eyes. "You must be talking about Professor Benjamin Halevi."

She got the response she was waiting for – it showed in my eyes, the quick turn of my head and my body language. "How could you know that?" I demanded. I had certainly not given her enough information to make that leap so quickly – or ever!

"I'm psychic," she stated, as matter-of-factly as if she had just said *I'm Jewish*.

"You're *what?*" I exclaimed, mouth agape.

"It's not so strange. I'm a religious person, and I also have certain gifts. The Bible is full of seers, not that I put myself in that category, but it's not a total contradiction." She laughed and said, "If only you could see your face!"

"Well, Rabbi...."

"Zahava, please."

"Okay, Zahava," I said, shaking my head. "So what can you tell me?"

"First of all, I'm not such a good psychic that I would give up my day job. Mostly I'm just intuitive, but occasionally I get brilliant flashes of insight. That's what happened this time. I just knew! It's a handy adjunct to the community work I do, especially with teenagers. Oddly enough, I was just thinking about that family the other day, about the boy. I believe his name was David."

The name echoed in my ears.

Zahava took a sip of tea before continuing. "There were some very interesting predictions made about the boy's future. After that, the family just dropped off the map, and there has never been another word about him. I was a rabbinical student at the time, so that was over thirty years ago. The whole King David issue caused quite a commotion, not only among Jews, but amongst Muslims and Christians as well. You see, King David plays an important role in all three religions.

"The Christian faith considers the biblical King David to have been a prophet who foreshadowed the coming of Jesus, and many believe that the return of David would herald the Second Coming of the Christ. King David is also considered an important prophet of Islam and even appears in the Koran.

"And, of course, orthodox and conservative Jews are still waiting for the Messiah, the future King of Israel, to arrive. They believe this 'future David' will unite the original Twelve Tribes of Israel and herald a Messianic Age of global peace. But to be the true Messiah, he must be from the Davidic lineage. Now here's where it gets intriguing," she said, leaning forward, a wave of intensity spreading across her face. "It turns out that the mother, Sara, is definitely from the Davidic bloodline."

Obviously, she thought this was a key piece of information, because she relaxed, finished her tea and signaled the waitress for a refill. *That's not exactly new information for me. I wonder what she would think if she knew that David was an Atlantean Priest even before he was King David...and that, in their way, all of the prophecies are true!*

Zahava shook her head. "It was crazy! There were a lot of religious zealots who believed this boy was very important, and all of them wanted a piece of him. It wasn't a pretty picture, that's for sure, and I'm not surprised they vanished.

"I can't tell you what Professor Halevi changed his name to, but if the family lives in Tiberias, I might be able to help you find them...or him. I know someone in Tiberias, or rather my sister knows someone, and he's pretty good at tracking down just about anyone. Also, he's rather indebted to my sister, so the mere mention of her name could go a long way in soliciting his help."

"That sounds great. How far away is Tiberias, and what is the best way to get there?"

"It's a little over an hour away, and I'll drive you."

"No, I couldn't possibly...."

"Are you going to make a habit of this 'no' stuff? Try saying 'Yes, thank you. I'd love it!' Besides, I'm not all that charitable. My sister lives there, and I've been meaning to visit her for ages. I have no plans for this evening and no early classes tomorrow, so this is the perfect time."

"Yes, thank you, I'd love it! I guess old habits die hard," I said, thinking about how I had gone through the same routine with Tina – many times!

There was that "hand of fate," again. David had written about it in the diary, and Mary had told me about it. So had Jeff! They had seemed to understand that when you're on purpose, you get what you need, when you need it. *And, boy do I need it!*

After quick stops at my hotel and her apartment to pick up what we would need for overnight, we were off. We passed date groves, vineyards and shepherds tending their flocks, but while the scenery was amazing and the conversation lively, I was antsy. After so many false starts, things were hopefully turning around, but I had already been looking – and not finding – David for three days now. *I really need this to work. There's so much at stake….*

Night was falling by the time we arrived. We stopped in front of a small hotel in the old part of the city not far from the waterfront. "This is a great little hotel, inexpensive but very clean and cozy." Zahava reached into her handbag and pulled out a small notebook and a pen. "I'm going to give you a phone number. Call it as soon as you're settled in your room. A woman will answer. Tell her you're a friend of Devorah Shalev and that you need to speak with Shimon. He's deaf, but he can read lips, so you'll have to see him in person. Once the woman hears you're a friend of Devorah's, she will arrange a meeting and tell you where and when to meet him."

She wrote down the number and handed me the piece of paper. "This must seem a bit unusual, and I guess it is, but Shimon's an unusual man. If this family is in Tiberias, he'll find them. Listen, I get you are on some kind of mission, and I know it involves the boy. I have a very good feeling about you… and about him. Whatever this mission is, I can tell you it's important. However, I think it might turn out somewhat differently than you expect. Just keep at it. Don't lose hope."

Our eyes met. "Don't worry," she said, leaning over and hugging me. "Shalom. May you always walk in peace." I hugged her back and thanked her. "Okay, now. Off you go." There was nothing else to say. I grabbed my things and watched as her car disappeared into the night.

The hotel was just as Zahava had described, clean and cozy – and it still had an old-fashioned dial telephone. *Well, just as long as it works!* I took a deep breath and dialed. A woman answered.

"Shalom. I am a friend of Devorah Shalev, and I would like to speak with Shimon."

There was a slight pause. "Would tomorrow morning be convenient for you."

"Yes, that would be fine," I answered.

"Do you know your way around town?"

"No, not really."

"Where are you located?"

"I'm staying in the Old City not far from the lake."

"All right then, take a cab to the southern section of Tiberias, to the Hamat Tiberias National Park. It's an archeological park, and there will be a small entrance fee. Tell the driver you want to go to the Severus Synagogue. The ruins of the synagogue are in the park. That's where Shimon will be. There are signs so you can't miss it. He is meeting someone there at nine o'clock. Look for two benches that face each other. He calls that his 'office.' He will meet with you when he's finished. Will you hold a moment? I have another call coming in." There was a slight pause. "Forgive me. I'm back now. What is your name?"

"Cassandra."

"Very good, Cassandra. Shimon is in his early fifties, has a medium build, grey hair and a beard. He will meet with you sometime after 9:30. He will be wearing a brown plaid jacket."

CHAPTER 75

The taxi dropped me off at the Hamat Tiberias National Park shortly after 9:00 the next morning. The park included the Hammam Suleiman Museum as well the ruins of not only the Severus Synagogue, but of an ancient hot springs, courtyards, columns and walls. The area was humming with tourists, most with camera in hand. I paid the entrance fee and found my way to the remains of the ancient synagogue.

A sign in English, Hebrew and Arabic announced that the original temple was built between 286 and 337 AD, when the Sanhedrin, the high Jewish court, was headquartered in Tiberias. I learned that five more temples had been built over the centuries, each upon the ruins of the other. The Severus Synagogue was uncovered in 1920 by workers who were building a new road. The site was preserved and archeologists have partially reconstructed the perimeter walls of the synagogue, but only to two to three feet in height.

Although there was no actual roof over the ruins, a partial structure supported by several poles covered a section of the ruins. I gingerly entered the ruins and walked toward the covered area. Beneath it, a low fence protected an amazing and very ancient stone mosaic floor.

A guide was in the midst of telling people that this was a zodiac mosaic, dating from the fifth century. The guide explained that the mosaic consisted of three panels. The central panel depicted the sun god Helios driving his chariot across the sky. A spectacular zodiac surrounded him, and images of four women, symbolizing the four seasons, appeared in each corner of the mosaic. The guide moved the group to another area of the ruins, but I remained transfixed by the stone floor. *Wow! A zodiac!* The mosaic clearly showed the relationship between events in the heavens and their effects on the earth. I had heard that many ancient cultures looked at things this way, but I never knew the ancient Jews had.

"Cassandra?"

I turned to face an attractive man with gray hair, a scraggly beard and a brown plaid jacket. "Beautiful, isn't it?" he said. "It's the oldest surviving mosaic floor in all of Israel and one of the most important archeological finds in the whole of Jewish history. Imagine, almost seventeen centuries…the history of this place! Incredible! I come here as often as I can.

"By the way, I'm Shimon," he added, handing me a bottle of water. "It's from the hot springs. The healing powers of the waters have attracted people here for thousands of years. So, did you hear why this place is called the Severus Synagogue?"

I shook my head.

"It's because archeologists found the Greek name Severus inscribed on a section of the mosaic floor. It's very faint," he said, walking to the far end of the mosaic and pointing toward the inscription. "The inscription shows the influence of the Greco-Roman culture of the time on the Jewish people."

I couldn't distinguish the inscription – and I wasn't much interested – but I wanted to be polite. After duly admiring it, I turned and said, "Thank you Shimon, but how did you know it was me?"

"Ah ha," he smiled. "You're here by yourself. You don't have a camera. You have a serious look about you. So I thought to myself, she must be Devorah's friend," he said, laughing and taking hold of my arm. "Why don't we go and sit down."

Shimon led me over to a pair of small, intricately carved stone benches that faced each other. He told me that, at one time, Tiberias was a great center of learning. "These benches are very old," he said, "some of the greatest Jewish sages probably sat right here.

"Look around," he suggested, with a sweep of his arm. "The other benches are very old too, but they have been arranged for the tourists. Originally, all of the benches faced each other like these do. Why? Because, you see, there is a tradition for not only rabbis, but for anyone who studies torah, to do so with a partner. They sit across from each other and study…and challenge each other…in order to reach a greater truth."

I looked appreciatively at the benches scattered here and there around the grounds. "That's fascinating!"

"You'll have to look at me when you speak or I will not understand what you are saying."

"Oh, I'm sorry. I forgot," I said, quickly turning back. "You speak so well that I…."

"Don't worry. It happens all the time. I didn't lose my hearing until the explosion. It was many years ago, but my speech, it was already well established."

Explosion! That's when I really looked at the man sitting opposite me and noticed a rather distinct scar running down his left cheek – and a face that while not old, seemed to have lived a difficult life. He felt me looking at the scar, and his hand seemed to move up, involuntarily, to protect it. I looked down.

"No, don't look away. I have Dr. Shalev to thank, because that is all I have to show from the accident. This scar, and of course…the loss of my hearing."

I must have looked bewildered.

"Devorah, Dr. Shalev, she came right after the bomb exploded. If it wasn't for her, many of us would probably be dead." He looked at me more closely. "Where are you from?"

"The United States, from California."

"The United States is very far away. People there think they understand what is going on in Israel, but really they have no idea. It's crazy! We are all relatives here, Jews, Christians, Muslims. We share a common ancestry and history, yet we cannot seem to get along. How can children grow up…how can they learn when they are afraid? Children listen to what they are taught, and if what they are taught is to hate, how can they learn to trust…to love? Where is our future? It is very sad. No, it is sick!

"I'm sorry," he said, the intensity of his look softening slightly. "At times I can get carried away. So, what can I do for you, friend of Devorah?"

His words were straight out of the diary. *Nobody, not even the planet, will be safe until all of this hatred changes! There's something very special about this man. I want to hear more.*

"First, let me say that I completely agree with every word you just said. And you are right. We live such a protected life in the United States. We don't… I don't…."

"I appreciate your words, but it's not necessary, really. It's not your fault that you were born where it is safe. I do not want to talk about it anymore. So, how can I be of help to you?"

"Well, there's a family I'm trying to locate. They moved here some thirty years ago from Jerusalem. Their name was Halevi, Benjamin and Sara Halevi, and they had a little boy named David. The problem is that they changed their name when they moved here, and I have no idea what they changed it to."

Shimon pulled out his iPhone and used it as a hand-held computer, which seemed oddly out of place in our ancient surroundings. He tapped something into it and began to scroll. He muttered to himself, tapped something else and continued to scroll. "I have Benjamin and Sara, but the boy does not show up on my list."

"He left a long time ago."

Shimon was persistent in his search. "I see that Benjamin is a math tutor, and he and his wife Sara are now known as Ben and Sara Barak. They live at...." He changed his menu and continued scrolling. His brow furrowed, and he scratched his head. "Hmm!" he said, looking at me with a strange expression. "They do not live here anymore, but...I don't understand." He looked back at his "computer." Some time passed before he spoke again. "It seems they moved away two years ago, but they gave no forwarding address. They just disappeared."

"What do you mean, 'disappeared?'"

"Perhaps that is the wrong word. They just do not show up on any of my current lists."

"What kind of lists?"

"I have information about people...many, many people. I need the information for my work."

"Your work? What kind of work do you do?"

"It's...it's not work exactly, it's more like my purpose in life."

Purpose in life! "How interesting! What exactly do you mean by 'your purpose?' How did you find it? I'm serious...I really want to know."

"It's a long story, but if you insist. I'll try to be brief. It started from the explosion," he began, his hand unconsciously rising again to touch his scar. "I was in a café with some friends when a bomb exploded. Bodies were flying. I was thrown against an Arab man. When I tried to push myself up, I saw that my hands were covered with blood. Then I saw a sight...I will never forget this sight. The man I was leaning against...his legs were...one was lying sideways and the other was blown off at the knee. The man was literally bleeding to death. Blood was everywhere. I almost vomited. I screamed for help and looked around frantically. A woman was bending over someone else, and I hollered for her to hurry over.

"The woman made her way towards us, stepping over broken chairs and shattered glass. She pulled on my shirt and said something to me, but I couldn't hear her. She took off her own shirt, grabbed a sharp piece of glass and ripped the shirt in half. She tried to stop the Arab man's bleeding by using the fabric to tie tourniquets around what remained of his legs. The fabric was instantly soaked with blood. I couldn't look at that, so I looked at the man's face. I will never forget that face. He was in shock, his face smooth and relaxed. Think how sometimes the body can protect itself!

"Medical help began to arrive. Some people were strapped to gurneys and carried away. Others were covered with white sheets until they could be taken. They thought my injuries were not so serious, so I got to sit there and watch. But something was wrong...very wrong. I could see people screaming, but I could not hear a thing. Finally the woman who was the first to arrive, the one who tore off her blouse, came to me. She was wearing a large doctor's jacket that someone must have given her.

"She asked if I was alright. I could see her lips move, but I heard nothing. I told her about my problem and was immediately taken to hospital. The woman was Dr. Devorah Shalev. She had been down the street when the bomb exploded and hurried over. Without her, many more of us would not be alive.

"There you have it. Except for my hearing, I was good. My family would have to make adjustments. I would have to make adjustments. I could learn to read lips. Small price to pay for being alive! But I was angry. Angry at the price I had to pay, angry for those that died, angry for those who suffered for...I don't know how long...then died anyway. And I was angry for the ones who would be crippled for life. I could not get the face of the man whose legs were blown off out of my mind.

"I am sorry, Cassandra. I think I have not been very brief. But now I am going to get to the point of my story."

"Don't be sorry. I can't even imagine...."

"Don't try to. It cannot be done. Anyway, many months went by until one day I decided to find out if the man had lived. The officials had the names of course, but I had no idea what his was. It was my wife who suggested I contact

Dr. Shalev. As it turns out, she had kept in touch with him, because…well, after all…she had saved his life. She told me he had lost both legs but had been released from rehabilitation and was doing remarkably well.

"So I went to see him. Of course, it had been very hard for him…for his family. Everything had changed. But he had to go on…for them. What he did, people said it was a miracle. Except no, it was no miracle. He took a choice. He was going to live…to live a full, productive life. And it was going be a happy life. It was not easy. Where his legs were blown off, it made it hard for him to wear the prostheses. Even now, he can wear them only for a short while before they bother him. He had every right to be angry. So how did he live his life?

"He looked around at his children…at the friends and neighbors who came to help…and he was afraid for them, for their safety. He said to himself, *No more! This hatred has got to stop! The fighting…the killing…it has got to stop! That's what my life's work must be.*

"When he tells me this, I say to him, 'You're crazy. What can one person do that will make a difference in such insanity?'

"'But I'm not one person,' he says. 'You will be with me, and soon there will be others.'

"Me?"

"'Yes you, my friend. We almost died together…now we are brothers. We must show the world a different way.'

"Now I'm thinking, here's Ibrahim, that's his name, with his legs blown off, wanting to help people understand each other, respect each other, even to love each other as brothers. And I…I want to kill the bastards who did this to us. 'How do you do it?' I ask him.

"'Well Shimon,' he says, his face softening, 'I've tried, but I cannot be happy and angry at the same time. For me, it's impossible. Sometimes, when I get really, really frustrated, I get very angry…but then I am not happy. And everyone around me is miserable. Those people already got my legs. Do you think I am going to let them get my life as well?'

"The more he talked, the more I understood. My anger didn't make one bit of difference in the world, and more importantly, it didn't make anything better. It was wasted energy. So I start to think…if I have all this energy to waste, better I should use it for something good.

"That was it. Our fate was sealed. We each had made the adjustments we needed to make so we could continue to support our families, but our life's 'work' was to open channels of communication between the Arabs and the Jews.

"We began with meetings in our living rooms. It was just a few people at first, those of us who already knew and trusted each other. Each of us met with other people, and the idea began to grow. Now we have small groups working everywhere…many, many people, both Arabs and Jews. And all these people, they know many other people. But we have to be a little careful. We can't let our names get into the wrong hands. Some people are crazy! I don't know, maybe they like to sell guns…maybe they like power…or maybe they just like to hate. They're happy with the way things are…with the fighting. We don't want them to stop us.

"So, I keep track of everyone I can, and so does Ibrahim, what they do and how they can be helpful to each other. I put each person in a category…either they understand and are on our team, or they need maybe to be educated. No one is our enemy, but there are those who are stuck in hatred. We have to be very careful with these hateful ones.

"Now, friend of Devorah," he said, holding up the iPhone clutched firmly in his hand, "the information I have in here is handy but limited. Ibrahim has access to our other sources. Let me make a call and see if we can meet with him." he said, texting his friend.

At first I was torn between my fascination with this unusual man's harrowing experience and my impatience to find out about David. But as Shimon's story had unfolded, I was moved beyond words. I found myself clinging to every syllable he uttered but for vastly different reasons than he might have thought.

What he and Ibrahim are doing is exactly what David had written about in the diary. *They may not be aware of it, but by organizing people to come together in this way, to come together in love and understanding, they are helping to shift the energetic balance of the planet.*

"I put in a code when I need Ibrahim quickly," Shimon said, "so he should be calling soon. Listen to me," he laughed, holding up his phone again. "All these years I can't use the telephone, but I still think of my tap-tap-tapping as 'calling.' If you're going to be deaf, this is a good time for it. And this," he said, holding his phone to his chest, "this is a great tool to have. It's my 'seeing-ear' dog.

"And if we're lucky, we may be able to find your Mr. Ben Barak. It is good that he is a tutor. Especially, we like to be in touch with men and women who work with young people. They can teach music or math, coach swimming or basketball, but they can teach peace as well. They are with the children when they are still impressionable…. Wait! I feel the phone. Let me see…. Yes, it is Ibrahim."

I watched Shimon carefully as he read, scrolled and tapped away, looking for a hint of what they might be 'saying.'

"Ibrahim is in a meeting but he has already alerted our people to begin the search. He will call you tonight, between 8:00 and 9:00 tonight. Where can he reach you?"

Oh my god! Almost ten hours to wait! I can't stand it! I did my best to hide my distress as I gave him the information.

"I can see you don't like the wait, but these things cannot be rushed. There are many people involved. Maybe I can…." Shimon said, looking at his watch. "No, I cannot. I would like to show you around Tiberias, but I must go. However, I can tell you where are the interesting places to pass your day." Shimon jotted a number of things I should see, and we said our goodbyes.

Ten hours…! Oh, David! God, my stomach is in an absolute knot. I tried to follow Shimon's list, but all I could think of was David. I counted the hours until it was time to go back for the phone call.

CHAPTER 76

The phone rang at 8:45 that evening. "I'm so sorry to disappoint you," said Ibrahim, "but none of our people have been able to find out anything about the Barak family. We lost touch with them about two years ago. There is no record of their death, they seem to have simply vanished."

"What does it mean...they *vanished?*"

"It could mean anything. Perhaps they emigrated to another country. Perhaps... You see, sometimes there are things we just don't know."

"So there is no way at all that you can track them?"

"No, I'm sorry. There really isn't. Is there any other way I can be of help to you?"

"No. Thank...thank you for your time. And all the people...."

"We try to be of help. Shimon said you were a lovely lady. I wish you all the best in your search."

I felt like I was drowning – gasping for air. Two seconds later I was furious. *Another friggin' dead-end! What am I supposed to do now? How am I going to find David? What's will happen to him if I can't...?* I had tried everything I could think of, and even some things I couldn't. Why had I assumed it would be easy? Perhaps I had been trying too hard. What if I wasn't supposed to find David, what if he was supposed to find me?

As I threw myself on the bed and reached for a pillow, a horrible thought hovered in the back of my mind. *Maybe the diary is only a story, and I've been on a wild goose chase from the beginning.* My father's frequent words to me as a child, "You live in a dream world," echoed in my ears. It could be worse than that. *All this talk about Atlantis, priests, priestesses and changing the world.* Could it just have been some desperate attempt to have a life? *I've become obsessed with other peoples fantasies. I can't believe I could think I would be the key to saving the world. What I need to save is myself! The only sane thing to do is to let the whole thing go and get home as soon as I can.*

My wake up call came early the next morning, but in my efforts to leave,

I was stymied at every turn. The morning buses to Tel Aviv were already full, and I had to wait forever to get a seat on a later one. I spent two and a half hours on a crowded bus before suffering through the grueling airport wait for a plane back to Cairo. By the time I arrived, it was too late to catch a plane to the United States. *Damn! I have to endure another night here,* I groaned. Even the Mena House didn't seem warm and inviting.

I had some food sent up to my room, but I couldn't even look at it. A call to the airlines brought the joyful news that the first available seat wasn't until 1:45 the next afternoon. *Great! I can't even get out of this miserable hole!*

My hands mechanically packed my suitcase. I was in a daze. My body felt like it was folding in on itself. It was hard to give up such a deeply held goal. *Well…I have plenty of time in the morning. I guess I could still go back to the village and look for Rashid one more time…but that's it. I'm not going any further with this. It's over. Finished!* I had already put way too much time into this craziness. Besides, it was people like Shimon and Ibrahim who were going to change the world, not me!

As I zipped my case closed and plopped it on the floor, I noticed the red message light blinking on the hotel phone. *Shimon!* I sprinted to the phone and punched in the message code. A moment later I heard Tina's bright and cheerful voice. My heart sank. I listened numbly as she told me how much she loved and missed me, and then I heard a break in her voice and realized she was crying. I sank onto the bed and listened intently to her next words.

"I'm so sorry, Cassie, your brother called me when he couldn't reach you. He called…he called to say that your mother had died…. It was that Mad Man disease. He said it happened very fast, and he…." That was all I heard before I dropped the phone and began to wail like a wounded animal. *How can this have happened? I talked to her just a few days ago….*

My wail turned to uncontrollable sobbing, then to dry, heaving moans. Somehow I managed to call home. My father couldn't come to the phone, so I talked to my brother. Or rather, he talked. I couldn't get out more than two words at a time. It was hours before I slipped into the welcoming relief of sleep.

CHAPTER 77

It looked like late afternoon as my dreamer's eye followed a male figure walking down a winding path through a lush green forest. The figure turned to face me. It was David, this time dark and bearded. His blazing blue eyes seemed to stare right into mine. The scene changed, and David appeared in one location and then another – virtually all over the world. He was always surrounded by a small band of people.

I had the ability to see energy and understood that everything I saw – every person, animal, plant, even inanimate object – radiated its own unique pattern of energy. It was evident that whatever a person felt was reflected in his or her energy field. Unfortunately, most of the patterns emanating from the people I saw were erratic and distorted.

I saw glimpses of the major cities of Europe, the United States, Asia and Africa. Many of the places were familiar to me, yet it was as if I were seeing them for the first time. All of the glamour was gone. Cities that I had always yearned to visit now appeared gray and lifeless.

The energy from the earth itself was very weak. It was constantly being depleted by the unhealthy, erratic and confused thoughts and feelings of the people. I became claustrophobic and choked by the dirty air and the frenetic activity. Although the locale changed, each new place seemed exactly the same as the one before – very unpleasant.

Images of David returned, and as before he was always at the center of a small group of people. Sometimes he was in the countryside, other times in hotel rooms or private homes. The faces changed, the locations changed, but the energy patterns did not. Wherever David was, the energy flowed in harmonious ways and the mood was always calm and peaceful. In fact, there was a certain humming to the energy itself, as all of the different personality types, ages and nationalities melded in a commonality of purpose.

I was never able to hear any of the words exchanged, but frequently I saw large maps being unfolded, studied and avidly discussed by group members. In these settings, David's own energy appeared boundless.

Occasionally, I saw him alone in the open air, frequently near water and always where nature appeared at her most pristine. This was the only time and place where he allowed himself to relax and be nourished. When he was with others, he was always putting out energy, reassuring people and tending to their needs. Yet, even when he was alone, he was never completely relaxed.

I could feel hidden eyes upon him. He was constantly being watched and he was aware of it. The "watchers" were not benevolent. It was as if they were prevented from harming him – but just barely.

Then I saw David in what appeared to be a country in the Middle East. He was being forced to enter a small, clammy prison cell. His captors, who only appeared as lurking shadows, laughed menacingly as they hurled insults at him. It was evident that he had been beaten.

As soon as his captors left, he dragged himself, dirty and tired, to stand before the small, barred window of the tiny room. Once there, he stared out at the blackness of the night sky – as if waiting for a sign from the heavens.

At that moment, a tall figure whose face was almost entirely hidden by the dark cowl of his long robe appeared beside him. A strange glow emanated from within the cowl of his long robe and surrounded him like a halo. David looked into his eyes. The apparition nodded. "Yes David… now," was all he said.

Then, with that particular quality of movement that takes place only in dreams, the scene suddenly shifted to the base of the Great Pyramid. I saw David standing with another figure – a woman. They quickly embraced before turning their attention to the steep-walled pyramid that stood before them. Silently, David and the woman began their careful climb up the precipitous, weathered stone face of the pyramid. Once they reached the top, they stretched out their arms into the empty flat space where the capstone belonged.

For a brief moment, the outline of an exquisite gold and crystal capstone glowed brightly in the velvet darkness of the night. A great explosion of light quickly followed, and I saw, superimposed over them, the image of a spinning globe. It grew larger and larger, and in it I saw many of the ancient stone sites. At each site were gathered groups of people. They formed giant circles, holding hands singing and snaking their way through the stones, forming very particular and unique geometric patterns.

The entire globe began to sparkle. Tiny, very bright pinpoints of light were everywhere. Singing voices joined together in one beautiful sound – a great tone that grew and grew. The sound rose, swelling in volume until the entire planet vibrated with it.

High above it all, I could see David and the woman lit by the light of the glowing capstone. Their images became larger and larger. The woman turned – her face was mine.

The two figures merged into one, long, cascading stream of geometric forms. Then I saw a calendar with a date circled in red – it was tomorrow.

I awoke abruptly, the geometric forms dancing before my still-closed eyes and the tone vibrating in my ears. It was the most incredible sound I have ever heard. It seemed to contain all languages within it. Intuitively, I understood that the swirling forms held a depth of information far surpassing words, but their message was clear: *The time is now! The energy of a New Era is upon us.* The time for action had arrived.

It was the darkness just before dawn. My eyes were raw and my body leaden. *What in the...?* Then I remembered Tina's message and the conversation with my brother, and the misery started all over again. I have no idea how long I lay there before my sadness turned to rage – a rage that propelled me out of bed and ready to take action against John.

I snapped on a lamp and tore open my suitcase, searching for the sturdiest clothes I had. I jumped into faded jeans and a tee shirt, grabbed a sweater, put the talisman around my neck and the room key in my pocket. I made myself take the minute needed to tie my shoes, and then, as David had so graphically described in the diary, I tiptoed out of my room, "like a thief in the night," gently closing the door behind me.

My heart ached for my mother and family, but I had to meet David. It was my destiny! *We have to stop John...we have to! I have to do this for you,*

Mom. I pushed all the clashing thoughts and memories from my mind as I waited for the interminably slow elevator to deposit me on the ground floor. As soon as the doors opened, I bolted out of the hotel and into the crisp morning air. I took a deep breath, and like the wind, ran toward the pyramids. With the barest hint of dawn at my back, I could just make out a lone figure near its base.

I ran and ran and ran, feeling the sand shift and part beneath my frantic feet. I thought I would never make it – and yet I ran some more. Panting and short of breath, I slowed and stopped. There, just yards in front of me, stood David. It was as if he had stepped right out of my dream. I was overwhelmed by a love so powerful it seemed my heart would burst. Tears streamed down my face as I walked slowly toward him. There were no words – there were not even thoughts. I was transfixed by the blueness of his eyes, the bristling blackness of his hair and beard. It was a moment of incredible stillness and beauty.

"We're back home, my Love, my Diantha. You see, I, too, know your real name," David said with a smile. "Here we are, rejoined after so many eons of time." He took me in his arms and held me close. Our kiss was so achingly familiar it lit a candle of remembrance in some long-dark corridor of my soul. I have no idea how long we stood locked in that deep embrace. I saw images of Atlantis as well as some ancient place not of this world. It was like the very desert where we now stood, but on its horizon there were two moons rising.

We separated slowly, fingers still entwined, and looked into one another's eyes – seeing both past and future, each a bit reluctant to let the other go. "I knew you would come, Diantha. I have been waiting all these many lifetimes…just for you. There were moments in the darkness of the night when I feared you would not hear my call. What is left to do I can only do with you at my side."

"Shhh…." I said, gently putting my finger to his lips, moved by the side of him that could still question. "I am here now." I looked again into his eyes, and an entire vista opened. I saw the last few hundred million years – back to the time when we were all one collective thought. It was a time before incarnation itself. I saw the primordial past when we both came here to seed Planet Earth with our ancient bloodlines. It was a time when Earth was still fresh and teaming with all manner of life – a time before those who would become Hu-mans had fully embodied. We gave a part of ourselves to those ones, and human life took off in a different direction than it might otherwise have gone. Now our very seeds were coming to fruition.

"Yes! Now you see...you understand," said David. So aligned were our two souls that he knew his vision was now mine.

"You know what we must do." It was as much a question as a statement.

"Yes," I whispered. I had seen it in the dream and I could feel the closeness of the wave – the energy of a New Era – approaching. The Earth was already trembling in anticipation. He took me in his arms and held me for one more unending moment. No more words were necessary. We moved apart and began to walk the last remaining steps to the base of the Great Pyramid, ready to begin our ascent toward its apex.

Suddenly, a burst of deep maniacal laughter thundered through the air. It hurled itself against the stone facing of the Great Pyramid and then rebounded with a deafening echo – an echo that almost knocked us to the ground.

David grabbed my arm. "Quick, we have to teleport out of here!" We tried but couldn't do it. "Run," he said, pushing me forward. "Head for the small pyramid...there's a secret passageway."

We took off around the side of the large pyramid. From the corner of my eye, I caught the visage of three figures dressed in dark clothing as they materialized from the remnant of night. Each carried a luminous object in his hand.

"They've got crystal laser pistols," David yelled. I heard their sound as the ammo whizzed past my head. I ran faster, staying hidden in the pyramid's shadow as the sun cleared the earth to the East.

I heard a yowl and knew David had been tagged. "Keep going!" he called out, "I'm alright." I heard his labored breath behind me, so I could tell he could still run – *but for how long?*

We rounded the first pyramid and ran towards the second, aiming for the third and smallest pyramid. But standing directly – and starkly – in front of us was John, the High Priest Carmac.

"Back again, are we? Only, this time you're here for me!" he bellowed. I looked frantically in all directions, but we were boxed in. I darted anyway and felt the searing burn of a crystal as it whizzed by my right shoulder.

"Okay men, that's enough. Go get them!" commanded Carmac. Large, hulking arms grabbed me from behind and forced me to the ground. I struggled, but it was no use. The man quickly kneeled beside me, pinning me down with one sharp knee and deftly binding my wrists behind my back. He reached for my ankles and bound them as well.

I sensed Carmac above me. "Well, my pretty! Seems we meet again. I see you finally found your friend. I'm sure you want to see how he is since his little…mishap. Boys, bring David right here by the little lady's side. And turn her over! I want her to have a good view of her lover boy."

They swiftly turned me on my back and then put David face down on the ground next to me. His wrists and ankles were bound as well, and the bloody evidence of his wound was quickly growing on his upper thigh.

Carmac rolled David over with one booted foot. "Did you really think you could out-smart me, David? How dull of you! Where is your great hulk of an extraterrestrial friend now when you need him? Oh…I forgot…they agreed to non-interference. Such a silly game! Because you know I'm going to do nothing but interfere."

Carmac turned his attention toward me, tapping the ground with his dusty boot just inches from my face. "And you, Cassandra, or should I say, *Diantha*, since we have no more secrets here. You should have taken me up on my offer when I made it. Now that I have the two of you together, and your codes are activated, there's nothing I can't have just for the taking. I don't need your cooperation, I have other ways of getting what I need. And don't think you can teleport or levitate, or do any of your Atlantean magic with me. I've already shut you down. Just wait, I have a little something to show you that will both shock and terrify you all at once!"

"Okay boys, take them away," said Carmac, signaling toward his men, "And, you may as well bind his leg. I don't want him bleeding to death before I have those codes."

One man went to work on David's leg and the other came for me. They blindfolded and gagged us then, throwing us over their shoulders like two sacks of potatoes, carried us to a nearby jeep that had been modified to include an open flatbed in the rear. Then they tossed us in the back and locked the tailgate. The jeep bounced as Carmac and his "boys" climbed in, slammed the doors shut and started the engine.

CHAPTER 78

We rocked across the desert on huge tires, under a mercilessly blazing sun, for what seemed like hours. I had plenty of time to think, but I had no solutions. One thing was perfectly clear – Carmac wanted the codes and didn't need our cooperation to get them! He had a way to extract them directly from us. He was certainly confident about his plan, and if he had Atlantean technology, which he obviously did, I had no doubt that he could do it. Whatever he had devised, it would not be fun.

Once the jeep stopped and the motor was turned off, I could hear what they had in store for us next. "Geez, it's hot!" said one of the men.

"It sure is," replied Carmac. "Those two must be fried back there. Quick, get them some water! Let them have all they want and douse them with it before you bring them in. I don't need their cooperation, but I do need them alive and alert."

The cold water was shocking, but it was a relief. It sizzled as it ran off our steaming bodies and onto the bed of the truck. Our hands and eyes remained bound, but they untied our feet, and we were pulled to a standing position. One of the men said, "Okay, let's go!" They roughly half-walked, half-dragged us across the sand and into some kind of structure. It was cool inside. *This place must have really thick walls.*

"Throw them in the tank and rebind their feet," ordered Carmac. "They can't get out of there, but there's no use taking any chances. I'll let you know when I'm ready for them."

The sound of his laughter echoed through the building. Our captors moved us down a long hallway, first making a right turn, then a left. *I need to keep my bearings here. First a right turn...then a left.* We made another right turn and immediately stopped. I heard keys rattle and then slap against something metal. A lock turned and a squeaky metal door swung open. *Right turn...left...another right, and then an immediate stop. Door on left...*

David and I were forced to the ground where we lay on the cold hard floor, hands and feet bound and eyes blindfolded. The heavy metal door swung shut, a key turned in the lock and two pairs of footsteps receded into the distance. My body was tied up, but my mind was still working. I "felt" around, but my senses could only detect darkness, a musky dampness and silence.

Exhausted but hyper-alert, I listened for David's breathing. "Mmmm," I called. "Mmmm...mmmm," he answered. I inched my body along the floor. His "mmmm" got closer. Moving slowly, I twisted and turned until my body reached his. The touch of his body was reassuring. At least we were both conscious – and in the same room.

The minutes ticked away. I tried to stay calm, but it was impossible. Every second seemed an eternity. *If Carmac gets the codes, that will be it! He wants people to live in chaos, confusion and fear. That's how he controls them. Nobody will have a chance to choose another way.*

My body shuttered as I thought about the horrible things that would happen if the new energy couldn't enter the Earth safely. It would be catastrophic! Those who managed to live through such an upheaval would be thrown back to scavenging just to survive. David and I only had the next twenty-four hours to ignite the capstone and clear the Grid. *If we don't...well...the diary had made it very clear....*

I winced as I saw an image of our world in flames but then the strangest thing happened – I saw David blowing out those flames. *Where did that come from? Can he be reading my thoughts? My god, I hope....*

My body shivered with excitement. I pictured the moon – he sent me stars. I pictured rain – he sent me a rainbow. *Amazing! Carmac might have shut things down, but we could still communicate. David, what are we going to do? How are we going to get out of this? Carmac....*

Heavy footsteps echoed in the hallway, coming closer with each second. I panicked. *David...!* The sound pounded in my brain as I tried to control my terror. I forced air deep into my lungs and let it out, focusing on each breath. Keys clanked against metal and the squeaky door opened. A strong light passed over my body as a pair of hands unbound my feet and pulled me up. My feet were numb and I nearly toppled over.

"Come," said a heavily accented voice. Hands yanked at me, and an arm shored me up and pulled me through the door. My feet folded again. One man held me while the other locked the door. Then, with one of Carmac's goons on either side, I was dragged down the long hallway.

CHAPTER 79

Carmac's men walked so fast I had no time to regain my footing. They gripped me so tightly my arms throbbed. We turned a corner and abruptly stopped. Another metal door creaked open, and I was dragged through a doorway. I was immediately assaulted by a light so intense it bore through my blindfold and a blast of noise so loud it made my head pound.

The two men shoved me onto a cold metal chair, unbound my hands and then used metal clamps to re-bind them to the arms of the chair. I recognized the cacophony of sound. A television – no, many televisions – were blaring, all tuned to different news channels and all competing with one-another. "Today a third war broke out in the Middle East...and on the home front a suicide bomber...in Zimbabwe an outbreak of Cholera...Mad Man disease is now showing up in all parts of the world...the incidents of rape are up on...."

Carmac's maniacal laughter echoed through the room. *I don't need to see him...I know who it is!* My blindfold was ripped off, and a strong light was directed at my face. It was blinding. I closed my eyes against the searing whiteness.

"So, my pet, I bet you didn't think I could do it," Carmac wheedled. "Ha! You have no idea who you're dealing with. You're dealing with me...Carmac... and I've been waiting a long time for this little meeting of ours. You're mine now, and I can do anything I want with you," he said, prancing like a peacock. "Thanks to you, my little pearl, I'm going to have complete control of Earth!"

He leaned over me, thrusting his face mere inches from mine, momentarily shielding me from the blast of light. He held his hand up and I could see the back of his wrist. The sight of a tattoo with a lightning slash across it, the tattoo that signified his alliance with the Forces of Darkness, made me shiver. "You, my pretty, can make this easy...or I can make it painful. Very, very painful!" His impatience was palpable, and his angry voice competed with the piercing sounds swirling incessantly around the room.

What's he going to do? I can't let him get the codes! I just can't! I have to buy some time. "Okay Carmac, you win. But I can't see...and the televisions are so loud I won't be able to hear what you want me to do." I tried to make myself sound very meek – and very scared. It wasn't difficult.

He shoved the light aside and stood before my chair, glowering down at me. "Hmm! It's not so easy to be willful and flippant when I've got you tied to a chair, is it?"

I pulled myself together and cast my eyes down. "No, you're right...it... it isn't," I answered submissively. "You're much more powerful than I had imagined."

Carmac's eyes narrowed as though he were sizing me up. "You think I haven't been watching you and all your foolishness! Running around to this place and that thinking you could make a difference...that you could save the world. You and your little friend! Ha! Ever thought about why my men were following you, and why they broke into your room in Peru? Because I told them to, that's why! I was just messing with you. I got the diary when I really wanted it, didn't I!

"I, in my brilliance, knew I could get you at anytime, but I waited…day… after day…after day. I'm a very patient man. I can wait for what I want, but now the time has finally come. Yes, indeed! We're all here together again, just like a little family, you, David and me."

"You're right, Carmac. I guess we didn't make any difference. You're too smart for us. We never had a chance. But I can hardly hear you. Can't you turn down the televisions?"

I've got to think of something else! What…?

"Televisions!" he shouted, his face twisting and contorting. "What are you talking about? Televisions! This is my art gallery! My creation! Planet Earth as I've orchestrated it!" He looked around the room at the wall-to-wall televisions, pride oozing from his pores. Gesturing broadly toward first one screen then another, he said, "Look over here! And here! And here! Chaos, confusion, rape, disease and murder brought directly to Earth by Yours Truly. Don't you just love it? It's all my doing! Everything!"

Carmac cackled like the Bad Witch of the North before reigning himself in. Gangling arms folded against his chest, he glanced intently at his "art," nodding in approval as his eyes took in each screen. "It's fun to see the results of your handiwork. It's taken a lot of effort, but what can I say? I don't regret a minute of it. He paused then quickly spun toward me and shrieked, "I have offices all around the world set up just like this. I never turn the televisions off! Do you hear me? *Never!*"

He grew silent and began pacing back and forth, considering something. I remembered his long-legged walk and had to turn away. Quickly looking around the room, I could see that the walls, floor and ceiling were made of cement, just as I had suspected. One of Carmac's men was parked on either side of the only door. The whole place wasn't much bigger than the waiting room at my chiropractor's office. It was claustrophobic. A large, high-tech instrument panel lined one wall beneath the televisions. Thick metallic coils, suspended from various points along the low ceiling, ended about a foot above Carmac's head. I spied a small monitor that showed the room where I had just been. David was still laying inertly on the floor. I shuddered.

"Humph!" Carmac snorted. "Well, we do have work to do, and I don't want you distracted, so I'll turn them down…slightly." He signaled one of his men, and the room immediately became quieter. Rubbing his hands gleefully together, he snapped, "Alright then, let's get down to business.

"Bring me a chair," Carmac ordered, "the one with wheels." He snatched the chair as soon as it arrived and placed it directly in front of me. Swinging it backwards, he straddled it. "I'll get right to the point. I need those codes and I need them now. Once I have your half of the equation, I have another technique in mind for David. Simple magnetics. It'll be child's play to pull the codes directly from him. After all, it's Atlantean technology. I was a High Priest at one time, remember?" he said, becoming visibly taller in his chair. "I knew all kinds of shit back then. The trick's been to not lose it over all this time."

"Carmac…."

"Quiet!" he shouted. He signaled his other goon who immediately rolled over a small metal table the height of a two-drawer file cabinet. On top sat what looked like a thicker-than-usual laptop computer. He opened it, and I saw a standard blank screen, but where the keyboard should have been, rows of little gold metal coils were hooked up to a maze of small crystals.

He touched something, and the entire wall in front of me receded revealing a small well- hidden room. In the floor of this area, there was a door. It now slid open, and very slowly, a marble alter rose from deep within the ground. Crowning the alter was a great crystal, glinting in its multi-faceted glory, the light from its hundreds of angles shooting out in all directions.

Oh my god! It's the Great Crystal of Atlantis! The one my aunt cracked! Now it was alive again – and glowing. I could see lines of energy connecting, not only to the device he was working on, but to every other piece of electronics in the room.

"Thought it was dead, didn't you? Cracked and finished!" Carmac sneered. "It was, but I wanted it for my own use. Unfortunately for you, I've had time, many millennia of time, and I, only I, have managed to repair it. Way back then, we wanted it broken, and I was the one specifically chosen to make sure that happened. Your aunt may have been the Crystal Master, but to me she was a stupid, lovesick cow. I could get anything I wanted from her for just a little flattery. I got her to push more and more energy through the Great Crystal, until she cracked it. Ha! You should have seen her face. But that's all history."

"You...you really are powerful, Carmac." *Bastard!*

"That's the least of it!" he muttered to himself. "Tens of thousands of years.... You can't even fathom what I've been through."

I mustered up a sad, sympathetic look but his eyes were vacant and glowing. Damn! *He's in his own private world! He's not buying anything I do.*

"Yeah, it's been hell," he commiserated with himself. "Of course, there was always lots of entertainment," he added, with a sheepish grin. "But it all gets old after the first few hundred years."

Carmac turned his chair and began to fiddle with the computer-like-device. "This device is all mine. The rest of it may be Atlantean technology, but this... this, I developed myself. It's fantastic!"

I felt myself panic. *What do I do now? Stop it. Stop! Breathe! Think!*

"Carmac, I know I can't stop you. I can't do anything, but before you begin, could I please stand up for a minute. My legs...my back...they're so cramped. It's hard for me to concentrate. Your two men are right here. Tie my hands...I don't care. Please? You've shut down our powers. You know I can't do anything."

His eyes bore into me.

"I'll just shake my legs and twist my back. That's all. Please!"

"Release her!"

His goons removed the metal clamps holding my arms and unbound my feet.

With a sigh of relief, I shook each leg several times. I arched my back and then slowly lowered my head toward the floor. Standing back up, I made a slight pivot and kicked the goddamned cart across the room. It crashed against the wall, and the computer-like-device bounced and slipped halfway off.

"You bitch! You damn bitch!" Carmac's face crumbled into a hideous scowl. He rushed to his computer while his goons yanked me back to the chair, clamped my arms and rebound my feet.

Carmac shouted and swore as he examined the computer. At last, he gasped, "Ha! I made this thing so perfectly that nothing can destroy it. But you, my little pretty," he hissed, as he pushed the cart back into position, "you are going to pay dearly for that little trick of yours. But first you're going to give me the codes." He reached over and roughly stuck a patch with a little battery device to the inside of each of my forearms, just below the elbow.

"Done! Fantastic! Now my device is keyed into your energy signature. When I give you the signal, you will close your eyes and 'see' the codes. The codes will appear in a long series of digital binary commands composed of zeros and ones. This entire room is built to amplify your perception. And these coils," he said, pointing to the thick metal coils hanging from the ceiling, "will help you verbalize what you see. My device will record the codes as you say them, and these little beauties…." Carmac stopped and looked down lovingly at his computer – at the rows of gold metal coils connected to the maze of small crystals. "These little beauties will translate the codes into geometric symbols.

"I'm quite sure you'll do as I ask, my dear, because if you don't speak the numbers out loud and clear, you will start to feel a shock down your spine. But don't thinik that's it. The pain will continually increase like a scorching rod being slowly jammed down the neural tube in the center of your spinal column, burning you from the inside out. It won't take long before the burning will radiate out even further. It will move down your arms and legs, first numbing them then eventually paralyzing your entire body.

"After all that, if you are still foolish enough to refuse to talk," Carmac said, glaring at me, "the device will render you unconscious, but it will have already captured your energy signature and the codes will come anyway. Of course, by that point, you will be dead. Too bad! David will miss you."

Carmac flipped three switches on his "computer" and said, "Okay, now give me those damn codes!"

I had no time to think. A tingle ran through my body, and my eyelids became heavier and heavier until they fully closed. A series of ones and zeros appeared, just as he had said. I tried not to look at them, but immediately, what felt like a burning arrow struck the base of my neck just above my spine. More numbers appeared, but I didn't utter a sound. The fire began to sizzle down toward my lower back. The pain was so intense, I could barely breathe. I didn't know that I could utter a word, even if I wanted to.

Then I saw another row of numbers below the original set, but there was something different about them. *Oh my god! They're from David! He's sending them to me!* I focused on the lower row and started to say the numbers out loud. My breath was labored, but I managed. "Zero…one…one…." The pain subsided, and I was able to hear David's voice. *Good! Just repeat the numbers as I send them to you.* "One…one…zero…one…zero…" Both sets of numbers zipped by, slowed and finally stopped. I was dripping with sweat.

"See what a good girl you can be when you want to!" Carmac said, as if he were talking to a child. My skin burned as he ripped the batteries from my arms. I opened my eyes and saw him staring at the computer. I could see that it was continually running the stream of numbers David had telepathically sent me.

"Fascinating, isn't it? I have some adjustments to make, but it won't take more than an hour. When I'm finished, I'll bring in your pal David, and we'll complete our little exercise."

He opened a drawer in the metal cabinet and pulled out a complicated looking contraption with trailing wires and cables. "See these electrodes? They're my invention, too. The beauty of it is that it's so simple. One end of it hooks up to David, and the other plugs right into my computer. Your codes will act like magnets to pull his codes right out of him.

"And if you think that's amazing, watch this!" he said, sauntering over to the high-tech titanium instrument panel lining the wall under the televisions. He sat down on a large swivel chair, turned some switches, and a number of colored lights winked and blinked. "This panel controls everything! I can make anything happen anywhere in the world from right here. Before your…ah… 'little visit,' I set it to transform your binary codes into geometric forms. Oh good, here comes the first one. Great! That's fantastic, even better than I had imagined."

I strained to see what he was talking about and then gasped. *That looks like one of my glyphs!* I was so shocked, I almost choked. *How could the codes look anything like my glyphs?*

"Thank you my dear," he said, still flipping switches. "After your pathetic display, you settled down and did an excellent job. I would have hated to mess up that beautiful face of yours, not that it will do you much good. I've set the machine to neutralize both you and David once I have all the codes. By the time you two leave here tonight, your minds will be as vacant as an empty parking lot." He chuckled to himself. "Okay then, time for you to go back. Oh, but before you go, I want to show you my latest invention."

Carmac rolled his chair a few feet, then opened a concealed door under the instrument panel and pulled out what looked like a pair of wide silver bracelets. He gazed at them admiringly. "Ah, yes! They are beautiful, aren't they? They're titanium handcuffs, and they're hooked right up to this circuit board along with the rest of the security. It's impossible to escape from them. Absolutely impossible! And you, my dear, have the honor of being the very first to experience them." His maniacal laughter echoed through the room. "Okay boys, take her away," he bellowed with a wave of his hand "I have work to do."

His goons gagged and blindfolded me, rebound my hands with the new cuffs and shoved me back down the long hallway. They dumped me onto the cold cement floor, locked the door and clumped away. I listened for David's breathing, and when I was sure the men were far enough away, I scooted over to him.

Are you okay? Did they hurt you? he asked.

I'm fine, I answered.

Did you get the codes I sent you?

Yes, just in time, I replied. *But it's no wonder we couldn't teleport ourselves away. It's amazing we can still communicate. He has all kinds of equipment and everything is hooked up to some kind of instrument panel. He can control everything from there…all over the world. And, he even has the great Crystal of Atlantis, the one my aunt cracked. He brought it back to life! And he's got this place locked up…*

Stop! Stop! Slow down!

I'm sorry. I...

We haven't got much time...less than twenty-four hours to get back and climb the Great Pyramid.

I know.

I have an idea, but we'll have to work fast. We gave him phony codes. The moment he hooks me up to his machine he'll realize there's something wrong.

Our attention was diverted by footsteps pounding down the hall. *Why are they coming now...he said it would take an hour?* The doors clanked open and someone stepped over my body and wrenched David from my side. I yelped in silent pain – a pain as real as a ripping of my own flesh. I could actually feel his body as it dragged across the floor. Then the door slammed shut, the key turned in the lock, and the footsteps faded down the hall. I lay there stunned – all concentration gone, hardly able to think.

CHAPTER 80

A gentle breeze brushed against my cheek, but I was too numb to pay any attention. The breeze persisted and increased, until it caught my awareness. Although my eyes were still blindfolded, I could "see" the outline of a tall robed and hooded figure standing over me. Somehow I knew it was Zev Moab, but there was something unexpected – something strange about him. His body was filmy – not quite real.

He put a long finger before his lips, silencing my inner thoughts. "Careful now," I understood him to say, "I am going to help you up." In an instant I was standing at his side, but when I looked down, my body was still lying on the floor – bound and gagged.

"I don't...how...?"

"You are in your *etheric* body," your energy body," he answered. "This is the only way you can travel with me, and there are things I need to show you."

"But...but what about David?"

"He will be alright for now. We won't be long. We are going to enter an alternate time-space reality…a different dimension. It may seem like a good deal of time has passed, however on your Earth, it will be only moments."

Zev Moab reached for my hand, and we effortlessly lifted up from the ground, piercing the ceiling of the building. Then, like two birds, we quickly rose into the blue sky above. We ascended higher and higher until the earth grew small beneath our feet. Still higher we rose, passing through asteroid belts and unearthly streams of colored light. And still we flew, surrounded by a rush of twinkling stars, straight through a multitude of heavens.

We traveled further and further before we gradually began to slow. I could see shapes of some sort off in the distance. As we grew closer, the shapes took on a distinct form. We slowed even more and then stopped, suspended in mid-air. We had entered into a new and completely different place.

Stretching out in all directions, as far as the eye could see, lay a vast plain of stark and even whiteness. And on that plain stood a great legion of robed and hooded figures that looked exactly like my companion. Two huge angels towered above the ranks, white wings glinting gold in the light of some unseen sun. One angel flanked each side of the many rows of *hooded ones*. The angels were still, rooted like great trees, arms crossed over their massive breasts, each hand resting upon the opposite shoulder.

All, angels and *hooded ones* alike, remained tall and straight, heads bowed and eyes gently closed. Emanating from them flowed one long, sonorous and continuous humming sound – "Huuuuuuuu." It rolled over and over upon itself – ancient, constant, yet always new. "Huuuuuuuu." It came and it came, like some great ocean wave rolling in from the sea, only to be followed by another and another and another – endlessly.

Across the plain, at least one hundred yards away, stood tall, grey amorphous beings, their arms and legs, bodies and heads going in and out of focus. When in focus, there was something reptilian about them. From their hands, which shifted and clawed, dangled sharply defined filaments of some kind of glossy fiber. The filaments went down and down, through the whiteness, until they became lost in the vast and empty space below.

Above their heads circled large bird-like creatures. They were greenish-black, had the yellowish head of a cock, the tail of a snake and the body of a bird with huge leathery wings. Despite the strangeness of the birds, my attention was constantly drawn back to the grey beings and their reptilian hands. My eyes were riveted on them. My belly contracted in terror – like some animal being hunted – and still, I could not look away. My mind was entangled in a heavy web of fear as I struggled to find words.

"Those things, whatever they're called, look like ghouls. Who are they? What are they doing?"

"They are the Forces of Darkness, and they are meant to terrify by their appearance."

"And the ones on the other side, the *hooded ones*...the ones making the humming sound?"

"Those are the Forces of Light. Both groups are fighting for the Hearts and Minds of Hu-mankind. They have been in continuous battle since the first moment of creation. You read David's diary – you understand all that has happened. The difference – and it is a huge difference – is that the struggle has now reached its crowning moment, and the very future of Hu-mankind is at stake.

"To complicate matters, many of the ancient reincarnates from Atlantis, those who chose to follow the Forces of Darkness, are now back upon Earth. The Dark Ones are continuing their attempts to control those reincarnates by constant manipulation of their thoughts and dreams. They are fighting for their will, enticing them to rejoin their host. For, unbeknownst even to themselves, the reincarnates have come back to make that fateful choice again. Will they honor the interconnection of all Life and choose for the good of all? Or will they, once again, see only separation and think merely of themselves?"

I looked at the rows and rows of robed and *hooded ones*, then at the hordes of menacing figures. "What exactly are they doing with those filaments?"

"Ah! Even as we speak, the Dark Forces are pulling upon those ancient Atlantean Hearts and Minds – trying to convince them, yet again, to join their cause."

"Do they only want to control the Atlanteans? Or, do they try to control everyone that way?"

"Everyone! And you can see, by the condition of your world, they have done a very good job of it."

Thoughts of Carmac gloating over his televisions flew through my mind, until a sudden screech from one of the birds flying over the Dark Forces caught my attention. "What are those horrible birds?"

"They are not birds Diantha. They are known as *basilisks*. Stories about these lizard-like creatures are abundant in the folklore of your planet, however, what Hu-mans think they know about them is not true. They were never living creatures of blood and flesh. They have always been spirit-creatures, giant thought-forms created by Hu-man fear, hatred and lust for power. They are given shape and a seeming form by the Dark Forces – and the basilisks do their bidding. Your image of the Devil is based upon these creatures. But very few Hu-mans have actually glimpsed their like, for to do so usually results in death.

"Mark my words – do not underestimate the power of the basilisks. It is these very creatures that you and David need be wary of now. They will fight to the end to preserve the Ways of Darkness on your Planet. You may think it is the extraterrestrial Forces of Darkness you need to defeat, and it is true that you must, but the basilisks are even more enduring – and mindless.

"Right now, the Forces of Darkness believe they are winning. But if they think the balance of power has shifted on your Planet, they will send the basilisks after you. Once the basilisks pick up your scent, they will stay the course. And – they are relentless! The only thing that will take them out of commission is if you and David successfully climb the Great Pyramid and ignite the capstone."

"But what about the angels and the Forces of Light? Why do they just stand there? Why don't they do something to stop them?"

"Because they cannot. They have chosen to honor the Law of Non-interference. They have deep respect for Hu-mans. They believe in the Hu-man Race – in their great hearts and their capacity for Love. They are holding the Light for Hu-manity by intoning the ancient sacred sound. This is the sound of creation – the sound that is encoded within the core of every Hu-man on Earth. This resonance holds the deepest secret of all – that Hu-mankind is

God in physical form.

"It is hoped that the chant will bring Hu-mans back to themselves, so they might remember, on a feeling level, that they are a part of the web of life – that they are interconnected one to another, to all things and to the Planet itself. Once they remember who they truly are, their hearts will open and, as a natural consequence, their minds will follow. And they will make the choices that support all life."

"But Zev, Carmac is interfering in such a big way…."

"Exactly! That is why I've brought you here today. There is something you do not yet know. Diantha, all this time, you thought you had to find David, and it is true, you did. You also thought he was the hero of this story, the one who was going to save the world. But in fact, it is you – you are the Special One the world has been waiting for."

"I'm the Special One?"

"Yes, Diantha, you are."

"But David is the person who has to enter the Hall of Records and clear the Grid. He only needs me to climb the Great Pyramid and ignite the capstone. The diary said…."

"Nothing in the diary has changed. Everything you read is true. It is David's responsibility to clear the Grid. But Diantha, you must understand that although the diary is complete, the story still goes on. The next step, the next thing that needs doing, can only be done by you – and you alone. This is something you could not have understood until now.

"Do you remember, back when you were in Callanish, Mary, the Great Mother, told you that you have an important mission here in this life, and it will affect everyone on Earth."

"Yes! But I never thought…."

"You weren't meant to fully comprehend it then – that was only the beginning of your journey of awareness. Mary's job was to unlock your consciousness and help you see new possibilities. You had to 'choose' every step that you have taken. You had to open yourself, to learn – to develop your powers. You have been determined – and fearless. You have done everything you have been called upon to do, and that has brought you to exactly where you are today. Now, not only are you ready to hear what I have to say, but you also have the capacity to do what needs to be done."

I started to speak, but he hushed me with a movement of his hand.

"Diantha, you have already learned that you have been given many gifts. Among them is the ability to feel and manipulate energy – to move an object simply by focusing your mind upon it. However, there is another aspect of this talent you have not yet learned about. It is the most potent and important of all your powers. You are also able to transform energy. Specifically, you have the ability to transmute the Hu-man energy field, to make it different. You can take in the dense, fearful and distorted energy of Hu-mankind and literally change it. You already do this quite naturally without even being aware of it. Now you are being called upon to use this gift purposefully – to use it on behalf of Mankind.

"You are not being asked to remove all of the negative energy. To do that would take away Hu-manity's capacity for Choice – their chance to evolve. You are being called upon to shift only a very small portion of it, just enough so that Hu-mans can see more clearly. Your action will act as a support system for the Race of Hu-mans. It will help people to help themselves. It will serve to lighten their load just enough to tip the scales and allow them to make the Choice – the Choice to remember and reconnect, the Choice for Love."

"But Zev…." I gasped.

"No 'buts,' my dear. I see your surprise, however I also see something else. I see your understanding. Yes, your part in the Plan –your destiny – was put in place even before the time of Atlantis. We did not know to what extent your abilities would be needed, but as it turns out, Mankind has not taken responsibility for itself or for the Planet as quickly as we had hoped.

"You are singular in this ability. David cannot do it. He holds the Masculine Energy for the Planet, and so he is able to take action. He can do the tasks necessary to clear the Grid so that the energy of this New Era can flow safely into Earth. You, however, hold the Feminine Energy. In fact, you are the conduit for the Goddess, her representative on Earth. Only you have the ability to hold the space for Hu-mankind to shift as the force of this New Era approaches."

"I thought more people understood...had already made the shift. I saw David...."

"It is true, many people are in various stages of awakening and change, but John and the Dark Forces have reacted to this by stepping up their hold on Earth. They create more and more problems for Hu-mans to contend with, making an already difficult undertaking even harder."

"I heard John rant about some of the things he's done to maintain control over people...starting wars and creating situations that keep people in fear. He's crazy! Can he actually do those things?"

"Yes, he does, and unfortunately, too many of them work. For instance, he and his so-called friends have seen to it that billions of Hu-mans throughout your world are still struggling just to survive. They live a daily existence of drought, famine, poverty and disease – far too busy worrying about their next meal to think about the future of the Planet.

"Then John, or Carmac since it is time to call him by his true name, and his cohorts purposely fostered a taste for materialistic consumption throughout the more developed parts of your world. They knew that many Hu-mans would become so deeply imbedded in their lifestyle, that it would be hard, almost impossible, for them to see the bigger picture.

"When a group finally recognizes the importance of committing to a different way of life, Carmac and those who do his bidding take over and create catastrophes of one nature or another. You heard him. He loves wars, dictatorships and devastation. He creates economic meltdowns and what look to be natural disasters. That causes Hu-man attention to be diverted back to surviving in the physical world – to putting out fires. People become overwhelmed and give in to Fear.

"When that's not enough, he creates something special, like the Mad Man disease. Did you know that only those who consistently live with a sense of Fear are vulnerable to the disease? Carmac appreciates the toll Fear takes on the Hu-man immune system. The Mad Man disease is not a biologically-based disease. It is an illness of 'frequency.' Of course, the epidemic increases Fear, but then, that was the intent.

"So, although many Hu-mans have done an extraordinary job of becoming aware, not quite enough have been able to fully make the shift that is needed at this point – the shift that will raise Earth's protective magnetic shield. The Dark Star Beings have been able to hold their ground better than expected.

"We Galactic Visitors have been watching over Planet Earth, watching and waiting for the moment when your special ability might need to be called upon. Unfortunately, things cannot wait any longer. The New Era is upon us, and you are the Special One, the one being called upon to assist with the safe harboring of the new energies."

"But…but Zev, how do I even begin to do that?"

"Your task is not as formidable as it sounds. You do not have to 'do' anything. You simply have to be yourself and open to it. Once you have opened yourself, the next step is simple. You choose to allow your powers to work through you. As you process the energy of the Hu-man Race through your body, you will automatically transform it. In essence, you are rebirthing Hu-manity – giving it the greatest chance of rising to its highest possibility. And you have the ability to do this without harming yourself."

I stood immobilized for many long moments, letting Zev Moab's words sink in. And as I did, a strange thing happened. I felt myself grow large, then larger still. I sensed the energy of Mother Earth flowing through my body. My focus expanded. I could feel all the lakes and streams, rivers and oceans, mountains and forests inside of me. All forms of plant and animal life, and finally Hu-mans themselves, entered into my being.

At first, everything was pristine and pure, as it must have looked to David when he first glanced into the crystal. Then, quite unexpectedly, I saw a view of the world as it had appeared in my dream, distorted and fragmented energy zooming in every direction. And Hu-mans – many of them – seemed to be stumbling around myopically encased in a storm cloud. The choice was obvious – there was nothing to figure out – nothing to weigh and sort. I looked up at Zev Moab, and he knew – he could see it in my eyes and heart.

I sensed Zev Moab's hand on my shoulder. Almost from a distance, I heard his quiet yet commanding voice. "I know what you have just seen, and I know you were about to accept your mission. However, there is one last thing I must tell you. By agreeing to this task, you enter into a great dilemma. You have to succeed for the sake of Hu-mankind, but if you do, you will incur the deepest possible wrath of the Forces of Darkness. Carmac is only the front man. Your success will have brought you to the full attention of them all," he said, glancing over at the Dark Star Beings still busily attempting to manipulate the Hu-man Race. "They will be on the lookout for you – for your energy signature – and they will use every ounce of their power to find you.

"So the situation is this, even if you succeed in your task, and then you and David climb the Great Pyramid, ignite the capstone, enter the Hall of Records and clear the energetic Grid, the danger to you will still persist. We can never fully extinguish the Forces of Darkness. They are vicious – and they will always be here. You will never know when they might regroup, gain a foothold once again, and retaliate. And Diantha, if they find you, they will punish you harshly. They will hurl your soul away to some Dark Parallel Universe, a place so distant that you will never, ever – throughout all of eternity – see David again."

Zev Moab paused, placing his other hand on my other shoulder. "The only hope I can hold out is that once you and David have entered the Hall of Records, your energy signatures will have become significantly rearranged, making you much more difficult to find."

My entire body stiffened as I tried to turn his words into something my mind could grasp, but I faltered. It was as if my mind itself had frozen. In some far-away place, the words, "…*you will never, ever…throughout all of eternity… see David again,*" echoed over and over.

Dear God…what should I do? I looked up at Zev Moab, trying to read his inscrutable face. I knew in the depths of my soul that he had spoken the truth. The Forces of Darkness could come for me at any time. I also knew, over and above anything else, that this task was what I had come here to do. My terror was as tangible as the beating of my heart. *But how can I walk away from my destiny?* I looked at David's dear teacher and friend, and in a soft but steady voice, whispered, "Yes."

Zev Moab looked deeply into my eyes, and then put one hand on either side of my face and gently kissed me on the forehead. "By making this decision, you are choosing to perform the greatest possible act of selfless Love."

The pull, the actual sensation of being hurled back through space, overwhelmed me. The searing pain of the Hu-man Race, the sorrow and disillusionment, the sense of aloneness and abandonment, coursed through my body. I saw deeply into their hearts and minds – their very souls. I felt the power of their inner battle – their need for Love and their Fear of it – their yearning to be joined together and their fear of losing their personal identity. It was the ego's battle to maintain control of the unknown and the unknowable. It was the archetypical battle between the mind and heart – the very battle the heart had to win in order for the Hu-man Race to free itself from the Forces of Darkness.

The energies of Love and Fear twisted round and round inside of me, until it seemed my mind itself would break and shatter. Now, deep within my being I understood how ancient, primitive and primordial these two opposing energies were – and how difficult it was to let the battle go and move into Trust. Emotionally and physically, the experience was far worse than anything Carmac had inflicted upon me.

With a crash, my spirit landed back in my body still lying on the cement floor. *Was that a dream?* But of course, I knew it wasn't. I lay in the cold, damp darkness unable to move, fully understanding the schism within Mankind, knowing the long journey it must take to become free. *I have the understanding, but has anything really changed?*

Then I saw the image of Planet Earth. A very slight, fog-like mist began to roll across its surface like a giant ocean wave. A myriad of images quickly flashed before my eyes as people around the world stopped what they were doing and looked around in surprise. It was clear they felt a change but had no idea what it was.

A series of television screens appeared, similar to the ones I had seen in Carmac's office, only this time they weren't showing violence and destruction. Instead of reports on gang violence and apathy, one screen showed a group of mothers patrolling the streets of some inner city neighborhood. Their signs read, *No more killing innocent children! Change begins now!*

Several other screens displayed images of a war-torn country. A bomb had exploded in the street of a village, and the toll had been high. Groups of people stood around mourning their fallen friends and family, while others tended to the wounded. However, instead of interviews hawking the rhetoric of war, now a different story was playing out. Two men, obviously enemies, were screaming at each other.

"This is your group's fault...no, it's yours." An old man, tears streaming down his face, walked up and pushed them apart. "Look what your fighting has done," he cried in anguish. "This was my last grandson. My sons are dead...my wife and daughter, too. And for what? Tell me, for what do you continue this fight?"

Neither man had an answer, but the arguing stopped. They put their arms around the old man, and the three of them stood silently together amidst the death and destruction.

CHAPTER 81

The handcuffs fell from my wrists, and the door swung open. *Oh my god, it's working!* Zev Moab had said I didn't have to change all the energy – I had to change just enough so that people could see more clearly. I took off my blindfold and undid the gag. My fingers struggled to untie my feet.

Faster! Faster! I need to move faster! The clock is ticking! Remembering the talisman, I ripped it from my pocket.

"John!" I commanded. His face appeared, twisted and contorted. "Further!" I could see that John – Carmac – and his men were struggling for air. The room was dark except for the glowing light coming from the Great Crystal. Carmac's body was sprawled across the giant circuit board covering the controls for the entire security system. *That's why my cuffs are off and the door is open. He must have accidentally hit the main power switch as he fell on the board!*

I ran down the long hallway stumbling, almost falling, on feet still numb from being bound. I reversed the directions I had earlier memorized...*left*...*right*...*left*. I could "hear" the silence before I opened the door. Carmac's men were still alive and moving, but they staggered about in a stupor. Large, grey amorphous forms were looming in the air all around them, filling the room like huge, drunken, smoky shadows. Their reptilian arms dangled limply at their sides, and the filaments had fallen to the ground. *Good!*

"Diantha! Over here...."

I pushed the forms aside and saw David hunched over Carmac. I rushed to his side. "Is...is he dead?"

"No, but a few minutes ago they all started struggling for air." He looked at me with a grin, pride and relief flooding his face. "I knew you could do it. The Dark Forces live on chaos, confusion and fear, so whatever you did must have shifted that. It's as though you've been able to cut off some of their food supply!"

"Let's hope so, and I met Zev...."

"You'll tell me later. Right now, we have we have work to do, and we have to move fast. A grimace flashed across his face as he straightened up and tested his wounded leg. There was even more blood where he had been shot.

"Here, let me help you," I said, giving him my shoulder to lean on. "Can you walk?"

"Slowly, but it's not too bad."

"What about Carmac? Should we lock him up or something? What if he...?"

"We can't do anything about him. It's up to the rest of the people on the planet now."

"But the Crystal...."

"I hate to leave it here, but we can't take it bouncing along in the desert. We'll have to come back for it later."

Supporting David as much as possible, we fled down the hall and out into the cool desert night. We found the jeep with the key still inside, and I jumped into the driver's seat. David directed me as we practically flew across the rolling sands. Our voices couldn't be heard over the roaring of the engine, so talking was futile, but we were excited, and laughed and poked at one other like a couple of kids.

"We're going to make it," David howled into the night.

CHAPTER 82

We had gone only a short distance when I screamed, but this time from fear. A group of great hulking amorphous Dark Forms swept down and surrounded the jeep, their reptilian claws scratching at the windshield. I swerved to the right, but one of the jeep's tires sank into the sand, and the vehicle tipped on its side.

"Ha!" Carmac's ferocious laughter invaded the silent desert air. "Get them out of there," he shrieked.

His men got me out and held me, while the Dark Hulking Forms, still moving slowly, righted the jeep and pulled David out. Carmac walked toward us holding a giant laser gun that was powerful enough to blow us up right then and there. He looked strange and horrible, his face distorted and ancient-looking.

"You fools! Whatever you did, it's stopped working. You forgot you're dealing with ME! You had me for a minute, whatever trick you pulled. You and your ridiculous powers. But I've got you now, and you will never win. Never!" He turned to his goons, and said, "Now chain them up and throw them in the back. The wave is coming! We've got no time to lose."

As the two men threw us to the ground and began to swaddle us, my mind called out to David. *What is it? What's gone wrong?*

It's something in you...something that has shut down your energy flow. It's put a stop to whatever you were doing. What haven't you let go of? Think... think back...all the way back to your time in Atlantis.

But we don't have time...you knew me then...help me....

I can't. You have to find the answer for yourself.

What could it be? Frantically, I probed my consciousness. I fought back valiantly against the fear and rage that wanted to strangle me as I blindly searched. *Back when I had been my Aunt Diantha, I had been weak. I had begun to enjoy my power too much. I let Carmac praise me...woo me...seduce me. Use me! Like so many other Atlanteans, I had allowed myself, slowly but surely, to fall under the influence of the Forces of Darkness.* Tears sprung to my eyes. I saw exactly what it was! *I broke the Great Crystal... I caused the destruction of Atlantis! Oh, god! It was me!*

I foraged back through the muddy banks of memory until I reached that ancient shore. I had been thrown from the Great Pyramid of Atlantis and lay shaking on the ground. Carmac loomed over me then, just as he did now. And David, the Prince Priest A-Ta, leaned gently by my side, one last time. My whispered parting words were meant to reassure him, but in the instant of dying, I had cursed myself. I had carried that ancient curse over the millennia like some heavy rock bound to my soul.

David, I know what it is...I remember. I judged myself...never forgave myself for cracking the Crystal...for the demise of Atlantis. My last thought... just before I died...I cursed myself. Now what can I do?

There's no time to think about what happened then, but now...now you have to forgive yourself. You had great talent and were given enormous responsibilities, but you were too young. You weren't ready. We should have protected you more. You did all that you were capable of doing at the time.

And Diantha, there is something else...something very important. The destruction of Atlantis wasn't entirely a mistake. Hu-mans had already begun their separation from Spirit. They chose, all by themselves, to follow the Forces of Darkness. You didn't do it for them. It was timing...simply timing. You have to let it go, forgive yourself...now...or it's all over.

As one of Carmac's men turned me and yanked me up, a deep Nooooo groaned from my very soul. *No...! It wasn't my fault...not my fault...not my fault. I forgive myself. Oh god, I forgive myself...I forgive....*

Our captors slumped to the ground, the hulking Dark Forms spread this way and that on top of one another. *So that was the missing piece.* As long as I hadn't forgiven myself, my energy wasn't free to fully connect with the rest of humanity.

The work I had done to lift the collective Hu-man Spirit couldn't "take." Now that I had forgiven myself – accepted and loved myself –others would be able to do it as well, and the Hu-man family could finally and fully reconnect!

Click-clack – click-clack! The locks on our chains slid open, and we struggled to free ourselves. David managed to unwind his hands and feet first. I was still working on releasing my legs when he leaned over, loosened the chains and helped me up.

CHAPTER 83

Back in the jeep, I gunned the engine and we raced against the dawn, heading straight for the pyramids. It was still dark but barely so, as we made our approach. We jumped out of the jeep and ran toward the base of the Great Pyramid. The sky began to streak with the first rays of light.

"Head for the east side," David called out. "It has a better foothold." We reached the eastern face of the pyramid completely winded, but there was no time to rest. Pushing forward, we cautiously began our ascent. Groping at the stone blocks in search of a secure spot to place each hand and foot, we climbed steadily.

I had scampered up about fifteen or twenty feet when I made the mistake of looking down. It was like standing on the top of a twenty-foot ladder. I looked up the Great Pyramid's steeply sloping walls toward the top, and the brutal reality of what lay before us seemed overwhelming. I froze.

David noticed and said, "Don't look down! Focus on where to put each hand…each foot. Step by step by step. It's doable. We just have to get into a rhythm. Come on, let's go."

Hand over hand, higher and higher we slowly climbed, grasping each stone securely before making the next move. The morning sun, having just cleared the horizon, was at our backs. We were almost halfway to the top when a single, loud screech punctured the air. Many more followed. The sounds became louder – and closer. I glanced in their direction.

Oh, my god, it's the basilisks! Before we had a moment to think they were at us – pecking at our skin and pulling at our hair and clothes, their leathery wings flapping.

"What the…." yelled David, holding onto the stone face with one arm and swatting them away with the other.

"They're basilisks," I shouted. "Zev Moab showed me…the Dark Forces… to keep us from…reaching the capstone." We fought, kicking and screaming, batting at them with our hands, trying not to lose our footing.

"We…won't…make it…this way. Have to…teleport up."

"We didn't…reprogram…the Great Crystal…our power…."

"I know. Just hold on. No! Start going down… just a little. Maybe they'll let up…buy me some time."

I took a step down. It was even harder than climbing up. I took another step and almost fell. I clung to the side of the pyramid and found that as long as I wasn't climbing up, the basilisks slowed their attack. But David hadn't moved downward, and their attack on him continued. *Buy me some time,* I remembered him saying. I took one step up the pyramid, then another. The basilisks pranced on me, circling over my head and pecking at my hair. I yelped as one of the creatures nipped my neck.

"David…can you do it?" I shouted.

"Working on it."

I climbed up one more step. The basilisks circled again, nipping, tugging, and pulling. *They can take us down in a second…what are they doing?* One of them shrieked in my ear, and I had the answer. *They're laughing at us! We're their game, their sport.*

I felt a sharp pinch on my upper leg. I shook my leg, but the basilisk wouldn't let go. I shook it again, but the creature hung on. Finally, it let go, and I tried to find my footing, but my leg was numb. I couldn't get a foothold. My fingers gripped the pyramid's wall so tightly they began to bleed. My foot continued searching and soon found its place.

Thank god, but how long…?

My eyes looked for David through the basilisks' flapping wings. He was leaning against the side of the pyramid, completely still and deep in concentration. One of the basilisks circling overhead swept down and grabbed at my shirt. I was thrown off balance and leaned back too far. My hands lost their hold. I grasped again and again, trying to get a grip, but my foot slipped. The basilisk let go, but it was too late. For a second, I felt myself sliding down the face of the pyramid. Then I wasn't sliding anymore – I was in free fall. Everything was happening in slow motion. My mind went blank. I couldn't even call out to David.

Suddenly, he was beside me, and in a flash we were leaning against the top of the Great Pyramid, hands and feet securely in position.

"How…?"

"I found a way!"

Nothing needed to be said – we remembered exactly what to do. As in days gone by, we stretched out our arms and, for an instant, saw the brilliant gold and crystal capstone glinting in the morning sun. Though the capstone was no longer visible, we knew it was still there.

"We did it!" David panted.

It almost seemed as if Atlantis was resurrected, and all the ancient karma cleared. That could never be, but something more marvelous had indeed occurred. The great and treasured crystal capstone was now fully activated and anchoring Light onto the Planet. Even more people would be able to evolve – to feel their connection with all Life. And we hoped, no we knew, with every fragment of our being, that Mankind would make the Choice – the Choice for Love.

A single loud screech shifted my attention. "What about the basilisks…?"

"They're leaving," he said. "Look to your left."

I carefully turned and watched as the Basilisks flew slowly away. They lumbered, wings too weak for their heavy bodies, and aside from that last parting call, there wasn't a sound.

Looking back at David, I shouted. "We made it! We really made it!" The eternal, sonorous, humming sound, *Нииииииии,* began to fill the air.

"Ready for our last step?"

"Definitely!"

In an instant we were standing at the pyramid's base, the incredible sound rising clear up to the heavens. Bloody and exhausted, we gazed into each other's eyes. David gently took my face into his hands and kissed me, then enfolded me in his arms. We shared the vision I had seen in my dream – large groups of people gathered at the ancient stone sites around the world. They formed giant circles, holding hands and chanting – snaking their way through the stones and forming very particular, unique geometric patterns. They were energetically feeding the planet. And we had our work to do, as well.

Reluctantly, we parted from our embrace, and David led as we crept along the pyramid's base until he found the hidden doorway he was looking for. With the greenish-gold light that had no source illuminating our way, we climbed down winding steps leading into the inverted underground pyramid.

The light led us down three levels, each one several stories high. At the third level the light turned and we followed it a short distance. It stopped in front of a wall built of granite with a large, deeply recessed archway in its center.

"The Hall of Records is in there," David whispered, "behind this granite wall."

CHAPTER 84

From within the silent shadows of the ancient archway, a figure emerged. The figure stepped forward into the light and greeted us with a smile. The smile was unforgettable. It belonged to Rashid, the camel driver who had slipped the diary into my camera bag, the single act that had started this whole journey. But instead of wearing the clothing of a camel-driver, Rashid was now dressed in the long robes of The Brotherhood.

Rashid looked exactly as David had described him in the diary. He had materialized from a mist and had guided David through the passageways and into the hidden room within the Great Pyramid. *Of course, he would be the third one who would enter the Ancient Hall…he's one of its guardians!*

"Ah," Rashid said with a bow and a twinkle, "I've been expecting you."

"Rashid, if I had known who you really were, I would have accepted your invitation for dinner," I said, laughing. He opened his arms, and we all embraced. Then he asked us to move a few steps back from the wall and pointed to the area just above the arch. The light shown upon a golden plaque – the plaque that had once been dedicated to David. However, now it read:

> *David and Diantha,*
> *Lights of The New Era*
> *Who have been accordingly prepared*
> *That they may bring forth*
> *The Ancient Wisdom*
> *From Darkness into Light.*

I was surprised –and yet I wasn't. I knew that both David's codes and mine were needed to enter the Hall of Records. And we all understood that time was of the essence. As in some ancient sacred dance – known to us both but long forgotten – David and I turned to face one another. Automatically, our hands began to rise upward, but as mine did, I was astonished to see my glyphs fly out of my fingertips. They floated above my head before sweeping around to hover beside me.

David and I stood, palm facing palm, willing the codes to come. They rushed out of our hands, and soon we were surrounded by geometric forms similar to the glyphs I had drawn – but different. These glyphs swirled around and then shot through the wall. A moment later the primeval locks clicked open and the granite slab within the archway parted before our very eyes.

Rashid, David and I entered those ancient sacred underground vaults mentioned so often in the diary. As if with some pre-knowledge, David walked directly to a giant bas-relief of a mandala embedded in the wall to our right. He formed a symbol with his fingers, casting a shadow within the center of a larger shadow formed by the mandala itself. An opening immediately appeared where the shadow had been, and a small keyboard made of deep-green jade and ivory slid out. Nothing supported the keyboard – it simply hung suspended in mid-air.

David struck three notes on the keyboard, and a strange and eerie sound emerged, both unsettling and comforting all at once. I detected the sweet smell of rain and a rustling sound, like wind moving through bamboo. A great crackle of lightning flashed though the chamber followed by the roar of thunder. I heard the distinct clicking sounds of a pod of dolphins and the moaning of a great humpback whale. Then silence.

I turned quizzically to David, who seemed very far away – watching something I could not see. When he came back to himself, he looked at me and smiled, his blue eyes sparkling like a starry night.

Rashid whispered, "David has more work to do. Come, there is something you need to see."

Moving trance-like, I followed him and found myself before a gilded wall. Upon it, jumping out at me like some fierce energetic beings, I saw my glyphs. "Those…those are my glyphs! *What…?*"

Our gentle guide placed his hand on my shoulder and said, "You know what they are, don't you?"

"Well…I was told they were Pleiadean glyphs, and that they had been seen on some stones on Easter Island. But I could never find them."

"They are a part of the ancient knowledge from the Pleiades. You channeled them because you were meant to learn from them. And you did! They instructed you as they came through you. Instinctively, you understood they were related to the sacred sites. It was time for the peoples of Earth to know them also…and to learn from them. That's why you put them in your art show. It was the beginning of their journey out into the world. In truth, they are your gift to the Race of Hu-mans.

"Unlike the codes you and David just used to enter this Sacred Chamber, the glyphs you channeled are for everyone. They're meant to light the way for all people in these times of upheaval and change. They hold very specific energetic patterns meant to assist in the evolution of consciousness on Planet Earth."

David had finished his task and quickly joined us. Rashid took each of our arms and led us into a small, dark alcove on the far wall. Gradually, the dark nook became quite bright, lit by the greenish gold light that had no source – but blazing much more brightly now. Rashid waved his hand, and with a *swoosh*, all of the information from all of the walls, even those down the hallway leading to the Sphinx, came rushing toward us. It was the stored knowledge on the history of Atlantis and all great civilizations of Earth, as well as the deepest mysteries of our sacred Planet. As we watched, the information pulled itself together into one neat, energetic package, and David and I solemnly took this information – these energetic keys – into our beings.

As we did, we felt one final rush of energy, akin to that of racing waters released from a great dam. We understood the importance of this movement immediately. The last blockages of the ancient Grid had been cleared and the Earth Power System entirely restored. What could have been a crisis – a cataclysm – was now merely one collective sigh of relief. The New Era could now safely unfold.

The diary, as a sort of mirage, glowed before our eyes. It was open to the very first page, the page that seemingly started the journey into Oneness for David and I. But then something strange happened – the words slowly, then rapidly, began to un-write themselves. When the last word had vanished, the diary disappeared as well.

An image of Carmac and other members of the Forces of Darkness suddenly appeared, but they were no longer ferocious – they were all about the size of elves. We opened our arms and took them inside ourselves. We understood that we needed to embrace not just the Light but the Darkness, too. There was only one way to heal it – we had to take it in and make it ours.

David held me in his arms once more. Time stood still as millennia were washed away, and it was as though we had never been apart

* * * * * * * * * * *

David, Rashid and I laughed as our personalities danced, one with the other. And each of us felt the Grace as our minds linked up, once again, with the timeless Brotherhood. From our state of Oneness, we watched with satisfaction as the seeds of the Ancient Wisdom began to enter the peoples of Earth. We were proud and we were grateful, for now we could stay the currents of Darkness. All of this was possible because enough people had become fully present and accountable. Enough Hearts and Minds had made the leap – *the Choice* – for Love. Now new energy could permeate the land, and the world would thirst no more.

"There is no stopping it now, my friends," said Rashid. "The tides of awareness have turned. The Last Age of Darkness lifts, as Earth and her inhabitants, together as one single life form, step into their rightful place at the End of Time – the End of History as we have known it on this Planet.

"Indeed, now we step into a New Era of Light."

EPILOGUE

And so even now, when it looks to the uninitiated eye as if long shadows are cast upon the land, every day more Hu-mans wake up to the hidden knowledge of who they truly are. And as they do, they are joined synchronistically with others who slumber no more. A new Crystal Grid, comprised of Hu-man consciousness, grows stronger with each passing day.

It was apparent – David and I both knew – our future task was clear. We would walk in service upon the plane of Earth until its graduation, and then we would silently move on.

And so it came to pass that the days grew into months, and the months grew into years. David and I were called upon to work with group upon group of awakening Hu-mans. Sometimes a summons came from one those who barely understood. They would call out to us in their Dark Night of the Soul – a time when twin specters of Doubt and Fear came to haunt their dreams. Others were very aware of what was required, and we were more formally invited. Many of them were those ancient Atlantean souls who had come to clear their karmic slate. It made no difference – the silent or spoken request was always the same. They needed to hear our stories and have us guide their inner vision as it searched to uncover the Light.

Inevitably, we would find ourselves sitting together high upon a mountain top, in a lush green valley beside a running stream, on a sandy ocean beach or under a star-studded sky in the crisp desert night. The pipe would be passed round the circle of new initiates. Then there would come that moment when David or I would look each one of them in the eye, offer them the pipe, and utter just one word – "Choose."

And while all of this is true, there is something else I want to share. I know that the Forces of Darkness can gather strength again and come for me at any moment. And, of course, I will go up against them, once again.

I've made my Choice – and I'm prepared.

The glyphs scattered throughout this book are from the workbook:
MEDITATIVE MAGIC, The Pleiadean Glyphs by Judith Diana Winston.
www.MeditativeMagic.com

BIBLIOGRAPHY

Carey, Ken: Starseed The Third Millennium
Cayce, Edgar: On Atlantis
Cremo, Michael A. Thompson, Richard L: The Hidden History of The Human Race
Fortune, Dion: Glastonbury of The Heart
Hancock, Graham: Fingerprints of The Gods
Heyerdal, Thor: Easter Island
Hillarion: Seasons of The Spirit, The Nature Of Reality
Jochmans, Dr. Joe aka Janlandris: The Hall of Records, The Eathfire Series
Lazaris: various materials on crystals – books and tapes / www.Lazaris.com
Michell, John: The New View Over Atlantis, The Old Stones Of Lands End
Penwick, Nigel: The Ancient Science Of Geomancy
Raphael: The Starseed Transmissions, An Extraterrestrial Report
Schwaller de Lubicz, R. P. The Temple in Man
Solomon, Paul, The Trail of The Ancient Mystery Schools / www.PaulSolomon.com
Steiner, Rudolph: Egyptian Myths and Mysteries
West, John Anthony: The Serpent in The Sky
Westwood, Jenifer (editor): The Atlas of Mysterious Places
Zinc, David: The Ancient Stones Speak

RESOURCES FOR YOUR CONTINUING CONSCIOUS EVOLUTION!

www.BarbaraMarxHubbard.com
www.DavidIcke.com
www.EmisaryOfLight.com
www.HeartMath.com
www.IntegralEnlightment.com
www.IntegralInstitute.org
www.JeanHouston.org

www.JeanHoustonFoundation.org
www.KenWilber.com
www.Noetic.org
www.PurposeAndDestiny org
www.TheShiftNetwork.com
www.ThriveMovement.com
www.WorldWideTippingPoint.com

www.ingramcontent.com/pod-product-compliance
Lightning Source LLC
Chambersburg PA
CBHW030846030726
47495CB00005B/1395